TO TED –
BEST WISHES
FRIEND AND FELLOW WORDSMITH

Letters From The Road

FIRST OF A SERIES SPANNING 7 DECADES

G Gordon Davis

ISBN: 149973980X
ISBN 13: 9781499739800
Library of Congress Control Number: 2014910125
CreateSpace Independent Publishing Platform
North Charleston, South Carolina

DEDICATION

Dedicated to the memory of my father, Wilber, who was far more than a road man. His innate goodness far outweighed his faults, however few. May he rest in peace.

ACKNOWLEDGEMENTS

To my wife, Sharon, for her honest criticism and unflagging support. I also want to thank the Palm Springs Writers Guild for their guidance and fellowship. I especially want to thank the members of my two weekly critique groups, who over the years have helped me craft this novel and five others. They know who they are, and they have earned my everlasting gratitude.

My road calls me, lures me West, east, south and north:
Most roads lead men homewards.
My road leads me forth.

John Masefield
Roadways
1878-1967

PROLOGUE

MARCH 11th, 1931

Chance Wick focused on the rain-swept highway ahead as he fumbled in his shirt pocket for the pack of Old Golds he'd bought while stopping for gas in Fort Wayne, Indiana. He shook a cigarette from the pack and placed it between his lips, then lit it off a Zippo with the cryptic message: "Doc. You Bastard. Velma" etched into its brushed-chrome case. "Doc" was Chance's nickname, a carry-over from childhood and still used by old friends like Velma, a long-time lover, but never by his second wife, the former Alva Korsvold. She thought the nickname was unbecoming to the highest paid man at Dakota Tamper.

He had called Alva from Atlanta two days before, promising he'd be home in time to attend the birth of his second child, but the first by her, his second wife. She told him to never mind what his physician father said about the baby being a week off. She said the baby was already kicking hard, and if Chance intended on witnessing its birth, he'd damn well better drop everything and head for home straightaway.

Dropping "everything" meant cancelling next week's important Gulf Line demonstration. It was scheduled to be the last following a successful three-week swing through the Deep South demonstrating vibratory ballast tampers for the Cotton Belt and Louisville & Nashville railroads.

It was dawn and raining when Chance left Velma's place in Cincinnati. She bitched like she always did when he left after an overnighter, but he hadn't dared stay a second night. With a renewed sense of purpose and middling guilt, Chance pressed his foot hard against the gas pedal and didn't lift off until the LaSalle and the heavy equipment trailer it towed were doing seventy. He tamped out the unfinished cigarette in the ashtray and glanced at his watch. Six hours since leaving Ft. Wayne, and the rain that hadn't let up had turned to sleet. He swore, slowed to sixty, and lit another cigarette off the Zippo. Bastard indeed.

The monotonous action of the wipers was hypnotic and Chance fought to stay focused – to stay on the goddamned ball – and concentrated on the big Packard phaeton he'd been following since the Indiana-Michigan line. Assuming the weather held, he could be home in another three hours. Yet, as was often the case in Michigan in March, the weather hadn't cooperated. When he reached Kalamazoo he found the roads buried under several inches of fresh snow. He slowed and fought to keep the swaying trailer from jackknifing and taking the lumbering LaSalle off the road and him with it. He swore again when he reached for his cigarettes and discovered he'd smoked the last one while listening to Rudy Vallee singing, *My Time is Your Time,* on the radio.

He scraped a hole in the frosted-over windshield with his fingernails and strained to see familiar landmarks now obscured by blowing snow that limited visibility to less than a hundred yards in any direction. He fought against the giddy sensation of vertigo as he closed the distance between himself and the Packard ahead, now the only reference point in the swirling drifting snow.

Chance allowed his jumbled thoughts to follow the familiar trajectory that took him back two decades to Highland Park, Michigan. He was twenty-one years old and eight months into a shotgun marriage to his first wife Marguerite, who like Alva, was also due to deliver any day. Since Chance worked construction at the time, and had little money, they were living with his parents. It was a given that his physician father would be delivering the baby at home – home births being a common practice in 1911.

There was a sense of malignant urgency in the air on that night of December 3rd. Chance, who had been drinking with friends at the Elk's Club, stumbled home to find Marguerite in bed and moaning with pain while trying to expel the baby. His father held a pair of forceps clamped around the baby's head, zealously pulling and twisting while the bedside clock ticked relentlessly toward midnight. Another five minutes and it would be too late. December 3rd was Dr. Wick's fifty-second birthday – a date they all knew he wanted to share with the grandson they named Early. Dr. Wick succeeded in meeting his self-imposed deadline, but in so-doing he also blinded Early with the forceps.

Chance felt equally to blame for the divorce that came two years later. By then, his wife had become an alcoholic and he nearly one. What tipped the scales was the day he'd come home to find Marguerite in bed with a man she'd picked up at the Elk's Club. The two were fucking only three feet away from where Early stood blindly in his crib with shit-filled diapers that sagged around his knees and crying for his mother. It was easier to forgive her indiscretion, than it had been to forgive her indifference toward Early.

He redirected his thoughts toward home. It was nearly three, and he feared Dakota Straits was getting the brunt of the storm. He took little comfort in the fact that his elderly parents lived with them. Apart from the potential danger his aged father posed, it was *they* who needed looking after, and he believed they would be of little help in any emergency. Because of its location halfway up the eastern shore of Lake Michigan, Dakota Straits received lake-effect snow that often exceeded a hundred inches a year. If the storm caused the power to go out and telephone lines to go down, Alva would be frantic, especially if she couldn't get to the hospital. Less worried would be Early. Lights or no lights, it made no difference to him.

It was five-thirty when Chance pulled into town. He turned up Shore Drive toward home and slewed to an uneven stop in front of the house. He left the ice-encrusted LaSalle and black demo trailer parked where they were vulnerable to any passing snowplow. After concealing the incriminating Zippo in the LaSalle's deep map pocket, Chance stepped out of the car and slogged through drifting snow to the front steps and climbed to the porch.

He quickly let himself into the house and paused in the vestibule to stomp caked snow off his black wingtips. The house was uncommonly quiet and he wondered why his homecoming was being ignored. Maybe it was because of the storm, or perhaps they hadn't heard him come in. He strode into the living room, expecting to find Alva and his mother Winifred hooking rugs on the couch by the front window. Neither were there, nor was his father, who could usually be found seated at his favorite wingback smoking a Dutch Master and listening to Lowell Thomas on the big Zenith. Even Early, who enjoyed listening in as he fingered one of his Braille books, was absent.

Only then did it occur to Chance that they might have taken his father's Hupmobile to the hospital. He cursed the storm for causing him to be late and hoped that Alva hadn't yet delivered, and was at the hospital where her own doctor could attend to her. He'd go there next, but first he needed a drink and a cigarette.

He turned for the kitchen and strode purposefully to cabinet where he kept his liquor and cigarettes. He found the bottle of Old Crow, unscrewed the cap and splashed three fingers of whiskey into a paper cup and knocked it back neat before lighting his first cigarette. He was still feeling the whiskey burn when he thought he heard a voice – or was it the wind moaning around the eaves? Chance flipped his unfinished cigarette into the sink and hurried through the house to the stairs, taking them two at a time until gaining the landing. He paused to listen before turning down the hallway toward the bedroom he shared with Alva.

He found her there – in bed and flat on her back with two heavy Hudson Bay blankets piled around her slim figure. The room smelled faintly of ether. Her upturned face was deathly pale under the wintry-half light coming through frost-glazed windows at her side.

He was about to look for his father when he saw Early, who sat in Alva's bentwood rocker in a far dark corner of the gloomy high-ceilinged room. Early was repeating the same question over and over again; "What's wrong, Granddad...what's wrong...?"

Chance's scalp prickled. As he was about to speak, to ask Early what the hell was wrong, Dr. Wick entered the bedroom from the adjoining bathroom. The naked baby boy he held in his hands wasn't breathing and appeared lifeless. Its mottled skin glistened sickly-blue under the cold light. Blood pounded in Chance's ears. He was only dimly aware of a steam radiator knocking somewhere in the house, and the howling wind that rattled the shutters and loosened shingles on the roof.

Early halted his incessant rocking and turned to face his father. "Dad?" he said. "What's wrong? Granddad was delivering the baby, but it never cried."

"Give me a minute, son," Chance replied, "While I try to make sense of what's happening." Then he understood. His father had fucked up again. Had it been a stroke? No matter. He reached toward his father. "Give me the baby, Dad."

"What?" Dr. Wick said. "*What?*" he said again, and took a step back with the baby clutched to his pin-striped brown vest. His expression registered confusion.

"Goddamn it, Dad! Give me my son!" Chance pried the baby from his father's arms and rushed for the bathroom. Then cradling his infant son in the crook of his left arm, Chance grabbed a drinking cup off the sink and placed it under the cold water tap. He spun the knob and waited the eternity it took for the cup to overflow with ice-cold water taken directly from Lake Michigan and dashed its contents in his son's blue face.

"*Breathe,*" Chance shouted. "Goddamn it, *breathe!*"

The baby's arms and legs flew out reflexively. A tiny fist struck Chance's looming chin, followed by the baby's shuddering gasp that filled its lungs with life-giving oxygen, and finally it cried.

Relieved beyond words, Chance held his wailing, squirming son at arms length – as if afraid the cigarette and whiskey smell on his breath might have long-lasting and unpredictable consequences on the boy's undeveloped brain.

Alva stirred awake at the commotion. "Chance, is that you? Is the baby okay?"

Chance knelt and placed their squalling infant son in her arms. "He's fine, now."

Alva smiled and drew the baby to her breast. "Look, he has your beautiful hands."

Chance grinned and said, "A chip off the old block, and a keeper for sure."

CHAPTER ONE

Keeper sat bolt upright in bed with his heart racing and gasping for air in the darkened bedroom. The pillowcase and bed sheets tangled around his feet were so damp with sweat he feared he might have wet the bed – a shameful thing for a ten year-old boy to have done. It had been the same recurring dream, of his father dying in a terrible car wreck while far from home.

Chance was gone now too – already on the road for three weeks and not expected home for four more days. Keeper looked forward to getting a picture post card or an airmail letter from his father when he was away, but there hadn't been either since the card from Memphis two weeks ago. Time seemed to stand still in the old house when Chance was gone, especially for Keeper. He believed the big house held secrets – even a certain indefinable sadness, and was likely haunted too. He was convinced of it whenever a door slammed when no one was around, or when blizzards set windowpanes to humming against the wind like a forlorn chorus of sailors lost to the icy depths of the Great Lakes.

There were diversions, of course. Keeper's grandfather, Dr. Edgerton Wick, still saw the occasional patient from his old practice at the house in the lake-facing library. Keeper sometimes watched through the keyhole while his grandfather diagnosed illnesses and gave shots. He once questioned his grandfather's use of a strange medical device called the 'Master Violet Ray.'

"It's quack medicine, boy," Dr. Wick explained, "and does no harm. I still have an elderly patient who insists it helps her digestion."

Keeper's mother, Alva, was distant and rarely spoke unless it was necessary. His blind half-brother Early was twenty-years older and they had little in common. Dr. Wick mostly stayed in his upstairs room listening to the radio and reading his Bible. He'd been acting more strangely than usual ever since his wife, Winifred, died of aspirated pneumonia the year before. Keeper believed that were it not for his best friend, Jonnie Prettyboy, he wouldn't have anybody at all to talk to.

A distant flicker of heat lightning over the big lake, followed by a low mutter of thunder, drew Keeper's attention to the open window opposite his bed. He reached under his pillow for the chrome-plated Ray-o-Vac he was allowed to have when his father was on the road and switched it on with a soft click. He aimed the brilliant beam of light toward the screen and held it steady until a moth fluttered into view. For several minutes, Keeper amused himself by making the moth follow the light.

"Hey Mr. Moth," he said. "Look out for spiders. They'll eat you up."

After tiring of the game he covered the flashlight lens with his hand, which made the bones in his fingers look like they were being x-rayed.

Keeper aimed the flashlight at a wall-sized Ringling, Barnum Bros. & Bailey poster that had pink elephants dancing on their hind legs against a dark blue background. They waved American flags in their curled trunks. Keeper's father brought the poster home following a road trip to New York the year before. That was when Keeper hid in the backseat of his father's car. They were ten miles away from home before Chance discovered him and had to turn back.

Keeper next flicked the beam of light toward a wall calendar sent by the Dakota Straits First National Bank. Next Monday, August 11th 1941, and his father would be home. Maybe this time he could talk him into having a picnic on the beach or playing catch in the backyard. If he was lucky, maybe they could go fishing up the Dakota River with his uncle, Neil Korsvold, and Jonnie Prettyboy, a rough-edged tomboy and his best friend in the whole world. Maybe this time his father wouldn't pass out drunk on the living room couch.

Keeper rolled onto his elbows and aimed the flashlight at a Triple A road map thumb-tacked to the wall over his bed. The map was studded with colorful pushpins, which he used to keep track of where his father had been, where he'd called from last, and where he was going next. A red push pin showed where he'd called from Atlanta. A yellow push pin showed where he was going next, to Cincinnati, Ohio. Finally tiring of his game, Keeper yawned and turned off the flashlight to the accompaniment of lightning strobing over the lake and more thunder, louder this time. A subtle shift of cooler air entered the room through the screened window. While he listened, waiting for the rain, he could hear his grandfather snoring, and Early occasionally groaning at some private dream of his own. He wondered if Early saw anything in his dreams, or if everything was black. The one time he asked about it, he was told to shut up, as if Early's blindness was the biggest secret of all.

Then other sounds came – the refrigerator door being closed, then the scrape of an aluminum pot being set on the stovetop. Keeper knew that on nights when his mother couldn't sleep, or after tiring of playing endless games of solitaire in bed, she went to the kitchen for a bowl of warm milk and crackers. Keeper thought he might want to be with her – to have a glass of milk and a windmill cookie. He wanted to tell her about his bad dream and ask what it could mean, but he didn't because he heard her crying, and it sounded like she might never stop.

Keeper rolled over and buried his head under the pillow so he didn't have to see or hear anymore. Yet the harder he tried to block everything out, the clearer the images became. He could imagine his grandfather sleeping on his back, his pale upturned face and the dark hole of his mouth as he snored. He tried to imagine what Early was doing because of the grunting sounds coming from his half-brother's room. He tried not to picture his mother sobbing in the kitchen, but hers was the clearest image of all. He sometimes wondered if his mother cried because his father was away, or because he was coming home.

A sudden flash of lightning so bright Keeper could see it from under his pillow was immediately followed by a percussive thump of thunder that rattled the windows. He flinched when something sharp pricked the back of his left hand. Thinking he'd been bitten by a spider, he quickly grabbed the flashlight and clicked it on. There, just behind the middle knuckle, a tiny speck of fresh blood and something else – a red push pin lying next to the pillow. Keeper aimed the flashlight toward the roadmap on the wall. Atlanta, Georgia was missing its push pin.

He scooped up the pin and closed his fingers around it – tolerating the pain when it jabbed him, but unable to stop the tears that followed. He closed his eyes and lay back against the pillow, listening to the wind-driven rain lashing the old house and trying hard not to hear his mother, who still wept in the kitchen.

CHAPTER TWO

Jonnie Prettyboy was thirteen that summer, when she asked Keeper why he had been so-named, instead of something more common and less likely to cause him difficulty later in life. He said it hadn't caused any difficulties so far. She'd said "Just wait," and went on to say not even a son of a bitch Chippewa would give a child such a peculiar name. Since Jonnie Prettyboy was Dakota Indian on her father's side and Lithuanian on her mother's, she felt eminently qualified in pointing out the subtle differences between the Dakota and the Chippewa. Yet by 1941, many of these differences had disappeared, typically through intermarriage and assimilation with the locals.

Keeper was oblivious to these cultural dynamics. Instead, what mattered to him was the fact that Jonnie Prettyboy not only taught him how to swear, she also willingly accompanied him to the weather-beaten horse barn behind his house. There, on rainy afternoons when they weren't playing at the beach, Jonnie Prettyboy allowed Keeper to pursue his favorite activity of playing doctor in the hayloft. There hadn't been horses, hay or oats in the barn for over thirty years, but a horsey smell still leached from the walls on hot humid days. Since his grandfather was a retired physician, Keeper called playing doctor "physical examinations" and liked to make appointments. It helped that his grandfather's gynecological instruments and old examination table with its foot stirrups were stored in the hayloft. They lent a certain clinical authenticity to the proceedings.

Having gotten her usual clean bill of health, Jonnie Prettyboy dangled her thin brown legs over the edge of the examination table and lit a Chesterfield with a kitchen match. She wore patched grass-stained khaki shorts and a man's faded denim shirt from the Salvation Army. The shirt was baggy and helped conceal the budding breasts that were beginning to embarrass her. She leaned back against a foot stirrup that looked like an oversized ore lock and took a deep drag off the Chesterfield. "So, who came up with your dumb name anyway, huh?" she asked.

Keeper carefully set aside his Ray-o-Vac and stainless steel speculum. "My dad," he explained rather proudly. "He said I was a keeper when I was born."

"Good thing you weren't a turd," Jonnie Prettyboy said, and laughed.

It was easily ninety degrees in the hayloft, and a thin sheen of sweat glowed on Keeper's freckled and sunburned face. Except for a wayward cowlick, the reddish-brown hair he'd inherited from his father stuck to his forehead like it was pasted on. His eyes were his mother's – a clear blue-gray color she called "Norwegian ordinary." He also wore khaki shorts, but his were new, as was his green tee-shirt, brown argyle socks and Red Goose shoes. "Do you want to make an appointment for next week?" Keeper asked with a hopeful smile.

Jonnie Prettyboy ran her fingers through the glossy sable-black hair she wore pageboy-style, like Prince Valiant in the comics. "I'd rather not," she said.

"It's because of your boobies, isn't it?"

Her pale-gray eyes glittered like new dimes. "Just shut up."

Keeper pulled up a four-legged metal hospital stool and sat to watch Jonnie Prettyboy smoke. "I'll never understand you," he said.

She blew cigarette smoke in Keeper's face, followed with a laugh that showed teeth white as pearl buttons. "Since you're a dumb shit, it's unlikely you ever will."

"Crap," Keeper said. No matter how cross she got with him, he never got mad or loved her any less. They met on the beach the summer before when he was digging a fort with a garden spade brought from the horse barn. The sugar sand kept caving in until she showed him how to shore it up with driftwood and waterlogged planks from sunken sailing ships. Is spite of a three-year age difference, the two immediately hit it off, especially when he learned she smoked and brought her cigarettes taken from his father's special cupboard.

Sometimes the two pretended they were taking a road trip in Dr. Wick's Hupmobile, which he seldom drove anymore. It was kept in the horse barn now – its keys left in the ignition and occasionally tempting Keeper into starting it. To keep "the battery up," as he explained it. Jonnie Prettyboy would sit next to him, smoking a cigarette and ridiculing Keeper's talk of getting married one day.

She took a last puff from the cigarette and pushed herself off the examination table. "I gotta go home and fix pa's dinner," she said, and crushed the cigarette under her foot. "If I'm late, I'll get a good whupping."

Keeper knew her "home" was a retired Pere Marquette Railroad caboose parked on an abandoned spur in the sand dunes just north of town, where she lived with her parents. He also knew through his father, that her father, Roy Prettyboy, was a welder at Dakota Tamper, and that he drank homemade moonshine out of Mason jars.

"Will I see you tomorrow?" Keeper asked.

"Will you bring me a pack of butts?"

"Sure."

"Then I'll come. Turd.

CHAPTER THREE

Chance always made it a point to send Keeper a picture postcard whenever he stopped at some scenic location, such as the Grand Canyon, or at a big city like New York or Atlanta. He began doing so when his son was eight and considered old enough to appreciate them. After scribbling a quick note, he'd drop it in the mail before moving on. Sometimes he'd make it home before the last postcard arrived, but usually not.

Keeper saved them all and kept them in a chest of drawers in his room. Now that he was ten, the drawer held dozens of postcards and airmail letters, all bound up in a thick rubber band. He looked forward to sharing the postcards and the occasional airmail letter with everyone, including his blind half-brother, Early, who couldn't read anything except the raised dots on his Braille books. Even though he was older, Early always listened with a tolerant smile as Keeper read the latest news from the road.

That day's card came with a hand-tinted photograph of downtown Atlanta, and was postmarked August 2, 1941. Keeper took the card upstairs and knocked on Early's bedroom door like he was told to do when it was closed.

"That you, Keep?" Early asked after several long seconds had passed.

"Yep," Keeper replied. "Want to hear Dad's latest card?"

"Yeah, c'mon in and lets hear what the bullshit artist has to say for himself."

Keeper entered the room and took a seat by the window that overlooked their horse barn and Lake Michigan beyond – a view wasted on Early. *"Dear Keeper,"* he began. *"Today I am here in Atlanta, the home of Coca-Cola. This morning I passed a chain-gang working alongside a county road. There must have been fifty colored boys shackled ankle to ankle. They were all sweating to beat the band and singing wonderful hymns while they cut weeds with hay sickles. Next time, I'll bring you along. Signed, Dad. P.S. Tell everybody I love them."*

"Is that all?" Early asked.

"Yep."

Early seemed disappointed. "Too short," he said.

"That's 'cause it's only a postcard," Keeper replied.

"Take it to Granddad," Early said. "Tell him his wayward son sends everybody his love."

Keeper was still puzzling over his half-brother's comment about their father when he found their grandfather resting in his bedroom. He was listening to Gabriel Heatter on a portable radio that looked like a small cathedral. The old physician sat in a rocking chair and appeared to be asleep. Keeper waited in the open doorway while listening to Mr. Heatter's familiar voice intoning, *"...there's bad news tonight."*

Dr. Wick wore the same clothes every day – a vested brown pinstriped suit with a starched white shirt and paisley-print necktie tied loosely around the collar. A red rosebud cut from the garden that morning was pinned to the lapel. A thin gold chain draped across his stomach held a gold watch and the key that wound it. The old man's waxy skin and carefully combed white hair looked transparent in the low light of a flexible gooseneck lamp. His eyes were closed behind the black-framed eyeglasses perched precariously on the tip of his nose. His mottled physician's hands gripped the cane he held across his knees like a shepherd's crook. A glass ashtray from the Upjohn company held the dead stub of a Dutch Master cigar.

Because of the dead cigar, the mothballed old clothes, and the scented rosewater his grandmother used until her death, Keeper thought the room smelled like the funeral parlor where his grandmother's services were held. He cautiously stepped forward. "Grandpa?"

"I'm awake," his grandfather answered in a sleep-husky voice.

"Another card from Dad came in the mail today."

Dr. Wick stirred and looked up at his grandson. His bushy white eyebrows quivered expressively above the black-framed eyeglasses. "Where is your father now?"

"Atlanta...that's in Georgia," Keeper explained. "Do you want me to read it?"

"That won't be necessary."

"But why?"

"Sodom and Gomorra," the old man grumped.

Keeper laughed. "That's what you said when he was in New Orleans. But you didn't say what it means."

Dr. Wick shook his head. "It means nothing but whores and thieves lying in wait for the likes of your father."

He wasn't sure what his grandfather was talking about, but it sounded exciting, and even a little bit dangerous. Now more than ever, he wanted his father to take him on a road trip. He longed to have his father all to himself for as long as the trip lasted – and if he was lucky, maybe it would last all summer long.

Keeper let his gaze wander toward the decades-old glass-fronted bookcases in the corner alcove where a double-hung window over-looked the street below. The bookcases held his grandfather's medical books and the brass Zeiss microscope Keeper secretly used to study the filigreed wings of houseflies and things he picked from his nose. His favorite medical book was the illustrated "Diseases of the Nose and Throat." A human skull grinned vacantly from atop one of the bookcases. Two framed diplomas hung over the double bed Dr. Wick shared with his wife, Winifred, until the day she died. A well-thumbed King James Bible lay open on the nightstand next to the bed. Keeper turned when Early poked his head through the open doorway.

"Don't listen to what Granddad says, Keep," he said with a laugh. "It's the whores and thieves that should look out for Chance Wick." Still laughing, Early turned back to his room with quick steps that belied his sightlessness.

Keeper waited until he heard Early's door close before speaking again. "Grandpa?"

"What is it now?"

"Will Early be blind forever?"

Dr. Wick pushed himself back into his chair and sighed. "It's late," he replied. "Please tell your mother I'll take my meal upstairs tonight."

"But, you're a doctor, Grandpa. Can't you make him see again?"

Dr. Wick turned down the volume on the radio. "The war will soon be coming to America," he said, simply. "Early will be spared its horrors."

Keeper tried looking into his grandfather's eyes, but they were closed again.

"Grandpa?"

"Close the door behind you, Keeper. I feel a terrible chill."

CHAPTER FOUR

Except for Keeper himself and Jonnie Prettyboy, hardly anyone else ever ventured out to the dilapidated horse barn. The stairs leading up to the hayloft were narrow, dangerous, and without a railing. Chance nearly fell down them one day after storing Dr. Wick's retired medical equipment up there. The horse barn also was where Dr. Wick kept his beloved 1938 Hupmobile Aero Sedan, down by the stables where buggies were housed before there were automobiles.

"Your father isn't taking you on some dumb road trip," Jonnie Prettyboy sneered when Keeper told her about the picture postcard his father had sent from Atlanta. "So don't kid yourself." Her shirt was open, exposing her budding breasts.

"He promised he would next time out," Keeper replied. He reached for a nipple.

She slapped his hand away. "Bullshit. And don't touch me unless I say it's okay."

"You're just jealous because your dad isn't a road man."

Jonnie Prettyboy began to button up her shirt, a boy's shirt with two pockets. One held her Chesterfields. "Maybe," she said, "but my pa is home banging ma every night."

Keeper looked impressed. "You mean you can hear them going at it?"

She shook out a cigarette and lit it off a wooden kitchen match. "Sure."

"What does it sound like?"

Jonnie Prettyboy scowled. "I don't want to talk about it."

Keeper understood he'd better change the subject. "I'm going to be a road man someday."

"I thought you were going to be a doctor."

"There's glamour and excitement on the road," he said. "My dad sees all the sights, eats at fine restaurants and stays at Hilton hotels."

Jonnie Prettyboy laughed. "All the more reason he won't take you, turd."

Keeper was beginning to wonder himself. His father had been promising him a road trip, even a short overnight one, ever since he turned nine the year before. He turned away from Jonnie Prettyboy to look out the nearest window that was latticed with cobwebs. The glass was as old as the horse barn itself – each slightly rippled with little bubbles of ancient air trapped inside. From his lofty vantage point, Keeper could see his mother, Alva, in her vegetable garden hoeing between rows of fat red tomatoes, carrots, snap beans and radishes. As usual, she wore a faded cotton housedress and one of Chance's old blue bandannas tied around her head.

Keeper turned his attention back to Jonnie Prettyboy. "My dad met a movie star once."

"Lassie?" she asked through a lazy cloud of cigarette smoke.

"Clark Gable."

"Bullshit."

"It was on a Union Pacific club car."

"Did your pa say, 'Hi ya, Clark! I'm Chance Wick, from Dakota Straits?'"

"I don't know about that, but he got his autograph."

"Prove it."

"It's in my room."

Jonnie Prettyboy frowned. "Is your brother home?"

Keeper shook his head. "He's tuning pianos at St. John's today. Why?"

"He makes me nervous, the way he looks at me."

"You dope. He can't see."

"But he acts like he does."

"He smells you."

Jonnie Prettyboy shuddered. "That's even worse."

Keeper laughed. "C'mon," he said, "but put out your smoke first." Then he led the way down the narrow stairway, past the Hupmobile and across the sunlit backyard. The house was quiet when they entered by way of the kitchen door. Keeper tiptoed to the living room where his grandfather dozed in his favorite wingback. The big Zenith was on and broadcasting the local news. Keeper silently motioned for Jonnie Prettyboy to follow him up the front stairs.

"*Jesus Christ!*" Jonnie Prettyboy exclaimed when she saw the Ringling Bros. Barnum & Bailey circus poster pasted to Keeper's bedroom wall.

"My dad brought that home from the road," Keeper explained.

"Lucky you."

"He always brings me something." Keeper pointed to a cast iron circus wagon on his dresser. The wagon was painted red, with yellow artillery wheels and a blue-uniformed driver that held the reins to four prancing white horses. A cast iron lion snarled from inside the caged wagon.

Jonnie Prettyboy affected a look of utter boredom and pointed to the roadmap thumb-tacked over Keeper's bed. "What's the map for, and how come the push pins?"

"That's so I can keep track of my dad," Keeper answered. "The blue pins are for where he's been, the red one is where he was when he called home last night, and the yellow is where he's going next." A red push pin stuck through the center of Atlanta, and a yellow push pin was jabbed into Cincinnati.

Jonnie Prettyboy opened the circus wagon's rear gate and plucked out the lion for a closer look. "So, where's the dumb autograph?"

Keeper opened his top dresser drawer and rummaged among collected postcards, letters and his balled-up socks and underwear, until coming up with a matchbook.

"Here," he said, and thrust it toward her.

She took it. "This says Union Pacific Railway. Clark Gable wrote his autograph in a fucking matchbook?"

Keeper nodded. "Read it."

She opened the cover and began reading aloud. "*To Chance, I owe you one. Clark Gable.*"

"Pretty neat, huh?"

"I think it's stupid."

Keeper grinned. "I'll show you something you won't think is stupid," he said, and led the way down the long hallway to his grandfather's room.

"What if we get caught?"

"Don't worry," he replied, and brought down the dusty ivory-white skull from its location atop one of the bookcases. He held it out. "See what I mean?'

Jonnie Prettyboy gave a low whistle. "Is it real?"

"Sure. Feel the teeth."

She extended a shaking index finger toward the skull but didn't touch it. "I...I don't think so."

"Scaredy cat," Keeper taunted.

"I'm not either."

"Then touch it."

"Put it down first."

Keeper giggled and placed the skull on his grandfather's cushioned rocking chair that had been strategically placed next to an open screened-in window that overlooked the street below. "Do it now."

Jonnie Prettyboy gingerly poked the skull as if it would bite back. "There," she said, as if satisfied she'd met the test.

"Now kiss it," Keeper said.

"No."

"Put your lips on its teeth and say, 'I love you, Mr. Bones'"

"You're crazy."

"Say, 'darling, I want your bony baby.'"

"Jonnie Prettyboy raised a fist. "I'm going to beat the living shit..."

"Shut up!" Keeper hissed. "My grandpa's coming!"

"I never should have let you bring me here!"

"In the closet!" Keeper grabbed the skull and quickly shoved Jonnie Prettyboy headlong into the closet ahead of him and closed the door.

She grabbed Keeper by the arm. "It stinks like death in here. Let me out or I'll fucking scream."

"In a minute," Keeper whispered.

"Do it *now*, goddamnit! I can't stand being shut in!"

"Okay. Just take it easy." He cautiously opened the closet door several inches and peered out just as his grandfather came shuffling into the room. Keeper watched, hardly daring to breathe, as the old man hooked his cane over the back of the rocker and sat down with a weary sigh.

"What's he doing?" Jonnie Prettyboy whispered.

"Nothing. Resting."

"I want to go home."

"Wait. He's rolling up his sleeve."

"I don't feel so good," she whispered.

"Be quiet," Keeper cautioned, and watched as his grandfather opened the familiar black valise at his feet to take out a small stainless steel box, a length of rubber tubing, and a brown glass vial. Keeper was close enough to read the label. It said morphine.

Jonnie Prettyboy whispered into Keeper's ear. "Now what?"

He felt her hot breath on his neck as he strained to watch his grandfather open the metal box and take out a syringe. "I think he's going to give himself a vaccination." He had seen his grandfather give shots before, but this time seemed different. It took a while to knot the rubber tube around his arm, but after injecting the morphine into a thin blue vein inside the left elbow, Dr. Wick let his head drop, sighed, and closed his eyes.

Jonnie Prettyboy crowded against Keeper. "That wasn't a vaccination," she said. "That was some kind of dope."

Keeper cautiously opened the closet door. "I think it was something to make him sleep." At that instant, a great horned owl swept past the open window to land in a towering maple nearly as old as the house itself. The owl's fierce yellow eyes seemed to be staring directly at Keeper, and he felt as if it could see everything he had ever done, or would ever do.

Jonnie Prettyboy pushed him hard. "Let me the fuck out of here!"

He stepped out of the closet with the skull still tucked under his arm. "Scared of owls too?" he said, but he was glad she was with him.

"You dumb shit. If an owl comes during the day, it means somebody's going to die before dawn!"

"You're just being Indian superstitious," Keeper replied, but he sounded uncertain.

She headed for the bedroom door. "I'm never setting foot in this creepy old house again."

"Wait'll I check downstairs."

"You're not leaving me alone with your grandpa!"

"He's sleeping. Besides, you don't need to be afraid of him. He delivered me and you and lots of other kids in town too."

"I don't care if he delivered Baby Jesus. I'm not staying in this house another fucking *minute!* Not only that, I don't think we should be going to the horse barn anymore either."

"Can I see your boobies before we stop?

"No."

"Then, can I touch 'em?"

"Maybe tomorrow," she said, "unless we drop dead first."

CHAPTER FIVE

Chance and Velma lay side-by-side on her bed. Both were naked except for Chance, who wore ankle-length black socks. The house still reeked of postcoital spunk and the two T-bone steaks he had oven-broiled for their dinner the night before. It was the same whenever he came through Cincinnati. He'd pick up the steaks and she provided the trimmings. Sometimes they'd have wine with dinner, but it was always book-ended with bourbon shots for him and gin and tonics for her.

Chance vaguely remembered calling home the night before, although the details remained sketchy because he'd been knee-walking drunk. He told Alva to expect him late the next day, a Friday, and not to hold dinner. He also recalled it being past midnight when he and Velma finally tumbled into bed.

Chance rolled toward her and placed a hand on the nearest breast.

She smiled at the touch. "You've got the most beautiful hands, Doc," she said.

He knew it was true. They resembled his father's when his father was much younger – strong and deeply veined. "Even with these calluses?" he asked.

Velma lifted his hand from her breast and traced the ridges with the tip of her index finger. "How does a white man get calluses anyway?"

He laughed. "In my case, it's from demonstrating ballast tampers and flexible shaft concrete vibrators."

Velma slowly walked her fingers down Chance's stomach. "How about another demonstration with this flexible shaft?" she asked with a throaty chuckle.

Chance glanced at his watch and brushed her hand away. "Sorry, Vel," he said. "The road beckons."

"Bastard."

"That too."

Velma pushed herself up on one elbow and leaned into his face. Her nutmeg-brown skin contrasted sharply with his. "Stay another day, Doc?" she wheedled.

Chance reached for the half-smoked pack of Old Golds he'd left on the bedside table. He shook out a cigarette for her before taking one himself and lit them both off the Zippo, a gift from Velma, who had it engraved with "Doc. You Bastard. Velma."

"You know I'd like to," he replied as he handed Velma her cigarette, "but I have to be home by tonight."

"Did I hear you say, 'I'd *like* to?'"

"C'mon, Vel, you know how I feel about you."

Velma blew a cloud of gauzy blue cigarette smoke into Chance's upturned face. "You know what, Doc? I don't think you feel anything about anybody."

He reached for the butt-filled ashtray on the bedside table and centered it on his stomach. "Maybe it's time you got married to some nice nine-to-five guy and have lots of kids."

Velma snorted. "Do I look like the motherly type to you?"

He picked a stray bit of tobacco off his tongue and flicked it away before answering. "I only meant that for us..."

She interrupted. "'For us,' meaning I stay out of sight in my crib? Why shit. We never go out. No movies, no eat'n out, no fucking nothin', 'count of I'm an uppity black bitch who says her mind. Truth is you can't risk being seen with a nigra. Right?"

"You seemed satisfied with our arrangement before," he countered.

"Like dropping in for a steak dinner and a couple of fucks every now and again? How's a real woman supposed to be satisfied with that?"

Chance stubbed out his unfinished cigarette in the ashtray and returned it still smoldering to the nightstand. He pushed himself to a sitting position with a grunt and swung his legs over the side of the bed. There were holes in the heels of his socks, and for a fleeting moment, he thought he might want to ask Velma to mend them. "I've got to be going, Vel."

"Maybe you shouldn't come back," she said.

"You don't mean that."

Velma rolled toward Chance and placed a hand on his shoulder. "I do, Doc," she said. "Time goes by real slow when your only company is a mirror."

Wordlessly, Chance pulled away and stood to dress. His undershorts, cuffed trousers and long sleeved Pendleton shirt with the double pockets were where he'd tossed them the night before, over a chair next to Velma's mirrored vanity. He dressed quickly and shuffled into the living room in search of his black wingtips. He found them under the coffee table and was tying them when he caught sight of Velma standing the hallway, hands on hips and scowling. She wore a white terrycloth robe tied at the waist with a green and red-striped silk necktie. He recognized the tie, a Christmas gift from Alva the year before. He wondered where he'd left it.

"Breakfast?" Velma said, "Something to hold you over on the road?"

"Coffee'll do."

She nodded. "I'll get it started."

"Vel?"

"Don't say anything, okay Doc?"

Chance wanted to say he hated like hell to be leaving, and to remind her business was business, but thought the better of it. Instead, he silently followed her into the kitchen and sat at the Formica and chrome Daystrom to wait while she made coffee. He watched her every anger-fueled movement with wary eyes, even wincing as she banged the aluminum coffee pot against the sink to fill it, and again when she slammed the pot down on the gas stove like she was killing a roach. Chance reached into his shirt pocket for a cigarette and tapped it on the table to settle the tobacco before lighting it off the Zippo. After taking a drag he held the cigarette toward Velma. "Smoke?" he asked with a smile that emphasized a carefully trimmed moustache.

"Another bad habit I'd like to break."

"Mind if I turn on the radio?"

"Suit yourself."

Chance got up from the table and turned on the Crosley portable that shared a countertop outlet with a toaster so old it had doors that flipped open. When the radio warmed up he set the dial to Don McNeil's *Breakfast Club*, Alva's favorite morning radio program. Chance was certain she'd be listening to it. He found the image to be more comforting than guilt-inducing. He returned to his chair where he could watch Velma sulking at the kitchen window while the coffee percolated.

"There's a war coming, Velma."

She ignored the pointed observation, and when the coffee was ready, she slammed a ceramic mug down on the Daystrom and filled it to the rim.

Chance carefully picked up the mug and blew across it to cool the hot coffee. "There'll be a great demand for our equipment."

"Like flexible shafts?"

Chance smiled. "Railroad ballast tampers. I'll be on the road more than ever."

Velma scowled and turned for the bathroom at the end of the hall. When she returned she held Chance's shaving kit like it was bread from the oven. The kit had his initials CAW stamped above the clasp in gold-embossed letters. "I mean it, Doc," she said. "Don't come back unless you're serious about us."

Chance set his coffee mug down and stood to take the kit from her hands. "I'll call from the road," he said.

"Don't bother," she replied, and turned away when he tried to kiss her.

"Have it your way," Chance said. He strode quickly through the house to the screened front door, opened it, and stepped out onto the porch. He was about to let it slam shut when Velma came striding toward him with her robe flapping open.

"Don't leave me Doc, you son of a bitch bastard! Don't!"

"Goodbye, Velma," he said, and turned away. With determined steps he strode down the frost-buckled concrete walk toward the high-mileage blue Lincoln Zephyr sedan with its attached black demo trailer parked at the curb. He quickly unlocked the driver's door and slid behind the wheel. He fumbled the key into the ignition, started the engine, and pulled away without looking back.

CHAPTER SIX

It was the hottest August day yet, and Keeper and Jonnie Prettyboy were playing at the beach, where they had been since early that morning. They were only a block away from Keeper's house – close enough to hear his mother if she called for him to come home, and far enough to say he hadn't heard her when he didn't want to.

He wore an itchy pair of navy-blue woolen swim-trunks and was scouring the shoreline for driftwood and any overlooked planks washed up from sailing ships that sank in storms years before. It took all his strength to drag his latest find across the sand to Jonnie Prettyboy digging into a low bluff with a garden spade. She wore a two-piece yellow and black polka dot swimsuit, and unlike Keeper whose pale skin was sunburned, she was deeply tanned. She looked up as he approached with another plank. This one sprouted a heavy bolt that was bent like a curved tusk.

"That's enough," Jonnie Prettyboy said. She was panting and sand mottled her sweaty body. She clambered out of the hole to help Keeper secure the latest plank next to the others, and left a crawlspace from which to enter and exit. "Now help me cover it."

After the two had layered several handfuls of beach grass over the planks, she shoveled sand over the grass to camouflage the fort. When the two were finished, they had a cozy hideaway invisible to anyone unless they were standing on top of it.

"Now go home and bring us something to eat," she ordered.

"What sounds good?" Keeper asked.

"Potato chips. Potato chips and coffee."

Since he knew a pot was always kept on the stove at home, he didn't question the request. "Right away, honey," he said.

Her pale-gray eyes flashed with sudden anger. "Where do you get off calling me honey?"

"I don't know," Keeper blurted. "It just came out."

"Never call me that again, *hear?*"

He offered a guilty smile. "I won't." He felt sad and embarrassed whenever he said or did something unexpected to upset his friend. He never meant to hurt her, but sometimes it was impossible to know what would set her off. Once, he had called her a "Redskin," not thinking it was a bad thing to say because he'd heard Red Ryder say it in a movie. Another time he told her she couldn't be a real Indian because of her gray eyes. That got him punched in the stomach. On the other hand, he never complained when she made fun of his reddish hair, freckles, and 'Norwegian-ordinary' eyes, or how easily he got sunburned, which he was right now.

"Bring some cigarettes and matches too," Jonnie Prettyboy added.

"Yes, sir," Keeper replied. He grinned and ducked when she raised a fist at him.

He ran through the hot sand, dodging horn-blowing motorists when he crossed the foot-scorching asphalt of Shore Drive, and raced up the sidewalk to his house. He circled behind his mother at work in the vegetable garden and let himself unseen into the kitchen through the screen door. Moving sneaky-fast, he took an unopened bag of potato chips from the pantry and held it under his arm while he poured several cups of hot coffee into a thermos.

He was halfway out the door when he remembered the cigarettes. He turned back and dashed to the cabinet where his father kept his liquor and cigarettes and grabbed a pack from the open carton of Old Golds. He was halfway out the door again when he remembered the matches. Juggling his contraband, Keeper snatched a book of wooden matches off the stovetop and carried it between clenched teeth. When he heard Early shuffling toward the kitchen, he froze.

"Mother?" Early called. "Is that you?"

Keeper pressed his back against the wall as Early entered the kitchen. Sand he'd brought from the beach on his feet crunched under Early's shoes.

"Keep, that's you, isn't it?"

Keeper held his breath as he sidled away from his advancing blind half-brother.

"You've been at the beach again, right?" Early said, and came toward Keeper with outstretched arms.

Without answering, Keeper ducked under Early's groping hands and bolted for the screen door. He let himself out with the door slamming behind him and ran through the backyard toward the beach and Jonnie Prettyboy, who he hoped still waited for him at the fort.

He crawled headfirst into the fort, relieved to find her still there, and placed everything he'd taken from the house at her feet before handing her the matches. "I feel like I'm married," he panted.

She ignored the comment and poured hot coffee into the red thermos cap before lighting a cigarette. "I've been thinking," she said. "I could fix up our fort real nice."

"It's pretty nice now," Keeper replied, looking satisfied as he poured a cup for himself in the beige-colored inside cap.

"Not nice enough to stay in."

His eyebrows shot up. "Stay?"

Jonnie Prettyboy took a deep drag off the cigarette. When she exhaled, tobacco smoke clouded her face and disappeared through chinks in the planking overhead.

"Sometimes I don't want to be around when my pa's drinking."

Keeper felt his stomach tighten at the thought, but he didn't exactly know why. "It gets cold out here at night," he said.

"I've been cold before."

"I've got a sleeping bag I could bring you."

She reached for the potato chips and took a handful. "You'd have to bring me chow too."

He seemed to consider the idea, as if weighing the risk of being caught against any potential reward, such as being allowed to touch Jonnie Prettyboy's boobies. "Okay," he said, and helped himself to the potato chips.

"Just remember," she said. "I don't eat anything that swims, crawls, or flies."

Keeper nodded to mean he understood and took a sip of thermos coffee. "What about in the wintertime?" he asked.

"I'll hit the trail south before it comes to that."

"My dad's been south," he replied. "When he gets home tonight, I'll ask him where…"

"Shut your big fat mouth right now!" Jonnie Prettyboy snarled. "You're not saying nothing to nobody about my plans."

Keeper looked away, intimidated. "What will you do for money?"

"I'll hook."

He immediately thought of his mother hooking rugs from colorful scraps of rags. "Rugs?"

Jonnie Prettyboy shook her head in apparent disbelief. "How can you be so fucking stupid?"

"I don't know," Keeper replied softly. "It must be inherited."

"Speaking of which, does your pa keep a roadmap in his car?"

He nodded. "He's a road man, isn't he?"

"Then bring it to our fort tomorrow, and don't let anybody see you, either."

"I won't," Keeper promised.

"When you come, make sure I know it's you by whistling."

"I can imitate a killdeer," he said, and whistled to prove it.

"You'd never fool an Indian with that fake shit."

"What if I do an owl?"

"What if I kick you in the nuts?"

"Okay," Keeper said. "I'll whistle like I was calling my dog, if I had one."

Jonnie Prettyboy rolled her eyes and sighed. "God, you're dumb."

He scowled. "Do you want me to bring the map, or not?"

She raised a fist, a warning. "Yeah, and not a word to anybody, or else!"

CHAPTER SEVEN

Keeper stood at the living room window impatiently waiting for his father's Lincoln to turn up the street. He had been maintaining his vigil ever since the dinner dishes had been cleared off the table and put away. Dinner had been the bucket of yellow perch Keeper had caught off the breakwall that afternoon, using a bamboo cane pole and shiners for bait. Behind him, Dr. Wick dozed in his wingback, and Alva sat on the couch hooking a rug for Early's bedroom. News of the war raging in faraway Europe and a place called Singapore in the Pacific muttered softly on the Zenith. To Keeper, its green tuning eye seemed to look accusingly into the room like an owl's eye.

"Your father's not going to get here any sooner by you watching for him." Alva said.

It was already dark, and Keeper was mostly seeing his sunburned face reflected in the window. "I'll recognize his headlights when he turns up the street."

"I'm not sure he'll recognize *you*," Alva said. "Your grandfather and I warned you about staying out in the sun too long. Now look at you," she scolded. "Burned to a crisp."

"I'm okay, Mom."

"What do you do on that beach all day long?"

"Play, that's all."

"With that Indian girl, what's her name again, Jonnie Prettyman?"

"Prettyboy," Keeper corrected, "and she's only half Indian."

"I wish you'd find some nice boys your own age to play with."

"Okay," Keeper replied. When he heard Early coming down the stairs, he turned to watch in case his half-brother stumbled. He knew it was bad to think that way, but not nearly as bad as when he deliberately moved their grandfather's wingback from its customary place, which caused Early to bark his shin against it and swear. Keeper was sent to his room over that dirty trick.

"Dad's not home yet?" Early asked of no one in particular.

Alva looked up from her rug hooking and checked her watch. "He's later than usual."

Early cocked an ear. "Maybe the traffic."

"Maybe the demo trailer had a blowout," Keeper mumbled under his breath.

"Don't say that," Early said

"I hate that trailer," Keeper replied. "It's ugly."

"It feels ugly too," Early added.

Keeper frowned as he contemplated his half-brother's uncanny ability to "see" with his fingers. Sometimes, he wished Early would wear dark glasses, so his blindness wouldn't be as noticeable, especially when he talked to someone. Then it looked as if Early was staring at an invisible spot two feet over people's heads. Keeper felt reasonably close to his half-brother, in spite of their age differential. He enjoyed Early's company, particularly when their father was on the road. In spite of having different mothers, Keeper could see they were related. Early had the same reddish-brown hair and facial features, but he was short – shorter than their shared father, who was six feet tall in his stocking feet. Early had the same beautiful hands too, making Keeper hope his would be beautiful when he grew up. Maybe then Jonnie Prettyboy would allow him to touch her boobies.

"Penny for your thoughts," Early said.

Keeper blushed, because he knew Early had a sixth sense and loved to tease him. "Mind your own bee's wax."

"Hey, Keep," Early whispered. "You got hair on your nuts yet?" He asked the same question at least twice a day.

"Like an organ grinder's monkey," Keeper replied, giggling because it was his stock answer to their ongoing joke.

Alva smiled. "What's gotten into you two?" she asked.

Early laughed. "Keeper said he needs a haircut."

"No, I didn't," Keeper whined.

"Doesn't he, Mother?" Early asked, and laughed as he groped to find Keeper's head.

Alva looked at Keeper with a critical eye. "Maybe. I'll ask Father."

Early cocked his head toward the street. "He's here now."

"Yay!" Keeper shouted. He ducked under Early's searching hands and ran through the house to the kitchen just as the Lincoln pulled up to the curb with the black trailer in tow. The clock on the wall showed seven-thirty. Keeper pushed open the screen door and bolted down the steps to greet his father.

"Dad!" he shouted.

"Hey, Keep!" Chance called back as he stepped from the car.

Keeper ran into his father's arms and buried his face in the Pendleton shirt that smelled of stale tobacco smoke, body odor – and ever so slightly of perfume.

"Did you miss me? Chance asked.

"Yeah," Keeper snuffled.

"I missed you more."

"Couldn't," Keeper replied with a hug.

Chance smiled and pushed his son away to look at him. "You need a haircut," he said, tousling Keeper's hair.

Keeper deflected the comment. "Can I bring in your suitcase?" He needn't have asked. Carrying his father's suitcase into the house was just as much his job to do coming home, as it was taking it out to the car when his father left for the road. At those times, Keeper felt like an accomplice to his father's leaving, and somehow responsible for the hollow, unsettled feeling that always filled the house afterward.

"How's everybody been?" Chance asked.

"Good," Keeper answered as he opened the Lincoln's trunk. Of course it was a lie. Too often he'd heard his mother late at night, slipping down to the kitchen for a bowl of warm milk and saltine crackers when sleep wouldn't come. Sometimes he heard her weeping while she played endless hands of solitaire in her bed. It was worse when it stormed, or when his father had just left on a long trip. Then there was his grandfather, who sat in his room reading a Bible and listening to solemn announcers like Edward R. Murrow on the radio talking about war all the time. Sometimes Early listened in while he fingered his Braille Bible and shared opinions about President Roosevelt, who Dr. Wick called a "communist," and "undoubtedly syphilitic" as well.

"I count on you to be the man of the house when I'm gone, Keeper," Chance said.

"That's me, Dad," Keeper replied as he lugged his father's suitcase into the house.

Instead of first going into the living room, Chance turned for the liquor cabinet and opened a bottle of Old Crow. As he poured himself a drink, Early entered the kitchen.

"Cheated death once again, huh Dad?" Early laughed and stuck out his right hand in the general direction of his father.

"Good to see you, son," Chance said. He took Early's hand and shook it.

"Did you bring company?" Early asked.

"No, why?"

"I smell 'Evening in Paris.'"

"Cincinnati," Chance replied too quickly. "I was given a 'see you next time' hug by a contractor's big-knockered accountant."

Early shook his head and scowled. "This time out was tougher on Mother than usual," he said. While waiting for a response, he poured himself a cup of coffee from the pot on the stovetop, and stopped when he felt the hot liquid touching the tip of the index finger he held over the cup's rim.

"I know it's hard for her," Chance replied. "That's why I count on you being the man of the house in my absence," repeating what he always told Keeper. He turned when he heard Alva calling his name from the living room, a tremulous; "Chance, is that you dear?"

"Be right there."

Early held out a hand to stop him. "We've got to talk about Granddad."

"Later, Early," Chance said, and strode into the living room to greet both his waiting wife and father, who dozed on and off in the wingback. In the background Gabriel Heatter intoned; *"There's bad news tonight..."* on the big Zenith.

Chance bent to place a chaste kiss on Alva's upturned cheek.

"How were the roads?" she asked.

"Not bad, considering there's a fifty-mile-per hour speed limit."

"Which you habitually ignore," Alva said. A mild reprove.

"That would be true, Alva dear. Otherwise, I'd still be two hundred miles this side of Cincinnati."

"Your favorite stopping-off place on the way home."

"It's convenient," Chance replied.

Alva turned back to her hooking needle and the unfinished rug spread out on her lap and forced a smile. "Do you stop there on the way out, too?" she asked.

"It depends on the time of day, Alva, but yes, sometimes I do."

"Have you eaten?" she asked after a minute.

"A cup of coffee this morning is all."

Alva plunged her hooking needle into the rug like she was spearing a frog, and said, "You must be starved. There's still some fish from dinner, perch that Keep caught off the pier today. Do you want it warmed up, or cold?"

Chance smiled. "Whatever's easiest for you, my dear."

CHAPTER EIGHT

Dirty breakfast dishes filled the sink and Don McNeill's "Breakfast Club" played over the kitchen radio. Dr. Wick was in the garden cutting a red rose for his lapel. Early was out tuning the local piano teacher's Baldwin, and Keeper was washing his father's Lincoln at the curb. With everyone else otherwise occupied, Chance and Alva lingered over coffee at the kitchen table.

"How much longer before Mr. Pettigrew takes you off the road?" she asked. It was a reasonable question. Chance had been promised a promotion for some time, along with less travel.

Chance tapped out a cigarette from the pack they were sharing and lit it off a match torn from a Union Pacific matchbook. "I don't look for that to happen anytime soon."

Smoke from the cigarette Alva held between her fingers hung in the air between them like a gauzy curtain – as if to mask the hopelessness she felt. "The boys need you at home, Chance," she said, "and so do I."

"This time I'll be home for two weeks catching up on paperwork. After that, I'm taking the Super Chief from Chicago to Albuquerque."

Alva's face registered disappointment. "My brother promised Keeper he'd take the three of you on a fishing trip up the Dakota River while you're home."

"No time."

"Find time."

"I'll make it up to Keep. I'll buy him something out west."

"Buying him things is a poor substitute for not having a full-time father."

Chance appeared not to have heard. "Keep likes Indian things. I'll get him a genuine beaded Indian belt and a pair of moccasins."

"That's another thing," Alva replied. "He's been spending too much time with that Indian girl, Jonnie Prettyboy, and it's not healthy. She has a mouth on her like a dock worker, and is a bad influence on Keeper."

"That's Roy Prettyboy's daughter. He works at the plant."

"That doesn't change my opinion."

"Nonsense, Alva. They're just kids."

Alva slammed her coffee mug down on the table. "I can't keep going on like this, Chance. Sometimes I want to run away from this goddamned house and its responsibilities and never look back."

"I'll get you help," Chance offered in a conciliatory tone of voice. "Someone to come in and help with the housework."

"I don't want 'someone,'" she replied on the verge of tears. "I want *you!*"

He pushed back from the table and went to the liquor cabinet where he poured himself a drink, taking it straight. "Why not have your sister come up from Detroit and stay while I'm out of town?" he asked. "She'd be good company, and Keeper would enjoy seeing his aunt."

"Chance, you haven't heard a goddamned word I've said!"

"Alva, I've got a job to do, and if *I* don't do it, Mr. Pettigrew will find someone else who will."

"Maybe that wouldn't be such a bad idea."

Chance turned for the sink and ran tap water over his cigarette before tossing the wet butt into the wastebasket. "I've got to run out to the plant for a few hours."

"Take Keeper with you. God knows he sees precious little of you as it is."

Chance smiled. "I intended to."

"I'll do your laundry and mend your socks after I wash the breakfast dishes," Alva said. "Your shirt smells like I wish I did."

He winced at the comment. "I'll pick up something for dinner."

"What about eating out for a change?

"Wouldn't be a change for me."

Alva sighed. "Get whatever you want, but I won't be cooking it."

"I'll get veal chops," Chance said as he grabbed a fresh pack of cigarettes from the carton in the cabinet and headed out the kitchen door.

"Hey, Keep," he called when he saw Keeper putting the hose away. "How'd you like to come with me to the plant for a few hours?"

Keeper looked up with a huge grin that split his peeling, sunburned face. "Can I drive?" He'd been "driving" since he was old enough to sit on his father's lap.

"Sure thing," Chance replied. Once he was settled behind the wheel, he patted his lap. "Hop on up."

Keeper slid onto his father's lap and gripped the steering wheel.

"Got 'er in neutral?" Chance asked.

Keeper wiggled the column-mounted shift lever. "Yep."

"Now turn the ignition key and press the starter button."

"I know how, Dad," Keeper replied. Once underway he grinned as he imagined himself on the road, a road man just like his father. "Can we take the long way?" he asked.

"You're driving," Chance said as he lit a cigarette off the dashboard lighter.

Keeper felt his father's strong legs moving up and down beneath him while controlling the clutch, brake and gas pedals. His father's warm breath on his sunburned neck raised gooseflesh and made his scalp prickle. For once, he didn't mind the smell of liquor on his father's breath – or the smoke from the cigarette either. It was as if he and his father were on the road together and headed to wherever Keeper decided they would go. And where he wanted to go right now was south to Georgia, where colored boys wearing striped uniforms worked on chain gangs and sang hymns.

He reluctantly allowed his father to take over the driving when they approached the plant, where they parked in front of the sign that spelled Wick.

"Good job, Keep," Chance said. "We cheated death once again."

Keeper beamed at the compliment. He enjoyed visiting Dakota Tamper almost as much as he did "driving" his father's Lincoln. The pungent smell of cutting oil, raw welded steel, rubber strapping, solvents, paint, and the freshly-cut lumber and packing excelsior in the shipping department was intoxicating. Rows of yellow ballast tampers, soil compactors and concrete vibrators filled the final assembly area, ready to be shipped to railroads and contractors around the world. Knowing that his father was responsible for sales always filled Keeper with pride, and made his father's long absences almost bearable.

"Wait in my office, Keep," Chance said as they entered the lobby. "I need to check in with Mr. Pettigrew, the boss."

Keeper nodded and took a seat in the swivel chair behind his father's desk. From there, he could imagine himself on the telephone, talking to customers and then dictating messages for secretaries to type. A large-scale map similar to the map he had in his room hung on the wall to his left. Colored pushpins identified dealer locations. Framed photographs showing his father on the job with contractors, and others of him drinking and smoking with dealers at conventions covered the opposite wall. Keeper was especially proud that his father kept a recent framed photo of the two of them on his desk. In it, his father, who always seemed to have a cigarette in his hand, wore a dark shirt and tie, and Keeper wore a sailor suit. It was the summer before Pearl Harbor.

The door to Orville Pettigrew's office was open, but Chance knocked out of respect for Dakota Tamper's founder and sole owner. "'Morning, Mr. Pettigrew."

Orville Pettigrew looked up from the Track and Structures trade magazine he was reading. "Good to have you home, Chance," he growled. "Come in and take a seat."

Fragrant burley smoke from the briarwood pipe he held between clenched teeth wreathed his bald head like a storm cloud. He wore twill jodhpurs, a white Western-style shirt and brown leather riding boots – his usual Saturday attire.

"Good to be back," Chance replied. After taking his seat, he pulled a pack of cigarettes from the pocket of the shirt he had put on fresh that morning.

"How are Alva and the family getting along?"

"They're all doing fine, Mr. Pettigrew. Thanks."

Orville Pettigrew didn't respond, but instead he leaned back in his swivel chair to puff on the briarwood while he studied Chance.

Chance tapped out a cigarette and lit it. For a long minute, neither man spoke, until he broke the silence.

"To be perfectly honest, sir, Alva's having a very difficult time."

Orville Pettigrew nodded. "I was about to call you a liar, Chance."

Chance forced a small grin and feigned interest in his cigarette.

"My apologies to Alva and the family, but make the most of your time while you're home."

"Sir?"

"It can't have escaped your notice, that we're being drawn into the goddamned war. Dakota Tamper will be busy, and so will you, more than ever."

Chance nodded. "I expected as much."

"I saw you pull in. Isn't that your son with you?"

"Yes. Keeper thinks the plant is magical."

"Call him in, Chance."

"Yes sir," he replied, and stood to call Keeper from the open doorway.

In seconds, Keeper was standing in the big corner office.

"Mr. Pettigrew asked to see you, Keep."

Mr. Pettigrew waved a hand. "Come in, son, don't just stand there."

Keeper nodded and stepped into the richly paneled office to stand next to his father.

"How old are you, son?" Mr. Pettigrew asked.

Keeper stood straight. "Ten, sir, but I'll be eleven pretty soon."

Mr. Pettigrew chuckled. "When I was your age, I was up before dawn milking cows, drawing water from the well and splitting firewood for the cook stove. Do you help out around the house when your father is on the road?"

Keeper stole a glance at his father before answering. "Yes sir."

"That's good," Mr. Pettigrew replied, "because your father will be traveling more in the days to come."

Keeper swallowed hard. "Yes sir."

Mr. Pettigrew turned back to Chance. "Chance, drop the demonstration trailer behind the plant and get the hell out of here. Enjoy the weekend with your family. We'll talk Monday."

———

Keeper loved every minute of shopping at Kroger's with his dad. He listened with pride while Chance bantered with the butcher over how the veal chops should be cut just so. He watched his father examine the produce for freshness and color, and rejecting any fruit or vegetable that showed the slightest bruise or blemish.

When they got home, and after helping his father carry the grocery bags into the kitchen, Keeper ran out to the Lincoln and opened the glove box where the roadmaps were kept. When he reached in he discovered something rectangular and smoothly metallic. Curious, Keeper wrapped his fingers around his find and removed it for a closer look. He recognized it to be a Zippo lighter with writing on it. He ran his thumb over the engraved message that read: "Doc. You Bastard. Velma." Keeper had heard his father's drinking friends call him "Doc," and he had also heard Jonnie Prettyboy using the word "bastard." But he had never heard of a "Velma." The only conclusion he could draw, without knowing what a conclusion was, was that Velma and his father were in some way connected, and not in a good way.

He flipped back the lid and thumbed the serrated wheel until a flame appeared. He stared at it until his hand shook, and when the lighter became too hot to comfortably hold, he snapped the lid closed and put it back where he found it. Then almost forgetting what he'd come for, Keeper hurriedly tucked the road map Jonnie Prettyboy had asked for under his tee shirt and returned to the kitchen, where he found his father pouring bourbon into a paper cup.

"Don't breathe a word to anybody about what Mr. Pettigrew said this morning," Chance warned after knocking back the drink. "I'll tell your mother later."

"Don't worry, Dad," Keeper replied. "I can keep secrets."

Chance smiled. "I almost forgot, Keep. I picked up something on the road for you." He fumbled in his trousers pocket and handed Keeper what appeared to be a sheriff's badge.

Keeper took it and turned it over in his fingers to examine it more closely. It was a perforated aluminum disc the size of a silver dollar, with his name, address and telephone number stamped around its perimeter. Horseshoes and four leaf clovers were stamped on its reverse side. "What is it?"

"A lucky charm."

"Okay."

"Just okay?"

"I mean, thanks. It's swell."

"I carry one just like it," Chance said, "for luck on the road."

Keeper wordlessly tucked the lucky charm in his pocket.

Chance smiled. "We'll take a trip together someday, Keep, and when we do, we'll be protected from the hazards of the road."

"Will they protect us from whores and thieves too?"

"Who the hell told you that?"

"Grandpa did. He said there were whores and thieves on the road, just waiting for the likes of you."

"Go out and play, Keeper," Chance muttered. "It's high time I had a talk with your grandfather."

CHAPTER NINE

Keeper knew Jonnie Prettyboy was waiting for him at the fort and probably mad because it was already past noon. After he changed into his bathing suit and a fresh tee-shirt he snuck downstairs to the kitchen and grabbed two glazed donuts from the breadbox. He let himself out through the kitchen screen door and ran through the backyard past the old horse barn with the donuts clutched in his sweaty hands. At the beach screeching gulls wheeled against a cobalt sky so deeply-blue it seemed to absorb light. When he reached the fort he gave the prearranged signal, four short whistles that were meant to sound like a killdeer in distress. When he heard an identical whistle from inside the fort, Keeper scuttled into the hidden entrance on his elbows and knees.

"Where the hell have you been? Jonnie Prettyboy snapped. "I've been waiting since sunup!"

"With my dad at Dakota Tamper," he panted. "I drove, too."

"Bullshit."

He held out a donut. It had sand on it from when he crawled into the fort. "I brought you some breakfast."

Jonnie Prettyboy snatched the donut from Keeper's hand and wordlessly brushed it off before greedily taking a bite. When it was gone, she washed it down with cold thermos coffee saved from the day before.

Keeper stared, curious, because it looked like she hadn't gone home. She still wore her two-piece bathing suit, and her eyes were red and tired looking. The potato chip bag was empty and there were ashes in the low depression where there'd been a small driftwood fire. Cigarette butts littered the sandy floor of the fort. "Did you stay here all night?" he asked.

"What's it to you?" she said, sounding mean.

"Nothing, I guess."

"Then shut up and give me that other donut."

Keeper handed it over without argument and pulled his knees up under his chin to watch as she wolfed it down.

"Don't stare at me like I'm some kind of freak!" she snapped. Donut glaze coated her lips like frostbite.

"Sorry," Keeper mumbled, and looked away, embarrassed again.

For several long minutes, neither spoke. Only the sound of heavy surf thundering ashore broke the silence – coupled with the distinctive beach-smell of sun-scorched sand, rotting alewives, and coal smoke pouring from the twin stacks of the outbound SS Dakota Straits.

"Did you bring the map?" Jonnie Prettyboy asked as she licked frosting from her fingertips.

Keeper pulled up his tee-shirt to show he had it. He peeled the map away from his sweat-sticky skin and handed it over with a pleased smile.

"Goddamn good thing, too," she said, with her meaning crystal clear that any future demands would be met unconditionally – or else. She held the map under a thin wedge of sunlight coming through a chink in the overhead planking and began to trace an index finger across the maze of intersecting blue and red lines that marked the U.S. highway system between Michigan and Florida.

"You're going to get me in big shit trouble," Keeper warned.

"Don't worry," Jonnie Prettyboy said. "I'm not a squealer like some people I know."

"Maybe not, but you can't stay here."

"Like hell I can't," she snarled. "And don't think you can get away with two donuts either. Come back tonight with some real chow, and more smokes too."

"But won't your mom and dad be looking for you?"

"Not after last night they won't."

Keeper was confused. "But you went home didn't you?" he finally asked.

Jonnie Prettyboy seemed to consider the question, as if admitting to it would be seen as a sign of weakness. "None of your business," she answered. With a scowl she shook a last cigarette from the pack Keeper had brought to the fort the day before and lit it off a kitchen match.

"Something bad happened, didn't it?" Keeper asked.

Glittering tears welled in Jonnie Prettyboy's pale gray eyes. They leaked down her cheeks to her chin and dribbled onto the swimsuit top covering her breasts. "Shut up, you little shit."

"Okay." Keeper wrapped his arms around his skinny legs and wriggled his toes in the cool sand. "I only wanted to help."

She rubbed her eyes with the heels of her hands, but never dropped the precious cigarette. "Son of a *bitch*!" she cried, and turned away, exposing a raised welt across her left shoulder.

"What happened to your back?" Keeper asked.

Jonnie Prettyboy choked back a sob. "I fell on some steps."

"No you didn't," Keeper said. "I'm almost a doctor."

"Swear on your life you won't tell?"

He held up his right hand like he was taking a solemn oath. "I swear."

She spit in the palm of her right hand and extended it across the driftwood fire ashes toward Keeper. "Spit and shake on it."

Keeper spit in the flat of his hand and slapped it against hers.

"If you squeal," she said, "you'd better look out for owls."

"I'm already a second class scout, and scouts don't squeal."

Jonnie Prettyboy didn't let go of Keeper's hand. Instead, she tightened her grip and held on as if to gain strength. "I went home like you said. Pa was drunk again and beating on ma," she began. "When I tried to make them stop, she screamed at me and said it was all *my* fault they were fighting."

Keeper's jaw dropped. "Your *mom* did that?"

She shook her head. "My pa did it, the fuck, with a leather belt."

"But...why?" He was almost afraid of learning the answer, as if knowing could bring more harm to her, and maybe even to him.

"You're too dumb to understand."

"I'll tell my dad," Keeper said evenly. "*He'll* know what to do."

"You'll do no such thing, Keeper Wick! You *swore!*"

"But what if it happens again?"

"Not if I never go home again, it won't. Besides, I cut him real bad."

Keeper wriggled his toes deeper into the sand as he considered what had happened, and what he could possibly do to help. "You could hide out in our old horse barn," he said at last. "Nobody but us ever goes out there anymore. Especially up to the hayloft."

"I suppose I could," she said after seeming to think it over. "But only temporary, while I make my plans."

"I'll come back for you tomorrow after dark," Keeper promised.

She drew on the last inch of her cigarette and exhaled in Keeper's face. "Don't forget the chow, and don't forget our secret signal either."

He coughed, nodded, and scuttled out of the fort on his hands and knees and back into the blinding sun. "I won't, honey," he said, and whistled again to prove he remembered.

"Don't forget my smokes!" Her warning sounded muffled from inside the fort.

"I won't, honey!"

"And quit calling me honey, you little turd! I'm not anybody's honey!"

Keeper crouched just outside the fort's hidden entrance. He was about to ask Jonnie Prettyboy if she wanted half a veal chop for chow that night, but decided not to when he heard her crying so hard it gave him goose bumps.

CHAPTER TEN

That night Keeper slept fitfully. Thoughts of how he might get Mr. Prettyboy to pay for what he'd done were shunted aside by yesterday's promise to Jonnie Prettyboy, of fixing her a hiding place in the horse barn where nobody would ever find her.

The long hot morning seemed never to end. As if things couldn't get worse, by mid-afternoon his father finally broke the bad news about more travel, which caused Alva to cry and take to bed with a brutal headache. Then he asked his father if he would play catch with him in the backyard, but by then Chance was drinking and said maybe some other time. Now Keeper prowled aimlessly through the silent house, killing time until going upstairs and finding Early. His half-brother was in his room seated at a card table and meticulously gluing together a bridge made of toothpicks and wooden tongue depressors. Had it not been for the cruel scar across his sightless eyes, it looked as if Early could actually see what he was doing.

"I heard you fooling around downstairs," Early said.

"There's nothing to do," Keeper complained.

"Come in if you like, but don't touch anything."

"I won't," Keeper promised. When he entered the room, he noticed Early's piano-tuning kit laid out with military precision on top of a mirrored chest of drawers. The kit consisted of a tuning lever, a tuning fork, a flat temperament strip and eight rubber mutes. A celluloid and pig-bristle hairbrush rested next to the tuning kit. Keeper idly wondered if his half-brother faced the mirror like a normal person when he brushed his hair. Quickly breaking his promise, he reached for the tuning fork and picked it up. After rapping it against the back of his hand, he held it next to his ear and hummed loudly to match the frequency.

"What did I just tell you?" Early scolded.

Keeper put the tuning fork back where it belonged. "Sorry."

"You start moving stuff around and I can never find it again."

"You can find those toothpicks okay."

"That's different."

"How do you know what it will look like?" Keeper asked.

"I can visualize it in my head."

When he tried to visualize Jonnie Prettyboy waiting impatiently at their hidden fort, it gave him a sick feeling in his stomach, especially when he remembered the ugly welt across her tanned back.

Early raised his head and sniffed. "You've been to the beach again, haven't you?"

"Why?"

"Because you smell like rotten fish, and that isn't all. You've been smoking."

"I haven't either."

"You know better than to try and fool me, Keep."

Keeper gulped. "It's from Dad, when we were in the car this morning."

"You're in trouble, aren't you? I can hear it in your voice."

"Nuh…no, not me," Keeper stammered.

"C'mon, out with it."

He turned away, as if Early could see how guilty he looked. "I have to go now."

"I'll find out sooner or later," Early warned.

Without a further word, Keeper backed out of Early's room and slunk downstairs past his slumbering father on the couch and into the kitchen. Moving quietly but fast, he took a paper shopping bag from the pantry and began to gather up food items. He chose a jar of his mother's homemade strawberry jam, a small box of Cheerios, two bottles of root beer from the refrigerator, a handful of graham crackers, the last donut and an apple. After remembering Jonnie Prettyboy's warning not to forget the smokes, he took two packs of Old Golds from the carton his father kept in his liquor cabinet.

With a final look at his snoring father, Keeper carried the bag of provisions out to the horse barn where he paused next to his grandfather's dusty Hupmobile Aero Sedan. Keeper looked through the grimy driver's side window to make sure the key was still in the ignition switch. He knew his grandfather always left the key where he could find it in the event he had to make a house call – even though the old physician hadn't made a house call in years.

Keeper hurriedly climbed the narrow and steeply-angled stairs and hid the shopping bag under his grandfather's gynecological examination table. It was hot in the hayloft, at least a hundred degrees by Keeper's reckoning. Over time, the musty barn-smell of long-gone horses and moldering oats had soaked into the walls like an invisible stain. Dust motes swirled in the sunlight slanting through rippled windowpanes, where it reached into spidery corners littered with the iridescent husks of dead flies. Hornets had built a papery-gray nest under the eaves, and their incessant humming sounded to Keeper like Early's tuning fork a hundred times over.

He had planned on bringing out his sleeping bag for Jonnie Prettyboy to use, but other than that, he had little idea what a thirteen year-old girl required in the way of necessities. Whatever it was, he needed to figure it out soon and bring the stuff without being observed by Early. Well, maybe not exactly observed. Since Early couldn't 'observe' anything, 'caught' might be a better word.

"Keeper?"

Keeper froze at the sound of Early's voice coming from below.

"I know you're up there, Keep."

He held his breath, not daring to make a sound. He heard Early's cane tapping at the foot of the stairs, an uneven but constant tempo, like a broken metronome.

"I'm not going to risk climbing the stairs, Keep, so listen closely. Jonnie Prettyboy's mother just called. She said her daughter disappeared from their home last night. She hoped you might know where she is."

Keeper blinked and wiped at the sweat stinging his eyes with the bottom of his tee-shirt.

Early called again. "Keeper, are you listening? Mr. Prettyboy has gone missing too."

Keeper went rigid with fear. What if Mr. Prettyboy was watching this very minute, waiting to be led to wherever his daughter was hiding so he could beat her again with his belt? And as badly as he wanted to get Jonnie Prettyboy before another hour passed, he thought he'd better wait until after dark. Then he could bring her back to the horse barn unseen, assuming, of course, that her father hadn't already found her.

———

Dinner was an ordeal for Keeper. Since he'd lost his appetite to worry, he only picked at his veal chop.

"Keep," Alva said with a concerned look. "Why aren't you eating?"

"His girlfriend is missing," Early volunteered; "and so is her dad."

Chance looked up with bloodshot eyes, evidence of his having finished the last of the Old Crow. "What the hell's this all about?"

"Mrs. Prettyboy called earlier," Early explained, "while you and Mother were napping. She said something happened between her husband and daughter last night. An argument of some sort. She tried to make it sound like it was nothing, but I could tell different. She hoped Keep might know where she is."

Chance scowled and reached for the cigarette smoldering in the heavy lead-crystal ashtray next to his dinner plate. "What do you know about this business, Keep?"

Keeper poked at his cold asparagus and half-eaten veal chop. "Nothing," he replied softly. "Just what Early said, is all I know."

Alva turned toward Early. "Did she say if she called the police?"

Early shook his head. "Didn't say either way, and I didn't ask."

Keeper swallowed hard and pushed his plate away. "Can I be excused?"

"May I," Alva answered. "Yes, and please bring down your grandfather's dinner tray."

Relieved to be excused and away from awkward questions, Keeper hurried through the house and climbed the front stairs two at a time to his grandfather's room. The door was ajar, and he could hear the evening news being broadcast over a cathedral table radio. A man named H.V. Kaltenborn was reporting that the German Army was advancing on Moscow, and that Stalin's capitulation was inevitable, whatever that was.

Keeper peered into his grandfather's room. "Grandpa? Are you awake?"

Dr. Wick sat slumped over the dinner tray placed across his lap and didn't answer.

Keeper pushed open the door and took small, hesitant steps toward his grandfather. As he reached for the tray, the old man stirred, as if sensing his grandson's presence.

"Do you smell it, boy?" Dr. Wick asked in a ragged whisper that sounded urgent.

Keeper sniffed at the familiar co-mingled smell of rum-soaked cigars, rosewater, mothballs and rubbing alcohol, but detected nothing new. "What smell?"

"Rotten plums," Dr. Wick rasped. "Rotten plums gone bad in the sun."

Keeper eyed the nearly untouched dinner tray and hoped his grandfather wasn't going to start talking about the old days again. "I don't know what you mean, Grandpa."

Dr. Wick coughed ripely into his dinner napkin until he gagged. "It's the smell of death, boy. Bodies stacked like cordwood at the curb faster than gravediggers can cart them away." The physician's bony, mottled hands trembled and fluttered uselessly over the dinner tray, as if to ward off some unseen horror.

"There aren't any bodies out there, Grandpa," Keeper said, but he shuddered at the thought, especially now.

"Surely you must smell them."

"You're remembering the Spanish flu epidemic, Grandpa," Keeper replied. He'd been told the story, of how his grandfather had tended sick and dying patients in Highland Park, Michigan in 1918. "Now if you're done, Mom wants your tray."

Dr. Wick waved a trembling hand over his unfinished meal. "Tell your mother smaller portions next time," he said. "I have no appetite these days."

As Keeper reached for the tray, his grandfather clutched him by the arm. "The Four Horsemen are nigh," Dr. Wick intoned. "We must pray."

"Do we have to?" Keeper asked.

Dr. Wick nodded and released his grip. "Bring me my Bible."

Keeper dutifully picked up the worn leather-bound volume that rested open next to the church radio and handed it to his grandfather.

Haltingly, the old physician began to read from Psalm 6: "*O Lord… rebuke me not in thine anger, neither chasten me in thy hot displeasure. Have mercy upon me…O Lord; for I am weak: O Lord, heal me, for my bones are vexed. My soul is also vexed: but thou, O Lord…how long…?*"

"Grandpa?" Keeper interrupted.

"What *is* it, boy?"

"Can I ask you something about Indians?"

Dr. Wick's eyebrows rose over the rim of his spectacles. "What of them?"

"Do they go on rampages and kill people when they're drunk?"

"Who told you such nonsense?"

"But weren't you in the middle of a rampage, when you were a telegraph operator in Canada?"

Dr. Wick nodded and put the Bible aside. "It was during the last Cree uprising in Ontario in eighteen hundred and eighty-five, and I don't believe they were drunk."

Keeper persisted. "But wouldn't a drunk Indian be dangerous?"

"Any drunk could be dangerous. Now please, take this tray to your mother."

With a sigh of relief, Keeper picked up the dinner tray and carried it downstairs to the kitchen where his mother was at the sink washing the dinner dishes. He knew he couldn't wait another minute. If Jonnie Prettyboy still waited at the fort, she'd probably kill him on sight. He cast a nervous glance toward the windows overlooking the darkened backyard. "Can I go out for a little while?"

"What can you do in the dark?"

Keeper offered a winsome smile. "I'll play hide and seek with Early."

Alva turned to fix him with a disapproving look. "Don't mock your blind brother."

"I didn't mean it in a bad way," Keeper said apologetically. "So, can I?"

"Very well, Keep. Don't stray, and come when you're called. There've been reports of Gypsies in town."

Keeper rubbed the goose bumps on his sunburned arms. Bad enough Mr. Prettyboy was on the prowl, he thought. Now there were the Gypsies to look out for. "I will, Mom. Promise."

CHAPTER ELEVEN

Keeper pushed through the kitchen screen door, allowing it to slam behind him as he ran through the darkened yard, dodging two lawn sprinklers then past the looming horse barn and across Shore Drive toward the lake. A half-moon rising over the eastern horizon illuminated the slender crescent of beach where he hoped Jonnie Prettyboy still waited at the hidden fort. The lighthouse at the far end of the breakwater probed the night with its multi-faceted Fresnel lens that both welcomed and warned ships sailing on the vast inland sea beyond.

The dark lake was oily-calm as Keeper cautiously approached their fort. He thought he heard his mother calling for him but ignored it. When he was within twenty feet of the fort's entrance he gave the secret killdeer whistle. When there was no reply he dropped to his hands and knees and crawled until he was at the fort's hidden entrance. Then he whistled again. Nothing.

Keeper was afraid he'd come too late. "Honey?"

"Shut the hell up!" Jonnie Prettyboy snarled from inside. "You want to give our position away?"

"Sorry," he whispered as he crawled headfirst into the dark and smoky chamber.

"Where the fuck have you been all day?"

Keeper pulled his legs up against his chest and rested his chin on his knees. "Something terrible is going on."

"If you've squealed...."

He interrupted. "Your dad has disappeared."

"You'd better be kidding."

He took a deep breath before giving Jonnie Prettyboy the bad news. "Your mom called this morning. She told Early that both you and your dad were gone. He said he didn't know if she called the cops or not."

Her response was immediate. "We've got to get the hell out of here right *now!*"

"I've got the hayloft ready," Keeper said. He hoped he sounded confident, because he was scared shitless that Mr. Prettyboy was Indian-drunk and out looking to kill his daughter, and maybe him too.

Jonnie Prettyboy quickly tucked the crumpled pack of Old Golds inside the waistband of her two-piece swimsuit. "Out, *now!*" she ordered.

With Keeper in the lead and Jonnie Prettyboy close behind, the two scrambled from the fort and quickly disappeared among the trees lining Shore Drive. Ducking and flattening themselves against the ground whenever headlights from a passing car swept into view, they cautiously made their way toward the horse barn.

Once there Keeper felt much safer and led the way up the steep and narrow stairway to the hayloft he had fixed up. "I brought you a flashlight," he said, but you'd better not use it unless it's an emergency."

"I'm not stupid, you dumb shit."

Keeper ignored her mean-spirited habit of always calling him a dumb shit. "I brought you a sleeping bag, some chow, a pack of smokes and two bottles of root beer. There's a pail for when you have to go."

"You almost thought of everything."

"Toilet paper?" Keeper asked.

"Kotex," Jonnie Prettyboy sniffed. "I started my goddamned period today."

"Period?"

"You dumb shit. It's when a woman menstruates."

"Menstruates?"

"Jesus. You're dense as a fucking forest. Doesn't your ma use Kotex?"

Keeper remembered seeing a Kotex box when he was rummaging around the bathroom one day, but he had no idea what it was for. "I guess so."

"Then get two pads. I'll need the belt too," Jonnie Prettyboy said, and then tapped her foot against the galvanized metal pail. "And bring me a comic book to read for when I have to use this."

"Yes hon…sir," Keeper stammered. He turned for the stairs and descended to circle the Hupmobile Aero Sedan glinting dully in the moonlight slanting through a broken windowpane. When he opened the garage door, a horned owl swooped past on muffled wings. "Holy crap!" he cried when he saw it. More scared than ever, he dashed across the yard while at the same time trying to avoid two lawn sprinklers that rotated with a monotonous and staccato hiss. When he entered the house he found his mother playing solitaire at the kitchen table. She had a drink in front of her and was smoking a cigarette.

"Where were you, Keeper? she asked softly. "I called and called."

"Sorry, Mom. I guess I didn't hear you."

"I could use some company tonight, sweetheart." Alva flopped over the queen of hearts, but couldn't play it.

"What about Dad?" Keeper asked.

She shook her head. "He's gone to bed."

"Early too?"

"I don't know where he is, hon. Sometimes he just up and disappears without a word. Day or night, it's all the same to him."

"I think he talks to ghosts."

Alva gave Keeper a curious look. "What kind of nonsense is that?"

"Lots of people have died in our house. I think grandpa will be next."

"Please, don't talk like that."

"Well, it's true. I just saw an owl, and you know what that means."

Alva sighed and shuffled the cards for another deal.

Keeper went on. "*I* almost died here too, but dad saved my life at the last minute."

"Don't be so morbid."

"I think we should get a gun."

"I think you should go to bed."

"Think about it, Mom. When Dad's on the road, the only protection we've got from Gypsies and drunken Indians is grandpa and Early."

Alva reached over to take Keeper's hand in hers. "Honey, nobody is going to harm us."

Keeper pulled his hand away and flexed his skinny arm muscles. "Just in case, I'm going to send away for the Charles Atlas 'Dynamic Tension' bodybuilding kit."

She laughed. "You're only ten."

"I'm almost ten and a half."

"Go to bed, Keep, and take a bath first. You smell like you've been camping out on the beach."

"I will," Keeper replied, and raced through the house and up the front stairs. He paused to look through the open door of his parent's bedroom and saw his father sleeping naked on top of the covers. The sight not only embarrassed Keeper, it made him wonder if his penis would ever grow to be as big. After gently closing the door, he stepped into the adjoining bathroom and clicked on the overhead light. He opened the medicinal-smelling cabinet that held the household's first aid items and sundry other bathroom goods until he found the Kotex box. Feeling queasy because he now knew what they were for, Keeper took two pads and stuffed them into his shorts He tried remembering what else it was Jonnie Prettyboy asked for, until he saw the white garter belt-looking strap, and took it too.

With a pounding heart he quickly retraced his steps down the stairs. He quietly let himself out onto the front porch and raced through the dark backyard to the horse barn. The door was ajar. He tried to remember if he had closed it coming out. He stepped inside and warily circled the Hup to stand at the bottom of the steeply narrow stairs.

"I'm back," he called in a hushed voice. When there was no answer he went up.

"Honey?" he whispered. "It's me, honey, Keeper, the dumb shit." He tossed the Kotex pads on his grandfather's examination table and sniffed into the musty barn smell. Something was different. Whiskey? Before he could speak, to ask Jonnie Prettyboy if she was drinking booze, he felt himself being grabbed from behind. He smelled adhesive tape and tasted coppery blood on the hand covering his mouth and nose. Hadn't Jonnie Prettyboy said she'd cut her father bad? He couldn't breathe.

"So it's 'honey' now is it?" Mr. Prettyboy's voice came low and threatening. "This'll teach you to meddle where you ain't wanted."

Jonnie Prettyboy whimpered from a dark corner. "Don't, Pa."

"Shut up, you slut."

Keeper kicked wildly at Mr. Prettyboy's crotch until connecting with something that made Mr. Prettyboy scream, "You filthy nut-kicking little bastard!"

Keeper teetered at the edge of the open stairwell, off-balance and flailing until his hands found and gripped Mr. Prettyboy's untucked shirttail. Then, with a final tug and twist, the two went tobogganing headlong down the narrow stairwell, with Keeper atop his flailing assailant. Their fall was broken when Mr. Prettyboy's skull hit the concrete floor with a sound like a twig being stepped on. Keeper frantically pushed himself away to stand, chest heaving, and staring down at Mr. Prettyboy, whose eyes were rolled back in their sockets and his head twisted unnaturally to one side.

Keeper smelled urine and guessed he'd pissed himself. He barely heard Jonnie Prettyboy as she slapped barefoot down the stairs to stand at his side.

She grabbed Keeper's arm. "Jesus Christ," she gasped. "Is he dead?"

"Gotta...call...cops," he said dully, like he was in a trance.

"*No*! We've got to *think*!"

"I'm a murderer."

"He would have *killed* us," Jonnie Prettyboy shrilled.

Keeper pulled at his piss-wet shorts. "I have to go in."

She grabbed Keeper by his skinny shoulders and glared. "And leave me here alone with him?"

"My mom will be looking for me, wondering why I'm not taking a bath."

"You're going to take a fucking bath...*now*?"

Keeper looked down at Mr. Prettyboy and shivered. Blood was beginning to trickle from the dead man's nostrils. It looked like black worms were crawling from inside his skull. "I'll come back after I get cleaned up."

"Then what?"

"I don't know," Keeper mumbled. "I never killed nobody before."

"You are the world's *dumbest* shit," Jonnie Prettyboy groaned. "I swear."

"They'll give me the electric chair, for sure."

"You dope. They don't have the death sentence in Michigan."

"How about chain gangs?"

"How about you go take your bubble bath?" she snarled. "When you come back, I'll have figured out something."

CHAPTER TWELVE

Keeper sneaked back into the house the same way he left, by using the seldom-used and never-watched front door. After he'd washed his shorts in the bathtub and scrubbed himself raw, he toweled off, brushed his teeth, and hurriedly pulled on his thin cotton summer pajamas. Satisfied he would meet his mother's scrutiny, he rushed downstairs to the kitchen to kiss her goodnight.

She still played solitaire and had a fresh drink in front of her. "You smell good, honey," she said as Keeper pecked her on the cheek.

He held his trembling hands behind his back and faked a yawn for his mother's benefit. "Guess I'll turn in, then."

She scowled. "You look like you're coming down with something," and beckoned for Keeper to come closer. "Let me feel your forehead."

He stepped back and forced a smile. "I just got out of hot water," he said, and headed upstairs before more questions came. Once in his bedroom, he pulled back the bedcovers and jammed two pillows under them, so it more-or-less looked like he was sleeping in case his mother happened to look in on him. Then he tiptoed down the front stairs and let himself out the door into the cool night air. The damp grass felt good on his bare feet, in spite of the scared feeling that constricted his throat and made his mouth so dry he couldn't spit.

He stopped to listen, and then pushed his way through the door into the horse barn, but he didn't immediately see Jonnie Prettyboy. "Where are you?" he whispered.

"Up here." Her reply came from the hayloft.

Mr. Prettyboy's dead body still lay at the bottom of the stairs. Keeper gulped. The bandage wrapped around the dead man's right hand looked like a bloodstained white mitten, and his rolled-back eyes were still open. Keeper was trying to gather enough courage to step over the body, when Jonnie Prettyboy came padding barefoot down the stairs.

"I think we should call the cops," he said. "They'd go easy on a kid, wouldn't they?"

"We're not calling no cops, so get that out of your head," she snapped. "What we're *gonna* do, is you're gonna help me drag my pa's body to your grandpa's car. He only weighs a hundred and twenty. On account of his drinking."

Keeper looked out a window toward the house, where his mother remained seated at the kitchen table with her cards. "Then what?" he asked.

"You said you can drive. Were you lying?"

"No. I'm an excellent driver."

"Fine. Now grab one of his legs and shut up."

Keeper looked hard at Jonnie Prettyboy, now seeing her in an entirely new light. Then, panting with fear and exertion, he helped drag her father's lifeless body to the rear of the Hup. He quickly unlatched the trunk lid and peered inside to see if it was empty. Except for a gallon can of antifreeze, it was.

"Grab him under the arms," Jonnie Prettyboy ordered. "You pull, and I'll push."

Keeper grunted under the weight. "Where are we going?"

"To the beach, stupid."

"Then what?"

She gave Keeper a pitying look, and said, "We're going bury him at the fort."

"We'll never make it through the sand."

"You got a better idea?"

"Give me a minute to think."

"We don't *have* another minute," Jonnie Prettyboy hissed. "Do you want to get caught like this? And what if your blind brother comes around?"

"Then we'd better hurry."

"Are you sure you know how to drive?"

"Pretty sure."

"*Pretty* sure?"

"Maybe it was on my dad's lap, but I know how."

Jonnie Prettyboy poked a stiff finger against Keeper's breastbone, and then a second time for emphasis. "All I can say is that you'd better not fuck this up."

"I won't," Keeper promised. He pushed at Mr. Prettyboy's left leg until it was bent double, then stepped back so Jonnie Prettyboy could close the trunk lid. Then, with a soft, "Ugh," he pushed open the rear-entrance barn door and paused to look up and down the cindered alley. The only sign of activity was trash burning in a neighbor's open-top steel drum. Then, satisfied they weren't being observed, Keeper turned back to where Jonnie Prettyboy waited by the Hup.

"You're wasting valuable time!" she hissed.

"I needed to be sure the coast is clear." He opened the car door, released the hand brake and put the gearshift in neutral. "Now, help me push it out."

Jonnie Prettyboy grumbled something under her breath, but did what he asked. Once they had the car in the alley, she jumped in beside him. "Just remember what I told you. Don't..."

"I know...I know," Keeper said as he adjusted the seat to its forward-most position so he could reach the pedals. Making sure the gearshift was in neutral, he turned the ignition key and pressed the starter, just as he'd watched his grandfather do so many times before. After four turns of the starter motor the engine caught and settled into a gentle idle. Not daring to turn on the headlights, he waited with senses so heightened he could smell the rum-soaked cigars his grandfather smoked, and even traces of his late grandmother's scented rosewater.

"This fucking car smells like old people and death," Jonnie Prettyboy grumbled.

"It's no wonder, considering," Keeper replied. He shifted into reverse and carefully backed out into the dark alley without lurching or stalling the engine, which pleased him enormously. He depressed the clutch with his bare toes, then snaked the shift lever into first with a slight crunch. This time he let out the clutch too quickly, which caused the car to lurch and buck unsteadily. He could hear Mr. Prettyboy's body thumping in the trunk, like he'd come alive and was trying to get out.

Jonnie Prettyboy's head jerked back and forth as Keeper tried to control the Hup. "Jesus Christ!" she cried. "I thought you said you could drive!"

"Take it easy, honey," he said.

"Goddamn you," she swore, and braced herself by placing both feet against the dashboard.

Keeper switched on the headlights once they were clear of the alley and turned for Shore Drive. "Keep a lookout for cops," he warned.

"*You* look out for cops," she snarled. "'Cause when this is over, I'm headed south."

"You want to run away?"

"And never come back."

"I'd go with," Keeper replied, "but I've got responsibilities."

"Bullshit."

"I'm the man of the house when my dad's on the road."

"Bullshit twice."

Keeper didn't argue because he had nothing more to add. When he got close to where he and Jonnie Prettyboy had dug their fort, he pulled over, turned off the ignition and set the brakes. After making sure they were alone, the two left the Hup to stand side-by-side on the low bluff overlooking the vast dark lake. The night air was humid and fishy smelling, and except for the soft rhythmic sound of waves scouring the shoreline, all was quiet. The great incandescent light at the end of the pier winked on and off while appearing to welcome the approaching lights of the carferry SS Dakota Straits as she steamed toward the harbor. The beach glowed white as phosphorous under an incomplete moon.

"I don't like the looks of this," Keeper whispered.

"We've got to work fast," Jonnie Prettyboy whispered back.

"Right," he replied. He hitched up his pajama bottoms and scurried around to the rear of the Hup. When he opened the trunk, Mr. Prettyboy's left leg and arm flopped out. "Holy shit!" Keeper shouted.

"Shut up!"

"I couldn't help it," he gasped.

As they heaved Mr. Prettyboy's body out of the trunk the dead man's shirttail snagged on a bumper guard. The corpse fell heavily and hit the asphalt drive with a sodden thump. Without pausing to rest, the two conspirators managed to drag the dead body through the deep sand to the fort's hidden entrance. The tracks they'd left in the sand looked as if a very large sea turtle had come to lay her eggs in the fort. The dead man's open mouth was choked with beach sand, and the white-marble eyes stared vacantly from their deep sockets.

"This feels like a bad dream," Keeper said when he squatted to catch his breath.

"It's the end of a real one for me," Jonnie Prettyboy replied softly. The Kotex belt showed just above her swimsuit.

He looked up, embarrassed when he noticed it. "C'mon," he said. "Help me push him in." When they had the body shoved to the back of the fort, the two pulled away the supporting pieces of driftwood planks, collapsing the fort on top of Mr. Prettyboy. Then using their bare hands, they quickly piled on more sand until only an indistinguishable mound remained.

Keeper threw a gnarled driftwood root on top of Mr. Prettyboy's burial place. "They'll never find him now."

"Even if somebody does," Jonnie Prettyboy replied, "They'll never be able to pin it on us."

"I'm scared they will."

"Keeper?"

"What?"

"You can call me honey now, if you want."

Keeper wrapped his skinny arms around her waist. "We'd better go now, honey."

They obscured their tracks on the way back by making it look as if kids had been running aimlessly in the sand. Because it looked like they were doing an Indian war dance, they both laughed. Laughing, Keeper thought, over a dead Indian. Strangely, he no longer felt scared, but proud, because he'd freed Jonnie Prettyboy from her father. He felt like the man of the house. The Hup fired to life with two cranks of the starter motor. Once underway, he switched on the headlights and turned for home and the horse barn.

She sat close with her legs tucked under her and her left arm draped protectively over Keeper's shoulders. "This will be out secret… forever," she whispered into his ear, and kissed him on his peeling and sunburned cheek.

He stole a quick glance toward Jonny Prettyboy, whose pale gray eyes seemed as bright as the moon itself. Thick, raven-black hair framed her face, her skin nearly as dark as the man they'd just buried. Keeper shivered, a slight tremor similar to those delicious quivers that came whenever he saw his name written, such as on the blackboard in school or printed on a report card. The sand between his toes was gritty and fishy-smelling. "What about your mom?" he asked.

"She'll be glad not to be getting the shit beat out of her anymore."

"So, are you going home, then?"

"Me and my ma don't get on."

"I don't think you can stay in the horse barn after this."

"I didn't say I wanted to."

Keeper sniffled. "You're going to leave me, aren't you?"

Jonnie Prettyboy turned to stare ahead – her profile a finely chiseled cameo caught in the cold moonlight slanting through the windshield. "I'll need clothes," she replied after a minute. "And a pair of shoes, a suitcase, and a carton of smokes."

"Where am I supposed to get girls clothes?"

"Jesus. How'd you get so fucking dumb? Bring me some of yours, and a scissors too."

"My life was simple before I met you, honey," Keeper said as he steered towards the alley behind the horse barn. A jackrabbit turned to meet the on-coming Hup, its ears alert, and eyes reflecting twin-points of light until zigzagging out of sight.

"Oh shit!" Jonnie Prettyboy moaned. "It's him." Early stood by the barn door facing them, but his blind eyes were sweeping somewhere overhead.

Keeper hit the brakes and stalled the engine. "*Quick!*" he ordered in an urgent whisper. "Jump in the backseat and don't say anything!"

"Fuck," Jonnie Prettyboy hissed. "I'm getting *out!*"

"*Wait!*" he called, but it was too late. She had opened the door and was gone. He turned back toward Early, who was shuffling toward the Hup and swinging his white cane until stopping when the cane rapped against the front bumper. *Tap...tap.*

"Is that you, Granddad, out for an evening's drive?" *Tap...tap.*

"It's me," Keeper said.

"I know it's you, Keep. Pull the car into the barn and get out... *now!*"

Keeper restarted the Hup and drove it back into the barn without stalling the engine again, a relief in case Early though him to be a bad driver.

"Who was with you?" Early asked.

"Nobody."

Early sniffed deeply and swiveled his head like he was listening to a distant sound. "Jesus, Keep. What do you take me for? The passenger door was open, and I heard somebody running. Light too, maybe a hundred and ten pounds, and barefoot."

Keeper thought fast. "My friend Pee Wee was with me. He got scared."

"Pee Wee have a nosebleed?"

Keeper tried to laugh, but couldn't. He knew Early could smell a fart in a windstorm. Now he wondered if Early smelled the blood from Mr. Prettyboy's nose. If not, maybe it was from Jonnie Prettyboy's menstruations. Maybe both.

"Are you in some kind of trouble?" Early asked.

Keeper's throat tightened. "Nope," he croaked.

Early placed his hand flat against the Hup's hood. "You didn't go far."

"Uh, nope."

"Goddamn it, Keep, I should tell Dad."

"He wants me to know how to drive, in case something happens when he's on the road."

"Give me the keys, Keep, and close the barn door."

Keeper reluctantly handed over the keys and turned to tug at the door until it was closed. "You won't tell, will you?"

"Pee Wee, huh," Early grunted. "You're as full of shit as the old man."

Keeper took it as a compliment and said, "Thanks, Early."

CHAPTER THIRTEEN

That night Keeper killed time by reading through his collection of Dick Tracy and Captain America comic books. It was past midnight before he finally heard Early snoring on the other side of the plaster and lathe wall that separated them. Only then was he able to comply with Jonnie Prettyboy's request for clothes and a suitcase – except he didn't have a suitcase. What he did have was an Official Boy Scout knapsack, which he hurriedly packed with a clean pair of fly-front undershorts, two pairs of knee-patched pants, two long-sleeved shirts, a pair of argyle ankle socks and a pair of scuffed brown shoes. He impulsively went to the sock drawer where he kept his father's cards and letters and dug out the hand-tooled wallet he'd made in scout camp. In it were four crumpled bills – a five and three singles.

He removed the bills, carefully folded them and slipped them into the breast pocket of his summer pajamas. He slung the knapsack over one shoulder and headed quietly down the back stairwell and into the kitchen. The stale smell of Alva's cigarettes reminded him he needed to filch a pack from the carton his father kept in the liquor cabinet. The scissors came from his mother's sewing basket, which he carefully placed in a pocket of the knapsack. After centering it on his back like he was going on a long hike, Keeper let himself out through the kitchen door and stood on the concrete stoop sniffing into the night air.

The backyard smelled loamy; of freshly-hoed garden soil and ripe tomatoes on the vine; of wet grass, worm casings; and of a cool breeze coming off Lake Michigan. A full and brilliant August moon spilled its light into a yard alive with fireflies signaling to each other in gentle bursts of lime-green phosphorescence. Beyond, and through the maple trees lining Shore Drive, the vast lake shimmered like hammered pewter.

He stepped off the stoop into the cool wet grass and followed his shadow on the way to the barn. He opened the heavy door and whistled, the agreed-upon killdeer signal, but since Mr. Prettyboy was dead it made him feel stupid.

"Up here, you dumb shit." Jonnie Prettyboy's voice came from the hayloft.

Keeper stepped past the gassy-smelling Hup Aero Sedan and climbed the narrow stairs to the hayloft. "It's me, honey," he whispered. "Keeper."

She sat out of sight in a far corner. "I didn't figure it was Western Union," she muttered, and added, "Where the hell have you been?"

"I couldn't come until Early was sleeping."

Jonnie Prettyboy said, "That creep. Why doesn't he get a tin cup and sell pencils?"

Keeper ignored the mean-spirited crack and stepped forward until he was silhouetted against the moonlight spilling through the broken window at his back. "I brought the stuff you wanted."

Jonnie Prettyboy came out of her dark corner to face him. She still wore her two-piece polka-dot swimsuit, and her eyes glittered like new dimes in the silvery moonlight. She giggled. "You look like the hunchback in some dumb movie I saw. Swung on bells like a fucking ape."

Keeper slipped his arms out of the straps and lowered the knapsack to his feet. "I didn't get to see the movie, and I didn't have a suitcase either."

"This is much better anyway," she replied. "Keeps my hands free in case of trouble on the road."

"Where will you go?" Keeper asked.

"South, like I've been saying all along."

"Aren't you a little bit scared?"

"Of what?"

"My mom says there's Gypsies around."

"Maybe the Gypsies should look out for *me*," Jonnie Prettyboy replied. She pulled the knapsack toward her and kneeled to open it. She first took out the pack of Old Golds and set it aside before removing the clothes, item by item. When she discovered the fly-front undershorts she held them up. "Aren't you the stud bull!" she said, and laughed.

"Where was I supposed to get girl's panties?"

"Actually, these are perfect," Jonnie Prettyboy replied. Rare approval sounded in her voice. Without the slightest sign of embarrassment she undid the top of her bathing suit, stepped out of the bottoms, and then dropped them both at Keeper's feet. "Burn these in somebody's trash barrel," she said. Except for the Kotex pad and belt, Jonnie Prettyboy stood before Keeper as naked as a Dakota princess on her wedding night.

Keeper cast his eyes downward, until his natural curiosity got the better of him. "This is how I'll always remember you, honey, except I still haven't touched your boobies."

She sighed. "Okay, but make it quick."

Keeper reached for a breast, a freshly-budded, raisin-tipped orb, but stopped short. "Maybe we should wait until we're married."

"Oh for Christ's sake." She grabbed Keeper's sweaty hands and pressed them against her peach-firm breasts. "Remember this."

Keeper felt his penis stirring, a fledgling erection that tingled like the time he touched it with Early's tuning fork.

Jonnie Prettyboy backed away. "That's enough," she whispered with a catch in her throat. She picked up the undershorts Keeper brought and stepped into them, followed by the pants, and then the shirt she'd selected, buttoning it but leaving the tail untucked. She sat to pull on a pair of argyle socks, and then the shoes, tying them in the moonlight puddling around her.

"Did you bring the scissors?" she asked without looking up.

Keeper wordlessly dug them out of the pocket he'd put them in and handed them over with the chrome-plated blades flashing wickedly in the moonlight.

Jonnie Prettyboy scuttled closer to the window – grabbed a handful of thick black hair, and began to cut until the floor around her was littered with tufts of shorn hair. It was as if some predatory weasel had caught and killed a black cat.

Now Keeper understood why she wanted the scissors. "Jesus, honey," he breathed when she had finished. "You look exactly like a boy."

"No shit, Sherlock," she said, and added, "I've changed my mind. Don't call me honey anymore."

Keeper offered an apologetic smile. "I'd drive you to the city limits, but Early took the keys."

"I'll count my blessings," Jonnie Prettyboy said, and reached for the pack of Old Golds. She peeled away the cellophane, tore off a corner of foil and tapped out a cigarette. She held the thin white cylinder between her first and second fingers like she'd seen Bette Davis do in the movie *Dark Victory*. "I need a light."

Keeper nodded. "There's some matches in the Hup. My grandpa lights his cigars with them."

"Then *get* 'em!"

Keeper hastened to obey before being ordered a second time. He found the matchbook with the name Upjohn printed on it in the glove box. When he returned to the hayloft, she had repacked the knapsack and sat cross-legged on the old examination table. Had it not been for the cigarette that seemed to float in midair, and her disembodied pale-gray eyes, he never would have known she was there. Silently, he handed over the Upjohn matchbook.

Without a thank you, Jonnie Prettyboy tore off a match, struck it, and cupped her hands to hide the flare. Once she had the cigarette going, she blew out the match with a puff of exhaled smoke that dissipated into the sudden dark that followed.

"It's time," she said at last.

Keeper fumbled in his pajama pocket for the bills and handed them over. "You'll need some money for the road."

She leveled her glittering eyes on Keeper and said, "Where'd that come from?"

"I saved some from my allowance and cutting grass and stuff," he replied. "It's all I had."

She rubbed an eye with the heel of her cigarette hand before taking the money. "You're the dumbest shit, I swear."

"How will we stay in touch?" he asked with a hopeful look that was lost in the gloom.

"We won't."

Keeper snuffled and wiped his nose on a pajama sleeve. "Everybody keeps leaving me," he said. "They either die in our house or take to the road."

Jonnie Prettyboy's cigarette glowed brightly when she took a deep drag, and then less so when she exhaled – on and off like a distant semaphore. "That's life," she said. "Might as well get used to it."

Keeper's chin trembled when he spoke. "Wherever you go, honey, someday I'll find you."

She took another long pull off the glowing cigarette and said, "Yeah, well, good fucking luck. Say your goodbyes, 'cause I've got to be going."

"Are you still gonna hook rides?"

"No. I'm gonna hop a southbound freight at the docks, so keep your stupid trap shut if anybody asks after me."

"I will," he mumbled, and slowly turned for the stairs. "I'll sure miss you."

"Me too."

"Honey...?"

"Shut up!" Jonnie Prettyboy cried. "Just shut the hell up and go!"

With sudden tears filling his eyes, Keeper stumbled down the narrow stairs, blindly feeling his way along the rough-sided wall toward the bottom. He deliberately stepped over the spot where Mr. Prettyboy fell to his death and paused next to the Aero Sedan. Its tarnished chrome glinted dully in a narrow wedge of moonlight slanting through the door he had absent-mindedly left ajar. As he was about to leave he thought he heard a cat meowing softly somewhere in the barn. He paused to listen into the gloom – until understanding it wasn't the forlorn cry of an abandoned cat at all – and that it was coming from the hayloft.

With unstoppable tears scouring his sunburned cheeks, Keeper pushed through the open door to follow the slewing tracks he'd left in the damp grass; an uneven trail leading back to the house that loomed chalk-white in the moonlight. When halfway across the yard, he stopped abruptly amidst seemingly thousands of fireflies surrounding him with glowing bursts of phosphorescence. Each seemed to be saying, *follow me! – follow me!*

Enthralled, Keeper turned to face the weathered horse barn and waited, but for what he couldn't be sure. The windows were unseeing and black in their sockets – except for the broken one up in the hayloft. There, the glowing tip of a cigarette could be seen winking on and off, until going out.

CHAPTER FOURTEEN

Mrs. Prettyboy came calling the very next afternoon. Her appearance did little to allay Keeper's concerns over his involvement in the disappearance of Roy Prettyboy. Mrs. Prettyboy was haggard from lack of sleep and wept uncontrollably. She pleaded with Keeper for any scrap of information that might lead to her husband, and especially her daughter, whom she feared had gone unwillingly with her father. As badly as Keeper wanted to tell Mrs. Prettyboy what had actually happened, he didn't. His fear of what Jonnie Prettyboy would do if she was found overrode his fear of being arrested for the death of Mr. Prettyboy. It would be better, Keeper reasoned, to 'keep his goddamned trap shut' just like Jonnie Prettyboy ordered him to.

Whenever he went out to the old horse barn to play in his grandfather's Hupmobile, he remembered when the two of them would spend a hot and deliciously secret afternoon together. When he climbed the stairs to the hayloft, Keeper always and deliberately stepped over a small brownish stain on the concrete floor from blood that had trickled from Mr. Prettyboy's nose. Keeper had scrubbed the stain with bleach, but there was still enough evidence, he thought, for the FBI crime lab to pin the death of Mr. Prettyboy on him if they ever came to investigate.

The deep-seated fear of being found out came back full-throttle, when Roy Prettyboy's badly decomposed body was discovered the next week, after a late-summer's storm when sand-scouring winds and high waves crashing ashore uncovered his burial place. Beachgoers thought the bad smell was coming from an alewife die-off until learning otherwise. The *Dakota Daily Clarion* carried the news in bold headlines, of how a local Dakota Indian had apparently died under violent circumstances, and that his wife was being held for questioning. On more than one occasion, local police had been called out to the abandoned caboose where the Prettyboys lived, to quell domestic squabbles that usually resulted in Roy Prettyboy knocking his wife around. When the county coroner discovered Roy Prettyboy's right hand had been badly cut, police found and took into evidence the butcher knife that had been used, and which still held traces of Roy Prettyboy's type "A" negative blood. Mrs. Prettyboy clearly had a motive, which led police investigators to also question her over the whereabouts of her missing daughter. She told them she had no earthly idea, and wept bitterly over her loss.

Keeper kept what he knew to himself, in part because of his loyalty to Jonnie Prettyboy, but also because he truly believed he was a killer, and wondered if ten-year old kids ever got the electric chair, never mind what Jonnie Prettyboy said.

"When was the last time you saw the girl?" Chance asked Keeper when the edition covering the story was delivered to the house. They sat at the kitchen table eating dinner – meatloaf hand-ground from fatty leftover steak tails, accompanied by fresh vegetables Alva had gathered from her garden.

"I don't remember," Keeper replied after gulping down a mouthful of meatloaf.

"That's strange," Alva said. "You two seemed tighter than ticks."

"She was just a friend," Keeper mumbled. "That's all."

"I haven't seen her around for days," Early said, chuckling and joining in with a favorite joke about being able to see.

"I always thought Roy Prettyboy was a pretty decent fellow," Chance said, and added, "although I understand he hit the bottle pretty hard."

Alva glared at her husband but said nothing.

Early's eyelids fluttered over sightless eyeballs that seemed to be looking at a spot somewhere over Keeper's head. "Never can tell about an Indian, huh, Keep?"

Keeper blushed and pushed away his plate. "I'm not hungry anymore," he said. "And besides, she was only half Indian."

"And which half might that be?" Early asked with a gummy smile that showed his teeth.

Keeper scowled. "You're a half-brother, so you should know."

Alva rapped a bread knife against her drinking glass. "That's enough, you two," she warned, and went on, "I just think it's terrible, for that poor girl to have lost her father that way, possibly even murdered by her own mother, for God's sake. Why, that's probably the reason she ran off. Who could blame her?"

"May I be excused?" Keeper asked, so softly he was barely heard. Accepting his mother's silent nod to mean yes, he pushed back in his chair and ran upstairs to his room, flinging himself across his bed, sobbing, and fell asleep in his clothes.

A uniformed officer and a plain-clothes detective came to the house the next day to question Keeper concerning the whereabouts of his friend, whom the detective at first referred to as a "half-breed." Keeper sat next to his mother on the living room couch, where Chance would probably be slumbering if he were home instead of at the office.

The detective took a seat in Dr. Wick's favorite wingback and pulled out a spiral notepad and the stub of a yellow pencil, prepared to take notes. The uniformed policeman stood by the doorway that opened to the formal dining room. "Now then, young fella," the detective began. "Where do you suppose Jonnie Prettyboy might be at?"

Keeper squirmed nervously and tried to think of the time he was up the Dakota River fishing with his father and uncle – a calm, peaceful and safe place to be.

"Shouldn't I have a mouthpiece?" Keeper asked.

The detective laughed. "Whatever gave you that idea?"

"I think it was in an Edward G. Robinson movie."

"Don't be disrespectful, Keep," Alva said. "This is a very serious matter."

"She *was* your friend, wasn't she?" the detective asked, turning serious.

"We played sometimes," Keeper mumbled.

"Where?"

"On the beach, usually." He wanted to avoid mentioning the horse barn, fearing where the detective's line of questioning might lead.

"Where on the beach, exactly?"

"All over."

"Over where Mr. Prettyboy's dead body was found?"

"I don't know. Maybe."

"Did you and your girlfriend dig forts?"

Keeper glanced toward his mother.

"Answer him," Alva said. "Tell the truth."

"Sometimes," Keeper replied, uneasily.

"Dig 'em deep, Keep?" the detective asked with an encouraging smile.

"Not that deep," Keeper replied.

"But deep enough to bury somebody, do you think?"

"Are you insinuating my son had something to do with that awful man's death?" Alva asked, alarmed.

"Of course not, Mrs. Wick," the detective said with a disarming smile. "We're just exploring all angles of the case."

"Can I ask you a question, sir?" Keeper asked with an innocent look.

With a look that suggested he was getting somewhere, the detective said, "Fire away."

He said, "Why aren't you out arresting Gypsies?"

"Yeah, okay kid. We've got that element under control."

"I don't think Keeper can help you," Alva said with a wan smile.

"A few more questions," the detective replied, and we'll be done." Then turning back to Keeper he said, "Did Jonnie Prettyboy ever talk to you about how things were between her folks?"

"Sometimes."

The detective held the stubby pencil over his notepad and said, "Well?"

"Answer the question, Keep," Alva scolded. "Did she?"

Keeper nodded and said, "I could tell it was hard for her."

"And why would that be?" the detective asked.

"She said she didn't get on with her ma."

"That's all?"

"That's all I know for sure."

"Listen to me, son," the detective said. "If you know *anything* that might lead us to the girl, tell me now."

Keeper crossed his feet and started to cry, mostly because he was afraid of what might happen to her if a bad man discovered she wasn't a boy at all, but a girl. "She said she was heading south. I think she was gonna hook a freight car down at the docks."

"Jesus," the detective groaned. "We'll put out an APB immediately, tell law enforcement across the south to be on the lookout for a thirteen-year old half-breed girl on the run."

After taking a shaky breath, Keeper turned to the detective and said, "You'll never find her that way."

The detective glanced at his watch and cleared his throat. "And why would that be, young fella?"

Afraid he'd already said too much, Keeper looked towards his mother for much needed reassurance and softly replied, "Because, you just won't, is all."

CHAPTER FIFTEEN

The war came to Dakota Straits with a viscosity of its own and brought change in an almost languid sort of way. Certainly, Pearl Harbor had been big news, but even that held little significance for Keeper until 1942. That was when his mother began using red and blue tokens and rationing stamps to purchase such basic goods as sugar, coffee, butter, beefsteak, and even eggs. Since his father was often gone and Dr. Wick ate little, and because the vegetable garden in the backyard was now called a victory garden, Keeper's mother made do. As for him, it had been three long years since Jonnie Prettyboy had hooked a freight car out of town. And since then had been no sign or word from his early childhood sweetheart. It was almost like she never existed, and he was slow to make new friends. In her absence he grew closer to his blind half-brother Early.

Other signs that the country was at war became evident when gold-fringed white flags with blue stars began appearing in the living room windows of homes where sons and daughters had gone off to the war. When a gold star flag appeared in a neighboring window, Alva told Keeper that the boy who lived there was killed when German fighter planes shot down his B-17. When Keeper heard that, he determinedly did his patriotic duty by collecting scrap metal, old tires and aluminum foil from chewing gum wrappers for the war effort. Even Dr. Wick wanted to make a contribution. His appeal to the local draft board offering his services in hopes of being commissioned as a high-ranking officer was turned down, a rejection that sent the old man into another towering rage against Franklin Delano Roosevelt, whom he called, "that syphilitic communist son of a bitch."

Chance traveled more than ever, but wherever he went, he continued his practice of sending Keeper letters and picture postcards. The latest airmail letter arrived in a crumpled pale blue envelope postmarked from Los Angeles, California, and dated August 15, 1943. It had come to the house late in the afternoon when the hot August sun was only a crimson glow beyond the western horizon. While Alva was in the backyard setting out the lawn sprinklers, Keeper rushed upstairs to share the letter with Early, who had taken a break while letting the glue dry on his latest toothpick and tongue depressor bridge and lay stretched out on his bed.

Keeper stood in the open doorway waiting for permission to enter. When Early sensed his presence he waved for him to come in. Keeper stepped into the gloomy room waving the flimsy letter as if Early could see and said, "Got another letter from Dad."

"Where's the bullshitter now?" Early asked.

"I don't know about now, but he was in Los Angeles when he wrote it. He was smoking too. You can even smell it on the paper."

Early sniffed. "Old Golds, if I don't miss my bet."

Keeper took a seat in Early's work chair and smoothed out their father's letter on his lap, prepared to read from it as soon as his eyes adjusted to the gloom. The soft mutter of Gabriel Heatter's voice announcing war news over the radio came from Dr. Wick's room down the hall. Heatter was saying there had been unfounded reports that the aircraft carrier USS Lexington had been sunk by the Japanese during the Battle of the Coral Sea.

Because it was getting dark, and because Early didn't have a desk lamp, Keeper had to squint in order to read the letter.

"*Dear Keep,*" he began. "*I'm staying at the Ambassador Hotel on Wilshire Boulevard. Yesterday I had a Cobb salad at the Brown Derby. I'll take you there someday.*"

"I wouldn't hold my breath if I were you," Early said.

Keeper continued without comment; "*I rode the Santa Fe Super Chief coming out. Boy, what a smooth roadbed!*"

Early scratched an ear and said, "Thanks to a Dakota ballast tamper."

Keeper swelled with pride at the thought of his father's wartime contribution to smooth roadbeds before continuing; "*I was lucky to get a stateroom with a fold-down bed. The car rocks like a cradle, and with those wheels clicking on expansion joints, sleep comes quick.*"

"The life of a road man," Early muttered under his breath. "Must be a bitch."

Keeper pressed on. "*When we were passing through New Mexico, I was having a whisky sour in the club car.*"

"Nothing new there," Early said.

"Stop saying mean things about Dad or I'll quit reading."

Early held up his hands, a sign that meant he was sorry.

Keeper resumed reading the airmail letter. "*You should see how modern club cars are these days. Chrome everywhere, with comfortable chairs and colored boys in white jackets serving cold drinks.*"

After waiting for the comment that didn't come, Keeper went on; "*I joined up with a swell bunch of fellows. Solid family men like me by the looks of the Rotary and Masonic pins in their lapels. We played gin rummy and caught up on the latest war news.*" Keeper paused. "What's gin rummy?"

Early folded his hands behind his head. "It's a card game. Keep going."

He took a deep breath. "*There was a young woman with us, Keep. She looked like Veronica Lake in that movie 'Sullivan's Travels,' you snuck off to see last year.*"

Early grunted, "Uh oh."

Keeper ignored the 'uh oh' and continued, this time with an image of Miss Lake in mind. "*Naturally I made an introduction. Turned out her husband was a Navy pilot who had been killed in action in the South Pacific. She was on her way to Los Angeles to collect his body and then return it to Indianapolis for his burial.*"

Early cleared his throat and said, "This isn't good, Keep."

Unsure of Early's meaning, Keeper kept reading; "*Her name was Mary Beth and she smelled like Palmolive soap. When I left for my compartment she was drinking Manhattans and smoking black market Lucky Strikes. I'm sure Early can explain what black market means. Very sad, this war. Going to San Francisco in two days. All for now. Give my love to everybody, Dad.*"

Keeper closed his eyes, sighed, and let the letter drop to his lap. He tried to imagine his father and the woman who looked like Veronica Lake smoking and drinking Manhattans and whiskey sours in the club car. He was an avid reader of the periodicals Dr. Wick subscribed to, and a recent *Saturday Evening Post* carried a full color Union Pacific advertisement showing the silver Super Chief headed west under cloudless skies while real Indians in buckskin looked on from their horses. In his mind's eye, he could clearly envision the Super Chief as it thundered past Oklahoma oil wells and Texas cattle ranches. Past Apaches on horseback who were probably wishing they were going west to California at ninety miles an hour aboard the Super Chief.

Keeper opened his eyes stared off into space, thinking how terrible it would be if it were *his* father who was riding like so much freight in the baggage car, instead of some Navy pilot.

"Did you tell mother about the letter?" Early asked, breaking Keeper's reverie.

He shook his head. "She was in the backyard when it came."

"Do us a small favor, will you Keep?"

"How small do you mean?"

Early laughed. "Let me hang onto that letter a little while, okay? The smell of cigarette smoke on that letter makes Dad feel especially close tonight."

"For me too," Keeper replied in a near whisper. He carefully folded the letter and returned it to the envelope before placing it in Early's outstretched hand.

"Good boy," Early said. "Meanwhile, let's consider Dad's letter to be our secret."

"I can keep secrets better than anybody," Keeper said as he stood to leave. It was almost bedtime and he wanted to wash and brush before being ordered to do so by his mother. She was lately crying over the littlest things, like running out of rationed butter and eggs before the next booklet came, and he didn't want to upset her further.

Early yawned. "Must be getting late, Keep. See you in the morning."

"I'll bet Dad made Mary Beth feel better," Keeper said as he stood to leave.

Early raised his head as if he could see Keeper's face, his smile lost to the gloom. "I'll bet he did at that, Keep, I'll bet he did at that."

CHAPTER SIXTEEN

Chance came home in the backseat of a taxi; smoking his last cigarette and exhausted from six long days of cross-country travel. He hadn't been able to get a seat aboard a commercial flight because of others whose wartime priorities exceeded his own. As a result, he had been forced to take the Union Pacific from San Francisco back to Chicago. His train arrived at the station late because it was often sidetracked for other trains rushing soldiers and military equipment to embarkation points on the West Coast.

From Chicago, Chance made his way north to Milwaukee via Greyhound bus. From there he booked passage home aboard the SS Dakota Straits. It had been a rough crossing, with six-foot waves that created chaos in the galley. A voyage that normally took six hours had taken a stomach-churning seven, and he was still feeling its effects.

It was late afternoon and Keeper was mowing the lawn when the taxi pulled into the driveway. When his father emerged from the backseat Keeper rushed to greet him shouting *"Dad!"*

Chance flicked his cigarette butt into Alva's zinnias that bordered the driveway and turned to greet his son with open arms. "Hey Keep!"

Keeper grinned, thrilled to be in his father's tight embrace. Chance was back and that was all that mattered for now. The long days and lonely nights – the hollow, unsettled feeling that seemed to fill the house during his long absences were all forgotten in the blink of an eye.

"How'd it go on the road?" Keeper asked once he'd caught his breath.

Chance managed a wan smile and stood back to admire his growing son. "It was rough this time, Keep, real rough."

Keeper hurried to retrieve his father's suitcase from the cab's trunk. "Did you see any movie stars in California?"

"Well, I saw Edward G. Robinson eating a club sandwich at the Brown Derby."

"Didn't you see any actresses, like maybe Veronica Lake?"

Chance laughed and rubbed Keeper's head. "No, but I had a drink with John L. Lewis on the Union Pacific."

"Is he famous?" Keeper asked as he struggled inside with the suitcase.

"He's the president of the AFL-CIO labor union and an ornery son of a bitch."

"Oh," Keeper replied, as if the name meant anything.

"Where is everybody?" Chance asked when he reached the kitchen.

"Mom's picking tomatoes in the victory garden," Keeper replied with a nod toward the kitchen window that overlooked the backyard. "Early's piano tuning at St. Stanislaus and Grandpa's up in his room listening to his radio and reading his Bible. That's all he does anymore, except sleep."

Chance nodded, as if understanding, and turned for the liquor cabinet. He poured three fingers of Old Crow into a paper cup and knocked it back in two hurried gulps followed by a splash of tap-water. He opened a fresh pack of cigarettes and lit one off a kitchen match on his way to the window that overlooked the backyard.

Keeper joined his father at the window. "We're having T-bones with garlic tomatoes and bakers for dinner. Mom saved up our meat coupons especially for you."

Chance pointed to a truckload of dirt piled next to the horse barn. "What the hell is that dirt doing out there?"

"The Gypsies did it," Keeper replied. They came last week with a dump truck. They said it was fertilizer left over from a big job. They told Mom she could have it for twenty bucks."

Chance groaned. "That's nothing but worthless fill dirt."

"It is?"

"Take my suitcase upstairs, Keep," Chance said, and turned for the door that opened into the backyard. "I'll have your mother unpack it later, after we've had a chance to catch up on a few things."

Keeper lugged the heavy suitcase through the house and up the stairs to the front bedroom. He hefted the travel-scarred bag onto the double bed his parents shared and thought about unpacking the suitcase, but didn't. He was afraid he might find the road present that might come later, when his father was feeling better.

When Keeper returned to the kitchen he glanced out the window to see his mother and father standing by the victory garden. Alva held the basket of softball-sized tomatoes she'd picked and was crying. Keeper went outside to see if it had anything to do with him.

"I'm not blaming you," Chance was saying as Keeper approached. "God knows you've got enough to worry about without me jumping down your throat every time some little thing goes wrong."

"It was the way you looked," Alva sobbed.

"Nonsense. I'll have someone from the plant haul away the dirt tomorrow."

"I knew I'd made a mistake as soon as they unloaded it," Alva said. "But by then it was too late, and I was too embarrassed to say anything."

Keeper wanted to tell his father that the Gypsies had almost sold his mother on seal coating the driveway with used motor oil. Early smelled it and warned her before it was too late. He said the same thing happened to a lady he gave piano lessons to.

"Can I say something?" Keeper began.

Chance held up a hand to cut him short. "You should have called the police, Alva." His tone was gentle.

"I know, dear," she replied tearfully, "but I was so ashamed."

"It's not a big deal," Chance said. "Sometimes even the best of us get taken."

Alva fiddled one-handedly with a loose thread on her dress – as if unraveling it would cause her bottled-up emotions to unravel as well. "The day is fast coming when you'll find out just how big a deal it is."

"We're all doing the best we can under the circumstances," Chance replied, and quickly added, "Especially you."

"Small consolation," Alva sniffed. "And while we're on the subject, something needs to be done about Dad."

"Can it wait until morning?" Chance asked with a look that suggested he didn't want Keeper to be present during any discussion about Dr. Wick.

"What *about* Grandpa?" Keeper asked.

"It's nothing for you to fret over, Keep," Alva replied, and handed him the basket of tomatoes. "Please take these into the kitchen like a good boy."

Although he knew something was wrong, Keeper was committed to keeping secrets. That evening, when he went upstairs to bring his grandfather's dinner tray down to the kitchen, he said nothing of what he'd overheard in the victory garden that afternoon. He found his grandfather slumped in his rocking chair listening to Gabriel Heatter, who was on the table radio saying, *"There's bad news tonight."* As if on cue, the siren at city hall began howling to warn Dakota Straits' citizens of another blackout.

"Air raid warning, Grandpa!" Keeper shouted, and rushed to pull down the blackout shades.

Dr. Wick gestured toward the closet with his cane. "Quick boy!" he rasped. "My valise!"

Keeper turned for the closet where he and Jonnie Prettyboy once hid to spy on his grandfather injecting something into an arm. He fumbled among the shoes until he found the medical valise next to a pair of brown lace-up shoes that looked very old. "What are you going to do?" he asked when he returned the valise to his grandfather.

"We must prepare for casualties!"

Keeper laughed. "There won't be casualties, Grandpa. It's a test."

"A test to try men's souls!"

"Maybe I'd better tell Dad to come up."

Dr. Wick clutched the worn valise to his chest and wailed, "Noooooooooo!"

Keeper now understood what his mother meant when she said something needed to be done about his grandfather. He was about to take the dinner tray down to the kitchen when Early came into the room.

"What the hell is going on up here, Keep?" he asked. "Enemy bombers wouldn't need lights to find us, with all this howling going on."

"It's Grandpa," he said. "Something needs to be done about him."

"Bring the Hup around!" Dr. Wick cried. "There will be causalities!"

"Tell Dad to call Dr. Wilberforce," Early said. "I'll wait here."

Dr. Wilberforce came within the hour to administer a sedative, something to calm his old friend and colleague. He left warning his son and daughter-in-law that Dr. Wick would soon need 24 hour care and to plan accordingly. By the time Chance and Alva retired to their room for the night they had carefully avoided any further discussion about Gypsy fill dirt or Grandpa Wick's precarious mental condition. His morphine habit was something else.

"Now can we talk about your father?" She lay next to Chance, who smoked a last cigarette before turning out a bedside reading lamp.

He shook his head. Can we save that conversation for tomorrow?"

"I'm talking about his using morphine."

"I had no idea he was using morphine."

"I'm not surprised."

"That he was?" Chance asked.

"That you didn't know."

He turned to face Alva. "What is that supposed to mean, exactly?"

"It means exactly what you think it means."

"Suppose you tell me."

"On those rare occasions when you're home," Alva replied, "you're either drinking or asleep. Either way, you're disengaged."

Chance took a deep drag off his cigarette. "My escape from reality."

"There's no escaping my reality," she replied sadly. "I love the boys and your father, but they occupy my every waking moment and leave me no time for myself. Besides, I'm already looking after your father day and night."

"He thinks I'm a failure," Chance said. "Do you think I'm a failure, Alva?"

Alva seemed to think before answering. "You're not a failure, Chance. You're only flawed."

Chance smiled like he'd just been handed a reprieve. "Can a flawed man make love to his wife tonight?"

Alva offered a rare smile and an even rarer proposition. "Not unless the flawed man you're referring to takes a much-needed bath."

Chance entered his father's room the next morning while Dr. Wick was using the bathroom and began to search for the morphine. He found two vials in the medical valise, as well as three others hidden in a pair of high-top shoes that resembled those worn by Woodrow Wilson. The valise was the same gold-initialed black leather bag given to his father by a proud and doting wife, Winifred, on the day he graduated from Chicago-Rush Medical School in 1900. The shoes were those worn while tending to patients during the Spanish flu epidemic of 1918.

Chance emptied the vials of morphine into the toilet his father had left unflushed. Then ignoring his feeble objections, Chance locked his father in the bedroom. Alva continued to bring her father-in-law his meals, but they were returned to the kitchen uneaten. She also emptied his chamber pot while he slept, soothed him while awake, and gave him sponge baths when he allowed it.

By week's end Alva entered her father-in-law's room, prepared to attend to his needs. To her great surprise he was freshly-shaven and obviously clean of the drug. He wore a white shirt, a paisley necktie and his carefully-pressed three-piece woolen suit, but with the fly left unbuttoned. It was a detail not overlooked by Alva.

Dr. Wick entered the kitchen unaided save for his walking cane. With a nod to all, he sat down to his favorite breakfast of Cream-of-Wheat, margarine on toast, rationed marmalade, coffee, and a soft-boiled egg served in a porcelain egg-cup. After cracking off the brittle skull of the egg with the blade of his table knife, he dipped his toast-point into the golden yolk and ate as if nothing had happened.

After finishing breakfast the old physician stood, hooked his cane over the crook of his left arm, and fumbled through his jacket pockets until he found and lit the rum-soaked cigar he'd saved for a special occasion. As soon as he had the cigar going, he wordlessly turned for the kitchen door that opened into the backyard.

After deliberately allowing screen door to slam behind him, he walked unsteadily toward the narrow strip of garden where Alva grew her American Beauty roses. There were eight mature bushes in all – each clinging tenaciously to trellises propped against the horse barn's weathered clapboard siding. There the old physician paused to cut a rose for his lapel with the pen knife he carried on a gold chain that reached across his vest. Then, with a contented puff off the rum-soaked Crooks he set off across the yard, unseen and wreathed in cigar smoke for a stroll toward the hospital two miles distant. Rounds needed to be made, and Dr. Wick was always on call.

CHAPTER SEVENTEEN

Chance was home for two months straight. Two months of sorting through paperwork at Dakota Tamper, and two months of drinking with his alcoholic friends in the neighborhood. As for Keeper, he was simply happy to have his father home, even though he seldom involved himself in any of his son's activities, or even professed interest in learning about them. He was simply a presence, disengaged and seemingly removed from the household's daily routine. He came home late from the plant, tired to the point of exhaustion and becoming quarrelsome when he had too much to drink.

Sometimes he skipped dinner altogether and went directly to the couch in the living room, where he'd sleep until being awakened by Alva to come to bed. On those nights she said he might just as well be back on the road, for all the good it did her.

On weekends the drinking started early. One Saturday morning, Chance allowed Keeper to drive him up and down Shore Drive in the New Yorker. It was a careless act that outraged Alva, but thrilled Keeper like nothing ever had. It was as if he and his father were setting out on a long road trip to exciting and adventurous places. Keeper envisioned their staying at fine hotels, eating juicy steaks, double-baked potatoes and sleeping on thick mattresses with feather pillows.

Chance came home from the plant late that following Monday. He was both tired and elated because they had tested a new ballast tamper. Chance told Alva it would revolutionize the industry. It had been his idea, he said, adding that Tamper owner Orville Pettigrew had doubled his salary.

"Neil called this morning," Alva said after congratulating her husband.

"What did your brother want this time?" he asked while pouring his first drink of the day. "Another, 'I'll pay you back next week,' loan?"

Alva shook her head. "Don't be a bastard. This morning he enlisted in the Navy. In two weeks he reports to the Great Lakes Naval Training Center at Glenview, Illinois."

Chance chased his drink with a splash of tap water and grunted, "Good for him."

Alva lit a cigarette. "He's taking you and Keeper fishing up the Dakota next Saturday."

"I have news for you, Alva. I don't fish."

Alva scowled. "I have news for you too, Chance. You *will* be going, and you'll be doing it for Keeper's sake."

Keeper of course was thrilled to have his father and uncle all to himself for nearly a full day up the river. It hadn't bothered him that Early declined to join them. In the unlikely event the flat-bottomed scow Neil had built himself suddenly capsized, Early explained he might not make it to shore, wherever that was.

It was a warm summer's day and cloudless, with a favoring breeze that took away the humidity and held down the biting black flies. Electric-blue dragonflies darted over the chocolate-brown surface of the shallow and gently-flowing Dakota. Its low banks were lined with old oak and softly-swaying poplar trees with papery-thin leaves rustling dryly in the gentle breeze.

Neil brought the tackle box that held his lures and treble-hooked spoons. Alva had put up ham and peanut butter and jelly sandwiches wrapped in waxed paper, enough for everyone, along with a fresh bag of potato chips and a Coke for Keeper. Neil brought twelve cans of Blatz beers in a cooler, not giving a damn that Chance didn't drink beer.

Neil sat at the stern operating the outboard. Chance sat on a kapok cushion looking uncomfortably out-of-place and sober in his long-sleeved shirt, trousers and black wingtip street shoes. Keeper squatted in the bow watching for sandbars and hidden snags, ready with the fish net in case a walleye, pike or northern trout hit the lure.

He looked over his shoulder and grinned at the sight of his father smoking a cigarette and looking as if he'd rather be anywhere else. His father often said; 'When I'm on the road, I want to be home, and vice the goddamned versa.' By the expression on his father's face, Keeper knew he was thinking, 'vice the goddamned versa.'

Oily-blue exhaust from the outboard covered the river's surface like ground fog, but to Keeper it smelled like the world's sweetest perfume. He watched his uncle squint against the sun's glare while intently scanning the riverbanks for sandbars and shallows, and for the deep quiet spots where fish hid under deadheads. Box turtles basked in the warm sun where muskrat and mink traps were set out in winter. The smell of cow manure in the pasture just beyond the low bank to the left mingled with the fish-smell that over the years had soaked into scow's wooden hull.

When Keeper bit into his first peanut butter and jelly sandwich, he wondered if he would ever be happier than at that very moment, or if the three of them would someday be together again, where everything would surely be different, yet the same as it always was.

CHAPTER EIGHTEEN

That fishing excursion up the Dakota River was the last for Keeper, who turned thirteen on March 11th 1944. And now it was already July. He hadn't killed himself either, in spite of having never heard from Jonnie Prettyboy. A distraction came from following his father's travels on the big Triple-A highway map he'd thumb-tacked to the bedroom wall. According to the push pins, Chance was heading for Cincinnati, Ohio, his last stop before coming home.

Keeper was eager to read their father's latest postcard to Early, who had joined him in his room after listening to war news with Dr. Wick. By June the allied armies had invaded Europe at Normandy, France, while at the same time the Marines were island-hopping in the Pacific and pushing the Japanese back. They were already ashore on Saipan, and the tide was finally turning against the axis forces. Neil Korsvold was serving as a corpsman with the 1st Marine Division in the South Pacific, which made Keeper terribly proud.

Keeper began, "*Dear Keep.*" His voice cracked, as it had ever since turning thirteen. One minute it would be high-pitched, and the next deep, almost like his father's voice.

"You're hurting my ears," Early joked when Keeper's voice broke again.

"Shut up," Keeper said, and started over; "*Dear Keep. Coming back from New York, I traveled on the Pennsylvania Turnpike. Finest road I've ever seen. Without the demo trailer to slow me down, I had the New Yorker up to a good hundred before being pulled over by a state trooper.*"

Early laughed. "The old man is having the time of his life."

Keeper laughed himself before going on. "*The trooper asked me what the big idea was, of speeding with a war on. I told him how it was when a fellow who's been on the road for so long always speeds up the closer he gets to home and his loved ones.*"

"What a bullshitter," Early said. "Does he say what happened next?"

Keeper read on. "*When the trooper heard that, he just told me to take it easy. See you soon. Tell everybody I love them. Dad.*" When Keeper finished reading the card, he placed it on his chest of drawers for reading later on.

"You're leaving something out," Early said.

"What makes you say that?"

"I can tell by the sound of your voice."

"Okay. There was a PS."

"Spill it."

"Dad said he'd be staying in Cincinnati for a few days."

"Why didn't you want me to know?"

Keeper seemed to think before answering. "I read a story about a road man who had a second family, and neither knew about the other."

Early laughed low in his throat and said, "Must have been a bitch on Christmas."

"I remember a Christmas when Dad didn't come home," Keeper said. "I think I was five."

"You were four," Early corrected. "Dad's train got stranded in the Rockies during a blizzard."

Keeper cleared his throat before asking the question that had been uppermost in his mind for a long time. "Do you think Dad has another family?"

Early rolled his blind eyes in apparent exasperation. "How could you think such a thing?"

"But he could, couldn't he?"

Early seemed to be looking at a spot on the wall beyond Keeper's right shoulder. "Not in a million years."

"I suppose you're right."

The half-brothers fell silent for several minutes, absorbed in their thoughts, until Keeper spoke.

"Do you think Mom and Dad still do it?"

"I know they don't."

"How could you know?" Keeper asked.

"Jesus, Keep. I can hear a mouse fart in the cellar. If they were doing it, I'd hear them, all right."

"I can't imagine them doing it anyway."

Early chuckled. "How do you think *you* got here?"

Keeper seemed to think before asking another question for which he had no ready answer. "Do you think they love each other?"

"That's an interesting question, but let me ask you this. When's the last time you ever heard either one of them tell the other, 'I love you,' or even share a hug and a kiss?"

Keeper slowly shook his head. "Never."

"Then that should answer your question."

"But, Dad always says in his cards and letters to tell everybody he loves them."

"He wants *you* to tell it, like second hand. Not the same thing as hearing it directly from the horse's mouth, is it?"

"I never thought about it like that."

"Then there you go," Early replied.

Keeper fell silent, digesting what Early had said, until asking the question that had been preying on his mind longer than any other. "Do you remember seeing anything before you went blind?"

Early's reply was quick and to the point. "No."

"Not even color?" Keeper asked.

"Describe color."

"Okay," Keeper said. "Red is warm, blue is cold, green is…well, green."

"And black is black, which is nothing," Early replied.

"But you were two-years old," Keeper said. "I can remember seeing stuff when *I* was two."

Early touched the red scar bridging his sightless eyes and said, "Let's drop it, Keep."

"You remember falling on the rake, don't you?"

"I never fell on a rake. Now get the hell out of here."

CHAPTER NINETEEN

It was a sultry Tuesday evening in Cincinnati, following a day so hot the fire department had opened hydrants to cool restive inner-city children. On the city's south side, Velma had opened every window in her thirty-six year old Sears-Roebuck bungalow to catch a welcoming breeze that caused the hollyhocks to scratch against the screens like a cat wanting to be let out.

At least that's what Chance thought when he heard it. He stood mixing drinks at the portable bar he'd rolled into Velma's bedroom as a step-saver. Except for his black ankle socks he was naked.

Other than for a single late morning foray into the kitchen to devour half-a-dozen scrambled eggs doused with Tabasco sauce, they hadn't left the bedroom since Chance came in off the road Monday night. Now heat lightning accompanied by the grumble of thunder in the distance foretold of rain on the way.

Velma lay stretched out on their shared bed cooling herself with a bamboo fan courtesy of *Elias R. Brown Eternal Rest Mortuary – No Theater Parking*. Perspiration glazed her hazelnut-colored skin and matted the long auburn hair that fell across her shoulders and breasts.

"So tell me Doc," she said with a scowl that deepened the crow's feet at the corners of her dark eyes. "Just how long will you be honoring me with your charming presence and scintillating wit this time?"

"If you play your cards right, I'd say right up until Friday morning," Chance replied as he dropped three ice cubes into Velma's gin and tonic. "I need to be home before dark."

She folded Elias R. Brown's complimentary fan and rapped it against an open palm. "If I was to play those cards you're talkin' about," she said, "I'd throw out the joker first thing."

"Very funny, Vel," Chance replied. He turned to hand Velma her ice-filled gin and tonic before rejoining her in bed. Careful not to spill his own bourbon on the rocks, Chance plumped up his pillow with an elbow and leaned back.

"I mean it, Doc," Velma said. "You know how I feel about your hit and run visits."

"If you'd rather I didn't…"

She placed a finger over Chance's lips. "Don't," she whispered.

He gently pulled her finger away and dipped it into his drink as if it were a swizzle stick. Then he put her finger in his mouth and sucked on it.

"Damn you," Velma groaned.

Chance smiled. "Tastes better this way."

Velma reached for Chance's slack penis and said, "Suppose I return the favor?"

"You can try, but it's not like I'm twenty anymore."

"Just wait and see," Velma replied. She turned to place her drink on the bedside table next to an alarm clock with two clappered-bells the size of peach-halves, then rolled over to slide face-first down Chance's stomach.

Bemused, Chance watched Velma at work through the amber-colored drink he held on his chest. The distortion made her head look detached and far away. It was as if he could distance himself from the act itself, a rejection of whatever guilt he might have felt, but didn't.

Unable to bring Chance to his fourth orgasm since Monday, Velma abandoned her efforts and snuggled close. "How about we take in a late movie, Doc? It might recharge your batteries."

The request surprised him. "You know the rules."

"Don't be such a stick in the mud."

"What's playing that can't wait until after I leave?"

Velma propped herself up on one elbow. "'*Meet me in St. Louis*,' with Judy Garland. It's gonna win an Oscar, for sure."

"I've been to St. Louis, and I've seen Judy Garland. Both are over-rated in my book."

"I'd like to have a peek in that book of yours someday."

Chance wordlessly placed his drink on the bedside table beside him and reached for an open pack of Old Golds. He shook out a cigarette and lit it off the Zippo with the engraved inscription: "Doc. You Bastard. Velma."

Velma reached for the cigarette and took a shallow drag before he could. "C'mon Doc," she wheedled. "Take me, please?"

"I can't risk it, Vel. You know my biggest equipment dealer is in Cincinnati."

Velma scowled and handed back the cigarette. "You won't be seen in public with a black woman. Admit it."

"You know that's not true," Chance replied. "I've always championed Negro rights."

"We be fine to fuck in de dark," Velma mimicked, "but not so fine as to take to de park."

Chance squinted through the swirling tobacco smoke caused by Velma's vigorous fanning. "That's enough."

Velma threw down the fan and swung her legs out of bed. "You really are a bastard," she muttered, and stomped off to the living room.

Chance smiled at the sight of her deep sacral dimples. "Oh, Vel?" he called. "Put something on the Victrola, will you? I'd like to request '*American Patrol*,' if you've got it. It's a Glenn Miller tune."

"I've got a request for you, too, Doc," Velma called back. "Next time you drop anchor in Cincinnati, and assuming I let you in, take off those goddamned black socks before you come to bed! You make me feel like we're making a French porn movie!"

"Now Vel," Chance called back. "You know my feet get cold because my circulation isn't good."

"You've got too goddamned *much* circulation, if you ask me!"

When she came back after putting Bessie Smith's recording of "*St. Louis Blues*" on the Victrola, she plopped down next to Chance with a smile that looked pasted on. "How long have we known each other, Doc?"

Chance knew it had been a long time, even going back to when he was between marriages. "Nineteen years?" he guessed.

"Twenty-one," Velma corrected. "And all these years I hoped there might be a future for us. Be honest, Doc. Was there *ever* a future for us?"

Chance stubbed out his cigarette in an overflowing ashtray. "How about we save that question for another time?"

Velma started to weep. "I'm forty-six, Doc," she sniffed. "Ain't no man gonna pick up with a woman my age."

"That's nonsense, Velma. You're a handsome woman. There's still plenty of time for..."

"Bullshit! You only come by to get your ashes hauled, and I'm guessin' I ain't the only one doin' the haulin' either. Doesn't your wife's pussy purr for action anymore? Or is it you, Doc? Maybe that pink willy of yours only works on us colored gals. Is that it?"

"Now Velma," Chance countered. "You know my personal life is off limits. Knowing I'm married is enough."

Velma cried "Fuck you!" and curled herself into a ball with her back toward Chance.

He touched her shoulder. "Listen, Vel," he began. "Maybe after the war..."

She stopped him with a furious backward kick that narrowly missed his flaccid penis but caught his thigh. "Fuck the war," she sobbed. "Fuck your vibrators, and fuck you too!"

Chance let his hand slide to Velma's rounded hip. "Maybe we *could* take in the late show at that. But sometime today I need to use your phone to call home."

"Sure thing, Doc. Anything you want. Just be sure to reverse the charges."

CHAPTER TWENTY

Chance arrived home late that Friday afternoon. He was tired but in a reasonably good mood, which carried over to the next morning. He'd even surprised Alva by showering and initiating sex before coming down to the breakfast table.

"It seems to me," she said to Chance over a third cup of coffee, "that once you get to Cincinnati, you'd want to get home as soon as possible, and not spend three more days away." She wore a faded blue housedress and seemed more tired than usual. The hair that had gone gray while she was still in her early thirties was kept in place with four tortoise shell barrettes.

"You know my biggest dealer is in Cincinnati," Chance replied. He gave a quick glance out the window toward the horse barn, where he'd seen Keeper go thirty minutes earlier. "What does Keeper do to amuse himself out there?" he asked.

"He plays in Dad's Hup," Alva said. "He thinks he's a road man, just like his absentee father."

Chance winced at the comment. "I may as well tell you now. We're demonstrating our new multiple tamper near Atlanta next week, and I need to be there."

Instead of complaining, Alva brightened. "Take Keep with you?"

Chance was quick to reply. "This is business, Alva, not a vacation."

She pressed harder. "All Keeper talks about when you're away is going on a road trip with his dad."

"A forced draft road trip to Atlanta and back wouldn't be any fun for Keeper."

"He'd love it. And besides, he's becoming a handful."

Chance shook his head. "I can't."

"Yes you can. Besides, having Keeper out from underfoot for a week or two would be a vacation for me."

The radio was tuned to Don McNeil's Breakfast Club, which made it sound as if Don himself was in on the conversation, when he said, "*That's right, breakfast clubbers, and remember, there's no vacation when it comes to collecting those pots and pans for the war effort!*"

Chance gingerly rubbed the bruised thigh where Velma had kicked him. "I'd have to watch him every minute."

"He's not a baby anymore. My God, Chance, he outgrows his clothes before he can wear them out."

"I'll give it some thought, dear. Meanwhile, not a word to Keep about this."

Dr. Wick interrupted the conversation when he shuffled into the kitchen with his cane hooked over the crook of his right arm. As usual, he wore his three-piece woolen suit and a crisp white shirt, but with a gravy-stained necktie. The pink rose he'd cut for his lapel the day before had shriveled overnight and looked like an abscess. He stopped when he reached the stove and extended a shaking hand for the aluminum coffee percolator.

"Let me get it, Dad," Alva said, and began to get up.

"Never mind, daughter," Dr. Wick replied in a voice that was loose and phlegmy. When he picked up the percolator it slipped from his palsied grip and fell to the floor, breaking apart and spilling precious rationed coffee and scattering wet grounds.

"Dad!" Alva cried. "I said I'd get it."

"Damn it, Dad," Chance said. "Ask for help next time."

Dr. Wick's expression was one of utter bewilderment. "What damn fool let the horse in here?" he cried, as if the incident had triggered some long-forgotten memory.

"It's all right, Dad," Alva said. Her tone was soothing. "You can have my coffee. I've already had two cups."

His eyebrows rose like white feathers caught in a sudden updraft above the black-framed eyeglasses identical to those worn by his idol, Dr. Freud. "Nooooooo," he cried with a stricken sound.

"Take it easy, Dad," Chance said, and got up to lead his father to a chair where he could look out the window and into the backyard.

"Mother will know what to do," the old man said.

Chance turned to Alva, who was already on her hands and knees moping up spilled coffee and loose grounds with a kitchen towel and a hot pad.

Dr. Wick tried to get up, saying, "I'll bring the Hup around."

Chance turned to address Alva. "How long has this been going on?"

She pushed back a stray hair with the back of her hand. "For too damned long."

He placed a gentle hand on his father's shoulder. "Let's have some breakfast first, Dad, and then we'll all go for a long drive."

Dr. Wick nodded and fell silent. He turned stiffly in his chair to face the horse barn, where his unseen grandson was imagining he was a road man behind the wheel of the Hupmobile Aero Sedan.

While Alva was wringing out the towel in the sink, Early came into the kitchen. He wore a threadbare bathrobe, carpet slippers, and mismatched socks. "Is something wrong?" he asked.

"Dad just had a little accident," Chance replied. "Nothing serious."

Early lifted his head and sniffed. "Coffee smells extra strong this morning."

"Coffee's gone," Alva said in a tired monotone," but you can have mine."

He approached the kitchen table with measured steps and took his usual seat opposite his grandfather. From there he could find everything – the salt and pepper shakers on the left, and the sugar bowl and creamer on the right. Alva placed her coffee cup in front of Early and tapped it so he'd know where it was. Once he was properly orientated, Early reached unerringly for the sugar bowl and poured several spoonfuls into his cup. He cocked an ear. "Where's Keep?"

"In the horse barn," Dr. Wick said, surprising both Chance and Alva, until adding, "He'll be bringing the Hup around momentarily."

"Dad," Chance said. "I think it might be useful if we had Dr. Wilberforce pay us another visit."

Dr. Wick's feathery eyebrows rose again. "Good. We'll need a fourth for bridge."

Chance shook his head, as if to deny his father's worsening mental condition. He turned his attention toward the yard as Keeper exited the weather-beaten horse barn and came loping across the yard on gangly legs. Alva was right, Chance thought. Their son was growing like a corn stalk in July.

"I think the Hup's battery's dead," Keeper announced when he came in through the kitchen door – a screen door that he let slam behind him. "I tried playing the radio, but nothing happened, unless a tube burned out."

"I warned you that would happen," Alva scolded.

"I smell rotten plums," Dr. Wick said.

Keeper turned to look at his grandfather with a concerned expression. "What's the matter with Grandpa?"

"He had an accident with the coffee," Alva replied.

Keeper leaned close to study his grandfather's face. "I think it's dementia," he replied softly.

"Where'd you come up with that? Early asked.

"I got it from one of Grandpa's medical books. It's the one Dr. Freud signed for him."

"Do you know what dementia means?"

"Sure." He circled a finger around his temple. "It means crazy."

CHAPTER TWENTY-ONE

By early evening Dr. Wilberforce had come and gone. His diagnosis of his old colleague had essentially been the same as Keeper's. This pleased Keeper, but caused Alva to have an anxiety attack that she at first thought might be her heart. Leaving Keeper and Early to their game of Chinese checkers at the kitchen table, she and Chance went into the living room to hear President Roosevelt delivering another fireside chat over the Zenith with the unblinking green tuning eye. Chance lowered the volume so as not to disturb his father, who was up in his room talking to his long dead wife, Winifred, which made for a very one-sided conversation.

"Dad's going to be more of a handful now," Alva said, simply.

Chance was working on the third double bourbon he'd taken during the past hour and a half. "I'll hire someone," he said. "A practical nurse, to come in and help."

"We've been over this before, Chance," Alva replied. "You know I won't have a stranger in the house watching my every move."

He ran his fingers through graying hair. "Then what am I expected to do?"

Alva settled into her chair. "Other than finding a job close to home?"

"I've *got* a job close to home," Chance argued.

Alva shook her head. "You've got a job that *takes* you from home!"

"Look Alva. Without a sheepskin, sales are the only option for men like me."

Not having a college degree was Chance's greatest regret, although by dint of his charm and native intelligence, it seldom showed. He was smart enough to have gotten a college diploma, had he not let himself become entrapped by the first woman he'd impregnated.

"I'd rather make do with less, than have you away so often," Alva said.

Chance scowled. "It's tough on all of us, but good-paying sales jobs like mine are damned few, and they all require travel. That's just the way it is."

"The way it *is*, isn't working," Alva countered.

"Early could do more," Chance offered. "He gets around pretty well."

Alva dismissively waved a hand. "Early isn't as self-reliant as you might think."

Chance rattled the ice cubes in his drink, as if annoyed. "Then ask Keeper to lend a hand. And remember, he can drive Dad's Hupmobile in a pinch."

"Keeper's not driving anything! He needs his father, not his father's responsibilities!"

"Maybe it's about time he learned to accept more responsibility," Chance replied.

"Rubbish. He's a thirteen-year-old kid who still hasn't picked up with other kids since that Indian girl disappeared."

"I'll talk to him tomorrow."

"Talk to *me*, Chance," Alva cried. "Tell me where and how this all ends!"

"Tell me how and when the war ends, and *then* I'll tell you," Chance replied, then tried a conciliatory approach. "Look. Write to your sister. Have her and her husband come up from Detroit."

"That's not the answer and you know it. Gas rationing wouldn't get them half-way across the state."

Chance knew it was true. An 'A' sticker would buy only four gallons of gasoline a week. And then there was tire rationing. Chance rubbed his forehead into deep furrows, as if to make the problem go away. "Then I'll do it."

Alva brightened. "Then you'll get my sister?"

"Jesus no, Alva. I'm talking about taking Keeper with me to Atlanta."

"I thought you'd forgotten," she said with a sidelong glance that suggested she had been disappointed before by his broken promises. After all, Chance had been promising Keeper a road trip ever since their son knew what a roadmap was.

"I hadn't forgotten," Chance replied.

Alva folded her hands in her lap. "Now I almost wish you had."

He reached into his shirt pocket for the second pack of cigarettes he'd opened since morning and shook one out. "Having second thoughts, Alva dear?" he asked after lighting it off the butt of the one he was smoking.

"Maybe I am at that," she snuffled. "I'm worried sick every day you're on the road. I worry when Keeper is at the beach. I worry about Dad falling down the stairs. I worry about Early burning down the house or getting run over. Even listening to war news makes me think about my brother, Neil, and it's becoming more than I can bear."

Chance sipped at his double bourbon while contemplating how best to reply to Alva when the air raid siren began wailing, another test to be on alert for enemy bombers.

"I'll get the upstairs lights!" Keeper yelled from the kitchen, "and no cheating, Early!"

"Don't run in the house!" Alva called. "You'll fall and break your neck!"

Once Keeper was out of earshot, Chance turned to Alva. "I'll make you a promise. When we get back from Atlanta, I'll ask Mr. Pettigrew to hire someone else for the road, and to put me behind a desk. That's where I belong anyway, managing."

"You'll *ask* Mr. Pettigrew?" Alva replied with hope sounding in her voice, "or *tell?*"

"I'll tell."

Alva looked dubious. "And if he says no?"

Chance turned off the floor lamp next to his elbow, plunging the room into sudden darkness. Only the Zenith's green cat's-eye showed, and it winked as Roosevelt's fireside chat faded in and out. "Then I'll quit."

For a full minute, neither spoke, as if considering the full consequences and implications of quitting, and what would happen to them if Mr. Pettigrew let Chance go. Only the air raid siren broke the silence, as if it carried yet another, more sinister warning.

"Do I have your word?" Alva asked, softly, expectantly.

His answer came two beats too late, but Chance hoped it would suffice for its brevity, if not sincerity. "Yes."

Alva sighed. "Then call Keeper."

Chance smiled in the dark. "Keep! Come down here."

Keeper called back. "Coming!" He quickly turned off his grandfather's table lamp, but he left the radio on because he knew the air raid warden would never see the glowing dial from the street.

"I'm not ready to retire," Dr. Wick complained. My Bible…"

Keeper interrupted. "It's an air raid alert, Grandpa. Lights out!"

"The Huns are bombing London again?" Dr. Wick replied with alarm.

Keeper laughed. "No Grandpa. It's a test."

The old physician cried, "Have someone see to Winnie!"

Leaving Dr. Wick to his senile ruminations, Keeper dashed down the front stairs to the living room that remained dark except for the green cat's eye and the ash glowing at the tip of his father's cigarette. "What do you want?" he asked.

"Two days from now, you and I are going to Atlanta," Chance said as casually as if he were discussing the weather.

"Are you serious?" Keeper asked. He wondered if this was just another hollow promise. Like promising to buy a football, or to go fishing, or go to a high school basketball game, or to do anything at all.

Chance knocked back the last of his drink. "Sure am, Keep."

"Wow!" Keeper exclaimed joyfully. "A road trip at last!"

"We'll be gone for a couple of weeks," Chance cautioned, "so you'll need to take your mother's suitcase and enough clothes."

Keeper excitedly punched the air with his fist. "I can hardly wait!"

"We'll send Mother letters from the road," Chance said. "Maybe even a picture postcard or two."

"And call too," Alva admonished. "I want to know *exactly* where you boys are every night."

"We sure will," Keeper said, and added, "Won't we Dad?"

"You can count on it, son. Now hit the sack. We road men need our sleep."

CHAPTER TWENTY-TWO

They came while Atlanta slept, up from their winter quarters in Zephyrhills: Red-eyed carnies hopped-up on Benzedrine and piloting wheezing Diamond T and REO trucks riding on balding pre-war tires and expired Florida plates. They were hard men who lived on and by the rules of the road – heavily tattooed and brick-red from the southern sun – men to whom the weather, luck and women had been unkind. Sweating canvas bags slung over REO and Lincoln bumpers held drinking water chilled by evaporation. Overloaded flatbeds hauling Tilt-a-Whirl and Ferris wheel girders and enclosed trailers carrying Caterpillar-powered generators tagged along on greased fifth-wheel couplings. On the sides of the trailers in faded red and blue lettering were the words:

ALL STAR AMUSEMENTS

&

TRAVELING CARNIVAL

Strung out for five miles in the wake of the procession were sun-faded Cadillac and Lincoln automobiles towing popcorn wagons, grab shacks, and Airstream trailers with aluminum skin pitted by the salty gulf air. The ragged convoy passed endless fields of cotton that looked like snowdrifts under a full blood-orange moon. Cotton blossoms bursting from knife-sharp husks waited for the rising sun to burn off the dew that dappled them like sweat, and for the colored pickers to come. They would already be up in their clapboard shacks, preparing a breakfast of boiled hominy, hog-belly fried in cast-iron pans, and hot chicory coffee poured from chipped stoneware pots. Bone-weary men women and children with bleeding fingers that never healed when there was a crop to pick. Unsmiling women in work aprons with heads wrapped in white cotton cloth. Gaunt men dressed in ragged bib-overalls, denim shirts and wide-brimmed fedoras to shield them from the baking-hot Georgia sun that already waited beyond the far horizon.

Ground fog shrouded weak headlights probing the narrow asphalt two-lane and the red Georgia clay shoulder. Beyond, and looming in shadowy silhouette were stands of cottonwood, black-jack oak, pignut hickory and loblolly pine. Each nearly indistinguishable from the other in the misty pre-dawn gloom. The sweet smell of blooming dogwood, hydrangea and honeysuckle was narcotic on the heavy, humid air, but was met with indifference by the carnies. The procession slowed as it neared Atlanta, passing shotgun shacks, crib joints, juke joints and rib joints alike, until arriving at Lakewood Park, where they would be setting up and where they would stay for the next two weeks. With military precision, the convoy assembled by rows as the already-hot sun broke the eastern horizon.

Weeks before, splashy posters announcing the arrival of the traveling road show had been plastered throughout Atlanta by the advance man – an ex-con and active Klansman now being held by the Atlanta police for having taken liberties with a fourteen-year old colored girl in his hotel room. By late afternoon the roustabouts had the midway nearly set up. Ready for the rubes were the hanky-panks with their gaffed games, the fun house and the gadget show with its crank-operated clamshell that cost a dime but never picked up the best prize. Along the midway, tents with freak shows featuring pickled punks in formaldehyde-filled jars were up, to include the iron lung show, the fat lady, the India rubber man, and the geek and the Alligator Boy. Over at the grind show tent, a hand-painted banner showing a nearly-naked blond woman holding a red parasol announced the attraction being offered. It read:

SEE THE AMAZING LULU LaRUE
Be Shocked & Amazed
At Her Titillating Delights
And Natural Wonders

Lulu rested on an unmade bed in her aluminum-shelled Airstream while waiting for the opening night's performance. The lacy black bra and matching panties she wore contrasted sharply against her radish-white skin. She sweated heavily in spite of the rotating table fan set to high speed at her elbow. With her was the darkly-handsome teenager with the astonishing pale gray eyes who had knocked on her trailer door in Zephyrhills, looking for work of any kind.

"I still can't get over what a goddamned pretty boy you are," Lulu remarked. It hadn't been the first time she'd been so moved to comment on Jack's sexually ambiguous good looks. Lulu had taken him in, mainly to protect him from the predatory roustabouts. But even before leaving Zephyrhills, Lulu found herself becoming increasingly attracted to the teenager whom she planned to incorporate into her grind show as a Nubian slave.

Jack held up a pair of diaphanous pantaloons and a rhinestone-studded green vest. The rest of the outfit included a pair of red caliph shoes, a turban and a gauzy veil. "I don't think I can wear these."

"It'll be perfect for the act," Lulu replied. "Put 'em on and let's have us a look."

"I'm embarrassed to wear them, Miss LaRue."

"Silly boy, I'll blind my eyes while you change." Lulu put both hands over her eyes and grinned wickedly as sweat dripped down her cheeks and onto her pendulous breasts. She had yet to see Jack undressed, and was looking forward to the opportunity of doing so.

"No."

"Look, kid. In this carny, everybody works or else they don't eat."

"Then I'll work for somebody else."

"You'll work for me and nobody else. Now, put on that outfit."

"I need a smoke first."

Lulu growled, "Not in the trailer. Now quit stalling and get changed."

"I fucking won't."

Stunned by the abrupt refusal and flushing red, Lulu swung her legs off the bed to angrily confront her unwilling assistant. "How goddamn dare you?" she hissed, and slapped her open-handed across the face.

"You fat pig! Jonnie Prettyboy howled, and punched back, hitting Lulu's left breast and dislodging it from its brassiere cup.

"If that fucking tit's bruised, you're gonna pay good!" Lulu bellowed. Enraged, she clawed at Jack's shirt, tearing away the buttons and exposing the breasts that Jack had been so carefully concealing with an elastic band.

For a long ten seconds, Lulu was speechless, until a gleeful smile dimpled her rouged cheeks. "Well, my...my... *my!*" she leered. "If you ain't the chocolate cherry surprise!"

"Get the fuck away from me!"

Lulu crossed her arms over her heaving sweat-slicked breasts while appraising her assistant in a new, critical light. "You're that half-breed runaway the cops up north are looking for, ain't you?"

"I don't know what you're talking about."

"Yeah you do. I seen the circulars. You're Jonnie Prettyboy, and you're suspected of murdering your daddy."

Jonnie Prettyboy made a sudden break for the door, until being grabbed by the neck. "Fucking bitch!" she screamed, and struggled to break loose.

Lulu panted from the effort of subduing Jonnie Prettyboy. "Any more funny stuff," she grunted, "and I'll turn you over to the Alligator Boy. Now, take 'em off."

Trembling with fear and pain, Jonnie Prettyboy shrugged off the torn shirt before stepping out of her jeans. Next she pulled the elastic band over her head and dropped it to the floor. Now she stood in the same fly-front shorts Keeper Wick had given her to wear three years earlier.

Lulu licked her lips and pointed to the shorts. "Them too."

Slowly, as if in pantomime, Jonnie Prettyboy hooked her thumbs over the elastic band and pulled them down over her hips to her knees. Then she stepped out of them, one leg at a time, until she stood completely naked and sweating in the Airstream trailer-oven.

Lulu reached for Jonnie Prettyboy. "Ohhh, baby," she crooned. "Come to mama."

Jonnie Prettyboy backed away with her hands over her face and sobbing.

Lulu pressed on. "Before we get fixed up for tonight's act, we're gonna have us a little party." Wiping sweat from her eyes, Lulu sidled over to the low dresser drawer next to her unmade bed and pulled out the bottom drawer. Inside was a half-gone fifth of Jack Daniel's and an obscenely large pink-rubber dildo loosely attached through its base to an adjustable strap.

Lulu reached for the sex toy and thrust it towards Jonnie Prettyboy. "Put it on, '*Jack*,'" she commanded.

"Goddamn you!" Jonnie Prettyboy cried. "*No!*"

Lulu sneered. "Either you do, or I call the cops. If you're real lucky, you might end up only doing a few years in juvenile detention."

"I won't do it," Jonnie Prettyboy sobbed. But the look of utter despair written on her tear-streaked face told a much different story.

CHAPTER TWENTY-THREE

For once Keeper didn't feel like an accomplice whenever he carried his father's packed suitcase down to the car. This time he felt like a co-conspirator as he placed the suitcase his mother had let him use next to his father's in the New Yorker's trunk. She cried of course. Early shook hands and joked that he'd keep a protective eye out for Alva and Granddad while Chance and Keeper were on the road.

Alva had arranged to have the local market home-deliver, and Dr. Wilberforce promised to look in on his old colleague as needed. Keeper had washed the New Yorker the day before, and it sparkled whitely as a new tooth under a brilliant morning sun that seemed forever suspended in a cobalt sky. The only fly in the ointment, so far as Keeper was concerned, was the black demo trailer hooked to the rear of the car. This time out the trailer held two generator-powered soil compactors, which they would be demonstrating in Cincinnati, their first stopover on the way to Atlanta. Also in Atlanta was the new Dakota tamper waiting to be demonstrated for the Cotton Belt Railway. It promised to be a busy two weeks for Chance.

Keeper waited until they were fifty miles down the road before asking the question uppermost on his mind. "Will I get to drive on this trip?"

Chance took a drag off his freshly-lit Old Gold and grinned. "Count on it."

Keeper leaned back with a contented smile and watched the scenery sweep past his window where dairy cows grazed in lush meadows amid butterflies and birds on the wing, and farmers on tractors looking skyward for rain.

He slipped a hand into his pants pocket and rubbed the lucky charm his father had given him, the one with the four-leaf clovers and horseshoes stamped on it. He rolled down his window to let the wind buffet his cheeks and drum loudly in his ears. He rested his arm on the windowsill and closed his eyes to the delicious sensation of a hot August sun on his bare skin. He allowed himself to dreamily wonder if the distant father he knew from Dakota Straits would become less so once they got to Atlanta: A father who would toss the football with him and take him to the movies and picnics on the beach. But for now, Keeper was simply content to be with the father he had.

The good weather lasted only as far as the Indiana state line. Then it was as if a dark-gray curtain had descended, bringing with it hard-driving rain that lashed the New Yorker and the trailer. Chance switched on the headlights and then the windshield wipers, which quickly smeared the June bugs and grasshoppers splattering the windshield like they'd been fired from a shotgun.

"This is the worst storm I've ever seen," Keeper said.

"Be glad it's not winter," Chance replied. "Then we'd be driving through a blizzard like I did on day you were born."

Keeper remembered the story. "Grandpa couldn't make me breathe. You got home just in time to save my life. And when you gave me to mother, you called me a keeper."

"All it took was a glass of cold water in your face."

"Okay if I turn on the radio?" Keeper asked after a minute of thinking how lucky he was.

Chance opened his vent window and flipped away his cigarette. "Fine by me."

Keeper turned on the radio and twisted the dial until finding a Chicago station. Lena Horne was on and singing *Stormy Weather*.

"How appropriate," Chance muttered.

They came upon the accident minutes later. A young soldier, wearing a rain-soaked khaki uniform, stood next to the shattered remains of a Buick Century four-door convertible. The soldier had a badly cut lip, and blood stained the front of his shirt and the single row of colorful ribbons over his left breast pocket. The Buick had apparently crashed into a rain-stalled Packard coupe, which because of its gray color was made nearly invisible in the downpour.

Keeper gawked at the sight of a bloodied woman slumped in the Buick's passenger seat with her hands held to her face. An ambulance was already there, and so was a state trooper, who stood in the rain directing traffic around the accident scene.

"Do you think she's dead?" Keeper asked as they crawled past.

"No, but it'll probably take a skilled surgeon to put her face back together."

"I hope we don't see another wreck on this trip. That was awful."

"I've seen worse," Chance replied without elaborating. He pushed the New Yorker hard to make up for lost time, and Keeper was unable to stop talking about the accident. He was even tempted to tell his father how Mr. Prettyboy looked at the bottom of the stairs in the horse barn. He was also thinking the dead Indian hadn't looked that bad by comparison.

"There's a fresh pack of cigarettes and a lighter in the glove box," Chance said, interrupting Keepers train of thought. "Get 'em for me, please?"

He opened the glove box and fumbled under a stack of dog-eared roadmaps for the cigarettes and the lighter he remembered seeing while getting Jonnie Prettyboy her map. Keeper was still curious about the message: "Doc. You Bastard. Velma." He had heard some of his father's friends call him "Doc," but he had no idea who Velma was.

Chance took the lighter from Keeper and struck a flame under the cigarette. "Not a word to anyone about what we saw today, Keep," he said.

"Why not?"

"Road life isn't as glamorous as you might think. Time you learned that."

"You never tell us about the bad side."

"It would be unfair to your mother," Chance replied. "She has enough to worry about as it is."

"She's probably worried right now," Keeper muttered, "especially with Grandpa going goofy."

"We'll call her tonight, from Cincinnati."

"Are we going to stop for something to eat pretty soon?"

"We'll stop for gas in Kokomo," he said. "You can buy a bottle of pop and a candy bar, or something."

"Okay."

"What do you like?"

"I like Cokes and Butterfingers best," Keeper replied.

Chance shifted into second gear and pulled out to pass a lumbering Greyhound. "I had no idea."

"I know *you* like smoking and drinking old stuff, like Old Golds and Old Crow," Keeper said once they were safely around the bus. It was hard for him not to think of crashing head-on into another car and leaving them bleeding to death in the mangled wreckage. He wondered how his mother would take *that* news.

"You could have added, 'to excess,'" Chance replied.

"But I didn't."

"Maybe you'll be a diplomat someday."

"I'd rather be a road man someday," Keeper replied, although he was becoming less certain by the mile and wondered if he had said it only to please his father.

Chance laughed, as if reading his son's mind. "Tell me that again in another week."

Traffic was much heavier when they reached Kokomo. "There's a Texaco station ahead," Keeper said, wanting to be helpful.

"Shell's my brand," but that'll do," Chance replied as he turned in to park next to an open pump. He turned to Keeper. "If you have to take a leak, now's the time to do it."

Keeper hadn't wanted to complain about needing to pee, and didn't need to be asked twice. He got out and hurried for the men's toilet located behind the station and just beyond the ladies toilet. A courtesy, he figured, since everyone knew women couldn't hold their water like men. When he entered his attention was drawn to a coin-operated condom machine bolted to the wall next to a single urinal. "Kilroy was here," and various other messages offering blowjobs and the telephone number of a "Donna" looking for a good time were scratched into the wall where a mirror should have been.

Fascinated by the variety of rubbers, black, ribbed, and otherwise, Keeper dug a quarter out of his pocket, dropped it in the slot, and pulled the knob for a French tickler. Unsure of what a French tickler was supposed to do that other rubbers didn't, he put it in his hand-tooled Boy Scout wallet in the hope of someday using it on Jonnie Prettyboy, who said she was headed south on that sad night in the horse barn three years ago. He had no sooner finished peeing when his father entered through the unlocked door.

"Go get yourself a Coke and a candy bar, Chance said. "I'll be out in a minute."

Keeper was still wondering what his father would think about the condom machine and the blowjob messages when he reached the red Coca-Cola tub. He lifted the lid to see several inches of water and a block of melting ice – but no Cokes – only five Royal Crown Colas and a single bottle of Nesbitt's orange crush. Disappointed, Keeper fished out a bottle of Royal Crown.

When he stepped inside the station to look for a Butterfinger he found two open boxes of candy bars on the counter next to the cash register. One box displayed Hershey bars, and the other Milky Ways, but no Butterfingers. After resignedly selecting a Milky Way, he took a crumpled dollar bill from his wallet and handed it to the attendant who had come in from refueling the New Yorker.

"What'cha you fellas haulin' in that trailer?" he asked after making change of Keeper's dollar.

"Vibrators," Keeper replied simply.

The attendant laughed. "Maybe I ought'a get one for my old lady."

Keeper felt his cheeks redden and wondered if the attendant's old lady was Donna. He thought about asking, but his father returning from the toilet prevented him from doing so. He also wondered if his father had bought any rubbers, and if he was going to use them on Alva. It was a troubling image.

After Chance paid for the tank of Ethyl and a quart of oil, he turned to Keeper. "Ready?" he asked with a hurried glance at his watch.

Keeper nodded and held up his purchases. "They didn't have Cokes or Butterfingers, so I had to take these instead."

"That's life on the road, Keep," he said as they returned to the car. His tone was easy and bantering, and he held his arm draped protectively over Keeper's shoulders. "You either take it or leave it. However it comes, the choice is up to you."

Keeper couldn't help but wonder where Jonnie Prettyboy was at that moment, and if she was having to 'take it or leave it.'

CHAPTER TWENTY-FOUR

"Where'll we stay in Cincinnati?" Keeper asked through a mouthful of the Milky Way he was trying to make last. The August sun was low on the western horizon, and Indianapolis lay twenty miles ahead.

The question seemed to catch Chance off-guard. Whenever he stayed over in Cincinnati, it was always with Velma at her place. "We'll find a hotel in town," he replied. "I'm bushed and need to wet my whistle before we eat."

Keeper was tired too, although not so tired as to be impressed by the sight of Indianapolis when they passed through. Colored men smoked cigarettes at a city parking lot, and Keeper guessed they worked there. "Look at those guys, Dad," he said. "They're the first Negros I've ever seen."

"You'll be seeing lots more ahead."

"Chain gangs too, like the one you wrote me about?"

"Maybe not chain gangs. But you'll see gandydancers working on the railroad."

"What are they?"

That's what railroaders call the men who line the tracks by hand and tamp ballast under the cross ties. They're mostly colored boys where we're going."

"I can't wait," Keeper replied. Then he fell silent, considering the events of the day, and what might lay ahead for them as they sped toward Cincinnati.

It was dusk when they reached the city limits. He watched wide-eyed as his father skillfully threaded the New Yorker and its demo trailer around clanging streetcars and yellow trolleybuses that glided silently on rubber tires. Within minutes, they had the Royal Cincinnatian in sight. When they pulled up at the curb, a colored valet wearing a doorman's uniform came out to greet them.

"Will you be staying with us overnight, suh?" he asked when Chance rolled down his window.

"Yes," Chance replied, and added, "That is, if you can find us a place to park."

"I can take care of that, suh. Will there be luggage?"

Chance jerked a thumb toward the rear of the car. "There's two suitcases, in the trunk."

The valet produced a silver whistle and blew a single blast that brought a bellhop.

Chance turned to Keeper. "Let's check in. They'll bring the suitcases."

Keeper's face fell when he followed his father into the lobby. It smelled sour, and the carpet was faded and threadbare. Overstuffed chairs and couches scattered around the lobby were stained and patched. Fake palm trees filled dark corners.

An elderly white desk clerk greeted them. "Do you have reservations?" he asked.

"Do we need them?" Chance replied.

"There's a war on, sir," the clerk said. "The Royal Cincinnatian is booked."

Chance reached into his pocket for his silver money clip and peeled off a ten-dollar bill. "Perhaps you can un-book something," he said, and winked.

The clerk took the bill. "I might be able to arrange something after all."

"Will there be a bath?"

"Of course, sir." The clerk unnecessarily rang a bell to summon the bellhop who held their suitcases, one under each arm. "Kindly take these two gentlemen to suite 205."

Chance and Keeper followed the bellhop across the lobby to a bank of four elevators. "How late do you serve dinner?" Chance asked once they were in the elevator and ascending to the second floor.

"'Lessen we runs out of food, usually 'til eight," was the reply.

When the elevator came to an uneven stop at the second floor the bellhop opened the door to lead the way down a poorly-lit hallway to its end. Sounds of men and women laughing and a radio playing swing music at top volume suggested a small party was underway in the room across from theirs.

"How long has that been going on?" Chance asked with a sour expression.

The bellhop unlocked the door and chuckled. "Only since yesterday morning."

Chance appraised the sparse room with a practiced glance. "The desk clerk said there was a bath. And where the hell are the beds?"

The bellhop nodded toward a curtain hanging over a doorway next to a mirrored chest of drawers. A dial telephone sat on the chest of drawers. "Bathroom's behind that curtain. I'll have your beds straight-away." He dropped the suitcases to the floor and opened a closet door. He reached in and pulled out a cot. "There's a 'nother like it in there," he said.

Chance kicked at one. "We can't sleep on those."

The bellhop scratched his head while seeming to think. "No suh, I 'spect you can't. But I might be able to step you and the boy up a notch for a small consideration."

"How small?"

"Five dollar, suh."

"Then do it."

"Each, suh."

Chance fumbled for the money clip and counted out two fives and handed one to the bellhop. "You'll get the other when we get the beds."

"Yas suh," the bellhop replied, and left.

Keeper took the only chair and scowled. "Is it always like this on the road?"

"No son. Sometimes it's worse."

Keeper pointed to a length of coiled rope under the window. "What's that for?"

"Nothing you need to worry about," Chance replied.

More curious than ever, Keeper went to the curtain that hid the bathroom and pushed it aside. He gulped at the sight of an ancient porcelain bathtub with claw feet, a pedestal sink, and a medicine cabinet with a broken mirror. Two thin face towels and two bath towels hung on a single rack over the toilet. A glass tumbler on the toilet tank, a sliver of soap on the sink, and a half-roll of toilet paper completed the inventory.

"I don't think we can stay here," Keeper said. "There's hardly any soap."

"Make do," Chance replied. "There's a war on."

"That's what I keep hearing."

The bellhop returned pushing two beds on wheels, with mattresses thin enough to allow them to be folded end-to-end. Sheets were already on them. "You gennelmens will sleep like kings on these, suh," the bellhop said.

Chance handed over the second five dollar bill, and added a ten to it. "If it's not too much trouble, see if you can scare up a bottle of Old Crow."

"If they ain't any, then what?"

"Anything but gin."

"Yas suh," the bellhop replied, and turned to leave.

"Wait, mister," Keeper said, and pointed to the rope. "What's that for?"

"Yas suh. That's for in case of fire." He left without explaining more.

Keeper went to the window overlooking the street below. "If there was a fire, Dad, there's no way we could get down on that rope without killing ourselves."

"That's another thing your mother doesn't need to know about."

"Maybe we should call and tell her we're here."

"Go ahead, and tell desk you want to make a long-distance call while I use the can," Chance said. "And remember, you've got a war-rationed three minutes."

Pleased to feel useful for once, Keeper placed his call to through the switchboard to Dakota Straits and listened to the phone ring at home until it was picked up.

"It's me," Keeper announced when he heard his mother's voice.

"Where are you?" Alva asked, sounding worried.

"Cincinnati."

"Are you and your father all right?"

"Uh, sure."

"What are you not telling me?"

"Nothing."

"You sound tired, Keep."

"It's been a long day on the road."

"Where is your father?"

"In the toilet."

"Where are you staying?"

"The Royal something or other. What did you have for dinner?"

"Meatloaf and snap beans, but your grandfather choked on something and upchucked."

Any reply was interrupted by a soft knock at the door. "Hold on, Mom," he said. "There's somebody at the door." He put down the phone and opened the door to admit the bellhop, who held a fifth of Four Roses. "Sorry, suh," he apologized, "but we is out of Old Crows."

Chance had heard the exchange, and came out of the bathroom to claim his bottle. "Has Old Crow gone off to war too?" he asked.

"Yas suh, I believe he done gone too."

Chance took the bottle back to the bathroom and closed the curtain behind him. With shaking hands he unscrewed the cap, poured several inches of whisky into the tumbler and drank it straight.

Keeper turned back to the telephone, prepared to ask his mother about Early, but the line was dead.

"Did your call get timed out?" Chance asked when he reentered the room.

"Yep, but I got to tell Mom we're fine."

"Good boy. Now let's eat."

The dining room was crowded, but they found a table for two close to the kitchen. After waiting twenty minutes without being waited on, Chance stood to intercept a tuxedoed waiter coming out of the kitchen. Chance held a five dollar bill folded lengthwise between two fingers. "If you ever come back, please bring us a menu," he said. "We'd like to order before water gets rationed too."

The waiter took the bill, and with a nod, he said he'd be back after delivering the colonel and his lady-friend their dinner order.

Chance followed the nod to where an obviously drunk Army officer in uniform sat with an equally drunk but attractive blond woman at a table set for four. Chance lit a fresh cigarette from a match torn from a book of Royal Cincinnatian matches. "War is hell," he muttered to no one in particular.

When the waiter returned, he dropped two menus on the table. "I'll be back for your orders in a minute," he promised.

Keeper picked up his menu and studied it.

"What sounds good, Keep?" Chance asked.

He was quick to answer. "A salad and a T-bone with a baked potato."

"Sounds good to me too," Chance agreed.

When the waiter returned Chance gave him their order, and added, "Bring me a double whisky straight up, and a Coke for the boy."

The waiter said, "We're out of steaks."

"How about pork chops?"

"I believe I can find two. "Do you still want the salads?"

Chance nodded. "Okay by you, Keep?"

"I'd rather have the sweetbreads instead."

Chance smiled. "Do you know what that is?"

"Oh, sure. We have them all the time when you're away."

The waiter tapped his watch." Will that be all, 'cause the kitchen closes at eight."

"What's happening on the home front, Keep?" Chance asked after the waiter left.

"Mom said Grandpa choked on his meatloaf and puked. She sounded worried."

"Mother's worrying days may soon be over. I told you mother that I'm going to ask Mr. Pettigrew to hire a road salesman, and to have me manage from the home office."

"But what if he won't?"

"I told her I'd resign."

Keeper frowned. "But, what would you do for a job?"

"I wouldn't quit unless I had something else lined up."

"But, you said you told Mother…"

Chance interrupted. "Sometimes you have to do the expedient thing."

"Does that mean you lied?"

"It only means I deferred the truth," he replied, and sat back when the waiter reappeared with their drinks.

Keeper wasn't sure what his father meant, and he'd added nothing to clarify what he intended to do in case he couldn't line up another job. Instead, he shared the silence with his father while sipping at his Coke until the waiter returned with their order.

"What's *that*?" Keeper exclaimed when he saw what was on his plate. He thought he'd ordered something along the lines of French toast, with powdered sugar and maple syrup on it.

"Sweetbreads," the waiter answered. "It's what you ordered…sir."

Chance laughed. "It's calf's thymus, Keep. Try it."

"I won't eat it," Keeper exclaimed flatly.

"Do you want to send it back for something else?" Chance asked.

"The kitchen is closed, sir," the waiter said.

Their conversation was interrupted by a commotion at the colonel's table. "Artie honey," the woman cried. "I don't *care* if there is a war on! This steak is as tough as a storm troopers boot, and they can shove it up their ass!"

Keeper turned to look. "*I'll* eat it," he said.

"What did you say?" Chance asked.

"I said I'll eat her steak."

Chance laughed and playfully poked Keeper on the shoulder. "Waiter," he said. "Bring it over before somebody changes their mind."

CHAPTER TWENTY-FIVE

It was 9:00 p.m. when Chance and Keeper returned to their room. With their hunger satisfied, both were intent upon getting a good night's sleep. But Keeper had questions. He lay stretched out on the fold-away bed wearing the pajamas his mother had bought him special for the trip and waiting for his father to finish using the bathroom.

Chance had stripped down to his boxer shorts and a pair of black ankle socks, causing Keeper to wonder if his father was going to sleep naked like he did at home. It was an uncomfortable thought, and he was relieved to see him crawl into bed without undressing any further.

The socks puzzled Keeper. "Why are you wearing socks to bed?"

"Because I've got lousy circulation."

"That's because smoking can cause athero...arterio... uh, hardening of the arteries."

"You don't say, Dr. Wick."

"Grandpa says it can cause a stroke," Keeper added.

"So I've heard. Now go to sleep."

"Can I get a glass of water?"

"If you must."

Keeper rolled off the fold-away and groped his way to the bathroom for the drinking glass that still smelled of Four Roses. He rinsed the glass before filling it from the tap and returned to place it on the floor next to his bed. With a final glance at the coiled rope bathed in the red neon light of the Royal Cincinnatian under the window, he crawled into bed and folded his hands behind his head. "When are we going to demonstrate the compactor tomorrow?"

"Mid-morning, in Covington, Kentucky," Chance replied. "Tomorrow night we'll be laying over in Knoxville before pushing on to Atlanta."

Keeper yawned. Sounds of traffic coming from the street below were muted and soothing, which made him feel sleepy, but something else continued to bother him. "I'm worried about what mother will do, if you have to lie to her," he said after carefully choosing his words.

Chance didn't immediately respond. He reached for the cigarettes and the engraved Zippo he had left on the floor next to his bed, propped himself up on an elbow and placed a cigarette between his lips. When he lit the cigarette, the Zippo's yellow flame bathed his handsome profile in its flickering light. "It's like this, Keep," he began. "Being on the road sometimes means a fellow has to keep two sets of books."

Keeper studied his father's face, as if seeking an answer. "I don't understand."

"It's like an accountant who keeps one true ledger for himself, and another very different one for tax purposes."

Keeper shivered with the delicious sensation of being allowed to share in his father's secrets, and of feeling closer to him than ever before. He dreamily watched as the glowing cigarette his father held moved in a tight half-circle to the ashtray, where it remained. "What kind of taxes?" Keeper asked.

"The kind the wives of road men collect. Now go to sleep."

"I'm not tired yet."

"I am."

"Will you tell me about Grandpa and the Indians again, Dad?"

Chance turned to face his son. "Then can we call it a day?"

"Yes."

"Your grandparents were in their early twenties when they married in Woodstock, Ontario, Canada in 1882. Their parents came to North America during the 1850s and settled in Toronto."

"I remember that part from before," Keeper said impatiently. "Tell me about later."

"I'm getting to that," Chance replied. "When he was still a young man, your grandfather worked as a telegraph operator for the Canadian National Railroad."

"Get to the uprising, Dad."

"That was called the Great Cree Indian uprising, when your grandfather sent urgent messages from his lonely outpost, tap-tapping in Morse code to headquarters."

Keeper stifled a yawn. "*That's* the part."

Chance took a pull off his cigarette before continuing. "One evening as your grandfather sent his messages, torch-carrying Cree Indians wearing war paint peered through the windows of his shack."

"Wow," Keeper said. "They must have scared the holy crap out of grandpa."

"He kept a cool head, Keep. For reasons he never understood, the Indians never harmed him, and only vanished into the night."

"Lucky," Keeper replied, "or else we wouldn't be here."

Chance chuckled. "Years later my parents would finger-tap secret messages across the dinner table to each other in Morse so my brothers and I couldn't understand them."

Keeper laughed. "Were you my age back then?"

"C'mon Keep," Chance yawned. "Let's save it for tomorrow."

"Okay," Keeper said, and closed his eyes. He could still see the ghostly image of the burning cigarette, and wondered if his mother was playing solitaire in her lonesome bed that very moment. He thought about Jonnie Prettyboy too, and wondered where she was, and if she was okay, or if the police ever found her. When Chance began to snore, Keeper yawned again and reached for his glass of water. Instead of finding the drinking glass, he felt something he couldn't immediately identify, until realizing with a shock that it had *teeth*! For the first time in his life, he understood his father wore false teeth, and had probably taken them out so he wouldn't choke on them in his sleep.

He closed his eyes and tried to imagine his father without teeth. He wondered what other secrets lay in store while listening to the sound of loud swing music coming from the room across the hall. After another minute, he heard the station being changed, a scramble of music, until stopping at Judy Garland singing "*Over the Rainbow*," and then another voice, a woman's, joined in, plaintive and just as sweet as Miss Garland's. At that instant, and for some inexplicable reason, Keeper felt an overwhelming sense of dread. It was as if every bad dream he'd ever had about being lost and alone was real. And for the first time since his best friend, Jonnie Prettyboy, had left him for the road, he cried himself to sleep.

CHAPTER TWENTY-SIX

Chance stood on Velma's front stoop, smoking a cigarette and waiting impatiently for her to answer the doorbell. The warm pre-dawn air was heavy with moisture that wouldn't burn off until the sun was well up. By then, Chance expected he and Keeper would be in Covington, Kentucky demonstrating the compactor. He was about to ring again, when the door swung open on squalling hinges.

"You've got a goddamned fucking nerve," Velma said when she saw Chance. "Come to stand on my doorstep at five in the morning like some randy rooster." She stood directly behind the screen door, her hazelnut colored skin contrasting with a white terrycloth bathrobe.

Chance smiled and flicked his half-smoked cigarette into Velma's geraniums. "The early bird catches the worm."

Velma snorted. "I'd call that bad news for the worm."

"Aren't you going to invite me in?"

"Give me one good reason why I shouldn't run you off."

Chance shrugged. "I figure the hundred clams I wire you every month is reason enough."

"I'm thinking it's time for a raise, Doc. Black market liquor is expensive."

"I don't have time to argue, Vel. I brought my youngest son this time."

Velma's eyebrows rose in disbelief. She looked past Chance to the white New Yorker parked at the curb. "Your kid is out there?"

"Good God, no," Chance replied. "He's back at the hotel, sleeping."

"You're a cold-blooded bastard, you know that?"

"I've been called worse. Now let me in."

Velma unlatched the screen door and waved Chance inside with an elaborate gesture. "Okay, Doc, what's your pleasure?" she asked, brightly, "Bed before breakfast, or vice versa?"

"Bed, and then I've got to be going."

"This is bullshit," Velma said. She let the screen door slam shut with a bang.

"What isn't anymore?" Chance asked.

"I don't know...nothing, everything." Velma approached Chance and pressed herself against him. Then, wordlessly, she took him by the hand and led him into her bedroom, and just as wordlessly shucked off the housecoat before climbing naked into bed. There, with heavy-lidded and languid brown eyes, she watched Chance undress.

"What the hell is *that?*" she asked when Chance opened his hand.

"A prophylactic."

"Black?"

Chance grinned. "It's ribbed too, for enhanced stimulation. I bought several in Kokomo."

Velma began to chuckle, a low, throaty sound. "Roll it on, Doc, and start stimulatin'."

Chance quickly took the familiar missionary position and began to methodically fuck Velma. He was proud of his staying power, if not for his inventiveness, and after climaxing, he rolled off and got up for a cigarette.

"Breakfast before you go?" Velma asked, sounding hopeful.

"No time," Chance replied after lighting his cigarette. "I need to get back before Keeper misses me."

"You never told me his name before."

"It wasn't deliberate, that I didn't."

Velma snorted. "I don't even know your wife's name, for Christ's sake."

"It's not important that you do."

"What *is* important, Doc?"

Chance took a lung-filling drag off his cigarette and exhaled through his nose before answering. "The road, Velma."

"It's always the fucking road!" she cried. "I don't know why your wife whatever-her-name is doesn't throw your cracker ass out!"

"Lots of reasons. And for Christ's sake, calm down."

"You know something, Doc?" she asked, and without waiting for a reply, went on; "Never, have I heard you use the word 'love,' as in, 'I love what's-her-name.' I take from that, that you don't."

"Don't presume any such thing."

Velma began to cry, a gentle wet sound like that of a small dog snuffling at the gap between a closed door and the floor. "You love *me*, don't you Doc?"

Chance stole quick glance at his watch and said, "I've got to be going."

Velma sobbed, "Why does it always have to end like this?"

"I'm sorry, Vel," Chance replied, and began dressing.

"You're always being sorry. Well, I'm sorry too!"

"Don't upset yourself like this."

"Goddamn you, Doc, I'm *already* upset!" she cried, and buried her face in her pillow.

Chance approached the bed and gently touched her on the shoulder. "I care very deeply about you, Vel," he said. "Maybe after the war…"

"Fuck you, Doc. Go. Leave. Close the door behind you and forget you ever knew me. If you come back, I'll call the police and have you arrested for illegal trespass and impersonating a human being."

CHAPTER TWENTY-SEVEN

When Keeper awoke to discover he was alone his first thought was that his father had simply forgotten and left without him. Nearing panic and heart racing, he stumbled for the telephone. Maybe the desk clerk had seen him. If not, maybe a call to the police would help. Maybe his father had been killed by the bellhop for his traveling money. Who knew? When he reached for the telephone he discovered a note written on hotel stationary. He picked it up to read:

Keep. I wanted to have the car gassed and ready to hit the trail as soon as we've eaten breakfast. If I'm not back when you get up, go down to the dining room and I'll meet you there. Dad.

Relieved to the point of tears, Keeper hurriedly brushed his teeth and washed his face before dressing for breakfast. Only after he stepped into the hallway and closed the door behind him, did he realize he didn't have a key to get back in. The room where he'd heard the woman singing "*Over the Rainbow*" was quiet. He turned the wrong way at first and walked to the end of the gloomy corridor before turning and retracing his steps to the elevators. He pressed a button to summon the elevator and waited several anxious minutes until he finally heard the car ascending to his floor. When the door opened he saw it was the same elderly bellhop at the controls that had carried their suitcases to the room last night. Keeper kept his distance, just in case the bellhop was a killer.

"Will we be waiting for the other gennelmens?" the bellhop asked.

"I'm meeting my dad in the dining room," Keeper explained.

"Dining room is full of hungry peoples jest now."

"Then I'll wait in the lobby."

The bellhop nodded and closed the door, followed by the safety gate before pushing the lever that sent the elevator on its slow, creaking descent to the lobby. After stopping with a stomach-turning lurch, Keeper tripped over the three-inch threshold and headed for the lobby where he hoped to find his father. When he didn't immediately see him, he wandered into the dining room to wait. As the bellhop had warned, the dining room was fully occupied. He looked expectantly toward the table he and his father had shared the night before, but it was occupied by a man who Keeper thought looked like Lou Costello from the Abbott and Costello movies. The man was smoking a cigar and reading a newspaper. Then he heard a familiar voice calling.

"Yoo hoo! Young man!"

Keeper turned to see the blond woman from the night before waving at him. She and the Army colonel were seated at the same four-place table where she had given up her tough steak. Keeper pointed at his chest and silently mouthed "Me?"

"Yes, you!" the blond woman trilled. "Come join us!"

Embarrassed at being singled out, Keeper hurried to their table and took the seat next to the woman. She and the colonel were eating egg and cheese omelets, and the colonel was preoccupied with making a sandwich out of three links of pork sausage and two burnt slices of toast. Keeper's mouth watered.

"Where's your daddy, handsome?" the woman giggled.

"He's gassing the car for the road," he replied, and blushed again when he inadvertently made eye contact. His mother never wore perfume, and this woman seemed to have bathed in it. As far as he was concerned, it smelled wonderful. When he felt the woman's soft warm thigh pressing against his, it was a very pleasant sensation that caused an equally pleasant stirring in Keeper's groin, and he hoped he wouldn't have to stand up.

"And where is the road taking you and your daddy?" the woman asked.

"We're going to Atlanta."

"I love Atlanta," the woman crooned, "don't I, Artie?"

"Bonnie, dear, you love anyplace where there's a man in uniform."

"Don't be mean, Artie," Bonnie replied with a look that suggested it wasn't the first time he'd been critical of her.

Keeper studied the shiny brass devices on the colonel's uniform. "Sir, are you in the infantry?" he asked.

The colonel looked at Keeper as if he'd just noticed him. "No, son, I'm in procurement."

Bonnie looked disappointed. "But Artie, honey," she said, "I thought you were an '*aveeater.*'"

"Jesus Christ, Bonnie. I said I was doing contract compliance for the Air Force."

Bonnie stuck out her lower lip and pouted. "It sounded way different last night."

The colonel looked up. "I believe that's your father heading our way."

Keeper turned to see his father striding toward them. He couldn't help but notice that the few women seated in the dining room had also turned to look at Chance, who smiled and winked as he approached. Keeper wondered if they'd still be attracted if they knew his father had fake teeth in his mouth.

"Sorry to be late," Chance said, and with an engaging smile toward Bonnie and the colonel, he introduced himself. "I'm Chance Wick, from Dakota Straits, Michigan." He shook hands all around and said, "Thanks for looking after Keep."

Bonnie looked puzzled. "Did you say Keep?"

"My name's Keeper," Keeper mumbled.

Bonnie giggled. "Why, how sweet!"

"Take a chair, Mr. Wick," the colonel offered. "We're about finished here. If you can find a waiter, there might still be an egg or two left in the kitchen."

Chance caught the eye of a passing waiter and waved him over. "The boy and I'll have grapefruit, orange juice, bacon omelets, and one coffee, black." He slipped the waiter a five dollar bill and said, "We're in a bit of a hurry."

"What line of business are you in, Mr. Wick?" the colonel asked after the waiter had left.

Letters From The Road

Chance gave the colonel his stock answer, but he was looking at Bonnie. "High-frequency low-amplitude vibrators."

"Lord have mercy," Bonnie said. "Pinch me if I'm dreaming."

Chance returned Bonnie's smile. "Sorry to disappoint you, Bonnie. My business is soil compactors, ballast tampers and concrete vibrators."

"And all vital to the war effort, correct?" the colonel asked.

"Very," Chance replied.

"My dad gets all the gas he wants," Keeper explained. "This is my first trip with him."

"Why, how sweet," Bonnie repeated. "And how old are you anyway?"

"I'm almost thirteen and a half."

She patted his thigh. "I'll bet you have lots of girlfriends, huh?"

Keeper squirmed uncomfortably at the closeness of her touch. "Not really."

The colonel stood to end the conversation. "Nice to have met you, Mr. Wick," he said, "but the war waits for no man. Good luck on the road."

Bonnie reached across the table for Chance's hand and took it. "Good luck in Atlanta, Mr. Wick. Maybe our paths will cross again someday."

"That would be my distinct pleasure," Chance replied. He reached into his shirt pocket for a business card and slipped it to her.

While Chance was making a show of helping Bonnie to her feet, the colonel turned toward Keeper. "You're a lucky fellow to have a father who cares enough to take you on the road with him."

Keeper offered an embarrassed grin and said, "Yes sir...real lucky." He would have stood too, a courtesy because of the glamorous Bonnie, but standing was out of the question with a boner that refused to go down.

CHAPTER TWENTY-EIGHT

Chance and Keeper had been on the road for six long hours, stopping only long enough for gas and to use the toilet. The demonstration in Covington that morning went well and resulted in a twelve-hundred dollar order for six tampers FOB Dakota Straits. By the time Chance ended the demonstration he was drenched in sweat while a dozen colored laborers looking on bantered amongst themselves on how amusing it was to watch a white man doing physical labor. "*Nigger, that ain't sweat,*" one said to another. "*That's bullshit!*"

Now Keeper was not only hungry, he was also bored and restless. "How long do we have to keep the demo compactor?"

"Until we're home," Chance answered

"Can't you just sell it and the trailer too?"

"No. I need them to sell *from.*"

"It feels like we're pulling a house." Keeper sat back in his seat wishing somebody would steal the trailer while watching grasshoppers big as hummingbirds smashing against the windshield and leaving gobs of yellow-green paste.

"We should be in Knoxville by four-thirty," Chance said after checking his watch. "If we drove all night, we could be in Atlanta early tomorrow."

"Would you if I wasn't along?"

"Probably," Chance replied.

Keeper felt a shiver of excitement. He could visualize the two of them as they sped alone through the night and having only to share the road with long-distance truckers. "Then let's do it."

"No. We'll stop for the night. I've had a crushing headache since morning, and I never get headaches."

"You said I could drive sometime," Keeper said. "How about now?"

Chance rubbed his eyes with the heel of his hand. "Maybe tomorrow."

"There's a place ahead," Keeper said. He pointed to a billboard and read from it aloud. "Plantation Motor Court. Twenty miles ahead. Cozy cabins. Hot Water. Bathtubs. Steam Heat. Flush Toilets. Radio. Telephone."

Chance grunted. "All the comforts of home, huh Keep?"

"Let's stay there. It's in Kentucky too, home of Daniel Boone."

Chance consulted his watch again before agreeing, "Okay. We'll call home after we eat. He fumbled in his shirt pocket for a cigarette until discovering the crumpled pack was empty, and pointed to the glove box "See if there's a pack of butts in there, will you, Keep?"

Keeper opened the glove box and dug through dog-eared road-maps without finding a fresh pack. "Sorry Dad, you're out. Besides, Grandpa says smoking is bad for you."

"Maybe you and your grandfather should mind your own business."

Keeper laughed. "How old were you when you started smoking?"

"How old are you?"

"I'm thirteen, Dad. I've been thirteen for five months!"

"Thirteen is when I started smoking Sweet Caporals."

Keeper quickly did the math in his head. "You've been smoking for forty years?"

"Yes, and drinking for thirty-three."

"Grandpa told me once that your lungs and liver were probably shot."

"Your grandfather was out of line. I've never been sick a day in my life."

"But you said you had a crushing headache."

"Maybe that's because of your constantly pestering me to drive."

"One more pester then I'll stop," Keeper said. "How come grandpa and grandma moved from Chicago to some crummy little town in Michigan?"

"Because I had a knack for finding trouble," Chance replied. "Or maybe it was the other way around. Either way, they thought rural living would keep me from a life of crime. It also might have been because your grandfather wanted to practice medicine as a country doctor."

"He said you made house calls with him. Tell me about that."

Chance smiled. "I was even younger than you, Keep. We had a horse and buggy, and a sleigh for when it snowed."

"Sounds like fun."

"Not in a blizzard it wasn't. In the winter we kept bricks next to a potbellied stove. When we had to make a house call I wrapped the warm bricks in blankets so we could put them under our feet. Of course, we were bundled up in heavy coats and lap robes too."

"What's the worst thing you ever saw, Dad?"

"I guess it had to be the farmer who got an arm tangled up in a shit...sorry...manure spreader. It was obvious he was going to lose the arm. Your granddad and I spread newspapers over the kitchen table, which was also used as an operating table. I might add that we only had kerosene lanterns for light."

"But how come newspapers?"

"Because newspapers were often the most sanitary thing available. While your granddad prepared for surgery, I gave ether."

Keeper exclaimed, "*You?*"

"It wasn't the first time either."

"How did it turn out? The operation, I mean?"

"The farmer learned to write left handed, and my schoolmates nicknamed me 'Doc.'"

At the mention of the name Doc, Keeper's stomach knotted. He wondered; could the name on the Zippo be the same Doc as his father? And if so, why was he a bastard? And who was Velma? How many times had Early suggested that the father they shared might be cheating on Alva while he was on the road? When he came to realize that his father and the Doc on the lighter were one and the same, he fell silent with his thoughts and less mindful of the lush scenery rushing past his window. The only sounds to break the silence between them was the crack of hard-shelled bugs hitting the windshield; the rush of air over the speeding New Yorker, and tires thumping over expansion joints on the two-lane concrete highway that lead Keeper and his father ever closer to Atlanta.

CHAPTER TWENTY-NINE

The Plantation Motor Court consisted of a whitewashed cement block office building and eight tin-roofed cabins hidden among the sycamore and black gum trees a hundred yards off US Highway 441. Were it not for the green neon vacancy sign above the office door, the Plantation Motor Court would have been virtually invisible to passing motorists. This included Chance and Keeper, who were actually looking for it in the dusky half-light of a late afternoon. For the past thirty minutes, the ominous sound of thunder growling in the distance and heat lightning strobing across a threatening Tennessee sky meant rain on the way.

Chance paid in advance for a night's stay. Now they silently unloaded their suitcases and carried them into the musty cypress paneled cabin that still held the heat of the day. Only after using the toilet and opening the single jalousie window in hopes of catching a cooling breeze, did Chance dig through his suitcase for the carton of Old Golds and the half-gone bottle of Four Roses he'd bought at the Royal Cincinnatian. His hands shook as he unscrewed the cap and quickly poured three fingers of whiskey into the cabins only drinking glass and knocked it back in a single, grimacing swallow.

"Don't you ever mix your booze?" Keeper asked disapprovingly. Seeing his father drinking until passing out at home was one thing. Having it happen on the road was quite another.

"Don't you ever mind your own business?" Chance replied as he tapped a cigarette from the fresh pack and lit it off his Zippo.

"When are we going to call Mom?"

"Later. After we've eaten."

"Why not now?"

"Because I need to take the edge off first is why."

Scowling, Keeper slapped at a blood-engorged mosquito feeding on his arm. "The longer we wait, the more worried she'll get."

"No lectures on the road, Junior," Chance grumbled. He turned for the bed closest to the window and sat down on its thin mattress with the bottle still in his hand. He kicked off the black wingtips still dusty from the Covington demonstration, propped his pillow against the headboard, and leaned back with groan.

"Do you still have a headache?"

"I do, but it should pass after a good night's sleep."

"Do you think we'll see that woman who gave me her steak? She lives in Atlanta."

"Remember what I told you about keeping two sets of books?"

"What about it?"

Chance poured another splash of whiskey into his drinking glass and rested it on his stomach. "Just don't forget, is all."

Keeper jumped at the sudden crash of lightning close by, followed by the explosive crump of thunder and rain drumming on the cabin's tin roof. "Which book are we keeping tonight?" he asked.

"The one that says smooth sailing and clear skies ahead."

Keeper scratched at his mosquito bite. "I think we should call mother now."

Chance gestured drink in hand toward the telephone. "Be my guest."

Keeper sat on the edge of his bed, picked up the phone and dialed for an operator. When he had long distance, he gave her the number in Dakota Straits and listened to the telephone ringing six times.

"Hello?"

"Hi Mom," Keeper said, cheerfully.

"I was upstairs."

"I almost hung up."

"Is something wrong?" Alva asked.

Keeper looked over at his father stretched out on top of the bed-covers with one stockinged foot crossed over the other and wiggling his toes. "Nope," Keeper replied.

"I've been so worried about accidents."

"It's been smooth sailing and clear skies all the way."

"Is your father close by?"

"He's right here."

"Put him on, Keeper, please."

Keeper handed the phone to his father. "Mom wants to talk to you."

Chance took it and cradled it under his chin. "Hi, dear," he said, sounding smooth and unruffled.

"Dad took a spill, Chance."

"How, where?"

"He fell off the toilet."

"That's almost a relief. I was afraid you'd say it was the stairs."

"I almost wish it had been. Dr. Wilberforce came right away. He said there were no broken bones, only bruises."

"How is dad otherwise?"

"He's very confused and talks gibberish."

"And Early?"

"Early scalded himself while pouring a cup of coffee this morning."

"And you, Alva dear?"

"I'm ready to kill."

"I'm sorry, Alva. When we get back, I'll…" Chance was interrupted by the crackle of lightning and rolling thunder overhead and quickly clamped his hand over the mouthpiece, as if to quiet the storm.

"What is that awful racket?" Alva asked.

"Just a little weather," Chance replied. "It's nothing to worry about."

"If anything happens to Keeper…"

"Keeper's fine, dear, and in case you're wondering, so am I."

"Where are you?"

"Tennessee. Knoxville."

Alva sighed. "All right, Chance. Unless there's something else, let me talk to Keeper again."

Chance handed the receiver back to Keeper and whispered, "Remember the books."

Keeper nodded and said, "Hi, Mom, it's me again."

"How much has your father had to drink?"

Keeper glanced toward his father, who was lighting another cigarette off the stub of the one he was smoking. "Today? One, mixed."

Chance smiled serenely behind the hazy-blue cloud of cigarette smoke hanging in the airless cabin. "Atta boy," he said, and took a sip of whiskey.

"Are you getting your sleep and enough to eat?" Alva asked.

"We're staying at fine hotels, sleeping on featherbeds, and eating steak dinners."

"You're getting to be as bad a liar as your father."

"Don't worry, Mom, everything's fine."

"Call again tomorrow night, Keep," Alva said. "You know how I worry."

"I will. Good night, Mom."

"Good work," Chance said after Keeper had hung up.

———

It was half past nine and still raining when Chance and Keeper returned to their cabin. They had gone into Knoxville for a dinner of pan-fried ham slices, grits with red-eye gravy and cornpone on the side. It was Keeper's choice. Chance, by then drunk, had allowed Keeper to drive the New Yorker back from the restaurant. Now bleary-eyed and flush-faced from the drinks he'd taken, Chance began undressing for bed.

"Aren't you going to take a bath?" Keeper asked.

Chance scratched himself through his underwear. "I bathe every Saturday night, whether I need it or not," he replied, and rolled into bed.

"When you were talking to Mom, it sounded like something happened at home."

Chance reached for his cigarettes and shook one out of the pack. "She said everything is just ducky," he replied, and lit the cigarette off his Zippo.

"We should bring her a present from the road."

"We will, and we've also got a lot of road ahead of us, so get ready for bed."

Keeper changed into his pajama bottoms in the bathroom before climbing into bed. "Can we listen to the radio for awhile?" he asked.

"See if you can find a weather report."

Keeper turned on the radio and drummed his fingers until hearing the distant-sounding voice of an announcer saying; "*This is your Grand Ole Opry. Stay tuned for Uncle Dave Macon and The Fruit Jar Drinkers. But first, a message from our family of fine sponsors, Oxydol.*"

With a satisfied smile he folded his arms behind his head and lay back to the sound of rain clattering on the tin roof. Lightning flickered through the canopy of sycamore and black gum trees outside the window and gave him enough light to see his father's profile and smoking the last cigarette of the day. "You've been everywhere, haven't you?" Keeper asked.

Chance's cigarette glowed brightly in the near-darkness. "Not everywhere."

"I mean in America."

"I've been to every state, if that's what you mean."

"Canada too?"

"Every province. I loved Banff. Someday I'll take you and Alva there."

"How about Mexico?"

Chance chuckled. "Baja California, Sonora, Chihuahua, and Nuevo Leon. Someday I'd like to see Australia."

Keeper shivered at the sound of his father's deep and disembodied voice. Their beds were only an arm's length apart. Close enough to touch. "Why Australia?"

The cigarette glowed again. "It's a beautiful country, Keep. I'm interested in their aboriginal mythology. I'd like to learn more first hand."

The Grand Ole Opry fiddled softly in the background as Keeper considered his father's comments. In spite of their physical closeness, it was almost like sharing the cabin with a complete stranger; someone who wore fake teeth and wanted to study aboriginal people, whoever they were. What more, he wondered, would he learn about his father over the days to come?

"If you could be anything you wanted," Keeper asked, "what would it be?"

"Maybe a writer."

"Do they make lots of money?"

"Some probably do. I keep a Remington Porto-Rite in the Chrysler's trunk in case inspiration strikes."

"Have you ever written anything?"

"No."

Keeper yawned deeply. The rain had lessened, and the mutter of thunder moving off in the distance was soothing. "Do you know any stories about aboriginal mythology?"

"One goes that the ancient Anangu people believed that when there was an eclipse of the sun, it was being eaten by the angry Karrkila, a giant war hawk with feathers of flint knives that could be shot out like arrows."

"That's hard to believe."

"If you think about it," Chance replied, "so is life hard to believe."

With only the glowing radio dial for light, Keeper watched his father take out his fake teeth and carefully placed them on the bedside table between them. "Can I ask you one last thing?" he asked.

"What is it now?"

"Do you and Mom love each other?"

"What makes you think we don't?"

"Because I've never heard you say it to each other, is all."

Chance sighed and tamped out his cigarette. "Some things just go without saying. Now turn off the radio and go to sleep."

Keeper obediently reached for the radio and switched it off, leaving the cabin in total darkness. He lay back with his arms folded behind his head, listening to the uneven patter of rainwater falling from the surrounding trees onto the tin roof above his head. It sounded like hundreds of clocks keeping time, counting the hours, minutes and seconds before heading back on the road. Tomorrow and they would finally be in Atlanta.

CHAPTER THIRTY

More than ever, Keeper felt as if the road was drawing him and his father deeper and deeper toward an unknown place, and he took great delight in the giddy sensation of being at once safe – yet not safe. The New Yorker's gleaming hood ornament seemed to lead the way down an endless ribbon of oil-stained concrete that was interconnected with every other highway, pathway and back alley in a continuous loop that had no beginning or end.

Every turn taken and every hill crested brought change. There were different names, different tastes, different songs on the radio, and different people talking differently. Even the land was very different; a foreign place that smelled both sweet and foul, as if something alien and corrupt had been buried nearby. Civil War battlefields guarded by concrete Confederate generals mounted on rearing concrete horses and waving bronze swords swept past the window. Abandoned graveyards studded with weather-corroded slabs of white marble stretched into the distance like tiles to an outsized game long-abandoned by its players.

Beyond the cemeteries, undulating fields of cotton rolled to the horizon under a sky so blue as to appear artificial. Scattered cumulus clouds offered scant relief from the sun for sweating colored people dragging burlap bags overflowing with picked cotton.

Keeper rolled down his window and stuck his hand into the wind stream like a make-believe airplane, diving and then climbing for altitude by bending his fingers. "How far to Atlanta?" he asked.

"Not far, only a few more miles."

"What if something happened and you couldn't drive?" Keeper asked.

"What would that be?"

"Because of your headaches."

"I always make it home."

"I'm thinking about home right now."

"Homesick already?"

Keeper nodded. "Grandpa could die before we get back."

Chance fumbled another cigarette out of the pack in his pocket and lit off the dashboard lighter. "There's always that possibility."

"Do we have to stay with your friend who's dying of cancer?"

"If he asks us to stay, we will."

"How old is he?"

"Forty-eight."

"How do you know him?"

"He's the cousin of my first wife."

"How come you never talk about her?"

"Because I don't."

"Neither will Early."

"Early doesn't remember her."

"He doesn't remember seeing anything, either."

"Let's drop it, Keep, okay?"

"What's his name, your first wife's cousin?"

"Jefferson."

"What's his first name?"

"That is his first name. His last name, believe it or not, is Burnside."

"What's his wife's name?"

"She goes by Honey."

"That's not her real name?"

"She was a 'honey' when she was younger, so everybody always called her that."

Satisfied with his father's answer, Keeper sat back in his seat and watched the late afternoon panorama of downtown Atlanta unfold beyond the New Yorker's windows. Tall buildings cast long shadows that muted color and darkened the bustling streets. On Peachtree and

Broad Street a sign advertising Coca-Cola loomed atop the Flatiron
Building. Streetcars passing on parallel tracks sounded their bells like
ships at sea as they merged into the busy confluence of Five Points.
Shiny, well-kept automobiles inched bumper-to-bumper through con-
gested streets. Except for the occasional uniformed serviceman on
leave, there was little to suggest a war was going on.

"Are we going to spend every night with Jefferson and Honey?"
Keeper asked.

"It's Mr. and Mrs. Burnside, and I'm sure they'll insist."

"It'll be almost like home."

Chance turned to look at Keeper questioningly. "How's that?"

"Ever since I was born, there's been somebody dying around me,
and Mr. Burnside is dying."

"C'mon, Keep, knock it off"

"Your mom and mom's mom died in our house, and so did some
cancer-eaten sea captain, in the same bedroom you and mom have
now. Who knows how many more people died in our house? I almost
died there too, like you always say. Grandpa will probably be next."

"Don't be morbid."

"It's true." Keeper considered mentioning Mr. Prettyboy's sudden
death in the horse barn too, until deciding not to. Still, the memory of
that terrible night three years before stirred fresh thoughts of Jonnie
Prettyboy, and Keeper wondered if she had made a clean break to the
south. He wished he could be with her right now – up in the horse
barn, until thinking maybe she wouldn't want anything to do with him
because of the age difference. By now, Jonnie Prettyboy would be sixteen, and maybe even married.

"Be on your best behavior tonight," Chance said, breaking Keeper's
train of thought, "and tomorrow I'll get us a room at the Hilton for the
rest of our stay."

Keeper yawned. He was both tired and hungry. "How much further to their house?"

"Only a couple miles more, off Fair Drive near Lakewood Park."

In spite of it being oppressively warm and humid, Keeper felt an
involuntary chill when they pulled up in front of the Burnside place.
The house was small and showed signs of neglect, no doubt due, he

thought, to the poor condition of Jefferson Burnside. A lone fruit tree stood in front of the single-story house. Yellow jasmine and trumpet honeysuckle vines with blood-red blossoms grew in wild abandon around the house. Their fragrance on the heavy evening air was sickly-sweet and cloying. A yellow bug light cast its light on low wooden steps leading up to the open front door. A patched screen door held back the swarming mosquitoes.

Chance turned off the ignition, and after taking a last pull off his cigarette, flicked in into the street. "This is it," he said.

Keeper took a deep breath and let it out with a ragged sigh. "Do we have to?"

"Yes."

Reluctantly, Keeper stepped out of the New Yorker and followed his father up the walk toward the house. He knew he smelled shit. It wasn't an ordinary shit smell either, like the gas station restroom in Kokomo, but a sick-shit smell. Mosquitoes swarmed over a wooden rain barrel squatting like a headless Buddha next to the termite riddled steps.

Keeper coughed and covered his mouth and nose with his sun-burned arm. "Dad?"

he said, his adolescent voice quavering with dismay.

"I know," Chance replied. "Be a trooper."

A dog howled from somewhere behind the house, a deeply-reso-nant yowl Keeper realized could only come from a large animal, such as a bloodhound.

"Jeff always had a coon hound," Chance said, "even though he can't hunt anymore."

"Is it tied up?"

Chance slapped at a mosquito on his neck before knocking. "He keeps it in a pen out back."

Keeper was about to say that was a cruel thing for Mr. Burnside to do, to keep a dog penned up all the time, when he heard a woman's deeply-accented and husky voice calling from beyond the screen door.

"Ah'm comin,' jus' hold yoah horses."

Keeper looked past his father to see the woman he guessed was Honey Burnside hustling toward them from inside the house. She was barefoot, wore a gray chenille bathrobe, and carried a drinking glass half-full of what looked to be whiskey. A cigarette dangled precariously from the corner of her mouth and ice cubes rattled in the glass.

She kicked the screen door open with her foot. "Doc!" she shouted from the corner of her mouth. "You old son of a bitch!"

"Hello, Honey," Chance replied with a wide smile.

She took the cigarette from her mouth and advanced upon him with open arms. "Yoah a sight foah soah eyes!" she gushed, and kissed Chance on the mouth.

He disengaged himself from her tight grasp and turned to Keeper. "Honey, I'd like you to meet my son, Keeper."

"So yoah Keepuh!"

"Yes, ma'am," Keeper answered. And now he knew, beyond the shadow of a doubt, that the 'Doc' on the Zippo and his father had to be the same man. The question remaining was who was Velma? Because it sure wasn't Honey Burnside.

Honey waved an arm. "You boahs come inside befoah them damned skeeters carry us all off, an' let me have a look at you!"

Keeper followed his father into the house where the sick-shit smell was much stronger, and stood uneasily while allowing himself to be studied by Mrs. Burnside. Feeling not unlike a laboratory specimen, Keeper glanced around the living room. A couch covered in badly-stained brown corduroy was shoved up against the far wall opposite a floor-model Zenith that looked very much like the one they had at home. Nailed to the wall above it was a brightly painted Jesus on a cross. The radio was set on low volume, yet Keeper quickly recognized the familiar voice of President Roosevelt making another of his fireside chats. A coffee table in front of the couch was piled high with dated movie magazines, with Myrna Loy and Rita Hayworth on the covers of two, and a dog-eared copy of Life magazine.

Keeper turned his attention back to Honey Burnside. He could see how she might have been a beautiful woman, but now she was plain and hard-looking, with breasts that sagged like bags of birdseed inside her robe. Hair that looked bleached tumbled over her shoulders, and her red-painted fingernails were dirty and split.

"Yoah the spittin' image of yoah daddy, Keepuh!" Honey gushed.

Keeper blushed hotly. "Thank you."

"How's Jeff?" Chance asked.

Honey slowly shook her head. "Oh, he's gettin' on," she replied softly.

"I'd like to say hello now, if he's awake."

"Just go on in, Doc. It'll do him a world of good, seein' you again. Meanwhile, Keepuh an' ah'll get acquainted, won't we, honey?"

When Chance left for Jeff's bedroom, Honey moved to stand dance-close next to Keeper and took a long swallow of her drink, causing the ice cubes to clatter wetly against her upper lip.

"So it's Keepuh, is it?" she whispered in a low husky voice. "Yoah such a big boah, ah don't know whether to offah you a Coke, or somethin' stronguh."

"Uh…yes, ma'am," Keeper stammered. "A Coke, please?"

"And such a polite boah, too," Honey replied, and smiling, beckoned with a nicotine-stained finger for Keeper to follow her into the kitchen.

He paused in the doorway to watch as she opened the door to a monitor-top refrigerator that had obviously seen better days. A cork coaster under one of its legs kept it from wobbling on the warped linoleum floor when she opened the refrigerator for a bottle of Coke, which she held against her neck.

"It's so wahum, don't you think, Keepuh?"

Keeper blushed again. "Yes ma'am."

Honey laughed and popped off the cap using a bottle opener screwed to the wall behind the sink and handed the Coke to Keeper.

He took it – feeling the bottle's cold, slippery condensation in his hand. "This is fine, Mrs. Burnside."

"Now that we're acquainted, Keepuh, just call me Honey. Now, how about ah put in a teensy eyedroppah of bourbon in that Coke?"

"Uh, no thanks…Honey."

She sidled up next to Keeper until their bodies touched. "I know what yoah thinkin' Keepuh," she said. "It wasn't always like this, you know."

Feeling both aroused and embarrassed, Keeper backed away. "Like what?" he asked, although he guessed he knew what she meant.

Honey waved her arm in a sweeping half-circle, causing the ice cubes in her drink to rattle accusingly. "Like *this*, Keepuh," she sighed.

He was taken aback by Honey Burnside's sudden openness, and wondered what, if anything, he should do, until she decided for him. Shifting her highball to her left hand, she took Keeper's right hand and pressed it firmly against her left breast.

"Ah was Miss Georgia once, Keepuh."

Keeper felt himself growing hard. "Ma'am?"

"Ah had mah beauty," she sniffed.

Keeper hoped she wouldn't notice his jutting erection and reach for it. Anything was possible. "I think you're beautiful now," he mumbled. How easily the lie came, he thought, and when it came right down to it, he knew he was no better than his father. And since he had his hand on Honey Burnside's boob, maybe worse.

"Yoah too kind, Keepuh," Honey whimpered, "but ah know bettuh. Ah'm livin' in a dump with a dyin' man who's got cancer of the ass and shittin' in a rubbuh bag."

"I'm real sorry, Honey," Keeper replied, which made him think of Jonnie Prettyboy, which in turn made him feel a deep sense of loss and sadness, especially when Honey Burnside released his hand from her breast.

Honey pointed down the hallway. "Ah'm livin' a dead-end life now, wasted on that man in thayuh," she said. "Ah had it all, Keepuh. Fur coats and boyfriends with money and fast cahs like Duesenbergs and Stutz Bearcats."

Keeper wondered what kind of car they had now, and was about to ask.

"Ah drive a goddamned nineteen twenty-six Rickenbackuh now," Honey said, as if anticipating Keeper's question.

"I never heard of a Rickenbacker."

"Yoah too young, goddamnit. They were built by the World War One flying ace of the same name." Honey turned to pour herself bourbon over ice when Chance walked into the kitchen.

"God, but I need a drink," Chance said. Sweat beaded his forehead like glycerin on wax.

"Looks like hell, doesn't he, Doc?"

Chance nodded in affirmation. "Does Jeff's doctor say how much time he has left?"

She took a swallow of her iced bourbon and held the chilled glass to her cleavage before answering. "A month, no moah."

"I'm sorry, Honey."

"Ah reckon we all are, Doc."

"What will you do?"

Honey laughed. "Suppose ah can trade off mah good looks?"

Chance took a clean drinking glass from the drain board by the sink and poured himself three fingers of bourbon from the bottle Honey was working on. "You're a damned attractive woman," he replied. "Don't sell yourself short."

She snorted and hefted a sagging breast with her free hand. "Who's buyin' this, do you figure?"

Chance knocked back his bourbon in two quick swallows. "Look Honey," he said. "Why don't you join Keeper and me for dinner? My expense account can take the hit."

Fresh tears welled in Honey's eyes. "That's real kind of you, Doc, but ah have some modicum of pride left."

"Then let me buy something, and we'll eat in."

"Nonsense. Ah've got chicken legs in the refrigeratuh and grits in the pantry. Will that do?"

Chance gave Keeper a gentle nudge. "What do you think, Keep?"

"I think I'm going to be sick. Where's the toilet?"

CHAPTER THIRTY-ONE

Keeper woke after only two hours of restless sleep on Honey Burnside's foul-smelling couch. Because of the oppressive heat, he wore undershorts instead of pajamas. Yet he was slick with sweat. The house still reeked of Honey Burnside's deep-fried chicken legs that had come out greasy and so undercooked he only picked at them. The house also stank of the cancerous shit-smell coming from Jefferson Burnside's bedroom, and something else that reminded Keeper of overly-ripe fruit. He had agreed to sleep on the couch so his father could take the second bedroom, and Honey said she'd sleep on the easy chair in her husband's bedroom just in case he needed her.

The yellow bug-light by the front door illuminated the night-blooming jasmine and honeysuckle that grew outside the front window and they appeared as miniature luminaries trembling on a light breeze.

Keeper rubbed his eyes as he tried to recall what awakened him. Voices? He strained to hear. There they were again, coming through the thin plasterboard behind the couch. He got to his knees and pressed his ear flat against the wall.

"Is that a rubbuh, for Christ's sake?"

"Bought on impulse and ribbed for your sexual pleasure."

A low sultry chuckle followed. *"Turn on the light, Doc, and let's have a look."*

"We'll wake Keeper."

"Ah'll close the doah."

Keeper strained to hear while blood pounded in his flattened ear like a distant drummer beating a frantic warning. Then the sound of bedsprings creaking metallically under a shifting load, the snick of a latch, the muted click of a light switch, and then Honey again, whispering;

"*Oh mah Gawd!*"

"*What do you think?*"

"*Ah love it! Hold yoah horses while ah roll it on.*"

Keeper bit down hard on the fleshy crook of his index finger, hoping pain would be enough to stop the tears of rage and betrayal that spilled from his eyes and scoured his cheeks like acid.

"*Easy Honey, I don't want to pop off too soon.*"

"*How do you want it this time? Ovah, or unduh?*"

"*Over,*" and the springs, compressing, coiling and uncoiling – *squeak-squeak-squeak.* Then an impassioned growl; "*Fuck me Doc. Fuck me black and blue.*"

Keeper pushed himself off the couch and stumbled blindly down the dark hallway to where the voices were coming from, and where the fruity smell was strongest. He stopped, as if the closed bedroom door were an impregnable barrier. Finally overcoming fear of being terribly mistaken, he threw open the door and gasped in open-mouthed disbelief.

Honey Burnside's back was turned toward him and she was straddling his father atop a jumble of bed sheets. Except for the black ankle socks his father wore, both were naked. The soles of Honey Burnside's feet were dirty, and Keeper knew beyond a shadow of doubt that he would remember this moment for the rest of his life.

"Dad?" The word caught in his throat like a hot coal.

Honey swiveled wide-eyed at the intrusion. "Keepuh?"

Chance raised his head off the pillow to stare at his son with an uncomprehending look. "Oh God," he groaned.

Keeper blinked through a haze of tears that scattered light from a reading lamp on the nightstand next to the headboard. Its tasseled red-silk shade was skewed, as if bumped by an errant elbow. A half-gone bottle of Jack Daniels rested on the nightstand, and next to it sat an ashtray and two drinking glasses. Both were empty, and the ashtray overflowed with crushed cigarette butts.

As if in slow motion, for time itself seemed to have slowed, Honey Burnside rolled off Chance like she was dismounting a horse and turned to Keeper with a crooked grin that seemed to suggest he could be next. He felt remote and lightheaded, as if *he* were the guilty one, not *them*. He even wanted to say he was sorry for bursting in on them like he had.

And what the fuck, Keeper thought dizzily. What was that resting slack against his father's groin? A blackjack? Then he understood. His father wore a black rubber taken from the condom vending machine at the Texaco station where they'd stopped for gas in Kokomo.

Keeper couldn't move. His legs felt numb, unresponsive, and barely able to support his weight. He was dimly aware of Honey Burnside reaching across his father for the fifth of Jack Daniels on the bedside table, then upending the bottle and taking a deep slug from it while her sagging breasts grazed Chance's chest.

"Goddamn it, Keeper," Chance hissed. "*Get the hell out!*"

The harshness of his father's voice stunned Keeper, and he backed slowly away until bumping into the wall beyond the door. "*Why*, Dad?" he cried. "*Why?*"

"Someday you'll understand," Chance mumbled. "Now leave us, *please!*"

Unable to speak and not daring to try, Keeper turned for the living room. In his haste he nearly stumbled over his mother's suitcase where he'd left it open in a pool of yellow bug-light slanting through the living room window. With hot tears coursing down his cheeks he gathered up his traveling clothes and pulled them on. His shoes and socks were under the coffee table. He stuffed the socks in his pants pockets and jammed his feet into the shoes without bothering to tie them. Almost as an afterthought he closed and latched the suitcase, put it under his arm, and bolted for the front door.

Once outside, Keeper stumbled blindly past the sweet-smelling jasmine and honeysuckle until he reached the white New Yorker and the attached demo trailer parked at the curb. He paused for a moment, as if wondering which way to go, then turned in the opposite direction from which he and his father had come. Then he began to run, hesitantly at first, until he picked up the pace – fast, and then faster, away from the awful shit-stinking house, away from the former Miss Georgia, and away from his lying, cheating, son of a bitch father, a road man who kept two sets of books.

CHAPTER THIRTY-TWO

Keeper had no idea where he was, much less where he was going. The lights of downtown Atlanta glowed brightly in the night sky to his left, so he figured he was walking east. Not that it mattered. He was lost. The dark streets offered no solace, nor did the rundown homes that flanked the sidewalk seem welcoming. He set the suitcase down on the gritty sidewalk and sat on it to rest – to think. It occurred to him that the nightly call to his mother hadn't been made, and that she would probably be sick with worry over not hearing from them. He wondered if his father was at that very moment calling her from the Burnside's, and if so, what lies would he be telling her?

Keeper locked his arms around his knees, lowered his head, and cried until his until his throat hurt. He wept at the hopelessness of his situation until the mouth-watering aroma of grilled onions caused his empty stomach to grumble over the unmistakable sound of a Calliope in the near distance. Where there was a Calliope there was a carnival, and carnivals had hotdog stands. Keeper bent to tie his shoe laces, then got to his feet, picked up the suitcase, and shuffled off toward the source of the tootling Calliope. He would make his cheating, two-sets-of-books father pay for what he had done. Let him worry for a while – maybe forever, even.

Keeper was enjoying perverse sense of satisfaction in imagining his father trying to explain to Alva why he'd come home alone, and where their son might have gone, when he found himself standing at the carnival's entrance fifteen minutes later. A large multi-colored banner announced;

ALL-STAR AMUSEMENTS & TRAVELING CARNIVAL
TEN DAYS ONLY
ADMISSION FREE - ALL ELSE EXTRA

Keeper dropped the suitcase and dug into a back pocket for his hand-tooled Boy Scout billfold. The nearly forty dollars in traveling money he'd saved up from allowances and mowing the neighbor's lawns and shoveling snow was still there. So was the French tickler he'd bought at the Texaco station in Kokomo in the hope he'd some-day find Jonnie Prettyboy and use it on her. In fact, the only money he'd spent so far was for a Royal Crown Cola and a Milky Way. Keeper transferred a ten dollar bill to his shirt pocket, picked up the suitcase, and entered the carnival grounds to find the hotdog stand.

The midway teemed with jostling crowds looking to forget war news, rationing and other shortages for a few hours. Screams coming from the House of Horror competed with hollering sideshow barkers and Tilt-a-Whirl and Ferris wheel riders. To Keeper, the carnival held a thrilling, even dangerous appeal, with its kaleidoscopic lights and swirling action. It was almost enough to make him forget what had happened back at the Burnside house.

His attention was drawn to lurid banners announcing freak shows that could be seen within the tents lining the midway. There were pickled punks in formaldehyde-filled jars, an iron lung show and the Alligator Boy in all his scaly-green hideousness. There was the India Rubber Man and the Siamese twins, two young girls who appeared to be joined at the hip by a stretchy band of skin. Keeper wondered how they went to the toilet, especially if they had to go at the same time. He paused to watch as a boy his age tried to grab a wristwatch from a glassed-in box of cheap trinkets by manipulating a claw dangling from a slender chain.

Keeper stumbled on, caught up in the crush of people like debris on a slow-moving river, until arriving in front of the hotdog stand and forcibly separating himself from the human stream by using his suit-case as a rudder. With his stomach still growling to the delicious aroma of grilled onions, he approached a straw-hatted, red-faced fat man standing behind the hotdog stand.

"I'd like a hotdog with everything, please," Keeper said.

The fat man plucked a greenish-looking hotdog off the grill with a pair of tongs and laid it on a steamed precut bun. "Onions too?"

"Yes sir," Keeper replied. "Lots."

The fat man ladled out catsup and yellow mustard from separate jars before sprinkling on diced onions with fingers stained tobacco brown. "Piccalilli?"

"What's that?"

"Relish."

"Um, no…thanks."

"Two-bits," the fat man said.

Keeper reached into his shirt pocket for the ten dollar bill and handed it over.

"You ain't got two-bits?"

"No sir."

"I ain't runnin' a fuckin' bank here," the fat man said as he scowled at the line beginning to form behind Keeper.

"This is the smallest I've got, mister."

"Shit. Look kid. You've got an honest face. Break that ten-spot someplace on the midway and hustle your ass straight back here. Unnerstand?"

"I will, mister," Keeper mumbled through a mouthful of loaded hotdog. He grabbed the suitcase with his free hand and turned towards the Ferris wheel being operated by a toothless, tattooed carnie wearing grease-stained Levis, a western-style shirt and scuffed cowboy boots curled up at the toes. The cigarette dangling from his cracked lips looked hand-rolled.

"Fifty cents," the carnie barked, and held out his hand.

Keeper lowered his suitcase and gave him the ten.

"Are you shitting me?" the carnie asked. "You gonna ride the wheel twenty times?"

Keeper took a last bite of his hotdog and licked mustard and catsup off his fingers. "It's the smallest I've got," he replied, "but I could do twice."

The carnie looked down at the suitcase and kicked it with the upturned toe of his boot. "Suitcase stays here," he said. "Otherwise, it's four-bits for that too."

"Okay."

"Times two is two bucks. Yes, or no?"

"Yes," Keeper replied.

The carnie pulled on a lever to slow the Ferris wheel until an empty car swung into view and then brought the ride to a complete stop. After making change for ten dollars, the carnie swung the safety bar away so Keeper could clamber aboard with his suitcase.

The carnie laughed. "You look like you're taking a trip to nowhere, kid."

Keeper placed the suitcase on the seat next to him and put his arm protectively around it. "I am," he said with a catch in his throat.

When the carnie threw the lever that engaged the gears, the Ferris wheel jerked into motion, causing the cars to swing wildly, and for Keeper to grab onto the safety bar with his free hand. His upward progress was marked by several stops and starts as the carnie took on more riders, until finally Keeper was halted at the very apex. He felt as if he were floating and looking down at an insignificant world that sparkled brightly beneath him.

He could see beyond the midway to the lights of Atlanta and to distant dark areas he guessed were the cotton fields he and his father had passed coming in. The bustling midway below sounded far off. He tiredly closed his eyes and imagined being back in Dakota Straits and on the beach with Jonnie Prettyboy at their secret fort and listening to the gentle wash of surf only yards away.

He was nearly asleep when the Ferris wheel lurched again. He considered spending another two dollars on the ride, but rejected the idea when it occurred to him he would need enough money to take a Greyhound home. If he ran low on money, that meant hitchhiking, something he was afraid to do. When the wheel cycled down, around, and back to the top two more times he took a last look at the midway sprawled below his feet. But this time he noticed something different – a tent at the far edge of the midway with a banner that proclaimed;

"See the Amazing Lulu LaRue
Be Shocked and Amazed
At her Titillating Delights
And Natural Wonders"

A garish painting on canvas that stretched across the tent's main entrance showed a very buxom and scantily-dressed woman holding a red parasol over her shoulder. Keeper immediately decided that if it didn't cost more than two dollars, he would go to Miss LaRue's tent show and see her titillating delights and natural wonders close up. After that, he'd look for a place to spend the night and find a Greyhound station in the morning. He wondered if his father was out looking for him. By now, maybe even the police were after him too, and it gave him guilty shiver to think about it. When the Ferris wheel lurched to a stop at ground level, Keeper waited impatiently for the carnie to unhook the safety bar. Then he grabbed his suitcase and stepped out with his legs still shaking from riding the wheel so many times.

"Happy trails, kid," the carnie said with a toothless grin.

Without replying or looking back, Keeper elbowed his way into the crowded midway. He paused momentarily to get his bearings, and then turned for the hotdog stand. After giving the fat man the two-bits he owed for the hotdog, and surprising him with his honesty, Keeper headed unerringly for the tent of Lulu LaRue.

CHAPTER THIRTY-THREE

Chance paced back and forth across Honey Burnside's threadbare carpet, smoking a cigarette and debating the wisdom of calling home. It was just past ten in Dakota Straits, and he knew Alva would be worried sick over having not heard from them. And sure as hell if he did call, she would want to talk to Keeper. Better, Chance thought, just to keep his mouth shut until Keeper returned, voluntarily or otherwise.

Honey sat with her legs crossed on the soiled couch Keeper had recently vacated. "What are you going to do now, Doc?"

"He's run away once before. It lasted all of thirty minutes. If he's not back in another fifteen, I'll go looking for him."

"Ah'm so sorry," Honey sighed.

"It wasn't your fault."

"Yes, Doc, it was. Ah should' a known bettuh." She uncrossed her legs and pushed herself off the couch to light a filter-tip Viceroy off the Old Gold Chance was smoking. She rattled the ice cubes melting in her empty highball glass and said, "Ah badly need anothuh drink. You?"

Chance shook his head. "I believe I've had enough for one night."

"Ah think you shouldn't wait much longuh."

"Keeper needs to understand the world doesn't turn on him, and that his father is only human."

"What ah'm saying, Doc, is that this is a rough neighbuhood."

Chance went to the window overlooking the front yard, as if expecting Keeper to be standing by the New Yorker parked at the curb.

Instead, what he saw was the reflection of himself, a man suddenly old beyond his years, and it shocked him. "Keeper will be fine," he replied after a minute.

"Ah'm talking about the nigguhs, Doc," Honey said, and rattled her ice cubes for emphasis.

"I'd rather you didn't use that word."

"Yoah in the South, Doc. Down heah, there's colored ladies and gentlemen, and then there's the nigguhs. It's the lattuh ah'm talking about, and it's them Keepuh needs to look out foah."

"Maybe you're right at that," Chance replied. "I'll get packed."

"What'll ah tell Jeff?"

"Tell him I'm sorry, and that I'll try and catch up with him before Keep and I leave Atlanta. That'll give Keeper two days to come to his senses."

"What makes you think Keepuh will feel any differently in a couple of days?"

"I'll talk to him."

Honey slowly shook her head. "Doc, you haven't the slightest idea what that boah is thinking, do you?"

"Yes, I do. He's thinking his dad will come for him, which is what Keeper always wanted. And to be honest, so, I guess, have I."

"That calls foah a drink," Honey said, and turned for the kitchen to refresh her bourbon and Dr. Pepper. When she returned, she leveled her eyes on Chance and said, "You know something, Doc? You picked a hell'uva way to discovuh that every boah wants his daddy."

Chance nodded in agreement and left for the bedroom to pack. When he came out, suitcase in hand, Honey stood at the screen door, silhouetted by the yellow bug light and framed by the jasmine and honeysuckle. Her elongated shadow stretched across the living room floor and hid the stained carpet where it fell.

Chance stepped into Honey's shadow. "Any idea in which direction he might have gone?"

"Towards the city, ah guess."

"That would make sense."

"Does he have money?"

"Yes, I think so."

"Jesus Christ, Doc. How can you *not* know?"

"I mean, he's got *some* money, but how much, I don't know."

"Ah think you've got a lot of territory to covuh with Keepuh."

"I'll find him," Chance replied. "He can't get far on foot."

"That's not exactly what ah mean," Honey said. "Ah'm talking about the emotional territory separating you from yoah son."

Chance put a hand on Honey's shoulder. "Apart from what happened tonight, Keeper and I have never been closer. When I find him, I'll explain about us."

"How do you explain 'us' to a thirteen yeah-old boah?"

"Bribery comes to mind."

"You'd bribe yoah own son?"

"With a six-year-old Hupmobile, if necessary."

"Wouldn't he keep his mouth shut about us if you ask him to? Aftuh all, the boah loves his daddy, doesn't he?"

Chance shrugged and replied, "I'm less certain of that by the minute."

"How about you, Doc? Do you love him? In fact, do you love anybody?"

"I haven't time for this."

"Answer me, Doc. Are you guilty of that very human emotion?"

"If love means hurting those closest to you, then yes, I'm guilty as hell."

Honey held the iced drink against her wattled neck and sighed. "How many years have we known each othuh, Doc?"

"I'd guess around twenty, give or take."

"Twenty-foah, Doc. Evuh since Jeff came home from that fucking wauh with his gonads shot off."

Chance looked at his watch and scowled. "I've got to go, Honey."

Her eyes brimmed with tears. "Yoah not evuh coming back, are you Doc?"

"I can't. Not after this."

"Ah'll remembuh you fondly, Doc."

"And I you."

"When you find Keepuh, tell him for me ah'm sorry."

"I will," Chance replied, and brushed past Honey to stand on the low stoop.

"Drop us a note evuh once and a while, will you, Doc?"

"Count on it," he replied. Then, without looking back, he turned for the road-weary New Yorker sedan and its attached black trailer that waited at the curb.

CHAPTER THIRTY-FOUR

"Step riiiiight up!" the derby-hatted and spats-wearing barker in the monkey suit called at the top of his lungs. "Step riiiiiiight up, ladieeeees and gentlemen! The next show is about to begin! For only three American dollars, it will be your privilege to see what Egyptian King Farouk paid a queen's ransom to see!"

Keeper quickly joined the growing line forming in front of Lulu LaRue's tent. As he jostled for position, he bumped into the man ahead of him, a sailor wearing crisply-starched summer whites. The sailor pushed back. "Watch it, buddy!"

"Sorry, sir," Keeper apologized.

The sailor turned with a scowl. "Why, hell, you're only a kid."

Keeper looked admiringly at the First Class Hospital Corpsman rating on the sailor's sleeve, and the three rows of ribbons on his chest, including a Bronze Star and the distinctive Purple Heart. "I'm not a kid," Keeper protested. "I've seen naked women before."

"Maybe so, but ain't you a little young for this kind of entertainment?"

"Do you think they'll let me in?"

The corpsman appraised Keeper with a critical eye. "If this grind show was in Honolulu, there'd be no problem for sure."

Disappointment showed on Keeper's face. "I've got money," he said. "I could pay extra."

The corpsman tapped Keeper's suitcase with the toe of a highly-polished black shoe. "You runnin' away from home?" he asked.

"No sir. I'm running *to* home."

The corpsman laughed. "That's a new one on me, kid."

Keeper pointed to the corpsman's rating. "My uncle's a corpsman."

"No shit?"

"He's serving in the South Pacific right now. Maybe you know him."

"The Pacific's a big place, kid, and there's lots of corpsmen."

"His name is Neil Korsvold."

"Don't recall hearing the name. Is he attached to the Marines, or does he serve aboard a hospital ship?"

"I'm not sure, but last we knew he was with the First Marines, Eighth Battalion," Keeper replied.

The corpsman shrugged. "Sorry, kid, but I was with another outfit."

"That's okay."

"Listen, kid. You stick with me, and I'll take care of this shitbag carnie if he gives you any trouble."

"Thanks, sir," Keeper replied, and picked up his suitcase when the line moved forward. When the barker questioned Keeper about his age, the corpsman interceded, explaining that Keeper was seventeen and small for his age. Not only that, but the boy had just enlisted in the Marine Corps to defend his country and shitbag carnies like him.

It was hot in the sour-smelling tent. Wooden folding chairs with the legend "Fighting Iroquois" stenciled on the back were placed in front of a low stage that featured a raised leopard-skin platform located just behind the footlights. Keeper followed the corpsman to the front row, where they took two seats in the middle and settled in for the show. Spotlights mounted high in the tent canopy played over the stage and the two-man band seated off to one side. Moths fluttered and batted frantically against the spotlights until death-spiraling onto the stage. The drummer, a mummified old man who sat behind his drums, stared off into memories he couldn't save. The coronet player, a skinny black man with hollow cheeks, wore carefully-pomaded hair that glistened under the spotlights. Keeper watched transfixed while the black man absently fingered the spit-valve of his horn. Something yellow and stringy dribbled out.

Keeper turned to study the crowd filling the seats behind him. They were mostly men, he noted, but several were accompanied by young women who giggled nervously. His attention was drawn back to the stage when the drummer rattled off the opening bars of the Saint Louis Blues March – *Boom-boom-boom-ta-boom.* Then, from behind a canvas curtain that had the Mail Pouch tobacco advertisement painted on it, a red parasol appeared and began to twirl. After a few more drum beats, Miss Lulu LaRue herself emerged into the spotlights and amid the swooning moths.

The corpsman elbowed Keeper. "This is it, kid."

Keeper gulped nervously. "Yes sir."

Lulu sidled across the stage on high-heeled red shoes – moving slowly to the beat of the drummer – *boom-boom-boom-ta-boom* – and teasingly held the parasol in front of her large drooping breasts. Red, white and blue feather boas that encircled Lulu's neck dangled below her dimpled knees. Black net stockings with little holes in them were rolled high over her doughy-white thighs. A G-string hid her crotch but not all the hair. Cigarette smoke filled the tent. Keeper coughed into his hand. Nobody spoke. A girl tittered and the drum went – *boom-boom-boom ta boom.*

"Whad'ya think, kid?"

"Good so far."

"It'll get better," the corpsman promised.

Lulu continued to grind to the music, gyrating suggestively in front of Keeper before circling the leopard-skin platform. He watched open-mouthed as she began shedding her boas, one by one, until only her net stockings, G-string and the tasseled pasties that covered her nipples remained. Keeper leaned forward in his Fighting Iroquois chair, not wanting to miss anything – wanting to remember every lurid detail before he was struck blind like Early.

Lulu continued with her routine of deep, revealing squats and high-kicks before coming to sit on the edge of the platform. The audience offered up a smattering of applause, and Keeper joined in. Lulu looked at Keeper and smiled – an open red-lipped leer that revealed her gapped front teeth. No longer an anonymous face lost in the crowd, now it was *he* who had been singled out. When Lulu crossed her legs with an exaggerated kick, she exposed several holes in the soles of her high-heeled shoes. Keeper wondered if she'd worn the same shoes for King Farouk.

Then, ten too-short minutes after her act began, Miss LaRue stood and sauntered back to the Mail Pouch curtain and disappeared behind it with a little wave. Was this all? Keeper wondered. Three hard earned dollars for this? He stood; ready to leave, when the barker return to the stage.

"Laaaaadies and gentlemen!" the barker cried. "Miss LaRue and I wish to thank you all for your kind show of appreciation!"

"Bring the bitch back!" someone shouted.

The barker held up his hands. "In a moment, gentlemen. But first..."

"Get the fuck off and bring Lulu back!" someone else hollered.

The barker smiled widely. "I understand your impatience, gentlemen. Miss LaRue's second act will begin shortly. However, due to the intimate nature of this performance, I cannot allow the ladies to attend, lest it upset their delicate sensibilities."

The grumbling men with their girlfriends got up to leave. Everyone else, including Keeper, remained seated.

The barker rubbed his hands together like he was warming them over a fire. "Thank you, gentlemen, for staying. I admire your discerning and worldly tastes. Now, for an additional contribution of only five dollars, Miss LaRue will put on a show unlike any this side of Gay Parieee! As soon as I have collected your money...ahem, contribution, the next show will begin."

Already aroused, Keeper fumbled for his Boy Scout wallet and took out five crumpled dollar bills. Sweat trickled down the back of his neck as he handed over his donation, which the barker added to a fat wad of bills in his fist before hustling back to the stage. Keeper no longer cared if he had enough money left to take the Greyhound back home.

The barker shouted, "Gentlemen, please welcome back – Miss Lulu LaRue!" The two-man band stirred to life – *boom-boom- boom-ta-boom*, to bring Miss LaRue back from behind the Mail Pouch curtain. This time the patriotic red, white and blue boas were gone. After strutting around the stage three times, Miss LaRue stopped directly in front of Keeper, threw back her shoulders and began spinning her tassels like counter-rotating propellers. Everyone applauded. The corpsman put two fingers in his mouth and whistled.

While Keeper gawked and gulped, Miss LaRue made another shuffling reconnoiter of the stage. Without breaking stride she unsnapped the G-string and waved it as if it were a distress flag while moving toward the platform. There she stopped to sit spraddle-legged in full view of Keeper, who leaned forward in rapt attention while the corpsman seated next to him hooted. The drummer lit a cigarette and rubbed the eyes that had seen it all. The black musician exchanged his coronet for an oboe and began playing '*Salome*'.

It was a signal for the Mail Pouch curtain to part and reveal Miss LaRue's assistant, a pretend-Nubian slave wearing gauzy red pantaloons, red caliph's shoes and a rhinestone-studded green vest. A gauzy white veil hid the Nubian's nose and mouth, and a gold-colored turban rested atop closely-cropped black hair. The Nubian held a purple velvet pillow with gold tassels. Something lay across the pillow, and Keeper squinted to see what it was. It looked like one of the 10 inch date-nut logs his mother sometimes made and refrigerated before slicing and baking. Except this log was pink, and Keeper didn't think Miss LaRue was about to bake anything.

The corpsman jabbed Keeper with his elbow. "Now's where we get our money's worth!"

"What's that on the pillow?" Keeper asked

"Ain't you ever gone exploring in your mother's dresser drawers before?"

"No sir," Keeper replied. The Calliope sounded far away. "I wouldn't dare."

"Well, if you did, I'll guarantee you'd find one of them hidden somewheres. They're called dildos, and this one here is a strap-on model."

Keeper gawped wide-eyed as the Nubian approached to kneel in front of Miss LaRue, then bowed and held out the pillow as if the dildo were an offering to the gods.

Miss LaRue reached for the dildo and began to rub it up and down her thighs.

"Hot damn!" the corpsman shouted.

Now fully aroused, Keeper crossed his legs to conceal his erection. The only sound inside the tent came from the oboe, and from Miss

LaRue herself, who moaned in feigned ecstasy. Then, with a snap of her fingers, she beckoned to the silent Nubian, who took the dildo from her and strapped it on like a gun belt.

"This is better'n Honolulu," the corpsman said.

To Keeper, the slender Nubian looked freakish, with the jutting pink dildo that bobbed and waggled on its strap as if attached to an invisible string. The improbable sight made someone laugh, which broke the tension and spoiling the moment. Keeper turned to see who had interrupted what he'd been waiting for – paid eight precious dollars to see – and when he turned back to face the stage, he found himself staring directly into the vacant pale gray eyes of Jonnie Prettyboy.

CHAPTER THIRTY-FIVE

Seeing Jonnie Prettyboy again after an absence of three years stunned Keeper. How did she get here, he wondered, and what was she doing in Lulu LaRue's cooch show? Believing that only torture could have made her do it; he leapt to his feet and stumbled toward the stage screaming "Stop!"

"Jesus Christ, kid!" the corpsman shouted. "Not *now!*"

Keeper waved his arms at the uncomprehending Jonnie Prettyboy. "Honey!" he called, "It's *me!*"

As if awakening from a deep trance, Jonnie Prettyboy turned to stare wide-eyed at the gawky and unfamiliar teenage boy rushing the stage. The pink dildo waggled at her waist when she raised her fists. "Stay away from me, you crazy fucker!"

"No, no, no!" he cried. It's me, Keeper. Keeper Wick!"

Jonnie Prettyboy held her fists in mid-flail. "Keeper?" she replied, uncertain.

"We gotta get out of here!" he shouted.

Miss LaRue lurched to her feet, covered her fat breasts with her hands and screamed, "Hey Rube!"

The scene in the tent was total chaos. The drummer and coronet player ducked behind the Mail Pouch curtain just as the barker appeared at the entrance with a baseball bat clutched in his fists.

Jonnie Prettyboy pointed toward the advancing barker. "Look out, Keeper! He'll kill you!"

"Shitbag will have to get past me first!" the corpsman shouted as he rushed to the stage. He grabbed Jonnie Prettyboy by the arm and leaned in close to be heard. "Is there a back way out of here?"

She waved a hand toward the curtain. "That way!"

"Go," the corpsman yelled. "Both of you, and don't stop running until you can't hear the Calliope no more!"

"My suitcase!" Keeper cried.

The corpsman grabbed for Keeper's shirttail and held it. "No time!"

"I can't leave it!" Keeper shouted. "It's my mom's!" He twisted until he pulled free from the corpsman's grasp and jumped off the stage to snatch up the suitcase only steps ahead of the bat-wielding barker.

"Goddamn you!" the barker screamed while waving the bat. "Little fucking punk! Fuck up my show, will you!"

"Go!" the corpsman cried again, and pushed Keeper after Jonnie Prettyboy, who had already disappeared behind the Mail Pouch curtain.

The barker raised the bat high above his head. "You'll pay for this, sailor boy."

The corpsman waggled his fingers, an invitation. "C'mon, shitbag."

Miss LaRue rushed to intercede. "Wait, Francis!" she cried. "We don't need any more heat from the sheriff!"

Francis paused and blinked in apparent confusion, as if a third strike had just been called. "Huh?"

The corpsman laughed. "Yeah, shitbag. Here's there's a war goin' on, and you're threatening' a decorated man in uniform."

"Fuck you, swabby. I served on a sub chaser in the first war"

"And I'll bet your asshole still misses the action."

With the bat still held high, Francis took a tentative step toward the corpsman. "And you can kiss yours goodbye."

The corpsman held up a hand, as if to stop Francis in his tracks. "Tell me, shitbag. How old is that kid who's workin' for you and Miss Lulu here?"

"None of your fucking business."

Lulu reached for the bat, "Put it down, Francis, dear. Sailor boy makes his point." Then she turned for the corpsman. "If you're looking for a good time," she cooed, "I've got a gassed-up Lincoln and an Airstream parked outside. There's also a jug of Tennessee 'shine in that trailer, just in case your whistle needs wettin'."

The corpsman pushed his white cap low over the bridge of his nose and whistled. "That's a kindly offer, Miss LaRue, but what about shitbag here? Ain't he gonna make a fuss, what with his old lady takin' up with the U.S. Navy?"

Lulu laughed. "Francis?" she asked. "Why hell, handsome. Ain't nothin' he likes better'n watchin'."

CHAPTER THIRTY-SIX

Jonnie Prettyboy stumbled ahead of Keeper, mouth open and gasping for air. They had been running in the general direction of downtown Atlanta for the past ten minutes and were hopelessly lost. "Where the fuck are we anyways?" she panted.

"Gotta stop and get our bearings," Keeper replied. Not only did his legs ache from pounding down dark and unfamiliar sidewalks, they hurt from where his mother's suitcase banged against them.

Jonnie Prettyboy pointed ahead to a darkened storefront with a sign over the door spelled out Mr. Sam's Fresh Meats Cigarettes Beer & Wine in hand-painted yellow letters. A low wooden bench out front occupied much of the sidewalk. "Over there," she grunted breathlessly. "Got to rest a minute."

Keeper sat next to her where he could catch his breath and think.

"A cooch show is the last place I'd expect to see you," Jonnie Prettyboy said after her breathing slowed enough to talk. "How'd you wind up here?"

"I'm on a road trip with my dad," Keeper explained. "At least I was up until a couple of hours ago."

She kicked at Keeper's suitcase with the curved toe of her red caliph's shoe. "What's with the suitcase?"

"I'm going home."

"Alone and on foot?"

"I was planning on taking the Greyhound."

"What happened with your pa?"

Keeper shrugged and folded his hands in his lap. "I can't say."

"Can't," Jonnie Prettyboy replied, "or won't?"

"Won't."

She took Keeper's sweaty mustard-stained hands in hers and placed them in her lap. "If you and that sailor hadn't showed up like you did, I was gonna kill the bitch tonight."

"Why'd you let her do this to you?"

She drew a deep breath and turned to level her pale gray eyes on Keeper. "She said I was wanted by the cops for killing my pa. If I didn't do what she asked, she would 'a turned me over for the reward money."

"But *you* didn't kill your dad," Keeper sputtered. "I did."

"Don't matter. If the cops found me they'd of sent me back to Dakota Straits and my ma."

"The cops found your old man's body where we buried him on the beach."

"And?"

"They came to my house and grilled me."

"And?"

"They wanted to know what I knew, and where you'd gone."

"Goddamnit, *and?*"

"They put out an APB on you."

"You squealed?"

"I said you'd gone hooking in the south, but they're looking for a girl, not a boy."

Jonnie Prettyboy seemed to think. "You got a smoke on you?" she asked.

"No."

"Fuck."

"I've got some clothes in the suitcase you could wear, though."

She laughed. "Ain't this where we came in?"

He ignored the comment. "We could travel together; maybe even ride the rails to California."

"I rode the rails, and it ain't something I'd recommend. 'Sides, I travel alone."

"I'm just trying to help is all."

She kicked the suitcase again. "Open it."

Keeper put the suitcase on his lap, unsnapped the locks and opened it. A pair of Keds and his pajama bottoms were on top. "The stuff underneath is clean," he said. "Take what you want."

Jonnie Prettyboy picked up Keeper's pajama bottoms and wrinkled her nose. "Where the hell have you been? Your clothes smell like deep-fried chicken and skunk shit."

"That's because of the house where we stayed. Besides, you won't get far in those harem clothes."

"Shut up." She took the pair of Keds and began to dig through Keeper's things until she found clean undershorts, a pair of long pants, and a short-sleeved shirt. "Be on the lookout while I change," she said, and took the donated clothes around to the side of the store.

When ten minutes passed and she hadn't come back, Keeper became worried that she might have left him again, and got up to look for her. At the same time, he smelled cigarette smoke. "Honey?" he whispered into the dark. "Are you there?"

"I thought I told you to shut up and be on the lookout."

Keeper spotted the glowing tip of a cigarette where Jonnie Prettyboy stood hidden behind a cluster of hydrangea bushes. From where he stood, she looked exactly like a boy in his clothes. "Where'd you get the cigarette?" he asked.

"I learned lock picking from the carnies. Want a beer? I opened two."

"No. Wait. Sure." He advanced toward the glowing cigarette beacon and took the bottle, which he held to his face – enjoying the beaded condensation and remembering Honey Burnside doing the same thing with her bourbon and Dr. Pepper.

"Do you suppose your pa is out looking for you right now?" Jonnie Prettyboy asked.

"I don't care if he is or isn't," Keeper replied. He held the bottle under his nose to sniff the malty, yeasty smell, and then tipped the bottle to his lips and took the first swallow.

"Would you go back with him?"

He took another long bitter-tasting swallow and belched. "No, not after what he did."

Her silver-gray eyes glittered in the orange glow of her burning cigarette. "Tell me what your pa did."

Keeper lowered his eyes, as if trying to erase the awful memory. "I don't know that I can."

"Could it be worse than what that bitch Lulu LaRue made me do with her?"

"No, but close enough."

Jonnie Prettyboy snorted. "Bullshit," then took another gulp of beer, which she swished between her teeth like mouthwash.

"It's not bullshit at all," Keeper replied at length. "I caught my dad fucking Miss Georgia."

Beer spewed from Jonnie Prettyboy's lips in a fine mist. Then she laughed a smoker's husky cackle that ended in a coughing spell.

"I don't see what's so funny," he said, scowling.

"Jesus, what a dumb shit!" she groaned after catching her breath. "It couldn't have been 'some dame,' or 'the neighbor lady,' or even 'a hooker.' Oh no! It had to be Miss Georgia!"

"Well, that's who it was."

"Wouldn't she be a little young for him?"

"She was a *former* Miss Georgia."

"Well, *that* balances the fucking scales."

"Her husband is a friend of my dad's."

Jonnie Prettyboy took another swallow of beer, belched again, and then took a long pull off her cigarette. "Some friend."

"He's dying of ass cancer."

"Which explains why your pa mercy fucked the former Miss Georgia."

"It doesn't matter why. He cheated on my mom, and I'll bet it happened before."

"I think you ought to give your pa a break for helping out his friend."

"And I think we should shut up before somebody hears us," Keeper warned.

"You got any money, shit for brains?"

He was taken aback by the question. "Some, maybe thirty bucks. Why?"

"Give me half," she said, "and then we'll split up."

"I think we should stick together. Besides, I don't know how much I'll need for bus fare."

"That's your problem. As for sticking together, your pa's probably out looking for you and probably the cops too. I do *not* want to be around when they find your skinny ass."

"Where will you go?"

"Wherever the wind blows warm and the sun shines year 'round," Jonnie Prettyboy replied. After finishing the beer, she tossed the bottle aside. "Now, give me the dough."

When he fumbled in his pocket for the bills he'd neatly folded, Keeper touched the lucky charm his father had given him three years before. It was all he could do to keep from crying. After counting out a ten and a five and handing over the bills, he pressed the lucky charm into her hand.

"What the fuck's this?" she asked.

"It's for you, honey, for luck on the road."

Jonnie Prettyboy took the charm and examined it closely under the burning ember of her cigarette. "This won't do me any good," she muttered. "It's got your stupid name and address stamped on it."

"Then you won't ever forget me."

She sniffed and wiped her nose on the back of her hand. "You've always been such a dumb shit."

"I can't believe I'm losing you again."

"Yeah, well, them's the breaks."

Keeper rubbed away the tears gathered in the corners of his eyes. "Maybe our paths will cross again someday."

"Maybe, and then again, maybe not."

"Will you kiss me?" Keeper asked.

"Well, I suppose I owe you *something*," Jonnie Prettyboy replied. She stepped towards Keeper and said, "Make it quick, and don't try any funny business."

He closed his eyes and gently pressed his lips against hers. He tasted the cigarette she just smoked – and smelled the musky yet not-unpleasant female odor that reminded him of a puppy.

"That's enough," she said, and with a catch in her throat, pushed him away.

He laughed softly. "Can I feel your boobs one last time?"

"No. That's all you're getting, so shut up."

Keeper pointed to Jonnie Prettyboy's Nubian headpiece. "The turban," he said. "I want it."

She removed the turban and tossed it to him overhanded like a boy would. "You're such a dumb shit," she said. "Dumb...dumb...*dumb.*"

"Maybe so, he sniffed, "But I love you, and someday we're going to get married."

She snapped away the cigarette butt in a trailing shower of sparks. "Yeah, well I wouldn't go getting my hopes up, if I were you."

"My mind's made up," Keeper replied, "and nothing can change it."

Jonnie Prettyboy laughed. "Gotta be going, Keep. See you in the funny papers." Then she turned and walked away from him until she reached the end of the block and stopped under a street light, as if deciding which way to go. Then, without looking back, she crossed the street and disappeared into the dark Atlanta night.

CHAPTER THIRTY-SEVEN

Keeper slept curled up on the store-front bench until the rising sun woke him. Or was it the plaintive wail of a distant locomotive that had awakened him? He sat up and rubbed his eyes. His mouth tasted terrible from the stale hotdog with everything but relish he'd eaten the night before, and from the beer Jonnie Prettyboy had stolen for him. As he blinked to open his eyes, shielding them with his hands against a sun already hot, a shadow fell across the suitcase at his feet.

Hoping Jonnie Prettyboy had come back for him, he squinted to see a figure standing between him and the sun. It wasn't Jonnie Prettyboy, but it *was* a girl, and by his estimation, similar in size and age, but with much darker skin and better developed. Unlike Jonnie Prettyboy's short-cropped hair, this girl had little pigtails sticking out of her scalp like detonator pegs on an anti-ship mine. The short-sleeved, daisy-print cotton dress she wore was sun-faded and barely covered her scabbed knees. She was barefoot, with slender nut-brown feet and soles pink as bubblegum when she lifted a foot to nudge the suitcase.

"You'uns a runaway?" the girl asked.

Keeper tried to make out her features and blinked because of the sun's bright aura behind her head. By shading his eyes and squinting, he could make out full tulip-like lips under a broad nose and curious dark eyes. "I guess so," he replied.

The girl laced her fingers together. "Either you is, or you ain't."

"Then I am." He thought he heard the train whistle again, which made him feel sad and homesick, but he didn't say anything either way.

"What's your name?" she asked.

He was unable to take his eyes off her boobs. "Keeper," he gulped.

The girl giggled, showing front teeth like Chiclets. "That's a curious name. Keeper whut?"

"Wick."

The girl laughed again, soft and breathy like a summer breeze ruffling the leaves of a sycamore. "Like whut goes in a candle?"

"Yeah."

"You'uns lucky your folks didn't name you 'Candle,' then."

"Lucky, that's me."

She turned her attention to another bite on her arm and scratched it. "Was it you, Keeper Wick, come an' robbed the sto' las' night?"

"Somebody picked the lock?"

"I didn't say *how* they come in," she replied, scratching and not making eye contact, "but they was two bottles of Atlantic pilsner took from the cooler, an' a pack of Chesterfields."

"I don't know anything about it."

"Naw, I s'pose you wouldn't."

"Do you live here?" Keeper asked, relieved to be off the hook.

"With my gran'pap, over the sto'."

"You know my name," Keeper said. "S'pose you could tell me yours?"

"Spec I could at that."

He leaned back and waited to hear it. At the same time, he badly needed to take a piss in the hydrangeas, but didn't dare. Not now.

"Whut's that perched up on your headbone?" the girl asked, pointing.

He had forgotten the turban and touched it as a reminder. "It's from the carnival," he replied.

"Umm," the colored girl said, and ran her tongue over her lips as if tasting cotton candy. "Wish't I could go. I'd soar free as a sparrow on that Ferry wheel, flyin' 'round and 'round, 'till they had to shoot me off it."

Keeper laughed at the image. "I rode on it last night."

"Did you see to the edge of the worl' from up there?"

"It seemed like it."

"Lawd 'a mighty."

"So?" Keeper said.

"So, whut?"

"What's your name?"

The girl looked down at her feet and spread her toes on a sidewalk already hot under the Georgia sun. "Zinnia Day."

"Is that one name, or two?"

Zinnia locked her hands behind her back. "They's both."

"Nice to meet you, Zinnia," Keeper said, and extended his hand to shake.

She unlocked her hands from behind her back and gingerly allowed Keeper to take four slender fingers. "Likewise."

"I never met a colored girl before."

She yawned and stretched lazily. "I never met no white boy, neither."

Keeper was sure Zinnia wasn't wearing underwear. "Really?"

"Oh, I seen 'em all right, but not to talk to, or sleepin' on our sto' bench."

"I never saw a colored person in my whole life until Indianapolis."

Where you'uns from, then? The North Pole?"

Keeper laughed. "Same difference."

Zinnia shook her head. "You'uns come all the way from the North Pole jest to see colored folks?"

"Not exactly. I was on a road trip with my dad."

She scratched her head and frowned. "You'uns runnin' from your pa?"

"Yeah."

She looked down to study a large brown and red ant exploring the top of her left foot. "Reckon he's lookin' for runaway Keeper Wick right this minute?"

"Probably."

"Po'lice too?"

Keeper shrugged his shoulders. "Maybe."

"Po'lice won't look for no white boy here."

Keeper squirmed uncomfortably. "Can I ask you a favor?"

Zinnia brushed off the wandering ant with her right toe and crushed it against the sidewalk. "You can axe."

"I need to use the bathroom."

She hid her mouth behind a slender hand and giggled. "I'se could tell."

CHAPTER THIRTY-EIGHT

Chance stood in the police lieutenant's office, where he'd come only after spending most of the night driving aimlessly in a futile search for Keeper.

"Describe your son, if you would, Mr. Wick," the lieutenant said.

Chance rubbed his red-rimmed eyes before answering. "I'd say five foot six or seven, fair-skinned and freckled, with sandy hair."

"Answers to?"

"Keeper."

"How do you spell that?"

"K-e-e-p-e-r."

The lieutenant shook his head. "Eyes?"

"Blue."

"Date of birth?"

"Um, he's thirteen."

"You don't recollect the actual date?"

"March is the best I can do at the moment."

"Any identifying marks, such as birthmarks, deformities, tattoos, glasses?"

"Come to think of it, he's a little sunburned."

The lieutenant jotted down the information in a spiral notebook. "How long has he been missing, again?"

"This is the first time I'm aware of."

"I mean, tell me again, when it was you discovered the boy missing."

"I didn't discover it. I watched him leave."

"You didn't intercede?"

"I was indisposed."

"In the shower, taking a crap, or what?"

"In bed, naked, as it were."

"What time was that?"

"Sometime around nine," Chance replied, and reached for the open pack of Old Golds in his shirt pocket.

"It's a little premature to be reporting a person as missing."

"Missing is missing. His mother will be frantic."

"Not so you?"

"Less so."

"Why, Mr. Wick?"

"He's far from home. Keeper has to come back."

Where do you call home?"

"Dakota Straits, that's in Michigan."

The officer clucked his tongue and made a notation in his notebook. "Why do you suppose 'K-e-e-p-e-r' ran off like he did?"

Chance clicked open the lid on his Zippo and lit the cigarette. His hand trembled, a slight flutter, perhaps caused by the headaches that were recurring. "We had a disagreement."

"Concerning?"

"Relationships."

"Can you expand upon that?"

"It's very personal."

"It often is. Have you looked for your son?"

"Yes, most of the night and street by street."

"Would he have any special interests, Mr. Wick, something that might lead us to him?"

"Such as?"

The lieutenant scowled. "For example, could he have gone to a ballgame?"

"I'm not sure he's interested in baseball."

"How about the movies?

"I don't know, maybe."

"You don't know a hell'uva lot about your son, do you, Mr. Wick?"

"Other than that he's carrying a suitcase, I'm ashamed to say I don't."

"There's a traveling carnival in town. Would he have gone there?"

Chance brightened. "That's a possibility."

"I'll send an officer to check it out. Meanwhile, where can you be reached?"

"I'm kind of in transit right now. I'll have to get back to you."

"Excuse my language, Mr. Wick, but even if your boy *wanted* to come back to you, he'd be shit out of luck!"

Chance took another drag off his cigarette and stood to leave the station house. "Aren't we all?" he replied, "And some more than others."

CHAPTER THIRTY-NINE

Keeper sat in an ancient bentwood rocker watching the dull-black Lionel "O" gauge locomotive circumnavigating the room on silvery tracks that traversed tongue-depressor bridge spans and through tunnels of green papier-mâché. On each circuit, the engine passed a platform complete with a ticket station, cast-lead toy cars, cast-lead toy people waiting to board, and a black-faced porter carrying a cast-lead suitcase.

The coal-tender had New York Central painted on its sides, and was coupled to a string of colorful cars. They included a flatbed, a cattle car, a baggage car, a Sunoco oil tanker, two passenger cars, one of which was a sleeper, and a red caboose.

The locomotive featured a working headlight and a whistle that blew whenever the train entered a tunnel. It was blowing now, the very sound Keeper heard from the outside bench earlier that morning.

Sam Day held a gnarled finger on the rheostat that controlled the locomotive's forward speed. He wore a freshly-pressed sleeping car porter's uniform, in spite of the temperature that was climbing by degrees in the upstairs bedroom. "Mr. Sam," as he was called by everyone, including by now Keeper himself, was clearly in his element. He grinned widely, exposing his tusk-like teeth. In contrast to the tufts of cotton-white hair that showed under his porter's billed cap, his skin was as dark and wrinkled as a well-traveled Gladstone bag. His eyes were rheumy and of a color that nearly matched his remaining teeth.

It was as if an amber stain had leached throughout his system like sap in a tree.

"We'un's highballin' now, Mistuh Keepuh," he cackled.

Keeper grinned as the highballing New York Central Lionel raced around the setup in Mr. Sam's bedroom. Having enjoyed a hearty breakfast of scrambled eggs, grits, and his very first cup of coffee, all prepared by Zinnia Day, Keeper was content to be exactly where he was. Zinnia had absented herself to open the store below, where she was charged with selling chicken wings, neck bones, tripe, short ribs and hamburger meat out of the cold case.

"How many years were you on the railroad, Mr. Sam?" Keeper asked, curious because of the memorabilia that had been carefully placed around the room like a shrine to railroading. A framed photograph of a smiling sleeping car porter wearing a white jacket and holding a freshly-shined pair of men's shoes hung at the head of the bed. Keeper recognized the porter to be much younger Mr. Sam, with slicked-back dark hair.

"Since ought-eight," Mr. Sam replied. "Thirty-six years last January."

"You must have shined a zillion shoes."

Mr. Sam chuckled and sucked on a prominent front tooth. "Times two," Mistuh Keepuh. Dey comes in pairs."

"And beds too," Keeper added, because in the photograph, Mr. Sam stood next to a double-bunked sleeper behind an open privacy curtain.

"Upper and lower, Mistuh Keepuh. Ever time the berth gets made up it gets the mattress turned, and the sheets and pillow cases changed too."

"Must have been awful hard work."

"Better than choppin' cotton, but Lawd help you if they's a speck out of order."

Keeper watched the locomotive as it emerged from a papier-mâché tunnel with its headlight twinkling and lonesome-sounding whistle that gave him a knot deep in his stomach. "My dad travels by train sometimes."

"I declare."

Keeper dropped a special pill Mr. Sam had given him into the smokestack, and smiled when white smoke appeared. "He's been on the New York Central too, but mostly, he takes the Union Pacific when he goes west."

"He's a travelin' man?"

Keeper nodded. "His company makes ballast tampers for railroads."

Mr. Sam laughed. "Mistuh Keepuh, have you ever in youh young life seen gandydancers lining a track? Now, suh, that's hard work!"

"You might have even seen my dad, because he demonstrates them all over the country."

"Seen lot's of mens, lonely mens travelin'away from they families, mostly wishin' they was home, but they's some that turns into houn' dogs, drinkin' an' chasin' wimmins."

"My dad said when he's on the road he wants to be home, and vice-versa."

"He be on the road now?"

"Yes sir. He brought me with him to Atlanta."

Mr. Sam nodded and turned back the rheostat controlling the Lionel's speed, slowing it until it came to a stop at the ticket station.

"Gran'pap?" Zinnia called from the stairs. "They's two mens down here needin' a bottle of Mogen David on credit."

Mr. Sam placed a gnarled hand on his arthritic hip and grunted to stand. "Take your hand to the throttle, Mistuh Keepuh, an' no highballin' while I takes care o' bidness."

"Yes sir, Mr. Sam. No highballing until you come back." Once Keeper was alone he picked up one of the cast-lead passengers – a traveling salesman who wore a derby and a suit with a vest and carried a boxy sample case. Keeper clutched the toy salesman in his fist until tears filled his eyes. Then he threw it against the wall hard enough to break off its head.

CHAPTER FORTY

Chance Wick stood in the cramped confines of the telephone booth with the receiver held to his ear, doodling on the Atlanta Yellow Pages with a mechanical pencil and listening to the phone ring at home. In his mind's eye he could envision Alva out in her victory garden, hoeing the fucking weeds while Early stumbled blindly through the house to answer the phone before it stopped ringing. Except instead of Early, it was Alva who answered, and she sounded out of breath.

"Yes? Hello?"

"It's me," Chance said, simply.

"Where in the hell have you been?" Alva shrilled. "Not a word from you and Keep in two days! Put him on, this instant!"

"I'm sorry, dear, but Keeper isn't available."

"What do you mean, 'isn't available?'"

"He disappeared last night, while we were at the Burnsides."

"If this is your idea of a joke…"

"It's not a joke. He ran off."

"I *knew* something terrible was going to happen!" Alva cried. "I just *knew* it!"

"I've just given the police his description," Chance said. "I'm sure it won't be long before they'll…"

"You didn't alert the police until now? How in God's name could you have waited so long?"

"I thought I'd have found him by now."

"Are you with the police now?"

"No. I'm at the Georgian Terrace Hotel on Peachtree. I'm calling from a pay phone in the lounge while they make up a room."

"I hear laughter and a jukebox. Are you drinking?"

"I'll admit the thought has occurred to me, but no, I was having a Coke."

"Not that I give a damn, but Mr. Pettigrew called from the office this morning, wanting to know where in the 'effing' hell you are."

"I'll call him next."

"I hate to ask, but is it possible Keeper could have gone back to the Burnsides?"

"I've already called. Honey knows where I am in case he does. I might add that Jeff slipped into a coma during the night, and is not expected to live."

"I'm sorry for him, but as for that tramp knowing..."

Chance interrupted, "Never mind her. How's Dad?"

"I do *mind* her. As for Dad, he now thinks Roosevelt and Winifred are under his bed making love, but he called it something else."

"Look, Alva. I know how you feel about someone coming in, but..."

"No. Your father deserves the same level of care I gave your mother and mine."

"You're being a martyr."

"That's enough gratitude for one day. Have you thought to call the hospitals yet?"

"The police already have."

"Then get your goddamned ass back out on the street, and don't call again until you've found my son."

"Our son, Alva dear."

"Early is here and wants a word."

"One thing more..." Chance started to say.

Alva interrupted with a groan. "Oh God, Dad's calling again."

"Alva, dear, I seem to have forgotten Keeper's birth date," Chance said.

"Then ask Keeper when you find him!"

"It's bad," were Early's first words when he got on the phone. "Granddad is shouting that Winifred left some chocolate pudding on his rocking chair, and wants Mother to bring a spoon."

"Jesus Christ Almighty," Chance mumbled. He began to scribble a cartoon sketch over a chiropractor's ad showing Ignatz throwing a sputtering bomb at Krazy Kat.

"You can say that again," Early said.

"Are you doing the best you can to help Mother?"

"I've been cutting the grass," Early replied. "She said it looks great, except for where I got into the radishes. Also…"

"That's fine, Early," Chance said, interrupting, "but there are people waiting to use the phone."

"One thing more thing before you go, Dad. Remember Jonnie Prettyboy?"

"Vaguely."

"She was Keeper's best friend who ran away three years ago."

"It comes back."

"Right, but Jonnie Prettyboy never did. Word is the police have reopened their investigation of Mr. Prettyboy's mysterious death."

"After all this time?"

"Get this. Mrs. Prettyboy said her daughter had a motive for killing her father."

Chance thumb-clicked the mechanical pencil and returned it to his shirt pocket, ready to renew his search for Keeper. "I find that hard to believe."

"No it isn't," Early said. "Mrs. Prettyboy told the cops that her husband had been jumping his daughter's bones since the kid was ten."

CHAPTER FORTY-ONE

The Greyhound station consisted of a single ticket cage and shared a cinderblock building with the Bars & Stars Café & Lounge. The dual-purpose building was located between a Ford agency on one side, and a Texaco station with two island pumps on the other. Hot tar laid over newly-graded red clay infused the sultry late-morning air with a harshly-sweet petroleum smell. Lumbering dump trucks with hard-rubber tires followed the tar wagon, spreading crushed gravel before being compacted by a steam roller. The day was already hot, with the temperature registering 98 degrees as indicated by a Coca-Cola thermometer nailed over the front door of the Texaco station. A scruffy brown dog slept in the shade of a red and white-striped awning that protected the café's street-facing windows from the sun's heat.

Jonnie Prettyboy approached the café from the opposite side of the freshly-resurfaced street. She walked with an even Indian-like pace while being mindful not to get tar on the white Keds taken from Keeper. She'd been walking steadily since first light – having spent the night sleeping in an unlocked tool shed on the northern outskirts of Atlanta. Upon reaching the sidewalk she crouched next to the dog and rested her chin on her knees to study it. She'd never owned a dog, and imagined how wonderful it must be to have one, along with her own house and a backyard instead of living in an old caboose that sits on an abandoned siding in the dunes. Sensing her presence, the dog began wagging its tail, '*whap-whap-whap*,' against the sidewalk.

Jonnie Prettyboy extended her right hand and scratched the tail-wagging dog behind the ear. "Nice doggy," she said.

The dog raised its head and turned its watery-brown eyes toward Jonnie Prettyboy, blinking gratefully before closing them again.

"I'll bet you're mighty thirsty, Mr. Dog," she whispered.

The tail went, '*whap whap whap.*'

She got to her feet and opened the screen door to enter and waited until her eyes adjusted to the gloom. Once she had her bearings she went into the Greyhound waiting room and studied the posted schedule of departure and arrival times, and the various destinations and ticket prices. She estimated she had enough money in her pocket to buy a one-way ticket to almost anywhere, with enough left over to live on, assuming she ate bread and beans once a day and found work within a week. The next bus was inbound from Nashville, with a fifteen minute layover before continuing to New Orleans by way of Montgomery. Since the bus wasn't due to arrive for another hour, she decided to wait in the café, and took a booth by the window where she could watch the road.

A ceiling fan gave little relief from the oppressive heat, but she didn't dare unbutton her shirt below the collar lest her cleavage show. She shifted her gaze to four white men in coveralls eating potato salad and Spam sandwiches at the counter. There were open beers in front of them and they were laughing over some private joke.

A middle-aged blond woman accompanied by a young girl occupied the booth adjoining hers, and the woman was reading aloud from a menu. A hard-faced waitress wearing a snood with a yellow pencil harpooned through it stood behind the counter – joking with the workmen like she had all day and ignoring Jonnie Prettyboy. A Confederate flag hung on the wall behind the counter, as if waiting to be taken up once again and carried into battle. A sign under the flag read, Never Forget.

Jonnie Prettyboy thought if she had a glass of water, she'd take it outside and give the dog a drink from the palm of her hand. When she pressed her forehead against the window she could see it still snoozing on the sidewalk with its chin resting on outstretched paws like a mangy sphinx. She was about to tap on the window when the waitress appeared.

"Can't you read?" the waitress snapped. She pulled the pencil from her snood and aimed the eraser end toward a spot above the window.

Jonnie Prettyboy followed the pencil to see what the waitress was talking about, and saw a sign that read; White Only. After three years of living in the Deep South, Jonnie Prettyboy was no stranger to segregation, and in fact had been mistaken for a Negro on more than one occasion. But today she was both tired and hungry, and not about to be pushed around. "You serve only white bread here?" she asked. "Only white rice? Only white taters? Only white milk? *What* white only?"

"Goddamn, if you ain't one uppity nigra whut don't know his place!"

"Up yours."

The waitress paled and turned toward the workmen sitting at the counter. "Bobby Ray!" she shouted.

Jonnie Prettyboy leveled her glittering pale-gray eyes on the waitress. "I'd like to order something to eat, please," she said, "starting with a large glass of water."

"*Bobby Ray!*"

"Yeah, Bonnie?"

"This nigra just tol' me 'up yours!'"

The little girl in the adjoining booth peeked to see what the disturbance was all about, and when she saw Jonnie Prettyboy, she said, "Momma, there's a nigger with ghost eyes looking at me."

Bobby Ray pushed himself away from the counter and swaggered toward the booth. "You back-sassin' a white woman, boy?"

"I only said, 'up yours.'"

Bobby Ray pointed a thick finger at the window. "See that tar wagon yonder, boy?"

"I sure do, Bobby Ray. You thinking about taking a much needed bath?"

"Goddamn..."

"I'm callin' the sheriff," Bonnie said, "get this nigra hauled off to jail."

"Don't need no sheriffin' here," Bobby Ray snarled, and reached for Jonnie Prettyboy's shirt.

"I wouldn't do that, Bobby Ray," she said.

Before Bobby Ray could react, she had gotten hold of his wrist. With a fierce grimace she snapped his middle finger back at an acute angle and broke it. Bobby Ray gripped his crippled right hand with his left and fell screaming to his knees.

Jonnie Prettyboy turned to the waitress. "Bonnie?" she said. "S'pose you could fix me up one of them white bread Spam sandwiches and a glass of water I could share with my dog?"

"That," Bonnie replied, "will be the fucking day."

CHAPTER FORTY-TWO

Keeper twisted the rheostat to slow the whistling Lionel as it approached the station, then further, until the O-gauge locomotive was in full reverse and the drive wheels were grinding against the silvery rails. The result was a rankling but not unpleasant ozone smell and a rash of sparks that reminded him of his father thumbing the Zippo for a light. *Damn* his father! It was *he* to blame for everything that had happened! He was sure his father was out looking for him at that very moment, but less sure his father had called home to say what had happened. He figured his father probably *hadn't*, because it would have been impossible to come up with a believable reason why their son had run away while on a much-anticipated road trip. He'd let his father stew in his own juices for awhile. Let *him* be the one to feel guilty for what happened. He deserved as much, if not more, for having been caught fucking the former Miss Georgia.

"Reckon you'll be movin' on wid de afternoon sun, Mistuh Keepuh?" Mr. Sam asked when he returned from helping Zinnia with the Mogen David transaction.

Keeper looked up from the Lionel and smiled expectantly. "If it's okay with you, Mr. Sam, I'd like to stay another day."

Mr. Sam pulled out a blue bandanna from his back pocket and blotted his brow while taking a seat on the edge of his bed. "If you is in some kind of trouble wid de law," he said, shaking his head, "Zinnia an' me, well, we dasn't be mixed up wid it."

"I'm not a crook," Keeper replied, "and I'm not in trouble either."

"Zinnia says you runnin' away from your daddy."

"I am."

Mr. Sam coughed wetly into the bandanna. "Sound's lak trouble to me."

Keeper leaned back in the rocker, folded his hands behind his head and drew in a deep breath. Ozone from the Lionel and Mr. Sam's bottled tonics lined up on a chest of drawers mingled with the ripe smell of ageing meat that came from the shop below. "It's my dad who's in trouble," he explained. "Not me."

Mr. Sam frowned. "If you don't mind me axe'n, Mistuh Keepuh, how old is you?"

"I'm almost fourteen."

Mr. Sam chuckled. "Boys run away from they momma when they seven, an' from daddy when they's sixteen, so you is right on schedule."

"Does that mean I can stay?" Keeper asked. "I won't be any trouble."

Mr. Sam glanced towards the photograph of himself as a young sleeping car porter. "You don't know a speck about the South, does you, Mistuh Keepuh?"

Keeper shook his head. "No, but I'm learning fast."

"Does you know about Jim Crow yet?"

"No sir."

Mr. Sam laughed, molasses-rich and deeply resonant. "Zinnia was right. You *is* from de North Pole! No white boy *ever* be callin' a black man 'sir' down here."

"Is he a Southerner, Jim Crow, I mean?" Keeper asked.

"Jim Crow ain't a 'he.' Jim Crow is lessons taught by white mens to black boys from the time they's old enough to walk."

"What kind of lessons, Mr. Sam?" Keeper asked, curious.

"The kind that keeps black mens from steppin' out of line."

"Could you get in trouble just by me being here?"

Mr. Sam didn't immediately answer, and instead got up to rummage through a mirrored chest of drawers. Finding a briarwood pipe and a pouch of burly, he returned to sit on the edge of his bed, opened the pouch, and dipped the pipe into it. He tamped the tobacco down with an arthritic thumb, lit the tobacco off a kitchen safety match taken from behind his ear, and replied in a soft voice,

"In the South, Mistuh Keepuh, trouble has a way of findin' folks whut ain't lookin' for it."

"I'd stay out of sight," Keeper said. "Then tomorrow I'll head out."

Mr. Sam closed his eyes and took a cheek-dimpling puff of fragrant burly. Smoke wreathed his head like fog over unpicked cotton. "Zinnia got a say in this, you know."

"Yes sir."

"Then go downstairs an' axe her."

Keeper pushed himself off the rocker and took the stairs down to the shop where Zinnia was swatting blue bottle flies off the meat case. Other dead and dying flies speckled the yellow curl of sticky flypaper dangling above it.

"You look lak you got sumpin' on your mind," Zinnia said with a suspicious look.

"Mr. Sam said to ask you if I can stay until tomorrow."

She waggled the swatter at Keeper and smiled to show her Chiclets teeth. "Is it Mr. Sam invitin', or is it Keeper Wick axing?"

"It's me asking, but he said you have a say in it."

"Since us only got two bedrooms, I reckon I would at that."

"Don't worry about me," Keeper said. "I can sleep on the floor."

Zinnia shyly looked away but held her smile. "Firs' white boy I ever gets 'quainted with, and right off the bat he axes if he can sleep over."

Keeper blushed. "I didn't mean it like that."

"Lak whut?"

"I don't know, like, I had something in mind."

She raised her brown eyes to meet Keeper's. "Does you?"

He blushed more hotly. "No," he replied, but her question caused him to wonder if he really had.

"Does you think colored gals is easy?" Zinnia said as she swung the swatter at a fat blue-black fly circling the meat case.

Keeper shook his head. "My girlfriend is half-Indian," he replied.

"Whut's de girlfren's other half?"

"Lithuanian, by her mother."

Zinnia frowned. "Whut's a Lithuanian?"

"I'm not sure. White, I know that."

"Is it de white side you fren's wid, or de Indian side?"

"I like them both," Keeper replied.

Zinnia swatted at another fly, this one preened itself on the chopping block next to the meat case. She flicked the dead insect at Keeper with the tip of her swatter. "Is her skin red lak Tonto's?"

Keeper laughed. "Maybe, a little bit."

Zinnia pulled herself erect and smoothed her dress to show her developing figure to its full effect. "I bet she's pretty, huh?"

"Yep," Keeper replied, but he was admiring Zinnia's figure and trying to remember exactly what Jonnie Prettyboy's face looked like.

"Whut's her name?"

"Jonnie Prettyboy."

Zinnia snorted behind her hand. "Sorry I axed."

"I suppose you'd like to know how old she is too."

"Old enough, I bet."

"Sixteen," Keeper replied. "How about you?"

"I'se the same."

"Do you have a boyfriend?"

Zinnia frowned. "Cleotus, but he's been gone to de army nearly a year now."

Keeper nodded, as if to acknowledge he understood her loneliness and concern for Cleotus. "So, can I stay?"

She raised the swatter and brought it down hard over two flies coupling on the meat case. "You got jammies in dat suitcase, Keeper Wick," she said, smiling, "or does all you North Pole boys sleep raw?"

CHAPTER FORTY-THREE

Chance pulled up in front of police headquarters and parked where he hoped the car and its attached demo trailer wouldn't be ticketed. He'd been scouring the streets for Keeper without a break, and he was beat. He rubbed his eyes wishing he had a drink. He hadn't called home since the day before, nor had he returned the many urgent messages Alva left for him at the Georgian Terrace Hotel. Instead of calling home with no news, he periodically stopped off at the police station hoping that they might have either found Keeper, or had gotten information, however slim, that might possibly lead to him.

Chance locked the car, lit a cigarette off his engraved Zippo, and turned for the stairs that led to the police station's main entrance. It was high noon and hot. By now he had become accustomed to the institutional sounds and smells inside the station house. Scalded coffee, stale cigarette smoke and the sour stink of men being questioned in cubicles by crime-hardened detectives wearing leather shoulder harnesses stained by sweat and neat's-foot oil. Chance heard the lieutenant calling his name before he saw him.

"Mr. Wick? A minute, please?"

He acknowledged the greeting with a half-wave and hurried to join the lieutenant who stood in his office doorway. Chance appeared hopeful, as if he expected to find his son standing in a corner like he wanted to surprise him and apologize for causing everyone so much trouble.

The lieutenant motioned for Chance to take a seat, then picked up a cup of black coffee off his desk and took a tentative swallow before setting it back down with a grimace. "I'd offer you a cup, Mr. Wick," he said, "but I'm afraid this dog piss might change your mind about our fabled Southern hospitality."

Chance nodded. "Thanks anyway, but about Keep..."

"We don't have your son as yet, Mr. Wick," the lieutenant interrupted, "but we have several reasons to believe he's still in the area."

"Care to share them with me?"

"Well, for one, we know he hasn't taken public transportation out of Atlanta."

"Have you considered he might have hitchhiked?"

"Would he have?"

Chance took a deep drag off his cigarette. "On second thought, maybe not. Keeper's a small-town boy and painfully shy, so it's unlikely he'd be thumbing rides with strangers."

"That's kind of what we figured."

"What else have you got?" Chance asked.

The lieutenant picked up his coffee cup, took a sip, and then carefully lowered the cup over an old coffee stain left on the desk's marred surface. "He was seen at the carnival last night."

Chance flared. "Your men saw my son but didn't pick him up?"

"Eyeball witnesses, Mr. Wick, not us. They were a hot dog vendor, a parolee who operates the Ferris wheel, and in particular a Lulu LaRue, who apparently wants to find your son as badly as you do."

"What did they say, for Christ's sake?"

The lieutenant seemed to think before answering. "Well, the hot dog vendor said he was an honest kid. The parolee said your boy loved riding the Ferris wheel so much he paid extra for the suitcase he carried, and the cooch said he kidnapped her Nubian slave."

Chance groaned and rubbed his eyes with tobacco-stained fingers. "I believe I'll have a cup of that dog piss after all."

"Sure thing, Mr. Wick," the lieutenant said agreeably. "Give me a couple of minutes to scare up a clean cup."

Chance stubbed out the last inch of his cigarette and immediately lit another while trying to imagine Keeper at the carnival. So close, yet so far as to be a thousand miles away. And what to make of him having kidnapped somebody; a Nubian slave, was it? Nothing made sense anymore, unless... He looked up when the lieutenant returned with the coffee. "Thanks anyway," Chance said, and with a quick look at his watch, stood to leave. "If you find Keeper, I can be reached at the Georgian Terrace Hotel. Meanwhile. I'll be chasing leads myself."

"Such as?"

Chance offered a grim smile. "For the first time in my life, I'm going to ride a Ferris wheel."

CHAPTER FORTY-FOUR

"What the fuck do you mean I'm under arrest?" Jonnie Prettyboy howled as the red-faced policeman ratcheted a pair of chrome-plated handcuffs around her thin wrists.

"When a nigra commits assault and battery against the person of a white man in Fulton County, his black ass goes to jail," the policeman said.

"It was him, that fat-assed Ku Klux son of a bitch over there who assaulted *me!*" Jonnie Prettyboy yelled. All the while she glared at a grinning Bobby Ray, who in spite of a broken finger, seemed to be enjoying himself.

"Shut 'yer mouth," the policeman snarled, "or it'll only go worse on you."

"I only wanted to eat a quiet lunch and get some water for a thirsty dog, until that cocksucker came along."

"Assault and battery, disturbing the peace, using profanity in a public place, and worse, eating where nigras don't belong. Any one will get you hard labor on the chain gang, three years easy," the policeman said.

Her breath came in ragged gasps. "I was minding my own business and waiting for the next bus. Ask that lady with the little girl what happened. She'll tell you."

As if on cue, the little girl peeked over the top of her booth and said, "That nigger used really bad words, an' then he broked that man's finger!"

Jonnie Prettyboy swore. "Aw, shit!"

The policeman pushed her through the café and out the front door into the bright sun toward a waiting black and white. The rankling smell of hot tar hung on the stifling humid air. Heat waves shimmered over freshly-paved roadway like a distant mirage and caused the tar wagon to appear as if it were floating in midair. The scruffy dog slowly raised its head and wagged its tail, *whap-whap-whap*, as they stumbled past.

In a single fluid motion, the policeman opened the cruiser's rear door with one hand and sent her sprawling onto the back seat with the other.

"Fucking cracker!" Jonnie Prettyboy shouted.

The policeman reached in to grab a handful of her sweat-matted black hair. He roughly twisted her neck until they were face-to-face and then punched her with a hard-knuckled fist, a short jab that split her upper lip and bloodied her nose.

"Goddamn you!" she sobbed.

The policeman grinned to show an even row of too-white teeth that contrasted with his ruddy pockmarked complexion. "How was you planning to pay for that lunch, boy?"

She ran her tongue over the split lip and glowered at the policeman with glittering pale gray eyes. "Fuck you!"

"I'll bet we can add vagrancy to the pending charges," he said. "Let's have us a look-see." With a grimace, the policeman pushed Jonnie Prettyboy onto her back and jammed his hands into her pants pockets.

"Don't!" she hissed.

The policeman thrust his hands even deeper, fumbling and probing with thick fingers. "What the fuck?" he muttered.

When policeman's right hand reached her sex, she clamped her knees together and bit down on her lip to stifle a cry.

"You born without a 'Bama black snake, Boy, or was it cut off by another nigra?" The policeman withdrew his hand and the fifteen dollars he'd found in Jonnie Prettyboy's pocket. With a grin he stuffed the bills into the shirt pocket that held his badge. "Just like I figured," he laughed. "A vagrant after all."

"Goddamn you!"

The policeman kept his left hand deep in Jonnie Prettyboy's other pocket and pressed his fingers hard against her vulva. "You want to declare any hidden weapons, boy," he laughed, "or are you gonna make it hard for me?"

She struggled to pull away from the grasping policeman. Blood bubbled from her nostrils and dribbled down her chin onto Keeper's borrowed shirt. "No more. Please."

The policeman fumbled more deeply, until coming up with the lucky charm Keeper had given to Jonnie Prettyboy, and turned it over between his fingers. "The fuck's this?" he asked.

She blinked. "It's a charm, for luck."

The policeman flipped the token in the air, caught it and slapped it over the back of his hand. "You lose."

"Please, let me…" Jonnie Prettyboy began, mumbling.

"Say, boy," the policeman said, interrupting. "Let's unbutton that nice shirt so's it don't get all bloody, what'd ya say?"

She pulled back and yanked fitfully against the handcuffs that kept her hands pinned behind her back, a futile act that thrust her breasts forward.

Grinning more widely than before, the policeman unbuttoned Jonnie Prettyboy's shirt down to the last button and opened the shirt to expose her brassiere and the half-moons of her breasts. He grunted, an animal sound deep in his throat. "'Pear's to me like we need a more thorough search before we book your ass downtown." The policeman grabbed a breast and squeezed it.

She gritted her teeth and kicked hard at his crotch. It was a glancing blow that missed her target, the obvious bulge in his pants, and instead caught him on the inside of his thigh.

The policeman howled in pain. "You'll pay now, bitch!" and gave Jonnie Prettyboy a final downward shove. He slammed the door shut and strode around the rear of the cruiser to the driver's-side door and slid behind the wheel. Pausing to adjust his cap in the rearview mirror, he started the cruiser and pulled away from the curb and onto the freshly-paved roadway with the rear wheels spinning.

She cringed at the sound of gravel rattling under the wheel wells next to her head and closed her eyes to the sickening smell of hot tar. Superheated air blasted through the open windows and buffeted her face, now sticky with congealing blood. It seemed as if the cruiser was rocketing backward in time and space, back to the terrible café and Bobby Ray, back even further, to Mr. Sam's Market and Keeper Wick, and further yet, back to the carnival where Miss Lulu LaRue waited for her with the biggest dildo of all.

CHAPTER FORTY-FIVE

Chance hadn't eaten since a complimentary breakfast of coffee and a donut taken at the Georgian Terrace Hotel before resuming his search for his son, and even a carnival hotdog sounded good now. He waited impatiently until the couple ahead of him paid for their foot-longs before giving his order to the vendor. "I'd like one regular hotdog with catsup and mustard."

The vendor looked up from his grill. "Onions an' piccalilli too?"

"No piccalilli."

"One loaded dog no pick' comin' up."

The sounds and colorful sights of the bustling midway were lost on Chance. Instead, he wondered what Keeper might have been thinking on the night he was here, alone, scared, and on the run.

The vendor held out the loaded hotdog on a square of waxed paper. "That'll be two bits, mister."

Chance dug into his pocket and fished out a quarter, and inadvertently, the well-worn lucky charm he always carried, the one that matched Keeper's. As he ate, he realized his son had probably stood on this very same spot eating *his* hotdog, but with what? He realized he had absolutely no idea what Keeper liked on his hotdogs.

He turned back to the vendor. "I'd like to know if you remember a certain kid who was here last night."

"Are you shittin' me, buddy? I see three hundred fuckin' kids a night."

"This one you might remember. You trusted him enough to let him have a hotdog solely on his promise of paying you later."

The vendor scratched his head, a scowl creasing his sweating, sunburned face, until brightening. "He carried a suitcase and had a ten spot I couldn't break."

"That was him, my son."

The vendor seemed unimpressed. "You don't say so."

"I'm curious," Chance said. "How did he take his hotdog?"

"Like he was starving, is how he took it."

"I mean, what did he want on it?"

The vendor shrugged. "Ask him."

Chance nodded. "You've been a great help." Trying not to lose more onions off the hotdog he was devouring, he elbowed his way through the shifting throng toward the Ferris wheel, until the melodic tootling of a calliope drew his attention and caused him to alter course toward the merry-go-round. He stood outside the low picket fence that kept anyone who hadn't paid from jumping on for a free ride and watched the elaborately carved horses as they galloped in place.

White and black stallions with wild manes, flaring nostrils and glassy eyes plunged up and down on gleaming brass poles polished by generations of riders. He wondered if Keeper had ridden one of them – alone among strangers with his anger and solitary thoughts. Barely recognizing the guilt he felt, he turned away from the merry-go-round and headed for the Ferris wheel, a ride he knew Keeper *had* taken.

Chance approached the elaborately tattooed and deeply tanned carnie operating the giant wheel. "Excuse me," he said loud enough to be heard over the racketing engine that powered the ride. "I'm looking for a boy who rode your wheel last night."

The carnie scowled. "You another cop?"

"No, I'm the boy's father."

The carnie spat. "What's it worth to know?"

"Suppose you tell me?"

"Five bucks."

"Chance shook his head. "I call that highway robbery."

The carnie turned away. "Call it anything you want, bud."

"Wait," Chance called, and reached for his money clip. He peeled off the outside bill, a five spot, and handed it to the carnie. "He's thirteen, rather shy, gawky, with blue eyes and sandy hair. Oh, and freckles."

"Fuck me if that don't describe near every white kid in Fulton County."

"This one carried a suitcase."

The carnie gave a toothless grin of recognition. "Paid extra for the suitcase and rode the wheel for eight minutes."

Chance pressed on, eager to learn more. "Did he say where he might be headed?"

The carnie shook his head and turned his attention to the brake lever an arm's length away. He yanked it against his belly and held it there until the Ferris wheel slowed to a complete stop before answering. "Didn't say, didn't ask."

"Nothing else?" Chance asked when the engine fell to an idle.

The carnie shrugged. "Well, since he was runnin' away, I wished him happy trails."

"That was kind of you," Chance replied softly. He stood aside as the carnie unhooked the safety bar on the first car before allowing its occupants to get off; a soldier in uniform and the busty overly-perfumed peroxide blond with him. Chance turned to follow her with his eyes until the carnie snapped his fingers for attention.

"Hey buddy. You lookin' or ridin'?"

Chance stepped forward and held out another five dollar bill, "Take me up until this runs out."

The carnie took the bill and said, "No standin' and no rockin' the car. Got it?"

Chance nodded and stepped into the car that still smelled faintly of perfume. He gripped the safety bar while the carnie sequenced the Ferris wheel car-by-car, discharging riders and taking on others until the car was swinging back and forth far above the midway. He looked down, as if expecting to see Keeper had come back, suitcase in hand and waiting to board the next car.

The uneven wail of an approaching siren caught his attention, and he prayed to an indifferent God that it had nothing to do with his son. He tightened his grip on the safety bar as the Ferris wheel lurched forward and downward, carrying him toward a destination that would end exactly where it began. Nowhere.

CHAPTER FORTY-SIX

The dog days of summer that held Dakota Straits in its suffocating embrace seemed to never end. For weeks, the sultry and oppressively humid weather slowed life to a sluggish pace more typical of Equatorial climes than the American Midwest.

Alva had opened every screened window that wasn't painted shut in hopes of catching the slightest breath of cooler air coming off the big lake. Each morning before the sun got too hot to tolerate, she set out the yard sprinklers to keep the grass from turning brown. The repetitive sputtering as they rotated seemed to have a soothing, even cooling effect, and helped calm her nerves. Still, her latest attempt to reach Chance by phone at the Georgian Terrace Hotel thirty minutes earlier had again proved frustratingly unsuccessful.

Feeling more defeated than ever, she sat alone at the kitchen table watching two robins as they probed for worms in the victory garden. There, above the even rows of sweet corn, tomatoes, carrots, radishes and snap peas, a brilliant arcing rainbow caused by the jetting sprinklers shimmered in the still air. Ordinarily, Alva would have taken the rainbow as a positive sign. If not the proverbial pot of gold waiting at its end, at least there would be four-leaf clovers to be found – and with them word that Keeper was alive and well. To think otherwise was not an option.

She idly glanced at her watch, as if it could tell her more than simply the time. There hadn't been an airmail letter from her brother, Neil, for over two months. She focused on her Navy corpsman brother because doing so was only slightly less worrisome than thinking about Keeper. She tried consoling herself with the old adage that no news was good news, and knowing otherwise, turned on the radio to listen to Don McNeil's Breakfast Club for the distraction it offered.

Alva was smoking in earnest again, a pack of Old Golds daily. Now she was on her fifth cigarette since waking, and drinking rationed coffee taken black and unsweetened. Sleep was elusive and came only after playing solitaire into the late hours of the night until the cards blurred before her eyes. She also needed to keep her ears open in case Dr. Wick called from his room, needing assistance for one goddamned thing or another. It was almost like having a baby in the house, feeding him pureed vegetables and fruit taken from the victory garden, and having to bath him, sometimes with the help of Early, but more often not. Only the day before, Dr. Wick had wandered away from the house to the old horse barn. Alva discovered him there, seated behind the wheel of his Hupmobile. He was naked and discussing the weather with his long-dead wife, Winifred.

Alva tried to remember the last time she'd been out of the house, and then recalled a Saturday matinee she'd attended with Keeper. He'd been pestering his father to take him to see John Wayne in *The Fighting Seabees*. Chance was drunk again and refused, saying it was a waste of precious time while off the road. She hadn't much minded. She was desperate to get out anyway, even if it was to see a war movie.

Truth be told, she knew there was no real need *to* go out. She didn't know how to drive anyway, and didn't dare leave Dr. Wick and Early alone in the big house, Matson's market was delivering groceries once every week, to include her Old Golds as needed, and the bottle of Gordon's gin she had developed a taste for.

Alva's thoughts turned to the idea of taking a welcome bath – a long soothing bath in cool water and just the tonic to restore her flagging spirits. Dr. Wick was in his room sleeping after eating a surprisingly large breakfast, and Early was tuning at St. Jerome's, thereby allowing some precious time to herself. She stubbed out the cigarette and hurried through the quiet house to the stairs and took them up to the bedroom she shared with Chance. She was grateful to see that the lace curtains hanging in the open windows fluttered like luffing sails in a lazy breeze coming off the lake. Humming tunelessly, she entered the bathroom and opened the tub's cold water faucet. While waiting for it to fill, she returned to the bedroom to undress.

Now naked and feeling uncommonly vulnerable, Alva stood in front of the full-length mirror mounted on the closet door. She stared at her reflection critically, as if apprising a total stranger who was gray-haired and pale-skinned like her, but with no stretch marks to betray the fact she once carried a child. The stranger's breasts were small-ish like hers, with nipples resembling rose buds. They sagged a little, something to be expected of a woman who would turn fifty on her next birthday. Still, the legs were shapely enough. Alva ran her hands over a still-flat stomach, then down to a pubis thick with curly brown hair. She smiled and the stranger smiled back – as if confirming their shared desirability. She wondered – would Chance approve of this stranger?

She broke away with a gasp upon remembering that the bathtub was probably about to overflow, and quickly turned for the bathroom to turn off the tap. Relieved to have caught it in time, she unwrapped the bar of Ivory soap she'd been hoarding and stepped into the tub. Hesitantly at first, she slowly lowered herself until the water reached her breasts. Grateful for the wonderfully soothing and nearly weight-less sensation, she closed her eyes and allowed herself to relax. The muted sounds of screeching gulls and the shouts of children playing at the beach carried through the open window behind her. With a contented sigh, Alva lowered herself even further, until her ears were underwater and her prematurely gray hair floated over her shoulders like bleached seaweed.

It was as if she were in her own small archipelago, complete with uninhabited islands and a Sargasso Sea. The bar of Ivory floated like a white raft between her breasts. The only sound now was the slow and regular beat of her heart, a distant drum in her ears going: *lub dub...lub dub...lub dub.* If she could will it to happen, she would allow the stranger to stay submerged forever, unable to hear any unwelcome knock at the door, no whimpering cry for help from the senile Dr. Wick, not even the shrill ring of the downstairs telephone that lately carried only bad news, and which at that very moment *was* ringing.

CHAPTER FORTY-SEVEN

Keeper returned the receiver to its cradle, puzzled as to why someone hadn't answered the telephone. Even Early sometimes picked up if Alva was otherwise occupied, and he'd let it ring maybe a dozen times.

"Nobody tuh home, Mistuh Keepuh?"

"There's always somebody home, Mr. Sam," Keeper replied. "*Always.*"

"Mebby dey's out of earshot."

"No, something's wrong, I know it."

"Why is it you white folks always be thinkin' the worst?"

"We do?"

Mr. Sam grinned and nodded. "An' tighter'n a bull's asshole 'roun' a beehive, too, worried sumpin might fly in an' set up house keepin'."

Keeper laughed. "They're probably outside in the victory garden."

"Who's they?" Zinnia asked.

"My mom and half-brother, Early."

Zinnia frowned. "Like in the early bird catches the worm?"

"Right."

"How old is 'early bird,' anyway?" Zinnia asked.

Keeper grinned at Zinnia's play on words. "Thirty-four."

"A growed up man named Early, an' he ain't changed his name yet?"

"Could be he likes it."

"Sounds like a nigra name to me," she said derisively.

"I guess it does sound colored. He also happens to be blind."

"Does he beg wid a cup an' pencils?"

"No, he tunes pianos."

Zinnia seemed to think. "Whut about your daddy's name, I'se skee-red to axe."

"Chance," Keeper replied, giggling because he knew what to expect.

Zinnia collapsed with laughter, a high-pitched whinny accompanied by her bare feet slapping on the shop's plank floor. "Fat chance, take a chance, or a snowball's chance in hell?"

"Just plain Chance," Keeper replied.

"I declare," Mr. Sam said, chuckling.

Zinnia laughed so hard tears streamed down her ebony cheeks. "Lawd have mercy! Dast I axe your momma's name, too?"

Keeper couldn't help himself. He was having more fun now than he could remember. "Zucchini."

She let out a war whoop of laughter. "Your momma's named after a *vegetable?*"

"So what?" Keeper replied. "*You're* named after a plant."

Zinnia seemed to settle down. "Zinnia's are pretty. Is your momma pretty?"

Keeper had to think before answering. What he remembered from the old black and white photographs in his mother's scrapbook, he'd guessed she *had* been pretty once. Now, she was just his mother, and thirteen-year old boys rarely considered the relative attractiveness of their parents. "I guess so," he replied, lamely. "I mean, she's old."

Zinnia smiled. "Whut about me, Mr. 'Finders Keepers, Losers Weepers'? Does you think I'm pretty?" She straightened and thrust out her breasts, and then with an elaborately provocative gesture, she smoothed her clinging cotton dress over her hips. "Huh?" she asked, staring Keeper in the eye. "Is I?"

He blushed. "Yeah," he gulped, "I mean, sure."

"Now, Zinnia," Mr. Sam said, "you be leavin' Mistuh Keepuh alone. 'For you knows it, you'll be forgettin' they's a Cleotus off fightin' a war for you."

"I ain't heard from Mr. Cleotus in so long, I'se thinkin' he's found hisself one of them sex-diseased French gals to shack wid."

"Hush, chile," Mr. Sam warned. "Cleotus could be layin' in a hospital somewheres, wounded in action an' unable to write."

"Speakin' of layin'," Zinnia said, "Finders Keepers is layin' wid us tonight."

"I'll take the couch," Keeper quickly added. He'd already noted the layout of the tidy upstairs apartment, which included a kitchenette, a living room that boasted a garish Rococo-style couch covered in clear plastic, three matching chairs, also protected with clear plastic, and a folding-leaf dining table with four wooden chairs. There was one bathroom with a single sink and tub, and two small bedrooms, the biggest of which had a railroad track running around it.

"You is gonna take my bed," Zinnia offered with a sly smile. "Ain't often we gets overnight company, 'specially a boy comes down from de North Pole."

"I couldn't let you do that," Keeper replied.

Mr. Sam took a thoughtful puff off his pipe and solemnly shook his head. "Zinnia puts her mind to sumpin', ain't no changin' it."

"Dat's right, *'Finders Keepers,'*" she said with an air of great finality. "Ain't no changin' it a' 'tall, oncet it's set." As if for emphasis, she flattened another hapless fly that had come within striking distance of her deadly swatter.

Keeper turned at the sound of the screen door slamming shut and watched as two young colored men entered the shop. Each wore a high-waisted maroon zoot suit with baggy trousers pegged at the ankles and long draped coats. They also wore matching broad-brimmed pork-pie hats, long gold chains fastened to their belts, and pointy yellow shoes.

"Mr. Sam, my man!" the first one exclaimed, grinning and slapping his hands together.

Mr. Sam seemed clearly annoyed. "Who let you fools out? he asked.

"Why, is that anyway to greet a valued customer?" the man replied.

"Maybe Mr. Sam's forgotten the courtesies learned when he was shinin' white folks' shoes on the railroad," the second man said.

"Shut up, Oliver," Zinnia said.

"Well, if you ain't lookin' fetchin' today, Miss Zinnia," the first man said, cupping his crotch. "I'll bet ol' Cleotus be missin' his home front action right about now!"

"You shut up too, Leroy."

"Goodness me," Leroy replied in mock dismay, "such disharmony!"

"And such hostility, too," Oliver chimed in.

"Get out, both of you," Mr. Sam growled.

Leroy turned to Keeper like he'd noticed him for the first time and leaned in close. "The fuck you lookin' at cracker boy?"

"Nu, nothing," Keeper stammered.

"You lost, boy?" Leroy asked accusingly, "or did your momma 'bandon you 'cause you're so fuckin' dog ugly?"

"Leave him be," Zinnia said crossly. "He ain't done nothin' to you."

"He's a cracker, ain't he?" Oliver replied. "Give him time."

"I'll ask you hoodlums one more time," Mr. Sam said. "Get out an' leave us alone or…"

"Or you'll call the po'lice?" Leroy interrupted, laughing. "Go ahead. Me an' Oliver here will wait so's we can tell 'em how you is sellin' black market cigarettes an' bootleg liquor from under the counter."

"I think Mr. Sam's meat ain't lookin' too fresh, neither," Oliver added, sniffing the air with a look of distain. "Maybe it's high time the health inspector comes a'callin'."

"Jive-ass niggers!" Zinnia cried. "Take whut you want an' get!"

Leroy flashed a smile that displayed a prominent gold tooth. "Hear that, Oliver? he said. "Zinnia says to take whut we need."

Oliver turned to Mr. Sam. "Is that cool by you, Uncle Tom?"

Mr. Sam looked down at his feet. "Do like she says."

Leroy sauntered to the cigarette case and removed two cartons of black market Chesterfields, while Oliver grabbed two fifths of bootlegged Jack Daniels and put them both in a paper bag. Leroy added the Chesterfields, then turned to Keeper, said, "Take my advice, you dog-ugly fuck. Don't let the sun set on your cracker ass here."

CHAPTER FORTY-EIGHT

Chance was feeling unsettled after twenty minutes on the Ferris wheel, and the hotdog he'd taken with onions churned uneasily in his stomach. When he stepped away from the wheel and back into the jostling crowd he allowed himself to be swept toward the tent of Miss Lulu LaRue, where a derby-hatted barker announced the next show through a cardboard megaphone.

"Laaaadies and gentlemen!" the barker shouted. "Next show starts in ten minutes! Learn what Egyptian King Farouk paid a queen's ransom to see! Only three American dollars! Step riiiiight up!"

It occurred to Chance that Keeper might have stood at this very spot waiting to see something he had no damned business seeing. Yet he had to admit that however bad it was, it couldn't have been worse than what Keeper saw him doing with Honey Burnside.

The barker pointed at Chance. "How about it, mister? Pony up three bucks, or step aside."

Chance's cigarette dangled from his lips as he dug for the silver money-clip in his pocket and peeled off three singles. He handed the bills to the barker and left to follow several others into the canvas tent. He selected a seat in the front row and waited while more customers filed into the tent amid ribald laughter and jokes over the probability of Miss LaRue being an insatiable nymphomaniac. A Marine master sergeant in dress blues wondered aloud if the Shetland pony giving nickel rides to children across the midway also serviced Miss LaRue.

A sallow-faced man on crutches with a withered left foot dangling from the pant leg of his bib-overalls said nothing of the sort would be allowed in Mississippi, but added he'd gladly kick in to see such a thing happen. As for Chance, all he wanted was for Miss LaRue to allow him a few minutes after her cooch show to answer a few questions about Keeper.

He folded his arms, crossed his legs and leaned back in his seat to wait for Miss LaRue to take the stage. The sour smell of red-faced, tobacco-chewing men who came to leer and fantasize over having sex with the overly-ripe Miss Lulu LaRue – pony or no pony, filled the tent.

When a two-man band stirred into action with an off-key rendition of Glenn Miller's popular tune, *American Patrol*, Miss LaRue came mincing on-stage in a pair of high-heeled red shoes and net stockings rolled to the crotch. The sparkly top hat complimented the red, white and blue feather boas and tasseled pasties that spun and sparkled under the spotlights. Being patriotic, Miss LaRue waved two small American flags, and after ten minutes of teasing the restless audience, she turned and disappeared behind the Mail Pouch curtain. Amidst jeers and cat-calls, the barker returned to the stage with the announcement, that for an addition contribution of five dollars, a special performance for men only would immediately follow.

Chance fumbled for his money clip and grudgingly paid the five dollars to see what was so damned special. It wasn't long in coming, with the remaining men paying rapt attention while a Negro dwarf dressed as a Nubian slave came out from behind the curtain carrying a red velvet pillow, upon which rested a glistening black sex toy.

If this was what Keeper had seen, Chance wanted no knowledge or reminder of it. To the cries of, "Sit down, asshole!" he got up and hurried for the tent's exit. He needed time to think, and once outside he took a deep breath. What if the carnies had lied to the police about Keeper running off with their Nubian slave? Maybe the two were being held against their will, to be groomed for carnival life. Now, more than ever, Chance needed to confront Lulu LaRue, and probably her barker too. He reached for a cigarette and lit it, prepared to wait until her cooch show was over.

After grinding out the fifth cigarette thirty minutes later, he made his way to the back of Lulu LaRue's tent, where the red Lincoln V-12 and Airstream trailer he'd seen from the Ferris wheel were parked. No harm in snooping around while waiting for the show to end. It was nearly dark, the sky now gone to a deep lavender-blue. Low clouds caught the last crimson flash of a dying sun just as the midway lights blazed to life. The glittering pin-wheeling lights of the nearby Ferris wheel reflected off the highly-polished hood of the V-12 Lincoln, but less so off the salt-pitted carapace of the aluminum-skinned Airstream. Chance cautiously approached the trailer and tried the doors. They were locked, except for the right rear door, which he opened. He leaned into the Lincoln's baking hot interior and recoiled at the nose-rankling smell of cheap perfume and stale cigar smoke.

"What the fuck do you think you're doing, buddy?" The raspy voice came low and menacing from behind.

Chance slowly straightened and turned to see the cooch-show barker standing between him and the Airstream. The barker held a cigar clenched between his teeth and a baseball bat in his fists. Miss LaRue stood a safe distance behind the barker, as if waiting to see what developed. The leopard-skin robe she wore was moth-eaten. Chance held his hands palms forward, as if to show he meant no harm. The calliope sounded far-off, and the midway muted.

The barker advanced, bat held high in his fists. "You're looking to steal the Lincoln, ain't you?"

Lulu giggled nervously. "Beat the shit out of him, Vincent."

"I'm not stealing anything," Chance protested. "I'm looking for my son, who ran away the night before last."

The barker waggled the bat. "Runaways come through here ever fucking day."

"I'm willing to pay for any information that might lead to him."

The bat wavered. "How much?"

Chance lowered his hands. It was like being asked to place a price on Keeper's head. "Will five do?"

Miss LaRue shifted in place and folded her arms under her drooping breasts. "Beat the Holy Jesus out of him, Vince honey."

"Shut up, Lulu," the barker snapped without taking his eyes off Chance. "Make it twenty, and we'll talk."

"Twenty it is," Chance replied, and added, "Suppose we can move our conversation into your trailer?"

The barker lowered the bat and pulled out a key from his pants pocket and turned to unlock the Airstream's door. "Inside," he beckoned, "and no funny business."

Lulu went first, followed by Chance and then Vincent, who still clutched the bat in his fist. It was fiercely-hot inside the Airstream. Cursing loudly, Lulu switched on a table tamp before cranking open a ceiling vent and four jalousie windows to let out the heat.

Vincent snapped his fingers. "The money," he growled.

Chance shoved his hand into the pocket where kept the silver money clip. He dug it out and flipped through the tightly-folded bills until finding two tens and separated them from the others. Wordlessly, he held the money toward Vincent while looking askance at Lulu busying herself in the galley. "His name is Keeper."

"Don't mean shit to me."

"He's thirteen, tall for his age, with freckles, blue eyes and sandy hair."

"Throw a fucking rock out the door, you'll hit somebody looks like that."

Chance shifted his gaze toward Lulu pouring herself a bourbon and Coke over ice in a tall tumbler. He licked his lips. "Suppose that twenty could buy me a taste?"

"Don't see why not, now that we understand each other."

"Let him get his own fucking drink," Lulu shot back. "My pussy's sore and I've been on my feet all goddamned day!"

"I'll get it," Chance said, and joined Lulu in the small galley. Her loosely-tied robe fell open to expose sagging breasts and stretch-marked skin. If she noticed, she made no effort to cover herself, and pressed her breasts against Chance when she turned to join Vincent in the forward section of the Airstream.

Too exhausted and filled with guilt to be aroused, Chance helped himself to a lipstick-smeared tumbler on the drain board and poured in three fingers of Lulu's warm bourbon. He drank it in a single gulp, winced at the burn when it went down, and then rejoined Lulu and Vincent. "It was my son who interrupted your show last night."

"You've got a fucking nerve coming around here," Lulu snarled. "Punk not only broke up my act, he took my Nubian with him."

"I'd 'a stopped 'em," Vincent added, "'cept some swabby got inna way."

"Somebody must have seen where they went."

Vincent struck a match to relight the cigar that had gone out. "If anybody had, I'd 'a got the Nubian back by now."

"Her description might help me find them."

Lulu snorted into her drink. "Bitch in her mid-teens, skin almost like a high-yellow nigra, with short black hair and the godamnedest pale gray eyes you ever seen. Passed herself off as a fucking boy named Jack, 'till I figured it out."

Chance sighed and stood to leave. "Unless there's anything else..."

Vincent held up a meaty, calloused hand to interrupt. "You find that cock-tease Nubian, you'll likely find your kid too. Bring her back, and I'll pay you a hundred clams, no questions asked."

"Just like that, huh?"

Vincent grinned. "Just like that."

"I've got a question, Vince," Chance said. "How the hell does a guy like you live with himself?"

Vincent laughed. "If I knew why your kid ran away, I might be asking you the same question."

CHAPTER FORTY-NINE

It was dark and a light rain was falling when Jonnie Prettyboy opened her eyes. She lay on her back, sprawled among the kudzu where she could see the Big Dipper and the North Star through a gap in the cloud cover. With a gut-wrenching groan, she propped herself up on an elbow, turned her head and vomited until the dry heaves came. Where was she? She remembered the policeman stopping in the country somewhere, then dragging her out of the black and white, after which everything shattered into splinters of kudzu green, sky blue and red Georgia clay. Before everything went black, she remembered smelling Sen-Sen on his hot breath.

She touched her nose and split lip, both swollen and sticky with congealed blood. She hurt between her legs, and except for the too-small brassiere and Keeper's donated Keds and socks, she was naked. Her undershorts hung on a vine beyond her outstretched feet, the torn and bloody shirt dangled from a low branch to her left. The khaki shorts lay in a tangled heap just beyond her head. The sound of a passing car instantly raised her hopes of getting help. She struggled to her feet, retrieved the shirt and slipped into it. Fighting nausea, she reached for her undershorts, stepped into them and pulled them up over her legs.

With desperation overcoming her fear of the cop who raped her coming back, she set off through the sodden undergrowth toward the sound of another passing car, then cursed when she arrived too late to flag it down. Then the sound of another vehicle approaching, a truck, and loud. Its single dim headlight winked like a yellow semaphore through breaks in the kudzu. She stepped to the middle of the road and waved her arms. "Stop!" she sobbed. "Please, goddamnit. *Stop!*"

The truck, a battered stake model with canvas stretched over the back, skidded sideways on the rain-slick red clay. Its rear brakes squealed and locked up the wheels. When the truck finally came to a juddering halt, Jonnie Prettyboy stood in the single headlight's low beam and only inches away from the steaming radiator.

"You crazy?" The man's voice quavered. "I could'a killed you!"

She staggered to the driver's side and looked up with pleading eyes. "Please," she gasped. "You gotta help me."

The driver squinted to make out her features. "What is you anyways? Boy or girl?" The panel lights were dim but sufficient to illuminate his nut-brown face and knotted, work-scarred hands that still gripped the steering wheel.

"Take your pick," she replied, "But right now what I need is a ride the hell away from here."

The driver leaned from his window to better assess the clearly injured person who was standing alone in the road next to his truck. "You some kind of mulatto?"

"Yeah, now, can I hitch a ride?"

"I 'spose its okay," he replied, and reached across the cab to open the right-side door.

Without giving the driver time to change his mind, Jonnie Prettyboy limped past the yellow headlight and steaming radiator and climbed into the cab. She pushed aside a grease-stained paper bag smelling of fried chicken and sat down. The seat was still warm from whatever was in the bag.

"Is you in some kind of trouble?" the driver asked as he ground the transmission into low gear.

"I was," she replied, "but not as much as a certain fucking cop is gonna be."

"I'd sooner you doesn't curse," the driver said. "I'm a Pentecostal man."

"Sorry," she mumbled. Her head snapped painfully back when the driver stepped on the gas to send the unmuffled truck lurching down the rutted red clay road. For the first time since leaving Keeper (how long had it been, she wondered), Jonnie Prettyboy finally allowed herself to relax and closed her eyes to the almost comforting sound of the exhaust pipe roaring beneath her feet.

"You'se a girl, ain't you?"

She inhaled deeply of the fried chicken smell. "Yeah."

"Dast I ask what happened to you?"

"No."

The driver bent over his steering wheel, straining to see ahead of the bouncing yellow beam. "You'uns hungry?"

"No."

"You won't mind if I have myself a bite of supper?"

"Go ahead."

The driver reached into the greasy bag and retrieved a chicken thigh, plump and breaded, and held in front of Jonnie Prettyboy's face. "You sure you ain't hungry?"

Her mouth watered – her resolve melted. "How many you got?"

"Enuff."

"Maybe one, then."

"Hep yourself," the driver replied. "They's Cora's homemade cornbread too."

She put her hand in the bag and traced her fingertips over still-warm pieces of chicken and cut squares of moist cornbread. She wrapped her fingers around half a chicken breast and silently held it up as if it were a prize.

The driver smiled encouragingly. "Go ahead."

Jonnie Prettyboy greedily bit into the crusty breading and flakey-moist white meat. She chewed with her mouth open, ignoring the sting of seasoning on her split lip, and ate until only the ribs, cartilage, and keel bone remained. When she was finished, she flipped the carcass out her open window and then licked her fingers.

"Been some time since you las' fed, has it?" the driver asked.

"Couple days, I guess."

"Have some cornbread while you're at it."

Now that her hunger had been established, she didn't need to be asked twice, and reached for a thick-cut square, which she consumed in four bites.

"Lan' sakes!" the driver exclaimed, laughing. "I best watch my fingers 'roun' you!"

Jonnie Prettyboy allowed herself a tentative smile and a soft greasy belch. "That was good," she said, dabbing her mouth on the bloody sleeve of Keeper's donated shirt. "Thanks."

"I'se got coffee."

"I'd like that."

The driver fumbled under his seat and produced a thermos and handed it to Jonnie Prettyboy. "They's more cups under the cap. Take whichever size you want."

She unscrewed the top cap, pulled out the cork and set it and the nested cups aside. Without being asked, she half-filled the bigger cap with coffee and handed it to the driver.

"They's sweet cream in it," the driver cautioned, "'case you takes it black."

"Fine as it is," she replied. After pouring herself a cup with shaking hands, she blew across it before taking a tentative sip.

With the cup held firmly in his left hand and doing his best to steer with his left knee, the driver extended a calloused right hand. "Otis," he said simply, by way of introduction.

She hesitated – as if wanting to push back the memory of another man's fist, until taking the extended hand. "Jonnie Prettyboy."

"You ain't from 'roun' here, is you?"

"No."

Otis nodded. "You'uns not black, is you?"

"Indian on my pa's side, Lithuanian on the other."

Otis chuckled. "They's a case for avoiding hard liquor, if I ever heerd one."

Jonnie Prettyboy took another slurp of cream-sweetened coffee. "You got a cigarette on you, Mr. Otis?"

Otis chuckled again. He pulled out a pack of Kools from a pocket in his bib overalls and held it toward Jonnie Prettyboy. "Menthol," he said. "Not to everybody's taste, but you is welcome to have one."

She took the pack, tapped out a cigarette and placed in the corner of her mouth furthest from the split lower lip.

As if anticipating her next request, Otis produced a safety match from behind his ear, struck it off the dashboard and held it under the dangling Kools. "You' ain't said where you is goin', but I'se headed to town with a load of produce from Cora's truck garden."

Jonnie Prettyboy took a deep drag off her cigarette. "I was going downtown anyway."

Otis nodded. "You doesn't need to say, but does your troubles concern a colored man?"

"White. A white cop I'm gonna find if it takes me the rest of my life."

"Merciful Lord Jesus!" Otis exclaimed. "You doesn't stand a chance goin' up against a white man wearin' a badge 'roun' here! Don't matter *whut* he done!"

"You think so, Mr. Otis? Soon's we get to Atlanta, drop me off within walking distance of any police station. "Then we'll see about that."

"They's an old saying that goes, 'Revenge, at first thought sweet, bitter ere long back on itself recoils.' I'd caution you to think long and hard on that, Miss."

"Thanks, Mr. Otis, but I've been thinking about nothing else since early afternoon." What Jonnie Prettyboy couldn't allow herself to think about, beyond exacting revenge, was the likelihood of having been knocked up by a rogue, racist cop.

CHAPTER FIFTY

Keeper swabbed his plate clean with the last of Zinnia's cornbread and leaned back in his chair with a satisfied smile. "I've never had liver with bacon and onions before," he said. "I'm going to ask my mom to make it, especially the cornbread."

He caught an approving glance from Zinnia, who had earlier changed into a dark-blue cotton dress with a frilly white lace collar interwoven with a red satin ribbon. The dress made her appear as if she were attending a birthday party. She had also gotten rid of the spiky pigtails. Now her hair was combed back in glossy-black waves highlighted by two flickering candles placed at the center of Mr. Sam's dinner table.

Mr. Sam offered Keeper a contented smile. "Zinnia can pencil down the cornbread recipe, 'case your momma don't know how it's done."

"My mom will know how, I think."

"Not if she don't use bacon, cheddar cheese an' lard, she won't," Zinnia said.

Mr. Sam chuckled and took a generous sip of the bourbon over ice he'd been nursing. The drink was nearly gone now, and the ice melted down to three jellybean-sized nuggets. "They's peach cobbler for dessert, Mistuh Keepuh, assumin' you've got room on top of them four pieces of cornbread."

Keeper rubbed his belly and laughed. "I'll make room."

Zinnia pushed her chair away from the table, "I'll get it, Gran' pap."

"Thank you, Granddaughter," he said, and turned to Keeper with a concerned expression. "Mistuh Keepuh. I ain't one to impose on company, but oughtn't you be tryin' tuh call home again? Your people got to be terrible worried."

"I will, just as soon as I help out with the dishes."

"Zinnia don't need no hep with the dishes."

"Say's who?" she asked as she returned from the kitchen. She carried three china plates heaped with brown-crusted, nutmeg-sprinkled peach cobbler, and vanilla ice cream on the side.

"Mistuh Keepuh is our guest," he replied, "an' guests don't do dishes."

Keeper protested. "But, I always help out at home."

"In that case, s'pose you kin fix me up a fresh bourbon over ice?"

He was pleased to accommodate the old man. "Coming right up."

He handed the glass tumbler to Keeper. "The fixin's in the kitchen, an' the ice is where you'd 'spect it to be."

"You need any heppin' out, Keeper?" Zinnia asked with a sly grin.

"I can manage," he replied, and got up to leave for the kitchen. He found a nearly full bottle of Early Times "fixin's" next to the sink that had peach skins in it. He was surprised to see Mr. Sam wasn't kidding. They did have an icebox; a cabinet made of solid oak with chrome hinges. He opened the door where he guessed the ice would be kept and found a block of ice big as a milk crate slowly melting in the zinc-clad compartment, but no ice pick.

"Ice pick is in the second draw' to your right," Mr. Sam called from the dining room.

Smiling at his apparent ability to know exactly what he was doing, Keeper pulled open the drawer that held miscellaneous kitchen utensils, including the ice pick, and a snub-nosed ivory-handled derringer. He ran his fingers over the grip, feeling the smooth warmth of the ivory, and wondered if Mr. Sam had meant for him to find it.

"It's loaded, Mistuh Keepuh," he called from the dining room. "Dasn't be touchin' it, less you is plannin' on shootin' somethin'."

With a grin, Keeper reached for the ice pick, chipped a handful of splinters off the block and dropped them into Mr. Sam's drinking glass before pouring in two fingers of Early Times.

"One more finger will do jes' fine," Mr. Sam said, laughing.

Keeper returned with the finger-added drink, and with exaggerated ceremony, placed it in front of the old man.

"Thank you, Mistuh Keepuh. If you was a Negro, I'd say there was a bright future for you with the Pullman Company."

"Thanks, I guess. My dad takes his booze straight too, but without the ice."

"Your daddy's a drinkin' man, is he?"

Keeper nodded. The memory of his father and Honey Burnside fucking was still too fresh, too painful, and it hurt worse than any injury or illness. Even the mumps.

Mr. Sam raised his glass and took a careful sip before speaking. "Does he take more'n what's good for him, maybe?"

"Yes sir," Keeper mumbled. Unable to avoid Zinnia's questioning gaze, he returned to his seat and silently began devouring his peach cobbler, but stopped when sudden tears blurred his vision.

"See whut you done now, Gran' pap?" Zinnia scolded.

He scowled. "Ain't did nuthin' but axe a question."

She pushed her chair back and circled the table to where Keeper sat weeping. She put her lips next to his ear. "Hush now, Finders Keepers," she whispered. "Gran' pap ain't got the good sense he was borned wid."

Keeper sniffed wetly at the perfume Zinnia wore, and feeling a delicious tingle in his groin because of the husky sound of her voice and her warm breath in his ear. "That's okay. It's me who's sorry."

Mr. Sam cleared his throat to speak. "S'pose we run the Lionel a spell, Mistuh Keepuh? You can be the engineer while Zinnia clears off the dishes."

He was embarrassed by his unexpected show of emotion and humbled by their hospitality. "After I help with the dishes."

"Naw, you go on ahead," Zinnia replied, "you'd jest be in the way. 'Sides, you don't know where nothin' goes."

Mr. Sam chuckled knowingly. "Zinnia runs things 'roun' here."

"Yes sir," Keeper replied. Unable to finish his peach cobbler, he stood to follow him into his cozy bedroom, when a sense of homesickness became overwhelming.

With the wave of an arm, Mr. Sam directed Keeper to take a seat at the controls. "Take the throttle, Mistuh Keepuh. Once I get my pipe lit,' we're goin' highballin'!"

Keeper took his seat and leaned over the miniature train station where the locomotive waited and cast-metal passengers and redcaps stood frozen in time. As fresh, unstoppable tears spilled from his eyes and splattered on the layout like fat raindrops, he grasped the rheostat and cried, "All aboard! Everybody *boarrrrrrrd!*"

CHAPTER FIFTY-ONE

Chance sat in his underwear, chain-smoking Old Gold cigarettes and drinking warm Kentucky bourbon from a bathroom drinking glass as he struggled to write a letter to Keeper on his portable typewriter. It was his sixth effort, as evidenced by the wadded-up sheets of Georgian Terrace Hotel stationery that littered the floor. If Keeper somehow found his way home alone, Chance wanted a letter waiting for him to be read – something to explain his relationship with Honey Burnside – but so far everything sounded stupid, banal, and unconvincing.

Chance had also been calling the police on an hourly basis, only to hear the lieutenant patiently explaining he'd call if Keeper turned up, voluntarily or otherwise. Chance knew that calling Alva to make a clean breast of things was far overdue, but he couldn't bring himself to pick up the phone. Some things were better explained in person. Or by mail.

He selected another sheet of hotel stationary and began reading aloud as he wrote. "*Dear Keeper. Words alone cannot express my...shit!*" He balled up the stationary and threw it in the general direction of the wastebasket. He selected another sheet and began again. "*Dear Son, I'm sorry for everything. Please try and understand why...damn!*" He crumpled the paper in his fist and took another swallow of warm bourbon. "*Dear Keep,*" he intoned. "*Your father loves you very much. It's just that your mother and I...*" He hurled another piece of paper to the floor. And so it went, until the hotel stationary was gone and the bottle of Kentucky bourbon empty.

Chance reached for the telephone and dialed for room service. After waiting for what he thought was an inordinately long time, he heard the phone being answered by a youthful-sounding woman with a deeply southern accent that reminded him of Honey Burnside.

"Room service. How may ah help you?"

"I'd like a bottle of good bourbon and some stationary sent up to room two-twelve, please. Name's Wick."

"There's a wauh on, Mistuh Wick. Papuh is rationed, and good bourbon hard to find."

"I know that."

"Then why are you asking, suh?"

"Because I'm out."

"So is the Georgian Terraces Hotel."

"I'll make it worth your while."

"Out is out, Mistuh Wick."

"Okay, honey. What the hell kind of bourbon *do* you have?"

There was a pause before the reply came. "Foah Roses."

Chance grimaced. "I'll take it," he said, and slammed the receiver down on its cradle. He gathered up the discarded wads of stationary paper and began smoothing them out. The only alternative now was to type on the reverse side, something he feared would be taken by Keeper as a sign of drunken instability and unresolved anger. Maybe a different approach was required, something that would appeal to Keeper's keen intelligence and naturally forgiving nature. Perhaps a story such as the one he'd made up about the Australian aboriginals would work better. It would be a story of struggle, mysticism, and in the end, redemption and understanding. But first an explanation or apology was required, however weak.

"*Dear Keeper,*" Chance began aloud. He chose his words carefully, as if putting his failings and weaknesses down on paper was the greatest weakness of all. He went on. "*Of course I'm sorry. Ashamed even. I have no excuse. I've failed as a son, husband, and father. To say I've tried to be otherwise is a damned lie. All my life I've been searching for something, thinking maybe I'd find whatever it was on the road or in a bottle. Was it love? Acceptance? Happiness? I can now see it was none of these things. Rather, it was these very things I'd turned my back on. I am profoundly sorry, son, and I apologize. I hope that someday you'll find it in your heart to forgive me.*" Chance slammed the carriage back and reached for another cigarette, which he lit off the engraved Zippo before continuing.

"*Remember the story I told you when we were in Knoxville, about the mythical war bird in aboriginal history? I guess you'd call this another metaphor, because I can't find the words to explain myself any other way.*" Chance sighed and rubbed his forehead into fleshy ribs before going on; "*Even with the aid of his mulga-wood killing stick, it had taken Wati two nights under a full moon before reaching the top of the Great Rock Uluru. The airless night was...*"

Someone kicking at the door interrupted his thoughts. "C'mon in," he called, and smiled when an attractive brunette wearing a nicely-tailored white jacket and a pleated gray skirt stepped into the room. She held a fifth of Four Roses in one hand and a box of hotel stationary in the other.

"Mistuh Wick?"

"Guilty."

"Ah've found you a bottle and some writin' papuh."

Not minding that he was in his underwear, he reached for the silver money clip where he kept it and his wallet next to the telephone. "Was it you I talked to?" he asked.

"The very same," she replied with a smile that showed no sign of embarrassment.

Chance stood and returned the smile. "What do I owe?"

"Five-seventy foah the Foah Roses, and what evuh you like foah the papuh."

He peeled off a five and three singles and handed the bills to the woman. "Keep the change."

The woman swept a practiced eye around the room. "Travelin' alone, Mistuh Wick?"

"At the moment, yes."

"Road man, are you?"

"Does it show?"

"Does Henry Ford make cars?"

Chance laughed. "You guessed right," he replied. "I'm alone as alone can be."

"Ah gathuh you wouldn't mind a little company foah tonight?"

That came quick, he thought. "You gather correctly."

"Theah's a cozy little bar around the corner. It's called Dizzy's. Ah get off at nine."

Chance checked his watch. It was nearly eight now. There'd be plenty of time to follow up with the lieutenant later. "You've got a name, in case I need to ask?"

"Amaryllis," the woman replied with a smile that showed an overbite.

"Amaryllis," he repeated. "Pretty name."

Amaryllis held her smile. "Whut comes befoah 'Wick,' Mistuh Wick?"

"Chance."

"As in 'take a chance'?"

Chance laughed. "Call me Doc."

"Then ah guess ah'll see you at Dizzy's... *Doc.*'" Then, with a turn and a flair of pleated skirt that exposed shapely legs encased in a pair of rationed nylons, Amaryllis let herself out of the room and closed the door behind her with a soft click.

It was nine when he finally completed his letter to Keeper. Satisfied, he poured himself a splash of Four Roses before making a last call to the police lieutenant, only to find him unavailable. After leaving a message saying he'd be out for the evening, Chance dressed hurriedly and took the elevator down to the lobby. There he paused to buy a three-cent stamp from the concierge, pasted it to the envelope marked personal, and dropped it into a convenient mail slot. Then whistling tunelessly he crossed the lobby to the revolving front door and pushed his way out to the sidewalk. The fragrant night air was comfortably warm, with a gentle breeze that carried the sounds of a restless wartime city.

Were it not for Keeper being gone and the reason why lodged in the back of his alcohol-fogged brain, Chance would have been a reasonably content man. He was in his element again, alone and anonymous, with a snoot full of cheap bourbon and a pretty woman waiting for him. Whatever apologies, excuses or explanations he needed to make were in the mail.

CHAPTER FIFTY-TWO

Soft ambient light from a full August moon spilled through an open window and into Mr. Sam's bedroom where Keeper sat at the controls of the Lionel. Mr. Sam sat in a far corner, puffing contentedly on his pipe and listening to *Amos 'n Andy* on a cheap table radio. A telephone shrilled over the radio's tinny speaker until being answered by Andy. *"Hullo. This here is de Fresh Air Taxi Cab Company, Incorperlated. Andrew H. Brown, President, speakin.' No, Amos ain't here right now..."*

Zinnia, who had been listening from the kitchen, stomped into the bedroom and quickly turned the dial to a station playing sweet music. "Gran' pap," she scolded. "How can you listen to those fools?"

Mr. Sam's pipe flared. "They amuses me."

Zinnia snorted, "Humph!" She appeared ready to add more, until being interrupted by wailing air raid sirens. Almost immediately, city streetlights winked off as if extinguished by an unseen hand. Except for the moon's reflected light, the only other illumination came from the Lionel's headlight, the miniature lights inside the ticket station and the softly-glowing radio dial.

"Draw the shades, Granddaughter," Mr. Sam ordered, "an' bring us a candle when you've turned off our lights."

Zinnia obediently raced through the apartment, clicking off each light and blowing out the dinner candles before returning to Mr. Sam's room empty handed.

"Isn't you forgettin' sumpin'?" Mr. Sam growled.

"Ain't bringin' no candle, Gran'pap. 'Ain't a good idea when we might be gettin' bombed any minute now."

Pale moonlight pooled in Mr. Sam's lap and spilled down his bowed legs to his slippered feet. Only the orange smudge of his glowing pipe betrayed his frustration at having been disobeyed. In the heavy silence that followed, Billie Holiday crooned *Strange Fruit* over the radio while Keeper toggled the Lionel's lonesome whistle.

"Okay, Gran'pap," Zinnia said. "I'll bring one, but firs' pull down the shade."

Mr. Sam grunted. "You do that. Don't want no po'lice knockin' at de doe, haul us off to jail."

Keeper looked up. "Would they?"

"Done it before," Mr. Sam replied. "Folks livin' next doe got took up by the po'lice las' time it happened."

"We have air raid tests at home, too," Keeper said, "but nobody ever gets arrested."

The pipe flared in the shadows. "You got any coloreds back home?"

Keeper was beginning to understand. "No sir, only some Indians," which made him wonder where Jonnie Prettyboy was. When Billie Holiday's song ended, a short commercial for Ovaltine followed. After that, an announcer gave the latest eagerly-awaited clue for kids that had Orphan Annie decoder rings.

He felt his thoughts drifting toward home. He wondered what his mother and Early were doing, and if his father was out looking for him in the blacked-out streets of Atlanta. He was barely aware of Zinnia, when she sidled over to him and gently poked his arm.

"Whut you thinkin' 'bout, Finders Keepers?"

"About home, is all."

"Homesick, is you?"

"Yeah."

Mr. Sam cleared his throat. "None of my business, Mistuh Keepuh, but dast you care to say whut happened 'twixt you an' your daddy?"

Keeper figured it was time to tell them, no matter how hurtful. "I caught him and Miss Georgia doing it in bed. And before that, she even made me touch her boob."

Mr. Sam coughed. "I declare."

"Lawd have mercy," Zinnia said.

Mr. Sam clucked his tongue. "How well does you know your daddy, Mistuh Keepuh?"

"Too well," he mumbled.

The pipe glowed from the dark corner where Mr. Sam sat. "Maybe you jest think you does."

"What do you mean?"

"Does your daddy git on wid your momma?"

"I'm not sure."

"Does he work hard to set food on de table?"

"Yeah, I suppose so."

"Does he wear armor plates an' carry a sword?"

Keeper smiled to himself. "No."

"Does your daddy fly through de air lak Superman?"

Keeper laughed. "No sir."

"So whut you're sayin' is he's jest a regular human being, lak de res' of us."

"I don't think he's regular at all."

"How so, Mistuh Keepuh?"

"He drinks too much, smokes like a chimney, lies, cheats on my mom, and keeps two sets of books."

Mr. Sam chuckled. "Sounds lak some mens I know," he replied, "an' *they's* human as all get out."

"You should go to the po'lice, Finders Keepers," Zinnia said, "an' turn yourself in lessin' you get in real trouble."

"Maybe in the morning," Keeper replied, "after breakfast."

Mr. Sam sucked on a tooth and said, "You expectin' us to fetch you breakfas' too?"

"Nu, no sir," Keeper stuttered. "I've got money. I'll pay you."

"Mr. Sam's guests don't pay," Zinnia said.

"Then maybe I should leave now."

Mr. Sam raised a hand, as if to stop Keeper. "Zinnia is right," he said. "You is stayin' 'till tomorrow, breakfas' included." He yawned and rapped his pipe into a Union Pacific ashtray, scattering orange embers from the briarwood bowl. "Reckon its pas' time for us to be turnin' in."

"I have a confession to make first," Keeper said. "Then maybe you'll change your mind."

"That so?"

"It was me and my best friend Jonnie Prettyboy who stole the ciga-rettes and two pilsner beers from your store. "I'll pay you back before I leave."

"Well ah declare!"

"There's more. My mother's name isn't Zucchini. It's Alva."

"I *knowed* it!" Zinnia exclaimed with a gleeful hoot. "Ain't no white woman gonna get named after a *vegetable!*"

"I lied," Keeper said, "and I'm sorry. Not only that, when Miss Georgia made me touch her..., well, when I did, I got sort of...um... aroused."

Mr. Sam leaned forward with a deep chuckle and scratched his wooly white head with the stem of his pipe. "Sounds to me, Mistuh Keepuh, lak you an' your daddy got lots in common."

CHAPTER FIFTY-THREE

In spite of her eagerness to report the cop who had beaten and raped her, it had taken all of Jonnie Prettyboy's courage to enter the police station. Upon hearing the words "cop" and "raped" in the same sentence, the desk sergeant on duty had immediately called for more rank than his to deal with her.

"Can I get you anything?" the lieutenant asked after she had been led to his office and was seated in a metal folding chair placed directly across from where he sat behind a scarred wooden desk. The toothpick waggled between his teeth when he spoke. "A Coke, maybe a candy bar?"

"Coffee black," Jonnie Prettyboy replied. "And if it's not too much trouble, I could use a cigarette."

"Aren't you a mite young to be smoking?"

"You want my story or not?"

The lieutenant held up his hands in mock surrender. "No problem, kid. Coffee and a smoke coming right up," he said, and got up to leave.

Jonnie Prettyboy glanced around the sparsely-furnished office while the lieutenant was away. Other than for the rogue cop who had assaulted her, she had little experience with the police. Still, the station house had an almost familiar, even reassuring feel to it. She watched uniformed and plainclothes police officers as they bustled about their business, taking phone calls and trying to calm distraught civilians calling about abusive spouses, stolen cars and lost dogs. She scanned each face, hoping to recognize the pimple-faced son of a bitch with the good teeth who had beaten and raped her. She knew it was a long shot, and hoped it was worth the risk she had taken by coming to the police in the first place. Her hatred toward her assailant far exceeded her fear of being recognized by the police as a suspect in her father's killing. Still, it had been three long years...

Her thoughts were interrupted when the lieutenant returned with her coffee. "Here's your java, kid, black like you ordered." When he set the brimming mug down, hot coffee slopped over the rim and made a ring on the desk.

"Where's the smokes?" she asked.

The lieutenant reached into the pocket of his starched and crisply-pressed western-style shirt, took out an open pack of Camels and tossed it on the desk between them. A book of matches that advertised Nigger Hair tobacco was conveniently placed inside the cellophane wrapper. "Camels okay?" he asked.

"Yeah," she grunted, and reached for the pack. She shook out a Camel and tapped it against the back of her hand to settle the tobacco. To favor her split lip she placed the cigarette to the side and lit it off a Nigger Hair match.

The lieutenant sat down and propped up both feet on the desk, exposing holes in the soles of his cowboy boots. "Maybe we can start off by giving me your name." The toothpick waggled encouragement.

"Jonnie Prettyboy," she replied through a cloud of exhaled smoke.

"What are you?"

"What the hell is that supposed to mean?"

"Take it easy, kid. What I mean is, you're not a nigra are you?"

Her pale gray eyes flashed. "Is there a law against being colored?"

Up went the hands again. "Okay, kid, *okay*. Just trying to get a fix on you."

With the cigarette held between her fingers she picked up the coffee mug with both hands and slurped noisily while staring at the lieutenant over the rim. "I'm Dakota Indian by my pa and Lithuanian by my ma. Does that satisfy your curiosity?"

The lieutenant nodded. "Where you from, Miss Prettyboy?"

"Originally, or recently?"

"Originally."

She took a long drag off the Camel and exhaled towards the lieutenant. "Nowhere originally, and everywhere recently."

The lieutenant looked up from the yellow legal pad. "That's not at all helpful."

"It happens to be the truth."

"Okay. Tell me more about what brings you here, if you would."

She touched her face, trailing her fingertips over the cut lip, scabby nose, scrapes and bruises. "A cop is what brings me here. A fucking white-assed cop, who thinking I was colored, hauled me out of a restaurant, beat me, raped me and left me in the woods for dead."

The lieutenant dropped the ballpoint pen he was writing with, leaned back in his swivel chair and rubbed his eyes. "I knew my day was going too good."

"Sorry to fuck it up for you."

"I'd appreciate you didn't swear."

"Sorry."

"Were there witnesses?"

"Yeah. At the Bars and Stars Café and Lounge. A waitress named Bonnie, a fat-assed cracker named Bobby Ray, and a lady with a little girl, who I thought was cute until the brat opened her nasty little mouth. They all hate coloreds, so good luck."

The Lieutenant straightened in his chair and scribbled something in the yellow pad. "Isn't that the café over where the Greyhound station's at?"

Jonnie Prettyboy took another drag off the Camel and nodded.

"Describe the officer who allegedly assaulted you."

"Allegedly?" she shouted. "Son of a bitch, *look* at me!"

"Keep that up," the lieutenant said evenly, "and we'll be conducting this interview with you behind bars."

"Sorry. The cop had a face full of zits and Sen-Sen on his breath. Oh, and his teeth looked like a mouthful of Chiclets. How's that for starters?" She drained the last of the coffee and pushed the empty mug toward the lieutenant with a disarming smile. "Another, please?"

"Pete!" the lieutenant barked when a plainclothes officer passed by the open office door. "Bring this young lady a refill, black."

The officer scowled, but took the empty mug as ordered. When he returned with the mug slopping black coffee on the floor, the two were still at a standoff, arms folded across their chests and avoiding eye contact.

Jonnie Prettyboy reached for the coffee. "Thanks Pete."

"Nigras," Pete muttered under his breath, and turned to leave.

"Miss Prettyboy," the lieutenant began, "you're going to have to do better than to say the alleged, sorry, that the assaulting officer had a bad complexion, good teeth and Sen-Sen on his breath."

"I'm sorry too, because that's all I remember until he knocked me out."

"Could you tell if he was Atlanta PD?"

"That stand for 'Pencil Dick?'"

"The lieutenant's face flushed red. "Look Miss…""

"Sorry. Sorry…sorry…*sorrrry.*"

"Could he have been a state trooper, or maybe a county cop?"

"Could have been either one, I guess."

"What about his cruiser? Color?

"Your regular black and white."

The lieutenant nodded and made an entry in his legal pad. "Could be county, could be us."

"How about a lineup? I'd pick his ass out in a second."

"Let's get some additional information first. What can you tell me…?"

The plainclothes officer stood in the doorway. "Lieutenant?"

"Yeah, Pete?"

"Excuse me, sir, but did I hear you say 'Miss Prettyboy'?"

"Yeah?"

"*Jonnie* Prettyboy?" Pete approached the lieutenant and handed him a faded sheet of mimeograph paper with a blurry blue-toned image on it. The word **WANTED** was spelled out over the image.

Jonnie Prettyboy leaned forward. Even upside down she recognized her scowling face. She remembered the picture being taken when she graduated eighth grade, except this one included her physical description and the contact number of the Dakota Straits police department. She wondered if she could make it to the door before being tackled.

"This has been posted on the squad room bulletin board for the last three years," Pete said. "Surprised we didn't catch it right off. She's wanted for questioning by Dakota Straits PD regarding the murder of her father."

"Well now, Miss Prettyboy," the lieutenant said. "Ever hear of a kid named Keeper Wick? He's from Dakota Straits too"

Jonnie Prettyboy lowered her eyes. "Never heard of him."

"I'll take that as a yes," the lieutenant said, and scribbled something in his legal pad. "Like you, Keeper is a runaway. His father is looking for him, and so are we."

"Can't help you there."

"Then what would you say to being our guest until we clear up this little matter?"

"What about my complaint?"

"That depends on proving what you say happened, happened."

"If I tell you where that Keeper kid you're looking for might be, would you be willing to forget my complaint and let me go?"

"It's a little late for that, Miss…"

"Then how'd you like to arrest a pair of carnies for violating the Mann Act?"

The ballpoint pen between the lieutenant's fingers froze in mid-air. "What's that again?"

"I looked it up, lieutenant, sir. It's called the white-slave traffic act of nineteen-hundred and ten. It bans the interstate transport of females for immoral purposes."

The lieutenant smiled. "I'd like that very much."

Jonnie Prettyboy smiled back and reached for a Camel. "I thought you might."

CHAPTER FIFTY-FOUR

Amaryllis sat at Dizzy's bar smoking a cigarette with a martini up and a bowl of beer nuts in front of her. A pimento-stuffed green olive impaled on a red plastic sword rested inside the chilled martini glass. She looked up when Chance came through the door. "Ah was beginin' to think you'd stood me up, Doc."

"Not a chance," Chance replied, noticing, but not mentioning the gold band on her ring finger.

Amaryllis laughed. "Do you always play off yoah name?"

"Not deliberately, I don't." Chance took the stool next to Amaryllis and held up a hand to catch the bartender's attention. A colored piano player dressed in a tuxedo sat at a baby grand playing *Oklahoma* from the smash hit Broadway musical. He was accompanied by three obviously drunk men enthusiastically singing the lyrics in imperfect harmony. Chance felt at home in joints like Dizzy's, where he enjoyed the anonymity, the convivial atmosphere and the companionship, even if it was fleeting and often insincere. It helped take away the monotony of the road and allowed him to forget he was hundreds of miles from home and family. He loved the low lighting, cigarettes winking in dark booths, the soft clink of cocktail glasses, and the laughter that followed his jokes.

A bartender appeared and slapped a cocktail napkin in front of Chance. "What'll it be, buddy?"

"Double bourbon on the rocks."

"Comin' right up," the bartender replied, and turned to fill the order.

"You don't favuh a brand? Amaryllis asked.

He shook his head. "These days, you take what you get."

"Do you always take what you get, Doc?"

He reached for the pack of cigarettes in his shirt pocket and tapped one out. "Meaning what?" he asked with feigned innocence while digging out the monogrammed Zippo.

"Meaning, do you ever turn anything down?"

Chance thumbed the lighter. "Am I hearing an offer?"

Amaryllis laughed. "Nothing like cutting to the chase, ah always say."

"All things that are," he intoned from memory, "are with more spirit chased than enjoyed."

"How quaint. Was that under yoah high school yearbook picture?"

"How'd you guess?" He looked up when the bartender returned with the double bourbon. "Run a tab for me, will you please?"

The bartender pointed to the bowl of nuts sitting in front of Amaryllis. "Get'cha some beer nuts?"

"I'll pass, thanks." Peanuts tended to get under his bridgework, which was why he avoided eating them when in the company of strangers, and especially reasonably attractive women.

Amaryllis took a delicate sip of her straight-up martini. "So, Doc," she began. "What brings you to Atlanta?"

"Business."

She held up the skewered olive and put it in her mouth. "That's what ah figured."

"Aren't you going to ask what kind of business?" Chance asked, prepared to offer his stock joke about vibrators.

"Ah don't think so."

"Fine by me," he replied. He turned to watch as the piano player segued into a lush rendition of Cole Porter's *Night and Day*. The husky baritone was suggestive of a long-standing cigarette and alcohol habit.

"Ah love that song," Amaryllis said. Sudden tears moistened her eyes.

Chance tapped his cigarette into the ash tray between them. "Means something special, does it?"

She nodded. "How about you? Is there a special song in your life?"

"None I can think of at the moment."

"You aren't a very sentimental guy, are you Doc?"

"Sentimentality is the refuge of the lonely."

"Youh not lonely?"

"I try not to be."

Amaryllis raised the martini glass to her lips and took a sip. The highly polished gold band on her ring finger sparkled under the soft lights. "*Ah'm* lonely, Doc."

Not that it mattered, but he wondered if she would remove the ring from her finger before climbing into bed with him. "You're too pretty to be lonely."

She put down the drink and smiled. "You know what they say about appearances being deceiving."

Chance grinned and winked. "And judging books by their cover?"

"You have a family, Doc?"

He nodded. "Married, with two sons and a senile father at home."

"Miss them, do you?"

He rubbed his thumb over the Zippo's engraved: "Doc. You Bastard. Velma." "Of course."

Amaryllis smiled. "So," she said, "Yoah human after all."

Chance took another sip of bourbon, when the unpleasant thought intruded that maybe he should be out looking for Keeper instead of chasing strange pussy and leaving the search to an indifferent police department. "There are those who would dispute that opinion."

Amaryllis abruptly changed the subject. "Did anyone evuh tell you you've got the most beautiful hands?"

Chance set the glass down and held up both as if seeing them for the first time. He wondered when the trembling had started and hoped it wasn't serious. Being a doctor's son, he tended to self diagnose. "They're my father's hands," he replied after a moment.

"Do handsome hands run in yoah family?"

"Suppose we talk about you instead?"

Amaryllis stubbed out her cigarette in the ashtray she shared with Chance and turned to make eye contact. "What do you want to know?"

"There's a wedding band on your finger. Start from there."

"Ah'll give you the Reader's Digest version, Doc. Five months ago mah husband had his P-47 Thunderbolt shot down ovuh Germany. His wingman wrote to tell me how it happened. They were rolling in to strafe an ammo train when he got hit. His parachute was seen to open, but ah've accepted the fact he isn't coming back."

"I apologize for making an unfair assumption."

"Apology accepted. What's yoah excuse, Doc, for cattin' 'round on Missus Wick?"

Chance finished his drink and held up two fingers for refills – his and hers. "Other than she's frigid?"

"Have you evuh considered whose fault that might be?"

"Hers, mine, ours? It doesn't much matter anymore."

Amaryllis took his hand in hers and held it. "Sleep with me tonight, Doc?"

"Now there's an ice breaker."

"Answer me, damn it, befoah ah lose all shame and have to beg."

"Why, ah'd be honored, Miss Scarlett."

Amaryllis laughed, sounding relieved. "As an employee, the Georgian Terraces is off limits foah me. We'll have to go to my place. It's just around the cornuh."

Chance glanced at his watch. 9:30 p.m. Maybe the police lieutenant had been trying to reach him. "Give me a minute to make a phone call."

Amaryllis lit another cigarette. "Ah'll be waitin', Rhett."

The bartender appeared with the drinks. "You leaving, buddy?"

"Both of us, in a few minutes," Chance replied. He fumbled in his pants pocket for the money clip. He slipped out two fives and put them over the bar tab. "Keep the change," he said, and turned for the pay phone located opposite the baby grand where the tuxedoed musician played *Summertime.*

Chance closed the folding doors and dialed the number the lieutenant had given him, then waited impatiently until it was answered on the fourth ring.

"Yeah?"

"It's Chance Wick, Lieutenant. I've…"

The lieutenant interrupted. "Where the hell have you been, Mr. Wick? I've been trying to reach you for the past hour."

"I had to step out. Have you found my son?"

"No, Mr. Wick, but we have a Miss Jonnie Prettyboy in custody. I believe you know her from Dakota Straits?"

Chance's knees threatened to buckle. "She's a friend of Keeper's. Are they together?"

"No, but she thinks she knows where we might find him."

Chance fumbled for a cigarette, his thoughts tumbling wildly. The lieutenant's voice echoed in his ear, like he was calling from the basement. "She *thinks* she knows?"

"Yes sir. I thought you might want to come along while I check it out."

He could see Amaryllis sitting with her back to him at the bar, and wondered if he'd have another opportunity with her. "Give me thirty minutes," Chance said. "No, make it fifteen, and I'll be there."

"One last thing, Mr. Wick. Miss Prettyboy told us how her father died, and that your son could back her up, so it's extremely important that we find him."

"Are you saying my son had something to do with her father's death?"

"That's what we intend to find out."

Chance slammed the receiver onto the hook and quickly strode to rejoin Amaryllis at the bar. "I hate to spoil our evening, but something big has come up."

Amaryllis' face sagged with disappointment. "I've heard that line before."

"It's not what you think."

"Correction, Doc. It's always what I think."

"Not this time. Give me your 'phone number and I'll get back to you."

"Now *theyuh's* a familiar line too."

"I mean it. I'll make it up to you."

Amaryllis stubbed out her cigarette, grabbed her purse and stood to leave. "Make it up to somebody else, Doc. See you in the funny papers."

"Wait, please," Chance said. When he reached for the drink he'd left behind, he clumsily knocked it over, spilling bourbon and sending ice cubes skittering across the bar's mahogany surface.

"You got a problem?" Amaryllis asked, 'cause yoah shakin' like a leaf."

"Not anymore I don't," he replied. "My son and I are going home."

CHAPTER FIFTY-FIVE

At Zinnia's insistence Keeper agreed to take her bedroom for the night, or for as many nights as she and Mr. Sam would allow him to stay. The windows had been left open to catch any breeze, but the stifling night air offered none. A too-bright moon cut a sharp wedge across the upper half of Keeper's sweating body, keeping him awake. He had been studying a framed and hand-tinted studio photograph of Cleotus, Zinnia's boyfriend, where she had placed it on a chest of drawers between a bottle of "*Evening in Paris*" and a stuffed toy bear. The soldier wore the billed cap and uniform of an enlisted man, and his PFC stripe was clearly in evidence.

Keeper was wondering if Cleotus and Zinnia had ever done it together, when the bedroom door opened. He shifted his gaze from Cleotis to Zinnia standing in the doorway. She wore a white-cotton nightgown that didn't quite reach her knees.

"I can't sleep, Finders Keepers."

Keeper felt a shiver of anticipation. "Me neither."

"Reckon we kin talk a bit?"

"What about?" he asked.

"Whut ever you want."

Since he was in his undershorts, Keeper wondered if she intended on climbing into bed with him, or would continue standing a safe distance away. "I guess we could talk for a while."

Zinnia smiled and stepped into the room. She closed the door behind her and approached Keeper lying on the narrow iron-framed bed. "Move over, Finders Keepers," she said, and poked him on the arm.

He shifted over as far as he could without falling out of bed. "What are you doing?" he asked.

"What does it look like?" she said, and pulled back the thin cotton sheet covering Keeper's legs before sliding in next to him.

"What if Mr. Sam hears us?"

"Mr. Sam wouldn't hear a wind-up piano if it fell down de stairs playin' ragtime."

Keeper had to laugh. "I hope you're right, 'cause he's got a gun."

"He knows how to use it, too." Zinnia warned, and let her hand drop over Keeper's leg.

His stomach muscles tightened at the touch. "I like Mr. Sam a lot."

Zinnia raised her knees and kicked the top sheet away until it was piled up at the foot of the bed. "Mr. Sam likes you too," she replied, "An' so does I."

Zinnia's slender brown legs were slightly apart. Her nightgown had climbed above her thighs. Keeper wondered if she wore anything underneath. "I saw your boyfriend's picture on the dresser," he said, hoping to deflect a possible advance.

Zinnia snorted. "You mean ol' 'never-write' Cleotus?"

"Yeah, him. How long has he been your boyfriend?"

She giggled softly. "I'd say right about up 'til now." Her finger tapped close to the erection growing inside Keeper's undershorts.

"What does he do?" Keeper asked, "In the army, I mean."

Zinnia rolled on her side and traced an imaginary line down Keeper's chest to his navel with her index finger and circled it. "He drives a truck."

"Like in civilian life?"

"Naw, Cleotus chopped cotton in civilian life."

The finger was getting closer to the waistband of Keeper's undershorts. "Whu, what kind of truck?" he stammered.

"Ammo trucks, gasoline trucks, all kind of trucks, chasin' some general ever' which way 'cross Europe."

"That's the Red Ball Express," Keeper said. "They keep General Patton's tanks supplied."

"Yeah, thass' him, alright." Zinnia replied, yawning.

"That's a dangerous job. Those guys get shot at, bombed, strafed, all kinds of shit. Accidents too."

"Mus' be why he ain't wrote."

"You sound like you don't care what happens to him."

"Oh, I cares alright. Its jes' that Cleotus is there an' I'se here."

"I'll bet he's worried about you," Keeper replied.

Zinnia shrugged, causing her nightgown strap to slide off her shoulder and exposing her left breast. "Whut about you, Finders Keepers? Is you worried 'bout somebody right now?"

Keeper was now fully erect. "Probably, but I can't think so good right now."

"Maybe that half-Indian, half-white gal, whut's her name?"

The heady smell of Zinnia's perfume and the feel of her sweating body pressed against him caused Keeper's heart to pound dully in his ears. He closed his eyes and tried to conjure up Jonnie Prettyboy's features, but her face was like an image reflected in a pool of water until being disturbed by a stone dropped into it. Only her name remained a constant. "Jonnie Prettyboy," he croaked.

"S'pose you could forget her for jest tonight, Finders Keepers?"

Keeper reached for the dark-brown nipple jutting only inches from his face. He licked his lips and swallowed hard when Zinnia's probing fingers found his erection. "Forget who?" he asked.

CHAPTER FIFTY-SIX

The lieutenant slowed the unmarked police cruiser to a crawl and pointed a finger toward the shadowy façade of Mr. Sam's shop. "That's the place, Mr. Wick," he said. Killing the lights, he made a sweeping U-turn at the next intersection and pulled up to the curb. Only the swaying whip antenna mounted on the rear bumper gave any indication that the black Ford was not a civilian car.

Chance looked uncertain. "This doesn't look like the kind of place where Keeper would stay."

"Don't be too sure, Mr. Wick. Runaways ain't choosy about where they hole up, especially if they're suspects in a criminal case."

"Keeper hasn't committed a crime, lieutenant. He's on the run because of something I did."

The lieutenant turned down the volume on the squawking Motorola two-way and cocked his head to see Mr. Sam's darkened upstairs windows. "I said 'suspects.' Mr. Wick. And until we compare his statement against Miss Prettyboy's, that's all they'll be."

Chance fumbled in his shirt pocket for a cigarette and was about to light it, when the lieutenant reached over and closed his hand over the Zippo. "Don't." he said, simply.

"Sorry," Chance mumbled. "Wasn't thinking." He glanced toward the lieutenant, whose features were hidden under the shadow of the wide-brimmed gray Stetson he wore low over his forehead. Only the policeman's lower lip and chin caught the moonlight slanting through the driver's side window. The lieutenant chewed gum that smelled like licorice. "Got an extra piece?" Chance asked.

Wordlessly, the lieutenant opened his jacket, exposing the cross-hatched grip of black .45-caliber pistol carried in a leather shoulder harness. He reached into his shirt pocket, pulled out a crumpled pack of Beeman's Blackjack and tossed it to Chance. "Help yourself."

Chance fumbled a stick from the pack, unwrapped it with shaking fingers and popped it into his mouth before remembering gum stuck to his bridgework. Since he needed something to settle his nerves, he concentrated on chewing the gum between his front teeth. "Now what, Lieutenant?"

"We're going to have us a look-see around the property, and then we're going to see if anyone's to home."

"Wouldn't it be smarter to call for backup first?"

"If your boy's inside, I don't want to risk spooking him or whoever's with him. Now, let's go. Stay close and keep it quiet."

Together, the two stepped out of the unmarked cruiser. They closed the doors with muffled thunks and advanced to stand warily in front of the shop. A cardboard sign advertising Camel cigarettes was propped against the window nearest the door.

Chance instinctively reached for the pack of cigarettes in his pocket.

"You light one, Mr. Wick," the lieutenant warned, "and I'll have you behind bars before you can whistle Dixie. Now stay close and watch your step."

Chance followed the lieutenant into a backyard brightly-lit under the full moon, with sharply-defined shadows cast by cottonwoods looming against the night sky. He screwed up his nose at the rankling smell of a garbage can in the alley beyond, its contents ripening in the heat. A cat yowled at something. "Do you see anything?" he asked.

"Quiet!" the lieutenant hissed.

"Sorry."

"I thought I heard something. A groan, maybe."

"Where?" Chance whispered.

"Coming from inside. We'd better check it out."

"Could it have been a dog, maybe a cat?"

The lieutenant shook his head. "Sounds more like a kid getting his ashes hauled."

CHAPTER FIFTY-SEVEN

"Keep it down, Finders Keepers," Zinnia warned. "Dasn't be wakin' Mr. Sam wid you caterwaulin' lak a tomcat."

Keeper always assumed the first girl he'd have sex with would be his lifelong friend, Jonnie Prettyboy. Instead, it was with a colored girl he'd known for only two days. "I couldn't help it," he groaned. "I never felt anything like that before."

Zinnia giggled. "You sure you wants to go back to de North Pole?"

"Not anymore, I don't."

"*Hush!*" she interrupted. "They's somebody outside."

"I don't hear any..."

She put a hand over Keeper's mouth. "Down below, scrabblin' at de doe."

The sound of someone pounding on the front door echoed through the shop, then a voice, loud and authoritative. "You in there, open up!"

Zinnia rolled out of bed and stumbled to the open bedroom window. "It's the po'lice!" she hissed.

Keeper leapt from bed and rushed to her side. "How can you tell?"

"Fool! 'Cause they's a whip antenna on de Ford's back bumper."

"It's the police! Open up!"

"See?" Zinnia said.

Keeper pressed his face against the window screen, trying to see who was banging on the door and demanding entry. "Holy shit," he cried. "It's my dad, and he's with a cop!"

Chance looked up at the sound of his son's voice. "Keeper! I'm with an Atlanta police lieutenant. Let us in!"

"I hate you! Go away!"

The lieutenant continued to pound on the door. "Police! Open up in there!"

"Lawd have mercy," Zinnia groaned. "Look whut you done brought down on us now."

Mr. Sam came shuffling into the room. In spite of the heat he wore long-johns and carpet slippers. He positioned himself at the adjoining window and pressed his whiskered face against the screen. An ivory-handled derringer was in his shaking right hand. "Is that them fool zoot suiters come back to rob us?" he howled. Without waiting for an answer, he punched an elbow through the window screen, stuck the derringer through the ragged hole and started firing, "*pop – pop – pop*," in rapid succession.

"Gran' pap, *no!*" Zinnia cried.

Keeper felt as if everything was happening in slow motion, like the bad dream where he gets chased by Frankenstein and the Wolf Man. Mr. Sam's gun sounded no louder than when he popped a wad of bubblegum. The yellow-white sparks caused by the three bullets ricocheting off the sidewalk and slamming into the unmarked police car seemed no more dangerous than when he set off fire crackers on the Fourth.

When the policeman reached into his jacket and pulled out the biggest pistol he'd ever seen, Keeper discovered he couldn't move – transfixed by his need to see what would happen next. It came surprisingly fast. He blinked and jumped when he saw the muzzle flash, followed by the sharp report of the policeman's pistol. He ducked instinctively when Mr. Sam grunted upon being hit, then spun backwards to fall face-first across Zinnia's unmade bed.

She screamed and rushed to his side. "Gran' pap! Get up!"

Keeper stood flat-footed, unable to fully process what had just happened until hearing his name being called.

"Keeper!" Chance cried. "Are you all right son?"

Too frightened to reply, he pressed his back flat against the wall in case more shots were fired.

"You up there!" the lieutenant called. "Don't shoot! We're coming in!"

The sound of splintering wood and breaking glass filled Keeper's ears as he stumbled wordlessly past Zinnia and her wounded grandfather. He groped his way toward the old man's darkened room across the hall and took a seat at the controls of the Lionel. Blinking back tears, he reached for the rheostat and slowly advanced the throttle. The locomotive's headlight cast a pencil-thin beam of light down the tracks as it picked up speed. The light inside the ticket station glowed invitingly, as if to welcome the cast-lead passengers who waited frozen in time on the baggage platform. Keeper toggled the whistle, a forlorn wail as the locomotive entered the last papier-mâché tunnel. He was highballing now.

CHAPTER FIFTY-EIGHT

Chance stood in the police station lobby feeding two quarters and a dime into the pay phone, then waited for the long distance operator to answer. When she told him to go ahead with his rationed three minute call, he dialed home. While the phone rang, he beckoned for Keeper, who stood across from him, sulking, to come closer.

"It's me," Chance said when he heard Alva pick up.

"Where are you?" she replied breathlessly. "I've been trying to reach you for two goddamned days!"

"In Atlanta, at police headquarters. We've found Keeper."

"Oh, dear God! Is he...?"

"He's fine, dear," Chance replied, interrupting. "I've canceled the Cotton Belt demonstration. We'll be leaving for home just as soon as the police have finished questioning Keeper and Jonnie Prettyboy. Tomorrow, probably."

"Keeper and Jonnie Prettyboy? Questioning? Chance, for God's sake, what's going on?"

"Remember Roy Prettyboy?"

"Yes, of course."

"After three years on the run, Jonnie Prettyboy turned up in Atlanta. She went to the police for some reason, and they recognized her as being wanted for questioning by the Dakota Straits police about her father's death. Turns out her father's death was accidental, and Keeper backed up her story."

"How can our son be mixed up in that dirty Indian business?"

"Let it go, dear. I'll fill you in on the details when we get home."

"She's coming with you and Keeper?"

"That's the plan."

"Then you may as well prepare her now. Two weeks ago Mrs. Prettyboy opened an artery with a butcher knife and bled to death in that horrible caboose they called a home."

"What a shame. She was a looker, too."

"Well, you could hardly blame the woman, considering. And how like you to comment on another woman's appearance."

"Don't be so goddamned judgmental, Alva."

"Don't swear at me."

Chance beckoned for Keeper to come closer. "Say hello to your mother."

Keeper reluctantly took the phone from his father. "Hi Mom."

"You've put us through a lot lately. You know that, don't you?"

"Sorry."

"Your father said you'll be fine, but you don't sound fine."

"I'll be fine, Mom."

"I've been so worried. You could have been dead."

"I wasn't."

"Where did your father find you?"

"I was staying with colored friends."

"You have *colored* friends in Atlanta?"

"I make friends easily."

"You didn't always."

"I've grown up since then. How's Early?"

"He misses you."

"Grandpa?"

"He misses you too."

"Grandpa doesn't know from shit."

"*Keeper!*" Alva cried. "My God, what's gotten into you?"

"Nothing," he replied, and handed the telephone back to his father.

"That was short and sweet, Keep," Chance said.

"Nothing to say."

Chance put the telephone to his ear. "Alva? You still there?"

Alva's voice was unsteady, tremulous. "Something terrible has happened. I just know it."

"Believe me, Alva, everything's fine."

"Everybody tells me everything's *fine!*" Alva sobbed. "Fine, fine, *fine!*"

"Now, dear."

"I'm glad for you, Chance, because nothing's fine here! *Nothing!*"

Chance struggled to remain calm. "Jesus Christ, Alva. How can we so quickly go from celebrating Keeper's being found alive and unharmed, to fighting like two caged wildcats?" He took a deep breath and rubbed his eyes. Lately he had been seeing flashes of light and felt the symptoms of last night's headache returning. When the lieutenant fired his pistol so close to his ear last night, he thought his head was going to explode. The muzzle flash blinded him for at least two minutes, which scared him into believing he'd lost his vision permanently.

"Just bring Keeper home safely, Chance, "and don't stop unless it's for gas."

"In other words, like usual."

"Exactly. And this time don't lose my son."

He was about to reply, to complain about Alva's singular and possessive use of Keeper's relationship to her, but the telephone had gone dead. "Damn," he muttered. With a motion for Keeper to follow, Chance returned to the lieutenant's office and slumped into the closest chair.

"Trouble at home, Mr. Wick?" the lieutenant said.

"Are you a married man?" Chance asked.

"Twenty-one years come Labor Day."

"Then you should know that was a stupid question."

The lieutenant smiled. "Cops always ask stupid questions. That's how we get our man."

"When will we be allowed to leave? Keeper's mother is beside herself with wanting to have her...I mean...our son, back home."

"Freudian slip of the tongue, Mr. Wick?"

"Yeah, Dad," Keeper said. He stood in the doorway, waiting, watching and listening. "I'm sure old doctor what's-his-name would have loved to analyze you."

"Knock it off, Keep."

The lieutenant put down his ballpoint pen and fixed Chance with a steady gaze. "Remember when I once told you you didn't seem to know a hell'uva lot about your son? Seems to me you still don't."

"I'm tired, lieutenant. If it's all right with you, I'd like to take my son and Jonnie Prettyboy and hit the road for home."

"I see no reason to keep you here, Mr. Wick. Your son's account of how Mr. Prettyboy died squares with Miss Prettyboy's story of an abusive father, and is consistent with his cause of death, namely, a broken neck suffered during a tussle with your son."

Chance reached for a cigarette with shaking hands and lit it off his engraved Zippo before turning to Keeper. "I don't understand why you didn't report this to the police immediately."

"It's like the cop said," Keeper replied. "There's a lot you don't know about me."

As much as Chance wanted to upbraid Keeper for having caused everyone so much trouble and worry, he couldn't. He knew the blame for his son's running away rested squarely on his shoulders. "I guess you're right, son," he said, knowing it was a half-hearted admission of parental failure.

The lieutenant pulled out two stapled sheets of paper from a desk drawer and slid them across the desk toward Chance. "This is a release form for Miss Prettyboy. There's also a medical report attached that states her physical condition at the time she showed up on our doorstep. Sign it, and you will be fully responsible for her care and feeding until she can be returned to her mother."

Chance deliberately chose not to mention Mrs. Prettyboy's suicide. There would be a better time and place for that. He picked up the form to study the description of Jonnie Prettyboy's physical condition. It read like a car wreck. "What the hell happened to her?"

"She claims to have been assaulted by a cop, but has decided not to pursue it further."

"May I ask why, for Christ's sake?"

"Personal reasons, I suppose. Do you agree to the release conditions, Mr. Wick?"

Chance nodded. "Give me your pen."

The lieutenant rolled his pen across the desk. "Mr. Wick. A boy doesn't just up and run away from his father when he's hundreds of miles away from home. Whatever happened between you and your son is none of my business, but I'd suggest you look to getting things back on track pretty damned soon."

"Thanks for the unsolicited advice."

"There's more," the lieutenant said. "Buy a football. You might even discover something in yourself when you catch your son's first pass." Then he pointed to Keeper. "As for you, I recommend you take care who you make new friends with. Could've been you who got shot last night."

"Mr. Sam and Zinnia were the nicest people I ever met," Keeper said. "They would have let me stay as long as I wanted, too, until you went and shot him."

"In case you've forgotten," the lieutenant replied, "the old man fired first."

"I don't care. He thought you were a zoot suiter trying to break in."

Chance took a deep breath and sighed. "Come on, son, let's go home."

"I'd rather take the bus."

"You're not taking the bus."

"I don't want to be with you."

"Look Keeper. I'm sorry, okay? Just stop beating my brains out."

"If you had any brains, you wouldn't have done what you did."

"You're too young to understand," Chance muttered.

"What are you going to tell Mother?"

"Nothing," he said, "and neither are you."

"Who's Velma?" It was a question Keeper had been afraid to ask ever since discovering the engraved Zippo in his father's car. Now he was no longer afraid.

"A friend, is all."

"She called you a bastard. What kind of friend is that?"

"One who knows me all too well."

"Is she in your second set of books too, along with that old hag, Miss Georgia?"

"I've closed those books, son, but yes, she was."

"Velma was right," Keeper sneered. "And I'll tell you something else, *Doc*. Last night I started my own set of books."

CHAPTER FIFTY-NINE

Jonnie Prettyboy sat in the backseat of Chance's white Chrysler New Yorker, arms folded across her chest and glowering. She wore the last of Keeper's clean clothing; a short-sleeved, white-cotton shirt and a pair of button-fly khaki shorts. She was barefoot by choice. It was 9:00 a.m. and already hot. The windows were rolled down and the vent windows turned outward to funnel air and the occasional hard-shelled insect directly into the car.

"I don't know why I have to sit back here," Jonnie Prettyboy grumbled. "I can't see shit."

Chance adjusted the rearview mirror so he could see her slumped behind Keeper, who sat in the front seat with his sunburned arm resting over the windowsill. The torrent of hot air blasting through the open vent buffeted Keeper's face and mussed his reddish-blond hair into a wild tangle.

"I thought you'd rather sit back there, considering," Chance replied, "but I'll let you trade places with Keep the first time we stop for gas." He readjusted the mirror until his bloodshot eyes were staring back at him, and then dug out a cigarette from his shirt pocket and lit it off the dashboard lighter.

"Hey, Mr. Wick, sir" Jonnie Prettyboy called over the roaring wind. "S'pose I could bum a smoke off you?"

Chance turned and winced at the sight of her scabby lip and the reddish-purple bruises on her still-swollen face. "You're kidding, right?"

"No she's not," Keeper said. Without asking for permission, he turned the radio dial from a station giving the weather report to another playing something by King Oliver. It was a jazz tune he recognized from his stay with Mr. Sam and Zinnia.

Chance nudged the rearview mirror with his index finger. "I'm supposed to be responsible for your care and well-being, Miss Prettyboy."

"Right now," she replied, "my well-being depends on having a cigarette, and if you care, you'll give me one."

Chance had come to admire her guts and couldn't help but chuckle. He reached for the nearly-empty pack in his pocket and handed it over his shoulder.

She took it without a thank you, rolled up her window to deflect the wind and poked Keeper on the back of his head. "Give me a light," she said.

"You haven't changed one little bit," Keeper said. He punched in the dashboard lighter, waited until it popped out, and then held it so she could light her cigarette from it.

"Are we going to drive straight through to Dakota Straits?" he asked after plugging the lighter back in its socket.

"We'll see how it goes."

"I hope we do, because I don't want to sleep in the same room with you."

"Cut it out, Keeper."

"Do we have to take the stupid demo trailer with us?"

"Yes."

"I hate that fucking trailer."

Jonnie Prettyboy snorted in mock derision. "Goodness gracious, Keeper Wick, but you've got a mouth on you."

"Yeah, well, I learned it from you."

"That's enough, you two," Chance said. "We've got a long way to go."

Keeper folded his arms and settled back into his seat. Flying insects cracked against the windshield like soft-shelled peanuts, leaving yellow-green smears that quickly congealed in the windstream. In the open fields beyond, colored men, women and children of all ages picked cotton under a brilliant sun.

The overheated Georgia air was sultry-sweet and smelled of decay and road kill. The barbwire fence paralleling the highway was festooned with the season's second flowering of waxy-white Cherokee Roses. Ahead, dark clouds the color of eggplant roiled above the horizon to top out at nearly twenty-thousand feet, with probing flashes of lightning followed by thunder that rumbled like a distant battlefield.

"Chain gang!" Keeper exclaimed, and pointed toward two men on horseback a hundred yards off the main highway. They cradled shotguns in their arms.

Jonnie Prettyboy sat upright. "Where?" she asked.

"There, coming up on my side."

"I see 'em."

"Slow down," Keeper said. "I don't want to miss this."

Chance let up on the accelerator when they came abreast of the chain gang. The mostly Negro and three white convicts were digging ditches alongside the dirt road. They wore black and white-striped uniforms and were shackled together at the ankles. The mounted guards wore wide-brimmed straw hats with silver stars pinned to their crowns. The shotguns glinted like raven's beaks in the bright morning sun. Choking clouds of dry Georgia soil drifted shoulder-high, coating the sweating horses, convicts and guards alike in a thin layer of gritty ochre-colored paste. None of them looked up as the New Yorker passed.

Keeper's tiff with his father was momentarily forgotten. "*Wow!*" he exclaimed. "Did you see those shotguns?"

"I saw two cracker sons of bitches that could hardly wait to use 'em," Jonnie Prettyboy muttered from the backseat.

Keeper turned around to face her. "What's got into you?" he asked.

She blew cigarette smoke in his face. "Maybe I'll tell you sometime when you're older and more mature."

"I could tell you something too," he said with a smug look. "But because it's in my second set of books, I won't."

"Looks like we're going to be in that storm in another fifteen minutes," Chance said, changing the subject.

"Be careful, Mr. Wick," Jonnie Prettyboy replied. "Remember, you're responsible for my health and well-being."

"You're in good hands. I always make it safely home, and on time too."

She grunted. "So I've heard."

Chance adjusted the rearview mirror so he could better see her. "What else have you heard about me, for instance?"

"I understand you collect autographs of movie stars, like Clark Gable."

"Keeper told you."

"I showed her the Union Pacific matchbook where he wrote his name, saying he owed you one," Keeper explained.

"What did good old Clark owe you for?" Jonnie Prettyboy asked.

Chance looked into the mirror and smiled. "If word got out, it might prove embarrassing for Mr. Gable."

"I wonder if Clark Gable keeps a second set of books too," Keeper said.

Chance shot him a warning look. "That's enough."

"What's that second book talk all about?" Jonnie Prettyboy asked.

"Nothing," Keeper replied. "It's just road talk."

"Speaking of the road," she said. "By the looks of that goddamned storm brewing up ahead, I think we're going to be in for a hell'uva ride."

CHAPTER SIXTY

Chance and Keeper were finally coming home. That, plus a tattered airmail letter just received from her Navy corpsman brother Neil somewhere in the Pacific, restored Alva's flagging spirits like no gin and tonic ever could. Never mind that foulmouthed Indian girl was also coming home with the boys. She fretted only briefly over what Jonnie Prettyboy would do without her mother, dead by her own hand, or for that matter, where the poor girl would live. Certainly not alone in that dreadful caboose left to rot out in the sand dunes! She believed the state would turn the girl over to the juvenile authorities, who would surely place her in a down-state orphanage. They in turn would see to her welfare and education, even if she was a half-breed.

Having successfully put the idea of an orphaned Jonnie Prettyboy out of Keeper's life, Alva set about preparing for his and Chance's homecoming, in that order of priority. She cleaned the house from top to bottom, but not the cellar, a dark and low-ceilinged place where the claustrophobic Alva Wick would not enter in spite of her passion for cleanliness and good order.

It had taken every minute to clean the big house after Chance called from Atlanta. She'd started with the upstairs windows, laundering the curtains next, followed by dusting and then scouring the bathroom floor on her hands and knees, to vacuuming every bedroom, the hallway, and even the runner down the front stairs. Dr. Wick's room was the most difficult because he was there, and Keepers the easiest, because he wasn't.

Early complained bitterly when Alva moved his piano tuning equipment from its customary place in his room, causing him to be late for a tuning assignment at St. Jerome's, and to put off helping out in the yard until after dinner. After a week of intermittent rain, the grass had grown too long for Alva to cut alone. To make do she tied a rope around Early's waist so he could pull the mower like a mule while she guided it by the handles and told him where to go.

The downstairs came next, with more window washing, curtain laundering, vacuuming, toilet scrubbing until the house reeked of bleach. Satisfied, Alva next gathered up her cherished cruet collection from a walnut secretary in the living room and took them one-by-one into the kitchen where she lovingly washed them in the sink with vinegar and hot water.

Alva saved hoeing weeds in the victory garden for last, and scolded Early for blindly digging up her zinnias and five stalks of sweet corn. She briefly considered washing Dr. Wick's flat-tired Hupmobile, but gave up the idea after realizing he would never be allowed behind the wheel again. Instead, she gave in to the need for a long cool bath, thinking a simple meal of fresh garden vegetables and yesterdays salted codfish served cold would hit the spot. The big meal, the special dinner she had planned, would take their monthly allotment of meat. Four T-bone steaks with baked potatoes on the side and a garden salad complimented with a reasonably good French wine.

But at that moment, what Alva wanted most was a cigarette and a tall gin over ice. After the third one, she decided it might be a rare treat for Chance if she wore her best dress for the occasion, plus her pre-war silk hose and underwear. She hoped he would stay sober long enough to appreciate it. Then maybe he'd even forget the former Miss Georgia.

CHAPTER SIXTY-ONE

The big Chrysler New Yorker with the attached equipment trailer sped through the thunderstorm, then shuddered and swerved when caught in a gust of wind-driven rain. Chance gripped the wheel and lifted his foot off the gas until he could control the heavy trailer swaying back and forth on its hitch. He fumbled for the pack of cigarettes in his shirt pocket, until remembering he'd given the last one to Jonnie Prettyboy. Without taking his eyes off the road, he pointed to the glove box. "There's a pack in there, Keep. Get it please?"

"I don't think this is a good time for smoking," Keeper replied, but he obeyed his father. The sky was an angry gangrenous color, with low clouds looking like giant heads of moldy cauliflower.

"I could use one of those smokes myself," Jonnie Prettyboy said from the backseat, and added, "If it's not asking too much."

Chance stole a quick glance toward the rearview mirror while lighting his cigarette. "Sorry, but it is," he replied.

"Piss."

"Maybe we should pull over somewhere," Keeper said.

"I've been through worse," Chance said.

"Me too," Jonnie Prettyboy said agreeably.

Keeper turned to his father. "If we make it in one piece, will this be in your second set of books?"

"There's those secret books again," Jonnie Prettyboy said accusingly. "Tell me, what's the big idea anyway?"

Keeper turned to face her. "It just means there's some things people don't need to know about, is all."

She smiled innocently." You mean like us in the old horse barn? That kind of thing?"

Keeper flushed red and flinched as hail exploded against the bug-streaked windshield as if being shot through the large end of a funnel.

"Now it's my turn to ask," Chance said. "What *about* the horse barn?"

Jonnie Prettyboy giggled. "Yeah, Keep," she goaded. "Tell him."

He wasn't about to admit to their anatomy lessons, beginning when he was ten and she thirteen. "It wasn't anything, that's all."

Chance grinned. "Are you keeping a second set of books too, Keep?"

Jonnie Prettyboy laughed. "I wouldn't worry about it, Mr. Wick. Keeper isn't mature enough to have a second set of books."

"I'm lots more mature then you think."

"Oh really? I could tell you stories that would curl your hair."

"Okay, kids," Chance said. "Settle down. Nobody gets their hair curled today."

CHAPTER SIXTY-TWO

It was mid-afternoon and raining when Chance pulled into a busy Texaco station in Knoxville. While an attendant gassed the car, Keeper and Jonnie Prettyboy bought candy bars and Cokes for the next leg of their journey. Chance bought a pack of Old Golds and a tin of aspirin for the blinding headache that came while driving through the storm.

It wasn't until they crossed the Tennessee-Ohio line two hours later when the skies finally cleared. Chance was shocked to see uprooted trees and storm-damaged farm homes and out-buildings gave mute evidence of the tornado-force winds that had preceded them.

When they reached the outskirts of Cincinnati, Jonnie Prettyboy had changed seats with Keeper for a third time and was fast asleep in the front seat with her head against the windowsill and her hands folded in her lap.

Chance glanced at his watch. Nearly five o'clock and he badly needed a drink, not that he dared. His mouth tasted like an ashtray and the headache hadn't responded to four aspirins chewed whole. He knew the smart thing to do would be to pull over, get something to eat, and then take a much-needed nap. He remembered passing some tourist cabins ten miles back. Maybe they should turn around and catch some shut-eye before heading out at first light. But turning around while on the way home wasn't something Chance Wick ever did. Needing to refuel the car, he pulled into an upcoming gas station.

"Where are we?" Keeper asked.

"Cincinnati."

"I'm hungry."

"We'll get something to eat here," Chance promised. He stepped out of the car and ordered an attendant to fill the tank and check the oil. The sun that had intermittently followed them from Knoxville disappeared once again behind a glowering sky that rumbled and flickered with lightning.

Keeper followed his father out of the car. "You don't look so hot."

"I don't feel so hot."

"Maybe we should stop for the night."

"We'll see."

"Maybe I should drive. I can, you know."

"Maybe I'll take you up on that."

Keeper glanced toward the car, as if considering the challenge of driving with the heavy demo trailer hooked to it, when Jonnie Prettyboy appeared from out of the car. "Where the hell are we?" she asked with a stretch and a yawn.

"Cincinnati," Keeper replied. "We're going to eat and maybe wait until morning to hit the road again."

"Fine with me," she said. "I'm in no hurry."

"I'm gonna to drive too," he announced with ill-concealed pride.

She jammed her hands in her pockets and frowned. "Bullshit, you will."

"Let's eat before deciding on anything," Chance said. "If the weather holds and I feel up to it, we'll push on."

Jonnie Prettyboy studied Chance's sallow face. "Something wrong, Mr. Wick?"

Keeper answered for his father. "He feels like crap, which is why I'm gonna to drive."

"That's enough," Chance said. "If either of you need to use the toilet, do it now."

Without waiting to be asked a second time, the two turned for the restrooms behind the station. "I think something's really wrong with your dad," she said as they waited for whoever was using the toilets to finish their business.

"This has been a bad trip for us," Keeper replied.

"It's been a fucked up trip for everybody."

A white woman stepped out of the ladies' room. When she saw Jonnie Prettyboy's darkly complected face she said, "Nigra's shit out yonder," and gestured to an outhouse nearly hidden behind a stack of old tires waiting for the next scrap drive.

"Fuck you bitch," Jonnie Prettyboy muttered, and quickly disappeared into the ladies' room.

When Keeper entered the men's room he found a coin-operated condom machine next to the urinal. He locked the door to keep his father from busting in on him like he'd done in Kokomo and dug a quarter from his pocket. He inserted the coin and turned the knob that dropped a foil-wrapped French tickler into the tray. He wasn't exactly sure what a French tickler did, but he figured he'd learned enough by sleeping with Zinnia to give Jonnie Prettyboy something special for her second set of books once they got home.

She'd been waiting for him outside the door. "You got any money on you?" she asked, snapping her fingers.

"Some. Why?"

"Because I need traveling money, is why."

"But my dad's paying for everything."

"Not where I'm goin', he ain't."

Keeper shook his head. "I won't let you leave me again."

"If you love me like you say you do, you'll give me the money."

"No."

"You were a dumb shit when I met you, and you're a dumb shit now."

"I've learned a lot about women since then."

Jonnie Prettyboy leveled her icy-gray eyes on Keeper and sneered, "Such as?"

Keeper patted his wallet where he'd put the French tickler. "That's for me to know, and you to find out."

278

CHAPTER SIXTY-THREE

A harried waitress approached the table where Chance, Keeper and Jonnie Prettyboy waited to be served. She slapped down three plastic-jacketed menus like over-sized playing cards and began rushing through the special of the day – Swiss steak, peas and mashed potatoes with gravy. That done, she said she'd be right back and left.

The café was crowded with travelers and locals alike, all catching a quick bite before heading back out into the storm that was gaining in intensity. It hadn't been Chance's idea to stop, but rather Jonnie Prettyboy's, who insisted they eat or else. The "or else" was never exactly spelled out.

"I'm going to have calves' liver with bacon and onions," Keeper said brightly, and added, "With a cherry malt."

"Make me wanna puke," Jonnie Prettyboy responded with a disgusted look. "I'm gonna have the special."

"You're kind of special yourself, Miss Prettyboy," Chance said as he shook a cigarette from the crumpled pack of Old Golds.

"That's me, alright," she replied, and looked away. "Real special."

Keeper scowled. "Cut it out, Dad. Your flirting makes me sick."

"Just trying to be friendly, Keep." When he reached into his shirt pocket for the lighter, it slipped from his hand and fell to the tabletop with the sound of a hammer glancing off a roofing nail.

Jonnie Prettyboy said. "Oops."

Chance snatched at the lighter, as if able to take back what had just happened. "It's nothing," he said with a lopsided grin, and waved at the waitress who seemed to be ignoring them.

She returned to their table oblivious to the concerned looks being exchanged all around. "Have you all decided what you want?" She held a yellow pencil poised over her order pad, waiting.

Chance appeared confused. He studied the lighter as if it had betrayed him, an inanimate lump of machined stainless steel that could no longer be trusted. He absently ran his thumb over the engraved message: "Doc. You Bastard. Velma." "Coffee?" he finally mumbled.

"That's all?" the waitress snapped, as if she knew her tip would be reduced by a third. She next turned to Jonnie Prettyboy with a disapproving look. "What about you, missy?"

"I'd like a beer, but I'll take the special and coffee *black*."

Keeper didn't wait to be asked. "Calves' liver, with bacon and onions. And a cherry malt."

"Comin' right up." Then, with a final glance disapproving glance that focused on Jonnie Prettyboy, the waitress turned for the kitchen.

"Places like this make me nervous," she said.

"Restaurants make you nervous?" Keeper asked.

"No, just crummy little dumps where people make assumptions."

"I don't understand," Chance mumbled.

"What's that?" Jonnie Prettyboy asked.

"I couldn't hold on to the razor."

"You mean the lighter?"

"Whatever," Chance replied.

She reached for his hand and held it. "Take it easy, Mr. Wick. We've got a long ways to go yet."

"I think we should get him to a doctor now," Keeper said.

Chance stared dumbly at the Zippo. "It's the road shakes, is all."

"It's more'n that, Dad, way more."

Chance didn't reply. With nothing more to say the three stared morosely at the gathering storm outside the rain-lashed windows until the waitress reappeared with their orders. Keeper complained about his liver being almost raw and the bacon fatty, although the cherry malt was perfect. Because she was starving, Jonnie Prettyboy said nothing about her special being tough and the peas raw, with lumpy gravy on the mashed potatoes. Before they'd finished Chance spilled his coffee twice.

Having declined dessert, Keeper and Jonnie Prettyboy helped Chance to his feet and left the café for the parking lot and the New Yorker – stumbling when he stumbled – and arguing when he became belligerent and insisted upon driving.

"C'mon, Dad," Keeper protested. "You're in no condition to drive."

Chance tried pushing his son away, but the effort proved weak and ineffective.

"Dad, listen to me!" Keeper shouted over a sudden whump of thunder. "You're having a stroke!"

"I'll be fine once I'm on the road."

"You promised me I'd have a turn driving, and now's the time!"

"Better let him drive, Mr. Wick," Jonnie Prettyboy said. "'Cause I'm not gettin' in the car otherwise."

Chance lowered his head in surrender. "Go ahead," he mumbled. "Keys in pocket."

Keeper reached for the keys and hesitated when he felt the creepy warmth of his father's groin. He couldn't help but remember him fucking Honey Burnside with that black rubber.

"Hurry up," Jonnie Prettyboy snapped. "I'm getting soaked."

Keeper held up the keys, still attached by a beaded chain to his father's lucky charm, and said, "We gotta get him in the backseat."

With no protest or help from Chance, the two managed to get him into the backseat before taking their places up front. Before Keeper could start the car, a brilliant flash of lightning exploded a power transformer across the street, followed by another concussive clap of thunder.

"Holy shit!" Jonnie Prettyboy exclaimed when the streetlights, the café lights, and every other light for as far as the eye could see blinked twice and went out. With a final worried look at his father in the rearview mirror, Keeper started the car and pulled smoothly out into traffic working the gears without stalling. Because the trailer had a push-pull effect, he alternated between the gas and the brakes, which because of his inexperience only made the lurching effect worse.

Jonnie Prettyboy sat watching the wipers squeegee dead bugs from the windshield and keeping an eye on traffic. When oncoming cars flashed their high-beams she slapped Keeper on the arm. "You dumb shit!" she hissed. "You forgot to turn on the headlights!"

Chance coughed from the backseat. "Can I trouble you for a cigarette, Miss Prettyboy? Seems I'm having a lil' trouble back here."

"Sure thing, Mr. Wick," she replied, and turned to reach across the seat. "Can you come a little closer?"

Chance pulled himself forward far enough for her to reach into his shirt pocket. She took a cigarette from the pack, put it between her lips and lit it off the Zippo found in the same pocket. After taking a drag to get the cigarette going, she placed it between Chance's lips. "Okay now, Mr. Wick?" He nodded.

"Mind if I have one too?"

He silently shook his head, as if to mean he had no objection, because there was little he could do to prevent her from doing so anyway.

She lit her cigarette off the Zippo then slumped back in her seat to read the legend engraved on the lighter. "Mr. Wick, what is 'Doc you bastard Velma' supposed to mean?" she asked.

"It means I messed up my life, Miss Prettyboy."

The rain was coming down harder now, and whenever Keeper stepped on the gas, the vacuum-powered wipers slowed to a torturous crawl. In the gathering dusk, the soft yellow glow of dashboard lights caused the two to look even younger than they were.

"Are we gonna drive straight through?" Jonnie Prettyboy asked.

Keeper adjusted the rearview mirror until he could see his father, who appeared to be asleep. "We have to," he replied.

Jonnie Prettyboy yawned. "Fuck but I'm tired."

"Why don't you sleep for a while?"

"You need somebody to keep you awake."

"I'm not a bit tired."

"Maybe just for a minute," she said, and curled up to put her head in Keeper's lap. Within two minutes she was fast asleep.

In spite of his father's precarious condition, Keeper felt grateful – elated even. Now *he* was responsible – fully able to make life and death decisions. *He* would determine how fast they would drive, what direction to take, when to stop, and when it came right down to it, where to get rid of the hated black trailer.

Keeper's newly-found sense of *adultness* was further enhanced by the unintended effect Jonnie Prettyboy's head in his lap was causing him. If she woke up before his erection subsided, he knew there'd be the devil to pay.

CHAPTER SIXTY-FOUR

Keeper closed his eyes long enough to let the New Yorker drift off the pavement and onto the shoulder. When stones rattled under the fenders he opened his eyes in alarm and steered back onto the road hoping no one had noticed. The headlights pierced the empty darkness ahead – twin beams of light that reflected off road markers and the 45 MPH speed limit signs that he chose to ignore. The rain hadn't lessened, and the wipers slapped back and forth on their highest setting. The speedometer was pegged at 70. Too fast, Keeper thought, and lifted his foot off the gas until he was doing 50. He was still thinking how close he'd come to killing everybody, when Jonnie Prettyboy raised her head from his lap to look out the window.

"Where are we?" she asked with a yawn.

"You asked me the same question in Atlanta, remember?"

"You mean at Mr. Sam's shop?"

"Maybe someday I'll tell you about when I stayed with them."

"Fine. So anyway, where the fuck are we?"

"Close to Goshen, Indiana."

"Jesus. How long did I sleep?"

"Almost six hours."

She turned to look in the back seat. "Your dad too?"

Keeper glanced at the fuel gauge. The needle rested on empty. "He's been snoring for the past two hours. I'll wake him when we stop for gas."

"I need to pee, so make it fast."

Keeper pointed at an upcoming billboard featuring the familiar red Pegasus trademark of the Mobil Oil Company. "We'll stop there," he said confidently.

Chance's voice came sleep-husky from the backseat. "It'll be closed."

"It better not be," Keeper replied, but as they approached the station, he could see for a fact that the lights were out. With an empty tank, he had no choice but to pull up to the pumps. He could see they were the old-fashioned kind, with graduated glass containers on top of each pump. He strained to see inside the darkened station, hoping but failing to see an attendant. He switched off the headlights and the ignition, but left the radio turned to a farm report.

"Open or not, I have to pee," Jonnie Prettyboy said firmly.

"So do I," Chance mumbled. He opened the door handle with his left hand and fell out face first.

"Jesus Christ!" Jonnie Prettyboy exclaimed.

Keeper opened his door against the wind-driven rain and rushed to his father's side. She had gotten there first, and had her arms around Chance, struggling to get him to his feet.

"We've got to get him back in the car!" Keeper yelled against the wind.

"You dumb shit!" she cried. "What do you *think* I'm trying to do?"

The two boosted Chance to his feet and propped him against the side of the car, where he swayed unsteadily, blinking into the slashing rain and fumbling one-handed at his fly.

"Give me a hand," Chance said, "before I piss myself."

"I can't!"

"Goddamn it, boy...do it!"

"For Christ's sake!" Jonnie Prettyboy shouted. "I'll do it!" She quickly unzipped Chance, dug out his penis, and held it until he was finished.

"I can't believe what you just did," Keeper said after they got his grinning father back in the car.

"Yeah, well I hope *you* never need help in that department, chicken shit."

Keeper looked hopeful. "What if I do?"

"I guess you'll have to squat and pee like a girl," she replied with a laugh. Then she scurried behind the New Yorker to do her business on the lee side of the black demo trailer.

Keeper waited impatiently until she returned before going himself. "I think I pissed on my shoe," he said when he came back.

"How'd it get so dark?" Chance mumbled from the backseat.

"Because it's night," Keeper replied.

"I don't think that's what he means," Jonnie Prettyboy said. She pulled the Zippo from her pocket, held it in front of Chance's face and struck a light. "Do you see this, Mr. Wick?"

"It sounds like my…um…razor."

She turned to Keeper with a stricken expression. "Jesus," she whispered. "He's blind, just like Early."

Keeper turned to face his father. "Can you see anything, Dad?" he asked.

"It'll pass. Where are we?"

"Near Goshen."

"Nothing around here but the Amish."

"We just can't sit around doing nothing."

"What time is it?"

"Almost two."

"How much gas in the tank?"

"The gauge reads empty."

Chance grunted in acknowledgement. "Station'll probably open in a few hours."

"Maybe I can find a farmhouse and borrow some gas."

Chance coughed; a rheumy sound deep in his chest. "The only fuel the Amish use is coal and kerosene."

"See if we can get a weather report on the radio," Jonnie Prettyboy suggested.

"What good would that do?" Keeper asked. "We already know about the weather."

"Then put on some music to take our minds off this fucking, sorry, Mr. Wick, predicament."

"We'll run the battery down," Keeper said.

"Then we'll charge it back up when the station opens, you dumb shit."

"Would one of you get my bottle?" Chance asked. "It's in my... what's it in again?"

"Suitcase?" Jonnie Prettyboy asked.

"That's it."

Without waiting for Keeper to argue against his father's wishes, she grabbed the keys from the ignition and stepped back into the storm. She straddled the trailer hitch, unlocked the trunk and quickly unbuckled the leather straps that held the travel-worn suitcase together. Ignoring the red portable typewriter, she sorted through Chance's dirty socks and underwear until she found the half-gone fifth of Glenmore. After taking a long swig for herself, she slammed down the trunk lid and returned to the car.

Keeper glared when she handed the bottle to his father, but wisely kept his mouth shut. Instead, he fiddled with the radio until finding a station playing the new hit, *You'll Always Hurt the One You Love*, by the Mills Brothers.

"Perfect, don't you think, honey?" he asked with a sideways glance.

Jonnie Prettyboy cracked open the vent window and lit a cigarette off the dashboard lighter. "It's an old story. And I've changed my mind. Don't call me honey anymore."

"Like that song," Chance muttered. "Turn it up."

Jonnie Prettyboy reached across Keeper's knee and increased the volume. "How's that, Mr. Wick?"

Chance placed the open bottle of Glenmore between his legs. "Even better if I had a cigarette and a woman during my hour of need."

Jonnie Prettyboy laughed and fitted her cigarette between the first and second fingers of Chance's left hand. "Here's your coffin nail, but I'm afraid the only female around is me."

Chance responded with a throaty chuckle. "Suits me fine."

"Isn't she a little young, even for you?" Keeper asked.

"I'll admit to being an imperfect man, Keeper, but that was uncalled for."

He turned to look at his father. "How about what you did in Atlanta? Wasn't that uncalled for?"

"C'mon, Keep," Jonnie Prettyboy hissed. "Not here."

"No. Let me talk. Would it surprise you to know, Dad," he said, "that Honey Burnside wanted to fuck me too?"

Jonnie Prettyboy's face showed shock and disgust. "What's that all about?"

He didn't answer. "Would it, Dad?" he repeated.

Chance took a deep pull from his cigarette. In the dark, its brightly glowing tip painted his sallow face a sickly orange. "No, Keeper, it wouldn't."

"Do the women you fuck know you don't have any back teeth and wear a bridge?

"What do you want from me? A blood confession to all my sins?"

"You'd bullshit your way around that too."

"Son, don't..." Chance's voice trailed off.

"This is terrible," Jonnie Prettyboy moaned. "Please, stop it now."

"What'd you do for Clark Gable," Keeper said, "when he wrote 'I own you one' in that Union Pacific matchbook?"

Chance shrugged helplessly. "Somebody I met on the train wrote it. I thought you'd get a kick out of it, is all."

"Was that somebody a woman, by any chance?"

Jonnie Prettyboy groaned. "Keeper, *please!*"

"That's okay," Chance said. "Let him talk."

"I wanna know everything," Keeper replied. "Starting from the day I was born."

A sudden gust of rain lashed the New Yorker, rocking it on its suspension and swinging the Mobil sign overhead nearly horizontal on its supporting chains. Lightning forked beyond a tree line a mile down the highway, followed by a surge of rolling thunder and more lightning. Its strobe-like effect froze the three in their places as if sculpted from stone. Chance stubbed out the cigarette in the backseat ashtray and then fumbled for the open bottle between his legs.

"I'd been on the road. You weren't breathing when I got home. Your grandfather was unable to act, to get you to breathe." He raised the bottle to his lips and drank deeply of the cheap bourbon.

"You've already told me that story."

"He was haunted by the idea of making another mistake."

"What's that supposed to mean?"

Chance reached across the seat for Jonnie Prettyboy. "Can I trouble you for another cigarette, Miss...uh?"

"No more smokes," Keeper interrupted. "Answer the question."

Chance cleared his throat. "It goes back to when he delivered Early. It was nearing midnight, and because it was your grandfather's birthday, he wanted his grandson to share the same birth date."

"Sounds dumb to me. What happened next?"

"In his zeal to deliver Early, he blinded him with a pair of forceps."

"But...you told me Early fell on a rake when he was two years old."

"It was a lie, Keeper, a lie to protect you from the truth."

CHAPTER SIXTY-FIVE

Keeper stared dumbly at the neon station clock that had become an indistinct green smudge through the rain and condensation-coated windows. "You're lying again," he said. "Grandpa wouldn't do that."

"Sorry to disillusion you," Chance replied. "Doctors are human too. Even they make mistakes."

"Is that your excuse too?" Keeper asked.

"I don't know."

"What kind of answer is that?"

"The truth."

"I think you hate us."

Chance coughed into his bandanna. "That's not true and you know it."

"But you always say when you're home you can't wait to be back on the road."

"And vice-versa. Strange, isn't it?"

"Yeah," Keeper replied, "and stranger still, is when you're home you're either drunk or sleeping one off."

Jonnie Prettyboy pounded her fist on the dashboard. "Goddamn you, Keeper! I'm going to get out and walk. I'd rather get pneumonia than sit here and listen while you attack your dad, who by the way isn't doing too hot."

"Go ahead," Keeper replied. "This is none of your business anyway."

"It already *is* my business. Until I can make my break, your dad is responsible for my well-being."

"Uh, Keeper?" Chance asked softly, haltingly. "I'd like you to take, uh, Miss…uh…" His voice trailed off as he searched his brain for the name he'd already forgotten.

"Prettyboy," Keeper snapped. "Jonnie Prettyboy,"

"Yes, of course. I want you to take her in your arms and hold her as tight as you can."

"Why?" Keeper asked.

"Just do it."

"Okay, Mr. Wick," Jonnie Prettyboy said, taking the initiative. Stubbing out her cigarette in the ashtray, she slid across the seat next to Keeper, who looked sullenly out the window as forked lightning probed the distant horizon. She wiggled closer and draped her arm around his neck. The radio dial glowed dimly as The Ink Spots sang, *If I Didn't Care.*

"Are you doing it?" Chance asked.

"Yes he is," Jonnie Prettyboy answered. "Aren't you Keeper?"

"Yeah."

"I'm afraid I have sad news for you, Miss…"

"Sad?" she interrupted, "or bad?"

Chance coughed, deep and phlegmy. "What's the difference?"

"Sad means I might give a shit, bad means I probably won't."

"Then I'm afraid you'll have to choose."

"C'mon, Dad," Keeper grunted. "Quit playing games."

"Miss, uh, Jonnie," Chance stumbled. "Your mother is dead."

"Bad news comes fast nowadays," Jonnie Prettyboy said.

Keeper held her more tightly. "Couldn't you have waited until later to tell her?"

"Shut up, Keeper," she said, and turned to Chance. "How'd it happen, Mr. Wick?"

"She took her own life."

Jonnie Prettyboy took a deep breath and sighed.

"You didn't like her much, did you honey?" Keeper said.

"I hated what she'd become. But without her to sign off on me, the authorities will put me someplace where I don't want to be."

Lightning flickered beyond the horizon, followed long seconds later by a low rumble as the storm moved north and to the east.

Overhead, clouds parted to reveal a crescent moon set against a backdrop of glittering stars.

Keeper turned to face his father, ready to make a deal. Silence in exchange for helping Jonnie Prettyboy. "What are you going to do, Dad?"

"Keep her."

"What?"

"Not Keeper. Keep…her."

"Nobody keeps me," Jonnie Prettyboy snapped. "And I'm sure as hell not going back to Dakota Straits, either."

"We could fix up the horse barn for you, couldn't we, Dad?"

"Sure thing, Keep," Chance agreed before nodding off.

"See honey?" Keeper said. "That settles everything."

"If you knew what that fucker Lulu LaRue made me do," Jonnie Prettyboy replied, "you wouldn't think so."

"If I told you what Zinnia and I did, maybe that would even things out."

"Who the fuck's Zinnia?"

"Mr. Sam's granddaughter. She's sixteen and lives with him over the store you robbed."

Jonnie Prettyboy pushed away from Keeper and gave him a long questioning look. "You don't say so?"

"I do say so," Keeper replied, smiling. "Wanna hear more?"

"I'm listening."

"We hit it right off, Zinnia and I did."

"Did you play croquet in the backyard, or tiddly-winks upstairs?"

"Neither, but I got to highball Mr. Sam's Lionel."

Her pale gray eyes flashed with uncommon jealousy. "I'll bet you highballed Zinnia too, huh, lover boy?"

Keeper glanced at his father in the backseat, but he appeared to be sleeping. "I guess you could say that."

"You guess, or you know?"

Keeper nodded. "Did I say she was a Negro?"

"You just spoiled my first guess."

"Do you have something against colored people?"

"What do you think, you dumb shit."

"Sorry," Keeper replied. "I wasn't thinking."

"You seldom are. On the other hand, I've got a hard-on for certain white sons of bitches."

"Keep?" Chance's voice came tremulous from the backseat. "This has been entertaining as hell, but I've got a brutal headache. Better we should get back on the road."

"We need gas, remember?"

"I've been thinking. What kind of pumps are out there?"

"They're the old-fashioned kind, with those glass bottles on top."

Chance grunted in apparent recognition. "They don't require electricity to operate. There's a hand pump that forces gas into those graduated containers you see. When full, gravity feeds gas through the hose and into the tank."

"You could've told me that before," Keeper replied. He slid out from behind the wheel to examine the pump closest to the New Yorker. To his dismay, the pump had a padlock on it. "It's locked."

Jonnie Prettyboy rolled down her window. "Try the other one, numbnuts."

Keeper stepped to the next pump. There was a padlock on this one too, a rusty Yale. He kicked it in frustration, and again, until the bracket that held the padlock snapped off.

Jonnie Prettyboy stuck her head out the window. "You'd better hurry, Keeper!"

"Give me the keys," he said. "There's a lock on the cap so nobody will steal our gas."

She pulled the keys from the ignition and handed them over. "Look who's talking about stealing gas."

"This is an emergency."

"I think you should take your dad over to South Bend where there's a hospital."

Chance spoke up from the backseat. "No. Take me home."

"I don't know, Dad," Keeper replied as he unlocked the gas cap. "I think you're having a coronary thrombosis."

"Coronary throm-what?" Jonnie Prettyboy asked.

"It's a kind of stroke. I learned it from my grandpa's medical books."

"That's encouraging," she said. "Dr. Wick dispensing gas and practicing medicine at a Mobil station."

Keeper ignored the comment and began pumping furiously to fill the glass container with gasoline. Once he'd filled the tank he replaced the gas cap and locked it.

"Slip five dollars under the station door for the gas you took," Chance said before Keeper could get behind the wheel.

He pulled out his Boy Scout wallet and took the five dollar bill tucked behind the French tickler. He slid the money under the station door, and then paused, as if forgetting something. He turned for the demo trailer, quickly uncoupled the hitch and released the two safety chains that kept the trailer from running wild. Then he cranked the jack stem down, releasing the trailer.

"What was that all about?" Jonnie Prettyboy asked when he returned.

"I'm leaving the demo trailer here," he said flatly. "The factory can send somebody else to come and get it. All's I know is it won't be my dad."

It the backseat, Chance smiled and closed his eyes.

CHAPTER SIXTY-SIX

Keeper continued to feel a nagging sense of guilt for having left the hated demo trailer behind in Goshen, Indiana. If his father lost his job because of it, it would be his fault. Meanwhile, Chance remained curled up in the backseat, his right arm covered his eyes and he clutched the red bandana, into which he occasionally spit.

"Will Mr. Pettigrew will fire you because of what I did?" Keeper asked.

"Don't know," Chance replied after an uncomfortable wait.

"What will we do for money if he does?"

"We'll cross that bridge when we come to it."

Keeper slowed when he saw a dark blue Michigan state police car approaching from the opposite lane. It was the first real sign that meant they were getting closer to home. "Maybe we could move to Australia," he said, and breathed a sigh of relief when the trooper passed.

"We're not moving anywhere," Chance mumbled.

"But you said you liked the aboriginal culture. Maybe you could write a book about them. Jonnie Prettyboy could come too. We'd live off the land like they do, and eat snakes and berries and ostrich eggs..."

Jonnie Prettyboy interrupted. "You'd never eat a snake. Besides, a Jap sub would probably torpedo us before we ever got to Australia. And besides that, your dad is blind as a fucking bat."

Keeper shook his head as the reality of their situation sank in. "I can't believe we'll have two blind people in the house."

Chance coughed into the bandana. "Your granddad had a patient with same symptoms. Gave him three aspirins and ordered him to bed."

"You're kidding, right?"

"No. Vision came back next day. So did use of...arm. But he died five weeks later from lockjaw after stepping on a rusty nail."

"We're gonna need gas pretty soon. And aspirins for you."

"Where're we...now?"

"On highway one-thirty-one north. We passed through Kalamazoo fifteen minutes ago."

"Stop at Grand Rapids. We can get gas, aspirin...cigarettes there."

"There's still half a pack," Jonnie Prettyboy said. "I've been kind of hoarding them just in case Cannonball Baker here decided to drive straight through to Dakota Straits."

"Light one, please?" Chance asked.

She lit one between her lips and reached for Chance's hand. "Here you go, Mr. Wick," she said, and placed the cigarette between his fingers.

Keeper opened his vent window and waved away the smoke. "Last thing my dad needs is another cigarette."

"And the last thing I need is lip from you," Jonnie Prettyboy said, and added, "It's about time we stopped to pee and eat too."

Chance pushed himself upright and leaned forward as if he could see. "We can stop at...Rowe Hotel on Monroe. There's a gas station..." The sentence remained unfinished.

"What about your aspirins and smokes?" Keeper asked.

"Rexall store around corner from... Rowe. Lunch counter there."

"I'm not so sure we should waste valuable time eating."

"Pick up sandwiches to eat in car...save time."

"Good," Keeper replied. "I'm tired of fine dining anyway."

"You'll need...money." With the cigarette left to dangle from the corner of his mouth, Chance fumbled through his right pocket for the silver money clip and handed it to Keeper. "There should be...few hundred dollars here."

"How much should I take?"

Chance coughed. "Enough so I don't have to do...again."

Keeper gave the money clip to Jonnie Prettyboy. "Take a twenty, honey, while I get my wallet."

Jonnie Prettyboy scowled. "I warned you, goddamn it. Don't call me honey anymore."

"What did I do now?"

"Think about it," she snapped. "Atlanta…Mr. Sam's…Zinnia. Want more?"

Keeper flared. "You're nobody to talk, Miss Cooch Show!" He angrily thrust the wallet toward Jonnie Prettyboy. "Put the money in there."

When she found the foil-wrapped French tickler Keeper had hidden, she held it up between her thumb and forefinger. "What's this?" she asked with an accusing sneer.

He lunged for the rubber. "That's *mine!*"

Chance clutched the robe strap. "What the hell…going on?" he asked.

Jonnie Prettyboy held the rubber beyond Keeper's reach. "Were you expecting to use this on me, you dumb shit?" she taunted.

"What…happening, Keeper?"

"Its okay, Mr. Wick," she crooned. "He only wants to be prepared, just like the Boy Scouts. The miserable creeps."

"C'mon," Keeper whined. "Give it back!"

With a grin she dropped the rubber into her shirt pocket, and with Keeper's attention turned to a passing Cadillac, she quickly peeled off five twenties from the money clip and stuffed them into a pocket of the shorts she wore from Keeper's suitcase. Then she held the clip over the back seat. "Here, Mr. Wick. We took what we needed. Gimmie your hand."

When Chance tried to transfer the cigarette to his lips, it dropped from his fingers. "Can't hold…"

Jonnie Prettyboy leaned over the seat. "Right next to your left foot, Mr. Wick. It's burning a hole in the carpet."

"*Damn!*"

"Just stamp it out."

Chance moaned. "Can't move…leg."

She jumped over the seat and into the back again. She picked up the smoldering cigarette and tamped it out in the ashtray. "Are you sure about not going to the hospital, Mr. Wick? 'Cause I don't think you'll make it otherwise."

He shook his head. "We'll make it...won't we, Keep? Get me home...die in own bed."

Keeper looked into the rearview mirror – more scared and uncertain than ever – and said, "I'll get you there Dad. You can count on me."

Jonnie Prettyboy snuggled close to Chance and held his limp arm in her lap. "You don't mind me taking up space back here, Mr. Wick?" she asked softly.

"I prefer it, Miss, uh..." His voice trailed off, thick with phlegm.

"Never mind, Mr. Wick," she whispered, and allowed Chance to rest his head on her shoulder. "We'll have you home and in your own bed in no time. Just take it easy."

CHAPTER SIXTY-SEVEN

Chance slept with his head on Jonnie Prettyboy's shoulder while she stared vacantly out the window to her right. They had just entered the Grand Rapids city limits, and Keeper had no idea how to get to the Rowe Hotel. He caught Jonnie Prettyboy's eye in the rearview mirror before speaking. "You'll have to wake Dad. I need directions to the hotel."

Jonnie Prettyboy yawned and nudged Chance awake. "Mr. Wick?"

"Yes, Alva?"

"It's me, Mr. Wick, Jonnie Prettyboy. We're in Grand Rapids, and Keeper wants to know how to get to the hotel."

"Where…what street?"

"Still on highway one-thirty-one," Keeper replied, "just past the city limits."

"Make left on Market," Chance mumbled.

Keeper frowned and looked into the rearview mirror. "I thought you said the Rowe was on Monroe."

"Market runs into Monroe, I think. Damn."

"That's okay, Mr. Wick," Jonnie Prettyboy said. "We'll find it."

"I see Market up ahead," Keeper said.

"Rowe on right, gas station across…" Chance struggled to find the words, "parking structure."

"Do you want me to park there?"

"No. Pull up…get gas while one of you goes to Rexall for..sandwich."

"Can I get you a cigarette, Mr. Wick?" Jonnie Prettyboy asked.

Chance shook his head. "Lost taste for them."

"I kind of wish I would," she said, and without asking for permission, poked Keeper on the shoulder. Light a smoke for me, will ya? And don't lip it."

Keeper grunted and reached for the half-gone pack of Old Golds where she'd left it on the seat. He shook out a cigarette between his lips like he'd seen her do, lit it off the cigar lighter and held it for her to take. "Anything else, honey?" he asked, and coughed when smoke went into his lungs.

"Yeah. Get me a carton of smokes when you're in Rexalls."

"I've got an idea how to get you to quit."

"Who said I wanted to?" she asked.

"Just try closing your eyes when you smoke."

"Why the fuck should I do that?"

"I've never seen a blind person who smoked, like Early, for example."

"Would that be like eating with your nose pinched?"

"I think so."

"I hate to admit you're right," she said after trying it. "When Early starts eating with his nose pinched, let me know. That's when I'll stop smoking."

"You're impossible," he replied. When he had the gas station in sight he slowed before pulling up to the pumps, but hit the brakes too hard and stalled the engine, which ticked metallically in the sudden silence. Too tired to be embarrassed, he yawned and blinked to stay awake. When an attendant came out of the station, Keeper rolled down his window and pointed to the green rationing sticker pasted in the corner of the bug-splattered windshield. Green allowed for unlimited gasoline because it signified the car was used for the war effort.

"Fill it?" the attendant asked.

"Please," Keeper answered, and added, "With premium Ethyl," when he remembered.

The attendant peered into the backseat where Chance and Jonnie Prettyboy sat huddled together. "Is something wrong?" he asked.

"It's my dad," Keeper replied. "He's sick and I'm taking him home."

The attendant looked at Jonnie Prettyboy, who unflinchingly glared back. "She your sister?"

Keeper turned to look, as if to reassure himself she was still there. "She's my best friend."

The attendant nodded. "There's a lock on your gas cap."

"Oh, yeah," Keeper replied, and handed the keys to the attendant, who looked back suspiciously.

"You don't look old enough to be driving," he said.

"Well, I am," Keeper lied. "I'm driving on my learner's permit. It's legal as long as a parent is with me."

With a shake of his head, the attendant walked around to the rear of the car and unlocked the gas cap to begin fueling.

Keeper reached for his wallet to check on how much money he had. There was a ten and a five tucked inside. "I'll get the aspirin and sandwiches while we're getting gas," he said. "Do you still want a carton of smokes?"

"What do you think?"

"Dumb," Keeper said, and set off at a trot for the drug store. It was early, and several customers at the counter were eating breakfast. A waitress making change at the cash register looked up at his approach.

"Can I order two sandwiches to go?" Keeper asked.

She pointed to an illustrated menu posted on the wall behind the counter. "Take your pick."

He thought the club sandwiches looked good and pointed at them like the waitress had. "I'll take two of those," he replied.

"Have 'em for you in a minute."

"Where's your aspirins and cigarettes?"

The waitress gave him a long look. "Aspirin are on aisle three, and the cigarettes are on aisle five, but don't bother looking for them."

"Why not?"

"Because we don't sell smokes to kids, is why."

"They're for my dad," Keeper explained.

"If I had a nickel for every time I've heard that, I'd retire to Miami Beach."

"Then forget it, and please hurry with the sandwiches. We're double parked." After finding the aspirins, he circled the store, looking for what, he wasn't sure, until he came across a display of sunglasses. He took two and brought them back to the lunch counter. When the waitress returned with the club sandwiches in a brown paper bag, Keeper told her to add the sunglasses to his bill, along with the aspirins. When he got back to the car, the attendant was cleaning the windshield.

"How much for the gas?" Keeper asked.

"Your best friend paid for the gas and three bottles of pop," he replied as he handed the keys back to Keeper. "I checked on your dad. I think he's having a stroke."

"Are you a doctor?"

The attendant shook his head. "I'm a third-year dentistry student at Michigan State. My uncle owns this station and the parking structure across the street. I work summers for him."

"My dad won't let me take him to a hospital. He says if he's going to die, he wants to be in his own bed."

"Where's home?" the attendant asked.

Keeper pointed west. "Not far. Dakota Straits."

The attendant nodded. "Can I get you a candy bar or something?"

"No thanks. I bought some sandwiches."

The attendant put his squeegee aside. "What's your name, kid?"

"Keeper. Keeper Wick."

"Look, Keeper. Your dad needs to be in a hospital. Let me call an ambulance."

Chance grunted from the backseat. "Cut gab...take home."

Keeper snuffled. "See?"

"I understand, kid," he replied. "Your dad is the spitting image of my own dad. Get him home for me too, okay?"

CHAPTER SIXTY-EIGHT

Keeper held the New Yorker to 70 MPH as he drove north on US 31 toward Muskegon, not caring if he got a ticket. Jonnie Prettyboy sat next to him. She wore the sunglasses he'd bought at Rexalls. They'd eaten the last of their club sandwiches an hour ago and held their nearly empty Coke bottles between their legs. Chance had taken three aspirins before leaving Grand Rapids and was snoring in the backseat.

"I should've peed back there," Jonnie Prettyboy said.

"Me too," Keeper agreed. He was pleased to have her seated next to him again.

"Stop in Muskegon."

He stole a quick glance at his father. "Maybe we should wait 'till we get home."

"I can't pinch mine off like you can."

"Then cross your legs."

"Don't tell me what to do."

"C'mon," Keeper pleaded. "Don't let the road get to you."

"It already has."

"I'll stop at the first place with a public toilet."

"Public or not, I'll piss in the woods if I have to."

Keeper shrugged and stared tiredly down the highway. The sun glaring overhead made him appreciate the sunglasses he'd impulsively bought. Still, he was a fine one to talk about road nerves. The road had gotten to him too. The thrill of finally being able to drive had been replaced by fatigue and tedium. It seemed as if he'd been gone for months. He couldn't even remember what his mother's face looked like, or Early's, or even their grandfather's, much less the colorful circus posters his father had brought home from the road. He wondered how his father had come by them, or if there was a woman with him at the time. He made a mental note to throw away the Union Pacific matchbook with the fake Clark Gable autograph once they were home.

By the time they reached Muskegon, all he wanted to do was sleep for a week.

"There's a Greyhound station," Jonnie Prettyboy said, and pointed. "We can piss there."

Keeper pushed the sunglasses over his head and turned to park near an idling silver and blue Greyhound bus. A uniformed driver was loading suitcases and packages into cavernous bins under the passenger compartment. The destination scroll above the windshield spelled Atlanta in white letters on black.

"Ladies first," Jonnie Prettyboy said, Stay here and watch your dad." Without waiting for a reply she opened her door and hopped out.

"Make it fast," Keeper said, and turning on the radio and sat back to wait. Chance remained in the backseat, curled up in a fetal position. His hands were folded under his head and appeared to be sleeping peacefully. A commercial for Ovaltine was on the radio when Jonnie Prettyboy reappeared next to Keeper's open window.

"What took you so long?" he asked.

"Woman trouble," she replied. "Something you wouldn't understand."

"Don't be too sure," he said as he slipped out from behind the wheel and turned for the bus station. "And keep an eye on my dad," he called over his shoulder.

He ran through the waiting room to the men's room – dismayed to find men standing in line at both urinals and someone using the single toilet. He waited, shifting from one foot to the other, until his turn came. Finishing, he zipped up and ran back to the car, where he was stunned to see Jonnie Prettyboy holding his suitcase.

"Whu...what the hell?" Keeper stammered. "What are you doing with my mother's suitcase?"

"This is where we part company. I'll send your clothes and suitcase later, when I can get my own stuff."

"C'mon honey, this isn't the least bit funny."

She pushed her sunglasses high over her forehead and nodded toward the idling bus. Her iridescent silver-gray eyes glittered. "I'm going back."

"To Atlanta?"

"I've got unfinished business with a certain fucking cop back there."

"You can't leave now! We're almost home!"

"*You* are almost home."

"But…"

"I'm not gonna let the authorities put me in some fucking orphanage."

Keeper wiped his eyes, ashamed to be seen crying if front of five passengers boarding the Atlanta- bound Greyhound. "You can't. I won't let you."

She stepped toward him with a determined smile. "Sorry. Your dad is a swell guy. Tell him I'll send him his hundred bucks back when I find work. Oh, and by the way, I put the Zippo back in his shirt pocket."

Keeper smiled through his tears in spite of himself. "I don't think he'll need it anymore."

"So, she said, smiling back. "Wanna feel my boobies before I leave."

He laughed at their old joke. "Sure,"

She held her smile. "How'd you like something even better?"

He couldn't believe what he was hearing. "Are you talking about actual sexual intercourse?"

She set the suitcase down and nodded. "Yep."

"Where are we gonna do that, for crying out loud?"

She gestured toward the New Yorker. "On the front seat, you dumb shit."

"But the bus…my dad…?"

"The bus leaves in fifteen minutes, and your pa is sleeping dead to the world in the backseat." She waited hands on hips for his reply. "Well, Dr. Horse Barn? Yes, or no?"

Keeper turned to look in the backseat, relieved to see his father hadn't moved so much as a finger. "Well, okay," he replied uncertainly. "We'll have to be awful quiet."

"Like church mice," she whispered. While he stood guard, she climbed into the front seat, undid the shorts she'd borrowed from Keeper and pulled them down over he slender legs to leave the bunched around an ankle.

Keeper gulped and became instantly erect when he looked down at her splayed figure. "Jesus, honey, but you look good."

"Ready?" she whispered.

"You still got that French tickler you too from me?"

"Yeah, but you're not using that freak thing on me."

"Okay then." He quickly wriggled out of his shorts and crawled awkwardly on top. For a second he almost wished his father would wake up to discover he wasn't the only Wick who could fuck on the road.

"Ow!" she hissed. "Watch the fucking elbows!"

"I can't find your pussy."

"Jesus!" she said. "What a dope!" She reached for his thrusting erection and guided it toward the intended target. "There," she said as he entered her.

"Holy shit," Keeper whispered. "I don't think I can hold off for very long."

"Think about something bad."

"Like what?"

"Like having a car run over you dog, for example."

"But I don't have a dog."

"Jesus, you dumb shit. Then think about something just as bad."

Keeper continued his methodical thrusting, a technique learned from Zinnia Day, until coming up with an idea. "What if it was Early who gets run over?"

She made a pleasurable-sounding moan. "Even better."

Keeper discovered that by shutting his eyes, he could better visualize Early's mangled remains under the wheels of a Blatz beer truck. Even the chatter of passengers boarding the Greyhound seemed to fade into the distance. The only thing that mattered now was holding off until Jonnie Prettyboy said it was okay to get off.

"Oh...uh...uh...god," she grunted, "Don't stop now."

"I...uh...uh...won't," he whispered, but he did, coming in spite of Early dead under the beer truck.

She pushed him away to signal it was over and kissed him on the lips. "That was good," she murmured. After pulling on her shorts and zipping up, she stepped out of the car to stand under the tree-dappled sunlight that highlighted her closely-cropped black hair. With a final tug at her waistband, she grabbed the suitcase and turned for the idling Greyhound as the driver loaded the last piece of luggage.

"Wait, honey!" Keeper cried. "Will you write me letters from the road?"

Jonnie Prettyboy lowered the Rexall sunglasses over her pale gray eyes and paused after handing the driver her suitcase. "I might," she replied, smiling. "And then again, I might not."

CHAPTER SIXTY-NINE

When Keeper finally reached home, exhausted from the trip, he parked the New Yorker in the driveway with its overheated engine ticking metallically as it cooled. Ever since leaving the Greyhound station an hour ago, he'd been alternating between weeping over losing Jonnie Prettyboy and turning to look in the back seat where Chance remained curled up, silent and unmoving. When he stepped out of the car to wake his father, Keeper couldn't rouse him no matter how hard he shook him. Alarmed, he ran into the house to find Early drinking coffee in the kitchen. With a hurried explanation that something was wrong with their father, he led Early back to the car, where they carefully rolled Chance onto his back. His handsome face had become a death mask and his blackened tongue protruded from his mouth like a baked potato. The left side of his face was purple with congealed blood that filled the capillaries just under the surface of his skin.

Keeper couldn't help but think that his father needed a shave.

Alva heard the commotion and had come out to stand behind the two, but was unable to look. She held her hands over her eyes, wailing, "Oh God oh God oh *God!*"

Early held their father's cold and lifeless hands in his. "What the hell happened?" Tears streamed from his unseeing eyes.

"He probably had a thrombosis in his brain," Keeper replied. "It hit him when we were on the road. At first he couldn't see. Then his arm went numb, and then his leg."

Alva pounded on the New Yorker's hail-pocked hood. "I *knew* something like this would happen!" she cried. "The goddamned road took everything from me!"

Early held his nose. "Why do I smell shit?"

Keeper glanced at his weeping mother before replying. "Grandpa said people do that when they die."

Early nodded, as if understanding. "We'd better get mother in the house and call the doctor to give her something."

"We'd better call the undertaker too," Keeper added.

"Goddamned road!" Alva shrieked.

Keeper closed the New Yorker's doors to shield his father's body, then went to his mother's side and placed an arm around her. "C'mon, Mom. We'd better go inside."

"Goddamned road," she sobbed.

"Its okay, Mom."

Alva clutched at her son. "Oh, Keeper. Oh, dear, dear Keeper. What will become of us now?"

He had been wondering the same thing. "Did Dad have any life insurance?"

"He had a policy through the plant," she sniffed. "His employer arranged it is all I know."

Keeper wanted to sound reassuring, even though he felt otherwise. "I'll call them later, after things settle down."

Alva forced a smile. "Dear, dear Keeper, always the man of the house whenever…" She broke down again, unable to finish or stop the tears.

"I'll break the news to Grandpa," Early said.

"Let me," Keeper replied. "He'll probably want the details. Now, let's go in."

"And leave your father alone?" Alva asked tearfully.

Keeper tightened his grip around his mother's shoulders. "C'mon."

"Oh God!" she sobbed helplessly, uselessly.

Keeper silently led his mother past Early holding the door and into the kitchen.

"I'll call the doctor," Early volunteered.

"To hell with doctors," Alva sobbed. "I need a gin and tonic. Make it a double, and make it fast."

"I'll get it," Keeper said. Already he was feeling responsible, able to give the orders, and ready to make the important decisions his father always made. It felt good.

Alva reached for Keeper's face and squeezed his peeling sun-burned cheeks. "Dear Keeper, promise me you'll never leave again!"

"I can't do that, Mom, six years from now I'll probably be in college."

"I can't bear to think about it!"

"We'll talk tomorrow, okay?"

Alva sniffled. "Whatever you say."

Keeper patted her arm and turned to make the drink she asked for. Her gin was always kept in the freezer compartment with the ice cubes. He reached for the bottle, unscrewed the cap and poured a good six ounces into a clean tumbler, followed by a splash of tonic water and three ice cubes cracked from an aluminum tray

"You know what I want right now, more than anything?" He asked when serving the drink.

Alva gave him an expectant look. "What's that, dear?"

"A beer. An ice cold beer."

CHAPTER SEVENTY

The undertaker and his assistant came late that afternoon. Keeper watched alone from atop the back stoop as the two men removed Chance's stiffening body from the New Yorker and lowered him into the lightweight wicker casket used for transporting dead bodies to the funeral home. Keeper felt detached – almost as if watching a movie, while the two men tried straightening his father's arms and legs so they could close the lid. As they struggled, Chance's engraved Zippo slipped from his shirt pocket. Seeing the brushed stainless steel lighter shook Keeper from his reverie and he rushed to grab it before it disappeared into the hands of the undertaker's assistant, who had an unlit cigarette dangling from the corner of his mouth.

Dinner was uncommonly common, just as it always was whenever Chance was away. Keeper sat at the head of the table, a position his father occupied when he was home. Dr. Wick was brought downstairs and placed at his usual seat facing the backyard and the horse barn. Alva insisted he be dressed in his brown three-piece suit, and had cut a fresh rose for his lapel. She also insisted on using the paired candelabra, saying Chance would have liked a candle-lit dinner, and would have appreciated not wasting the champagne she'd saved for their return.

When Keeper broke the news to his grandfather, the old physician raged and asked who would harness the horses to his buggy in the event he had to make a house call. After doing the dishes

Alva withdrew into herself, typical of her Norwegian upbringing lest unfettered emotions become an embarrassment. By eight-thirty she was in her nightgown and in bed – her grief buffered by playing solitaire, accompanied by a tumbler of undiluted gin and fresh pack of cigarettes. Dr. Wick sat in his room listening to Gabriel Heatter, who for a change had good news about the Pacific war.

Keeper sat at the kitchen table with Early, finishing the last of the champagne and recounting highlights of the road trip; of the terrible weather and chain gangs and cotton fields where colored men, women and children labored under a broiling sun. He told about the sights and sounds of big cities, and of hotels where ropes were used for fire escapes. They both hooted with laughter when Keeper told of how he and Jonnie Prettyboy escaped from Lulu LaRue and the cooch-show barker. Early said he wished he could have been along, to have "seen" it all with them.

When Keeper told Early he'd had sexual intercourse with two different girls while on the road, Early insisted on knowing all the details.

"What self-respecting girl would want sex with a thirteen-year old kid?" he asked.

"She was respectable," Keeper replied, now on the defensive. "She was black too. Her name was Zinnia Day, and she was sixteen."

Early shook his head. "I hope you used a rubber."

"I actually had one, but stuff happened so fast I didn't have time to use it."

"Then you'd better have Granddad check you for the clap."

"She looked okay to me," Keeper replied, but now he wondered.

"Who was the second unfortunate girl?"

"You won't tell Mom?"

"Not in her present condition, I won't."

Keeper shook his head. "I mean not ever."

"Cross my heart and hope to die. So who was it?"

"Jonnie Prettyboy."

Early laughed. "The half-breed? And here I thought Dad had a nose for pussy. Damned if you don't take right after him."

"I'm no better than him either," Keeper replied morosely. "Not only do I screw around, I'm even drinking booze."

Early lifted his goblet, as if to toast Keeper's initiation into adulthood. "Almost forgot. An airmail letter postmarked from Atlanta, Georgia came today. Apparently it's addressed to you personally."

Keeper's first impulse was that Zinnia Day had written to him. "Was there a return address?"

"No, but Mother said Dad's handwriting was on the envelope."

"Did she open it?" Keeper asked.

Early shook his head. "You know better than that. I think she put it with her bills on the desk by the telephone."

Now Keeper's curiosity was aroused. Why would his father send him a letter from the road when they were together? He pushed his chair away from the table and hurried to the telephone desk. He fumbled through the stack of unpaid bills until he found the letter. He took it back to the kitchen and took his seat at the table. With shaking hands he tore open the envelope and blew into it before removing the letter.

"What does it say?" Early asked.

"Wait," Keeper replied. He quickly unfolded the letter and began reading aloud. "*Dear Keeper.*"

Early was already drunk. "Never mind the fucking salutation. Get to the meat of the thing."

"If you're going to keep interrupting me, I'll read it to myself."

"Okay, okay," Early grumbled, and refilled his goblet until foaming champagne wet his finger.

Keeper went on. "*I know this will be my last letter from the road. And I write this knowing full well I won't be around when you read it. Of course I'm sorry. Ashamed even. I have no excuse...*"

Early interrupted. "Are you talking to me?"

"No. It's what the letter says." Keeper smoothed the paper before going on. "*I have failed as a son, as a husband, and as a father. I've ...*" He paused to take a deep breath.

"What the hell's this all about?" Early asked.

"I'm not sure," Keeper replied, and pressed on. "*All my life I've been searching for something. I thought maybe I'd find whatever it was on the road or in a bottle. Love? Acceptance? Happiness? I can see now that I had it all. But instead, it was those very things I'd turned my back on.*"

"Jesus," Early groaned. "What a crock."

"There's more," Keeper said, and continued to read. "*You and Early are everything any father could hope to have and more. And my darling long suffering wife, Alva, was a saint to have put up with a man like me for a husband. She, and you boys, all deserved better.*" Keeper put down the letter and knuckled his eyes.

"I don't know if I can stand anymore of this," Early mumbled.

"We have to," Keeper said, and went on. "*The future belongs to you, dear son. If I am to be an example of how a man can disgrace himself in the pursuit of wine, women and song, then maybe my life can still serve some useful purpose.*"

"He must've been drinking," Early said.

"Shut up," Keeper replied, and continued to read slowly and carefully, as if wanting to speak in his father's own voice: "*I am no believer in any god or an afterlife. Here is here, and now is now. I am no longer either, but you are. Always apply yourself to the utmost. You are a smart young man with a bright and prosperous future. I hope you'll find it in medicine.*"

Keeper paused to collect his thoughts, remembering in vivid detail their time on the road together. Everything had started out so well, until little by little things got worse and worse until he found his father fucking Honey Burnside. There was no other word to describe it. 'Fucking' is what it was. It occurred to him that he wasn't so innocent either. He now believed that running away from his father could have caused the stroke that killed him. He shuddered to think that while he was fucking Jonnie Prettyboy on the New Yorker's front seat, his father might have been dying in the backseat only a few feet away.

Now a hot August sun slipped beyond the rim of the big lake, leaving the horse barn silhouetted like an alien monolith against a purple and gold-hued sky. The lawn sprinklers had been forgotten, and the sound of their repetitive hissing swept through open windows like ghostly feet shuffling through the backyard.

"Is there any champagne left?" Early asked.

"Nope." Keeper took a sip of his remaining champagne before continuing. He was getting drunk too.

Early pushed back from the table and shuffled for the liquor cabinet. "I'm going to help myself to Dad's bourbon. Keep reading."

He swallowed hard before going on. "*Always look after your mother, Keeper, and Early and your grandfather too. They will be depending on you in the days to come. Even in death I find guilt, shame and failure.*"

Keeper took another deep breath to clear his head. "*I can only hope that all of you will find it in your hearts to forgive a man who could never forgive himself.*"

He laid the letter flat in front of him and bit his lip to keep from crying. As he silently contemplated his father's words, a subtle shift of cool air washed through the open windows. The eight hand-dipped candles that guttered in their glass candelabra dribbled gnarled fingers of ivory wax across the linen tablecloth.

"Is that all?" Early asked when he returned with a bottle of Old Crow and a shotglass.

"No. Dad wanted me to tell everybody he loves them."

Early snorted. "Just like always, wanting you to say it for him."

Keeper allowed himself a small smile. "Yeah."

Early sat down and poured himself a shot of Old Crow to overflowing. "That was pure bullshit, Keep. Just like him."

"He knew he wasn't going to make it home alive," Keeper replied softly, "and it was probably my fault he didn't. The letter said what he couldn't say in person."

"Don't blame yourself, Keep. He always burned the candle at both ends."

Keeper wordlessly dug the brushed steel Zippo from his pocket and held it in the open palm of his hand where it glinted dully in the flickering candlelight. He rubbed his thumb over the engraved inscription; "Doc. You Bastard. Velma." He snapped open the lid, thumbed the serrated wheel and smiled when it lit on the first try. He reached for the lead crystal ashtray his mother had been using and pulled it toward him. He held the flimsy pale-blue airmail letter over the ashtray, lit it off the Zippo, and let it burn like the final chapter it was.

"Maybe you're right," Keeper sighed. "Maybe it was just another bullshit letter from the road after all."

—

COMING ATTRACTIONS

THE ROAD BEYOND THE DARK

THE FUNERAL STONES

TIN TOWN

THE FLAMINGO EXPRESS

SNOW COUNTRY

31729366R00186

Made in the USA
Charleston, SC
23 July 2014